# all we lost was everything

## Also by Sloan Harlow

*Everything We Never Said*

# all we lost was everything

SLOAN HARLOW

putnam

G. P. Putnam's Sons

G. P. Putnam's Sons
An imprint of Penguin Random House LLC
1745 Broadway, New York, New York 10019

alloyentertainment

First published in the United States of America by G. P. Putnam's Sons,
an imprint of Penguin Random House LLC, 2025



Visit us online at PenguinRandomHouse.com.

Library of Congress Cataloging-in-Publication Data
Names: Harlow, Sloan, author.
Title: All we lost was everything / Sloan Harlow.
Description: New York: G. P. Putnam's Sons, 2025. | Summary: After the tragic loss of her father in a house fire, eighteen-year-old River Santos feels stuck, but when new revelations about the fire emerge, she must confront painful truths about her past, relationships both new and old, and a dangerous revenge plot that may be lurking closer than she thinks.
Identifiers: LCCN 2024045672 (print) | LCCN 2024045673 (ebook) |
ISBN 9780593855942 (trade paperback) | ISBN 9780593855959 (epub)
Subjects: CYAC: Family secrets—Fiction. | Grief—Fiction. | Siblings—Fiction. | Romance stories.
Classification: LCC PZ7.1.H37137 All 2025 (print) | LCC PZ7.1.H37137 (ebook) | DDC [Fic]—dc23
LC record available at https://lccn.loc.gov/2024045672
LC ebook record available at https://lccn.loc.gov/2024045673

ISBN 9780593855942

1st Printing

Printed in the United States of America

LSCC

Design by Cindy De la Cruz
Text set in Adobe Garamond Pro and Proxima Nova

For the ones who fell off the summit,
looked up from the bottom,
and started climbing again anyway.

# prologue
# river

Every Friday, my mom played the lottery. She would stop at the gas station on her way home from cleaning whatever mansion was on rotation that week and buy scratchers for the largest pot on offer. She would win, here and there. Small amounts—sometimes the cost of the ticket, sometimes a little more. Once, she even won a thousand dollars. More often than not, though, she'd come up empty, and she seemed truly surprised every time it happened. I think she really believed that one day, the odds would be in her favor. That one day, she would be a millionaire and magically her life would be better—all our lives would be better. The never-ending debt from her unfinished college degree would be gone just like that. The need for my dad to take on a second and sometimes even a third job would disappear overnight. I could attend college without a single thought about tuition.

We would be rich and happy, but we would be responsible, the kind of family that wouldn't be destroyed from within by its newfound wealth.

When I turned fifteen and learned about the odds of winning the lottery—"one in three hundred million," my stats teacher had intoned—I told my mom she'd be better off saving her money instead of wasting it on tickets each week. She'd just waggled her eyebrows and said, "Someone's gotta win. Why not me?"

As far as I know, she never did win the lottery.

But I did. And all it cost me was everything.

## chapter 1
# river

Cemeteries are the greenest places in all of Scottsdale, Arizona. Even greener than the golf course at the nicest country club in town, which I only know because my mom worked there as a housekeeper when I was seven, and her boss used to let me eat ice pops from the snack stand at the thirteenth hole.

Ocotillo Ridge Memorial Park is no exception. There's no red dirt here, no gravel. No dusty scrub or faded mulch. Just a clear stretch of brilliant green grass, water shortage be damned. The sea of green is broken up only by headstones and a smattering of flowering trees that lace the air with the gumdrop smell of acacia and the grape-soda scent of Texas mountain laurel. Dad loved those pendulous purple flowers, that sweet smell. It's why I dipped into my GoFundMe money—the dubiously earned nest egg I'd vowed never to touch except in case of emergency—to secure him a spot here, so he could always be near those blossoms.

It's the trees I focus on now, the way they glow in the morning light. I don't focus on the way a priest is saying my father's name—*Jay San-TOS*—and how it sounds all wrong on his clumsy tongue. The way substitute teachers used to say my name, indifferent, not bothering to understand the vowels or pronunciation, because in an hour, that name would no longer exist to them.

If I focused on how wrong it sounds, I would have to focus on how wrong all of this is. That my dad is lying there, in a cedar coffin, waiting to be lowered into the ground, instead of standing here by my side. That my mother hasn't even called, let alone shown up for his funeral. That life as I knew it burned down to the ground just two weeks ago, when my house caught fire, taking everything with it—my guitar, my songbook, my diaries, my clothes, *everything*.

And most importantly, my father.

Because of the extensive damage, the fire department hasn't been able to tell us exactly what happened, just that it was probably electrical. Everything in our house was so old and half-broken, it honestly could have been anything. And once the fire started, it blazed hot and fast; my dad didn't even make it out of his bedroom. Everyone says it's a miracle I survived. That I'm so "lucky" that I somehow made it out of the house to the front lawn, where the firefighters found me passed out from smoke inhalation. I have no idea how I did it; all I have of that night are smoke-addled flashes, nothing that adds up to "daring escape."

And personally? I wouldn't call any of this "luck."

Through the fog that has enveloped me ever since I awoke in the hospital, I notice just how many people are here. I recognize most of them. Gertie, the owner of the diner I've worked at for years, presses a tissue to her nose. Teachers from Scottsdale Senior High School, where I'm a senior, as well as staff and students from Mojave Prep, where my dad coached football, stare solemnly ahead. His assistant coaches all stand in a line, wearing an impromptu uniform of slick jackets and ties; the players wear their varsity jackets despite the heat, their expressions grim.

Thank God Tawny's here. My best friend in the entire world. And after everything that's happened, sort of my only friend in the world. Everyone has been so kind and helpful, but Tawny McGill is the only person I can bear to be around. She's also the last person alive, it feels like, who knows me inside and out, who knows what I need without me even having to say it.

My ex, Noah Pierce, is also here, though he has studiously avoided eye contact with me since he arrived with his father. It's probably for the best, though, since Tawny would explode with protective fury if he got within five feet of me.

Next to the Pierces are a dozen guys from my dad's regular Alcoholics Anonymous meeting, the "anonymous" part of the equation having long since fallen by the wayside after years of backyard barbecues or the occasional person coming up to us during our weekly breakfast at the diner to share that my dad had literally saved their life.

As I look into the sea of tear-streaked faces around me, at this crowd stitched together by my father's love and support, I can't help that little voice inside me that asks: *But where is Dad?*

It's a familiar refrain from my life. Anytime I got up to sing, from my first concert at eight to my last one at seventeen, as I'd walk onto the stage, my heels echoing against old, scuffed wood, my first thought was always:

*Where is Dad?*

I would look out into the crowd, searching only for him. I'd find him: the mole on his left cheek; his thick, black hair; his dark, laughing eyes. He'd raise his hand, wave and wave. In that moment, I was a famous singer, a celebrity. I'd always wave back until Mom would tug down his wrist, embarrassed but smiling as she tucked a strand of blond hair behind her ear.

*Where is Dad?* I think again. Knowing the answer breaks me.

As if noticing that I am about to fall to pieces, Tawny leans in and whispers in my ear, "I've got you, River."

"We both do," Tita Anna whispers from my other side, lacing her fingers through mine.

Tawny puts an arm around my shoulder, tucking me in tight. It's the only reason I don't fly apart. I stay there, in her embrace, through the rest of the ceremony, as the priest finishes his sermon, and then as person after person steps up to share their memories of my father, of the profound ways he touched their lives. Tawny stiffens next to me with each speech, turning herself to rock so I don't break. She and Tita Anna do their best to form a barrier around me, but not even they can protect me from the end of the funeral, from the moment they lower the coffin—*my dad*—into the grave.

I'm not ready. I can't. I turn my head and bury my face in Tita Anna's black dress. *Not yet.*

As everyone files by us, murmuring rounds of *I'm sorry*, and *he was such a great man*, and *I will miss him*, I remain there, as still as the headstones surrounding us.

"We should go, love," Tita Anna finally says, brushing my long, dark hair off my face. It feels like only seconds have passed, but a look at my watch tells me it's almost noon, which means the ceremony ended an hour ago. Only Tita Anna, Tawny, and I remain, along with a cemetery worker who stands a respectful distance away, shovel in hand.

"Wait," I say, suddenly frantic, searching for words to put to my impossible feelings. As much as it's killing me to be here, the second I leave this cemetery, it will all become unbearably real. I cannot leave without my dad. I cannot leave him here by himself.

A hand finds my shoulder. Tita Anna. "He's gonna be okay. We can come visit him whenever you want."

"Can I get him a saguaro?" I ask, grasping at anything to hold on to for even one more second to make this moment less awful. There's a little space to the right of the rectangular hole in the sandy earth, a spot for life in this place that holds so much death.

"Of course," Tita Anna says, steering me gently toward the car. Tawny follows at my side, a comforting shadow.

While we're walking toward the parking lot, someone's phone buzzes and buzzes. I don't realize it's mine until Tawny nudges my handbag.

"Do you want to check that?" she asks me. "Or I could turn it off for you?"

"Oh." I pull out my phone, which is riddled with notifications.

I swipe away the litany of *I'm sorry*s and *If there's anything I can do*s in my texts, about to turn the device off, when a new alert from GoFundMe pops up.

Part of me is still a little embarrassed that a corner of the internet knows my entire sob story, detail after detail laid bare for anyone to see. But I can't deny how helpful the GoFundMe money has been. We were constantly behind on bills, and it turned out that our homeowners insurance had lapsed. Which meant that after the fire, I had literally nothing to my name, no money to rebuild the house, nothing physical to resell, no safety net whatsoever. The second I voiced concern about paying my hospital bill, Tawny waved a hand impatiently.

"Don't worry. It's all taken care of."

"But how?" I asked, bewildered.

She held up her phone, showing me the post she'd written on GoFundMe describing what had happened alongside a picture of me and my dad at the Prickly Pear, a local music venue where I often sang at open mic night.

"You didn't have to do that," I protested, but she just shrugged.

"It's literally the least I can do, given . . . well, everything."

For nearly two weeks leading up to the funeral and for days after, my phone kept buzzing with notifications. A five-dollar donation here. Seventy-five dollars there. Someone even gave five hundred. Some of the donations were from names I recognized, others from people in faraway states who had read about what had happened, and some of the donations were simply anonymous. Slowly, the total figure had ticked up, first into the hundreds, then the thousands, and finally, mind-bogglingly, into the tens of thousands. I was both blown away by everyone's generosity and thoughtfulness, and sickened by the thought that I was profiting somehow on this horrible tragedy. When I said as much to Tawny, she just laughed and shook her head.

"Only you, River, could take something good and turn it sideways. It's not your fault the healthcare system here is so expensive. Or that your parents didn't have untold generational wealth. It's not blood money—it's a lifeline. Just take it and say thank you."

So I did.

It takes a second now for the page to load, but when it does, I stop walking.

Tawny and Tita Anna don't notice for a few steps. Then Tita Anna turns around and dashes to my side when she sees my face. "Are you okay? Did something happen?"

I can't speak, so I hold up my phone and show her and Tawny the GoFundMe figure. Suddenly, those digits have many more zeros. Many, *many* more.

Because someone has just anonymously donated two million dollars.

# six months later

# chapter 2
# river

I'm sitting on a crate of fat, ripe oranges, huddled and shivering, squeezed between the towering shelves of produce in Gertie's Diner's walk-in cooler. My head leans against a cardboard box full of white onions as heavy and round as softballs. Through the small holes on the side, I can smell how fresh they are, how I'll weep when I slice into them tomorrow during prep.

Ironic, as I'm trying—and failing—not to cry right now.

It's all because of my first table. It had been a family: a mom, dad, and little girl with long, black hair. "Three slices of carrot cake," the dad had said. "I know it's kind of early for it, but we always do cake for breakfast on her birthday."

For one moment, the entire scene had shifted—for one moment, it had been me and my parents sitting there, ordering cake for breakfast like I'd done on every birthday for as long as I could remember. But just as quickly, the scene rearranged itself, and reality came crashing back in. It wasn't me and my parents sitting there—and it never would be again.

I'd barely kept it together before hefting open the heavy metal door and diving into the blissfully frigid air of the walk-in, where I've been hiding for ten very cold minutes.

Now I hear the walk-in door push open, the telltale flap of someone walking through the curtain of plastic strips. I can't see the doorway from where I'm currently hidden amongst the towers of eggs and bricks of cheddar, but I know who it is.

I wipe my eyes and take a deep breath, trying to get a grip.

"Sorry, Tawn. I'm coming."

But when I open my eyes, I give a startled exhale, my breath curling visibly in the cold air. Because I'm not looking up into the hazel gaze of my best friend. Instead, it's Logan Evans, the last person I'd ever want to catch me crying in a walk-in.

"You," I say, "are not Tawny."

"No," he says, "I am not."

He crosses his muscular arms, tilting his head at me as the chiller compressor roars to life. A lock of thick, dark hair falls over his forehead, nearly touching his raised brow. His jaw is set tight, making his face look even more chiseled than normal.

There's no denying it: Logan Evans is hot. He's been here seven months, and his beauty still catches me off guard.

Tawny had nearly dropped her stack of plates the first time we'd seen Logan talking to Gertie about the HELP WANTED sign on the front windows last year. "Who the hell is *that*?" she'd said. "He looks like a prince Disney had to fire for causing too many early sexual awakenings."

But on his first day, I accidentally crashed into him with a tray full of Diet Cokes. I'd scrambled for a towel to mop at his soaked shirt, stumbling over myself apologizing to him. But instead of accepting my help, he'd stepped back, as though my touch had burnt him. When I'd met his gaze, his expression had taken my breath away. There was an unmistakable fury etched into his features, like he *hated* me, even though he'd only known me for less than an hour.

After that, no matter how hard I tried to be friendly, he barely spoke to me, beyond what was necessary. "Can you refill the mayo?" was what passed for small talk between us.

"He knows he's hot," I'd complained to Tawny, watching him work a table with two giggling grandmas, hating the way my stupid heart hammered at the sight of his smile, hating how much I noticed him when he never noticed me. Hating the way I cared, even though I already had the perfect boyfriend. (I try not to linger on the "had." I try not to linger on thoughts of *him* at all.) "He uses that face like a weapon."

Now I wipe my eyes and turn to face Logan. "Sorry, just having a bad day."

Logan sinks into a squat until we're eye level, so close I can see flecks of yellow scattered in his bright blue irises. For one fleeting moment, I swear I see a flicker of warmth there. He reaches out his hand, and all of a sudden, I stop breathing.

Is Logan Evans, who has barely ever said five full sentences to me, who rarely smiles or shows any emotion toward me whatsoever besides irritation, going to *comfort* me?

But instead of touching me, he stretches behind me, grabbing something wedged behind my back. The motion knocks me off-balance, and I have to put my hands out to catch myself.

"Gertie asked me to get more oranges. We're out of juice." His eyes kick back to mine. "You're . . . sitting on our last carton."

Perfect. Just perfect. Just when I'm hoping this scuffed metal floor will open and swallow me whole, the walk-in door bursts open again.

"I took care of them, got them carrot cake slices. Honey, I can't imagine . . ." Tawny trails off, blinking down at Logan's back as he silently gathers oranges.

When his arms are full, Logan rises and makes his way out from between the shelves, nearly dropping an orange as he takes great care to not brush against either of us. He doesn't spare us a single glance.

Tawny's nostrils flare. "I swear, he acts like we ran over his puppy. Would it kill him to be nice?" She gives my face a good look. "Seriously. Are you okay?"

I sniffle, and Tawny hugs me. It feels good to hug her back, to be surrounded by the coconut scent of her shampoo, the warmth of her body in this icy chiller.

I shake my head. "All good. Minus the whole sitting-on-Logan's-oranges fiasco."

Tawny rolls her eyes. "Oh, screw him. He should be so lucky to have you sitting on his oranges."

When I'm ready, Tawny leads us back out to wipe down the stack of dirty menus at the front counter. I'm scrubbing a dubious stain on the dessert section when I notice the picture of Belgian waffles. *Noah's favorite.* I feel a pinch in my heart, like I always do, at just the memory of his name.

Perfect, beautiful, heart-gouging Noah.

"Stop thinking about him." Tawny cuts into my thoughts. That's the problem with having Tawny as a best friend: She can read my mind.

"I wasn't," I lie.

"You sighed no less than three times this past minute." Tawny tosses another wiped menu on the clean pile. "You really need better taste in men, Riv."

"You're one to talk, you know." I raise a brow at her. "At least I didn't carry a torch for the world's douchiest prom king."

"How dare you." Tawny playfully smacks me with a plastic menu. "I didn't carry a torch. It was more of a match. Besides, that was back when I was young and foolish."

"That was five months ago," I say, deadpan.

Tawny tosses her ponytail to brush playfully against my face. "Like I said. Young and foolish."

I pick up another menu and pick at a dried piece of yolk on the corner. "You know, if you had just asked him out, he would have said yes."

There's no way he wouldn't have. She's gorgeous, with blond hair that she's constantly dyeing different colors, hazel eyes, and a heart-shaped face. Tawny's not just beautiful; she's charming in a way that sneaks under your skin and pulls you firmly into her orbit.

If there is one bit of luck in my life, she's it, thanks to whatever scheduling god seated her next to me in Spanish class sophomore year. She was new that year, but somehow she ended up taking me under her wing, as if she were the one who'd been there all along. Other than Tita Anna, she's the closest thing I have to family now.

"Please." Tawny flicks a dismissive hand in the air. "Matt's old news, baby. I saw on Insta that he showed up to graduation completely blitzed, and when he walked, or should I say *stumbled*, across the stage, he tried to go to the podium to give a speech."

"Whoa." I blink. "What was his speech?"

"I think he just yelled, 'Roll tide!' over and over." Tawny shrugs. "See? Bullet dodged."

My laughter dies down, and I fall quiet. "Sorry you missed the live show. Sorry you missed the whole thing," I say in a low voice. I can feel the painful pressure from earlier come back, rising in my chest.

I couldn't stomach walking in graduation, not when neither of my parents would be in the audience watching me. In solidarity, Tawny had spent the day at the movie theater with me, hopping from one showing to the next, buying me popcorn and Sour Patch Kids, handing me tissue after tissue, all without ever making me feel like I was a mess.

"Hey. *Hey.*" Tawny gives me an earnest look, brows furrowed. "Don't you dare apologize. My place is by your side. Always." She reaches out, squeezes my arm.

"Besides, Mom wasn't gonna be there anyway. *Berlin*, that time. They had her working ten days in a row." She shrugs. "I can't imagine . . . just flying nonstop across the ocean. Back and forth, back and forth. What an exercise in futility."

Tawny's mom is a flight attendant. A busy one. Constantly taking overtime and extra shifts to make life as a single mom work. She's almost never home. It makes my heart ache for Tawny, though she tells me to save my pity for someone else. As far as she's concerned, the arrangement works out just great. Minimal supervision means she can live her life how she wants to without constant fights. "I swear we love each other more because we see each other less," she always says.

Well, used to say. She's careful never to say anything like that around me these days.

Logan passes us, carrying a stack of menus, his blue eyes piercing. "You've got a table, Santos. Three waters and a Coke."

"Oh," I start. "Thanks, Logan. You didn't have to . . ."

But he's not even listening, his back already to me, and I hate myself just a little bit for registering the muscles moving beneath his T-shirt, the way his jeans fit perfectly.

Shaking myself out of it before Tawny can notice this too and chide me, I go take my table's orders, apologizing profusely for keeping them waiting. They're incredibly kind and end up leaving a generous tip. I clutch the folded bills in my hand, my heart pumping faster. And I wonder, as I always do:

*Was it them? Could they have been the anonymous donors?*

It's a game I find myself playing nearly every day. But every lead I've chased for the last six months has been a dead end. Ex-players of my dad's who are now playing professionally. Members of his AA group. A secretly wealthy family member. I even checked with GoFundMe. *No, no, no, and that goes against our policy.*

"Not them," Tawny singsongs as she sweeps by, watching me staring dazedly at my tip.

And there's that pesky mind reading again. I quickly shove the bills in my pocket. "How do you know?"

She shrugs. "I mean, I don't. But, Riv, we've been over this. Why does it even matter who gave it? Money is money."

Part of me knows she's right, but the bigger part of me can't set aside the mystery. It feels like one more loose thread in my ever-unraveling life. And it feels different, somehow, from accepting the random twenty here and there. Two million dollars from *one* person? Who has that kind of money, and who would give it to *me* without expecting so much as a thank-you?

For the next hour, though, I'm blissfully busy and have no choice but to set that mystery aside. Tawny and I bob and weave around each other like figure skaters on a black-and-white-checkered floor. It's a synchronicity that comes from waiting tables here at Gertie's since I was fifteen and my coworker being my very best friend.

"Table six needed more ketchup. I brought them a bottle," Tawny says as she ducks under my tray full of iced teas.

"Saw that you got Mrs. Lewis. I dropped off her extra ranch," I say, hanging the next ticket in the kitchen.

A few times, I swear I feel Logan watching me, but every time I look up, he's absorbed in an order or ringing up someone's tab. Miracle of miracles, I don't have any more embarrassing meltdowns in front of him, and by the time we've grabbed our bags from the lockers and clocked out, Tawny's sufficiently cheered me up.

When we walk out the back door, we hear a low, raspy meow. A large, scruffy tabby cat rounds the corner, twitching a crooked tail.

"Tigery!" I gush, stooping to scratch behind his ears.

It's taken patience and a *lot* of Gertie's chicken, but the wary stray cat that's lived behind the diner has finally let me love on him. Tigery's been a huge comfort in the days since the fire. As soon as I get a place that allows pets, I'll pamper him with feather beds and spoon-fed caviar like he's a feeble princeling.

"You always sound like you're reuniting with your long-lost husband after decades apart," Tawny muses. "You saw him this morning."

"Well, maybe a few hours *is* a decade in cat years. And I don't know, Tawn. As far as husbands go . . . I feel like I could do a lot worse than Tigery."

Tigery flops on the concrete and stretches out his paws.

"River," Tawny says, "we are not in marrying-our-cat territory yet. Okay? And I don't think it will ever come to that." Tigery slaps his tail on the concrete, as if in agreement.

"Thank you both for the vote of confidence," I say.

After another scratch or two, Tigery is sated and trots off into the shade. I stand, brushing dirt from my legs.

"Thanks for today," I say, giving Tawny a hug. "Love you so much."

"Duh," she says, kissing my cheek. "Love you more."

I walk back to my car, feeling good—happy even. But as soon as I slam the door shut, silence envelops me, an assassin I should have seen coming. The Arizona June heat is already choking me and making the side mirror sag, the duct tape holding it in place softening in the sun. And with no Tawny, no murmur of customer voices, no ding of the diner door, it all comes back.

The thing that is always lurking, the thing that, for blissful short slivers of the day, I sometimes forget. It comes up right now, all of it, from the basement of my heart:

My mom is gone. My dad is dead. And my life will never be the same.

# chapter 3
# river

I can smell the stench of burnt food as soon as I open the front door. The sour-black smell cuts through the fog that surrounded me for the entire drive home, and for a second, I'm back in that night. In the billowing flames and black smoke pouring out the windows. I'm back where I can't breathe, can't see . . .

*No.*

I slam the door on the memory, digging my nails into my palms as I drag myself back to the present.

"Hey!" Tita Anna calls from the kitchen. "In here!"

Once my pulse steadies, I hang my bag on the hook by the front door and peek my head into the kitchen. Tita Anna is stooping in front of the oven, peering through the window.

"It's almost ready," she says.

"I think it was ready forty minutes ago," I say, pasting a smile on my face.

Her face falls flat. "Oh God. Does it smell burnt?"

I purse my lips.

"Ughh, okay, so the sad part is I was *actually* trying here." She shakes her fists at the ceiling. "Curse you, Super Mommy's Kitchen! Maybe if her recipe blog were more *recipe* and less ranting about her marriage . . ."

I grab oven mitts and flip on the fan above the stove.

"Stand by." She winces, pulling the oven door open.

I snatch out the casserole dish, and Tita Anna shuts the door before too much smoke can billow out.

We stare at the black goo in the tray.

"What . . . was it?" I poke it, and black crust breaks away.

"It was supposed to be chicken potpie casserole." She pushes up her glasses, shaking her head. "Man. Jay was always the one who could . . ." She clears her throat. After a moment, she straightens, adjusting her T-shirt. "Wanna go out? My treat?"

The exhaust fan roars on high. But the air is still charred, the smell making my heart race.

"Sure," I say. Because in this moment, truly anywhere is better than here.

I LOVE TITA Anna. She's a lot younger than my dad, still in her thirties, and ever since I was a kid, she's always had me rolling with laughter. She's technically my dad's cousin, once removed, but she came from a family of four sisters, moved out of her house the second she could, and always called my dad the brother she never had.

She works remotely as a project manager for a tech company, and she is as irreverent as they come. Right now, as we're eating at an Italian restaurant, she's telling me that for her new Zoom background, she recorded a video of herself walking into her home office, acting surprised someone's on a video call, and backing out of the room.

"What?" I shake my head, twirling my linguine. "Explain that to me again?"

"Okay, okay." She tosses back her long, black hair and sits forward in her chair. "So, when I set that video as my Zoom background, it looks like I'm just sitting in my bedroom, right? I'm in the video, actually me, and then when that recorded video plays, it shows me walking in, looking surprised at interrupting *myself* on a Zoom call, apologizing, and leaving." She snort-laughs, stabbing a ravioli.

"Don't choke," I say as she pops it into her mouth, still laughing.

"I won't," she assures me. "Anyway. No one's said anything. Not once. Not the client. Not my boss. I think they're afraid to. Like they think it's my sister or just another random Filipino woman in my house, and if they ask if that's me, they'll sound racist. Ugh, I'd love that. Except, I worry if I play that card, they'll expect me to speak Tagalog."

I shake my head, smiling down at my nearly empty plate. The waiter comes and refills our water, asks if I'm done. Tita Anna asks for a box and the dessert menu.

"So," she says, peering at me over a picture of a slice of limoncello cake.

"So," I echo, smiling tentatively.

Tita Anna sets down the dessert menu and scratches her chin, contemplating the ceiling.

"Our apartment sucks, doesn't it?" she blurts out after a minute.

I laugh, surprised. After The Accident, Tita Anna insisted I move in with her. It's been wonderful living with her. But the apartment itself? I would never dare say anything because Tita Anna's been so gracious. But the walls are so thin, I can hear exactly which YouTube videos our neighbors are watching. I can hear the click of their keyboard. There's a hole in the bathroom that leaks anytime the upstairs neighbor takes a shower. And worst of all?

No pets allowed, so no Tigery.

Even so, it's a small price to pay to live with Tita Anna.

And the fact that I could easily afford something better for both of us—could buy us a place if I wanted—is something that Tita Anna never, ever makes me feel guilty about. She knows that I don't want to touch the GoFundMe money, to turn the worst thing that ever happened to me into something that can be fixed with dollars. Especially when I don't have any idea where the money came from in the first place.

Which is why I say, "Honestly? Any apartment is the best apartment if it's with you."

"Oh, Rivvy." Tita Anna reaches across the table and squeezes my fingers. "I don't deserve you. And of course I agree." She leans closer. "But we can go anywhere. Be anywhere. As long as there's Wi-Fi, I can do my job." She leans forward, eager. "River, we could live in Rome. *Rome.* Just think: handmade pasta every night. Real limoncello. Wine from a vineyard that's only a short train ride away."

My heart cracks open. When Tita Anna sees my face, her eyes are shiny and sad.

We're both thinking about my dad.

He was constantly adding things to his bucket list. Most of them were silly. Play a chess game with the Pope. Be a guest star on an episode of *Law & Order*. Befriend a wild javelina and train it to follow him around like a familiar.

But there was one item that was real: a trip to Italy.

It was how he was going to celebrate twenty-five years of sobriety. We would start in Rome, because he had wanted to toss a coin over his left shoulder into the Trevi Fountain, then head to Florence and then Venice. He planned on eating three gelatos a day and feeding the pigeons in St. Mark's Square. When I told him it was now illegal, he insisted it was worth it to pay the fine.

Needless to say, he never made it there.

Tears spring to my eyes. Quickly, I brush them away.

"I . . . yeah. Yeah, maybe not. I wasn't thinking . . ." Tita Anna shakes her head. "But there are other places. California?" Her smile is small. Hopeful. "New York? The Great Smoky Mountains? Anyplace where if you leave cookie dough in your car in July, it doesn't bake into a black crisp? Or a place where there's no such thing as 'scorpion season'?"

There's a moment where I imagine it. New York, a place with actual seasons. Midnight runs to the bodega with Tita Anna for a pint of Ben & Jerry's. The countless bars with open mics every day of the week. Tita Anna chiding me for riding the subway late at night. It sounds wonderful.

But it's not possible. I can't leave. My life is nothing more than glass shards scattered amongst the saguaros in the Sonoran Desert, each piece a burning question. For me to keep going, I need to gather them all, fit the pieces together, see how it all makes sense. I need answers. And the answers will never be anywhere else but right here.

"I can't leave." I sigh. Tita Anna nods as if she knew this would be my answer all along.

"Is this about your mom?"

"Amongst other things," I say, thinking of Tawny, of the diner, of Tigery. "But, yeah. I mean, what if she comes back, and . . . and I'm not here?"

Tita Anna's face twists, but she doesn't say anything. She doesn't have to. I know what she's thinking. It's the same thing Tawny thinks, the same thing the police thought.

*Why hold on to someone who didn't hold on to you?*

My mother was the type of mom who read me stories every night, perfectly voicing every character, from Chester the cricket to Gandalf the wizard to Miss Honey from *Matilda*. The type of mom who threw her whole head back in laughter at my stories. The type of mom who kissed my dad when she thought I wasn't looking, who still celebrated not just their wedding anniversary, but the anniversary of their first date.

But my mom was also the type who struggled. I never had a name for the way her moods could swing from one extreme to the next. How she could be so resplendently happy sometimes and barely make it out of bed others. She called them her Blue Days, and the only thing that ever seemed to help was hiking. When she was doing well, she'd pull out all her trail maps and point at the blue veins of rivers and red arteries of roads, showing me all the routes she'd already taken, all the ones she still planned to take. When she wasn't doing well, she'd grab her backpack and go, often without even saying goodbye.

She was an old-school hiker, my mom. She never brought a phone. All she ever needed was the same pack she's had since she was a teenager, a compass, and a tune to whistle.

"I didn't even *have* a phone when I first started," she said once. "I used to send letters. I wasn't beholden to anyone. All I had to do was send a postcard every three weeks." *To who?* I used to wonder. Both her parents were dead.

Once I came along, the cards were for me. Whenever she was gone longer than a week, she'd come back with a stack of letters, wanting to watch my face as I read her words. "It makes me feel like you're there with me," she always said.

*So take me with you,* I'd longed to say, but I never could bring myself to, fearing that my presence would change whatever magic healed her on her trips.

Not long after my eighteenth birthday, Mom started getting bad again. Leaving the house without telling us where she was going. Breaking down into sobs if the dryer left her clothes damp after a full cycle. Sleeping in until four p.m.

When we woke up one morning in early October, I wasn't surprised to find her gone.

"Her hiking gear's missing." Dad had stared into the closet before he deflated with a sigh. "I suppose it was just a matter of time."

"She'll be better when she gets back," I said with more certainty than I felt.

When Mom wasn't back for Halloween, I felt my first flash of fear. Then Mom missed Thanksgiving. But when she missed Christmas, my dad called the police. He'd sat me down afterward and said, "Riv, I think we have to prepare for the fact that your mom might not . . ." His eyes shone with unshed tears. "That she might have left us for good this time."

I refused to believe it. Because no matter my mom's mood, one thing never changed: how much she loved me. I knew, in a way I felt so deeply but couldn't explain, she'd come back one day.

That maybe she already had.

A week after the funeral, someone left a bouquet of bluebells, my dad's favorites, at Tita Anna's doorstep. There was no note, but I knew they could only be from her. I couldn't bear to watch them wither, so I hung them upside down to dry. They now sit on my dresser in a Ball jar, so fragile that one touch and they'll crumble to nothing.

Tita Anna reaches out and takes my hand in hers. "In that case," she says, "maybe we should take a trip. Get out of here and give you a break from . . . everything, but with a return date."

I stare down uncertainly at the crumbs on my plate and picture my dad throwing them to a horde of pigeons.

"You know what?" I say softly. "Let's do it. Let's go to Italy."

"Yeah?" Tita Anna lights up.

It's splitting my chest in two, the idea of doing all the things Dad had wanted to do, all without him. But I also can't imagine a better way to honor his memory.

And maybe, if I'm lucky enough to win the lottery twice, my mom will be back when I get home.

# chapter 4
# river

Mom didn't give up her love of hiking when rattlesnakes made their way into her gear pack or stinging nettles scraped her skin raw. Dad didn't stop coaching when his players—or their parents, more likely—threw fits on the field. We're all forced to coexist with less than pleasant things.

Which is why I didn't quit on the spot when Gertie told us we were catering Tate "Most Punchable Face Award" Franklin's graduation party at his mansion in Scottsdale's most exclusive gated community.

Tate was easily the most annoying kid in our grade. His dad had been a quarterback in the NFL, and even if Tate didn't remind you of this fact every three seconds, there was his constant talk of trust funds and the red Corvette gifted to him on his sixteenth birthday to contend with.

Ten minutes during homeroom was more than enough with Tate

Franklin. Now I have to spend the next six hours wearing a stiff white button-down and a bow tie, offering him tiny sliders on a silver platter. At least I'll be working with Tawny. But also with Logan, who, as usual, is ignoring me.

He barely glances at me, as if I'm just a ghost carrying platters of deli rolls alongside him. All my old classmates are treating me like that, actually. Like I'm a disembodied tray offering refreshments. It's both a relief and makes me feel like shit.

"Just four more hours, Riv." Tawny straightens my bow tie at the refill station.

"I won't make it," I croak. Tawny shoots me a sympathetic look before scurrying off when an old classmate snaps his fingers at her.

"Everyone here's an asshole," I growl under my breath.

Logan, standing nearby, looks back at me for half a second. Just as I'm wondering if that's a smile playing on his lips, he turns back to a cluster of girls openly ogling him.

It's too hot today to be outside, so the party is in the house's grand foyer, an enormous room with a double-height ceiling, marbled floors, and twin curved staircases on either side. Us servers, though, have to cut a steady path from indoors to out, a barely contained chaos. One minute I'm at the grilling station, where Gertie flips tiny burger patties. The next I'm wiping up spilled Coke off the marble floor. Everything's a blur until I catch my name coming from a group of girls with glossy, elegant hair.

". . . wouldn't touch millions of dollars? That's absurd."

I blink. They're definitely talking about me.

"It's worse than absurd! It's dumb." The speaker is a tall girl who was in my gym class freshman year. "Did you see her? I'd rather *die* than be caught hunching around Tate's mansion, serving all my old classmates *tuna salad*." She examines her nails, her face twisted in disgust. "Like, why does she still work? What's she trying to prove?"

"Hell," one of the other girls says, "I'd carry tuna salad in my pocket if I got to work with *him*." I watch their heads all turn toward Logan, who, admittedly, still somehow looks beautiful in a uniform that is designed—and failing—to make him look invisible.

"Tuna salad, ladies?" I say, loud and icy. I take small satisfaction in the way they whirl around, looking like deer with perfect eyeliner caught in headlights. It's no surprise when they scatter wordlessly, not even glancing at the fish-stuffed bell peppers on the tray.

"Do I even want to ask?" Tawny says, coming up behind me, her narrowed eyes trained on the departing girls.

Before I can answer, Tate's dad saunters over, gesturing widely with a champagne glass. "River. So good to see you." His drawl is a little longer than usual, more syrupy. He's clearly drunk. And clearly used to talking while drunk. He flashes us a charming smile.

"At first I was surprised when Tate requested Gertie's for today. It's so common . . ." Mr. Franklin cuts himself off, coughing into his fist. Who knew he'd have such self-awareness?

"What I mean to say is, everything is just great, and Tate is so happy. Thank you so much for your hard work today." His glassy eyes get serious for a second. "You're just like your mom that way."

The back of my neck goes cold. I feel Tawny stiffen at my shoulder. How could I have forgotten? I was so caught up in my own feelings about tonight that it had completely slipped my mind.

Mom used to work for this man. She used to clean Tate Franklin's house.

Is it poetic or pathetic that I've taken her place, working for the same millionaire she did?

"Your mom was our best cleaning lady," Mr. Franklin says. "We really miss her here, you know." There's something almost wistful in his tone. As if catching himself, he straightens up, suddenly all business.

"She could make our silver spoons sparkle. And not once did she ever chip our antique china. Not once!" Mr. Franklin says, overly bright. "Do you even know how hard it is to find good help like that?"

The party continues raucously around us. Logan is only a few feet away, serving mini tacos to my old friends Audrey and Marissa. The piped-in music has changed from a Dua Lipa song to a sappy instrumental. Kailey Collins and her ex are making out not-so-secretly in the corner. But I barely register any of it, my anger narrowing the world to a thin point as this drunk man patters on about my missing mother's *cleaning abilities*.

"If she ever comes back, make sure you let her know that I'd be open to interviewing her again for her position."

He toasts us with his empty glass before stumbling off to the next guest.

I'm shaking with fury as I watch him go.

"What an unbelievable *jerk*," Tawny spits, vibrating with anger, her hands waving about. I'm caught off guard. Tawny's anger has always been *at* my mom. Never on her behalf. It's touching, really. I guess in the Rock, Paper, Scissors of shittiness, Asshole Ex–NFL Player beats Abandoning Mother in Tawny's eyes.

"Yeah," I agree, but she hardly seems to hear me.

"Condescending, elitist—" On the last word she throws her hands to the side, accidentally knocking the platter of tuna salad into my chest.

Tawny's hands fly to her mouth as I let out a low groan. A couple of girls from my Spanish class look over, snickering softly.

"Oh, River, I'm so, so sorry." She looks miserable with regret. I sigh.

"I know. I just . . . Tawn, tuna fish . . ."

"I'll go grab some rags." She rushes off.

I get on my knees, pulling out napkins to scoop the tuna scattered on the floor onto my ruined platter. A shadow falls over me, and I'm suddenly swallowed by the smoky smell of palo verde bark burning on a dark Sonoran Desert night. I look up to see Logan, and God help me now that I know he smells like *that*.

"Rough night?" he asks, bending down to help me clean up the mess.

"Uh, yeah," I manage, taken aback. This might be the first time Logan has said something to me that's not work related. "You could say that."

Logan pauses to look at me. "Seems like you've been having a lot of those lately."

I swallow hard. So he has noticed. Maybe I'm not completely invisible to him after all. He reaches into his apron and pulls out a clean rag, offering it to me.

"Thanks," I whisper, my fingers brushing against his as I take it.

I've never noticed before, but Logan has a small scar on his upper lip, just left of his cupid's bow. It's an angled divot, like a large thumbnail had pressed deep into the plush arch of that lip, and the imprint had stayed. It's unfair, really, that anyone should look as good as he does.

He clears his throat. "Listen, Santos—" he begins, but before he can say anything else, Tate's drunken bellow cuts through the room.

"Look who's finally here! About time you showed up, Pierce."

*Oh no. God, please no. Haven't I suffered enough?*

I don't know where I find the strength, but I turn around to face him. Noah Pierce.

The boy who broke my heart.

## chapter 5
# river

Noah is standing awkwardly at the double-door entrance, his eyes sweeping the room and instantly locking on mine before Tate engulfs him in a drunken hug.

I turn to Logan, but he's no longer at my side. He grabs an empty tray from a nearby high-top and disappears into the kitchen, his face back to its usual stony mask.

I follow suit, single-minded in my desperation to get away from Noah and the beating heart of the party, careless with where I'm walking. People have to walk around me, brushing up against me, nearly tripping to avoid me. Finally, I see the door to the powder room that Tate's mom showed us earlier, making clear that it was the only one "the help" was allowed to use. I'm nearly there when someone behind me says, "River?"

That voice stops me cold. Even half a year later, it's as familiar as my own. My stomach plummets to my toes then ricochets right back up to lodge in my throat, sticking there. When I turn to face him, I feel like I can't breathe.

I manage to plaster a smile on my face. "Hey, Noah."

"Hey," he says, rubbing the back of his head. *Screw him* because he somehow got hotter.

For a moment, we can only stare at each other, the sounds of the party filtering in from down the hall. I don't know what's going on in his head, but I'm barely holding on. His boyish handsomeness has evolved into something more adult, more confident. He still has the same silky blond hair, but his jaw is more angular, his cheekbones more pronounced. And even though his large eyes are the same electric green as before, I find that I can't read them quite as easily as I once did.

"What are you doing here?" I blurt.

That's not quite the question I had in mind. What I mean is: Why is he here in Scottsdale? Why is he at Tate's party? Why . . . well, a lot of *whys*.

But none of that makes it out.

Noah's mouth twitches. "Oh, well, you know. Tate heard I was back and strong-armed me into coming. He's a hard man to say no to."

"I don't know about that," I counter. "I think over half the female student body has said no to him at one point or another."

Noah laughs. "And with good reason. He may be my friend, but he's an ass."

This is familiar. Gentle teasing that usually ended up with him pulling me into his arms, his last retort murmured into my hair.

*It's not a year ago, idiot,* I remind myself. He's not here as my date. This is now, when I'm working a party with people who are carefully pretending they don't know me, drenched in tuna salad, standing in the nicest house I've ever set foot in, with a boy who shattered my heart seven months ago.

As if realizing the same thing, Noah stiffens and coughs into his fist. "Anyway. I'm back for the summer, helping my dad out at his practice."

Noah's dad is one of the top surgeons in the state and is just as skilled at investing his money as he is with a scalpel. Noah's always idolized his father. His parents divorced when he was little, and his mom and stepdad moved to California, but Noah wanted to stay with his dad. He declared premed even before he started college. Unlike his heartbreaker son, though, Dr. Pierce is actually a great guy. He was one of my dad's best friends and helped him structure strength-training and practice regimes to help his players avoid serious injury, and he did it all for free.

"Cool," I say. "Very cool. So cool. You here with Jonah?" I say, naming his best friend from high school. He, Tate, and Noah were all on the soccer team together. Ironically, Tate, the son of "The Arm," was such a weak passer that he'd had to find a sport where he didn't need to use his arms at all.

"Actually, some college friends." Noah jerks a thumb over his shoulder toward the foyer, not meeting my eyes. "Ben and Ryan. They're visiting for a few days."

Interacting with Noah feels like hugging a cactus. There's no way to do it without agony. Just the mention of two close friends of his I've never met makes me want to double over. If he hadn't broken up with me, I would know who they were. I'd be here with them.

I fiddle with the hem of my apron and drop my gaze to hide my pain as another awkward silence descends. I knew I'd run into him eventually. It's a law of the universe. If there's someone from your past you're desperate to avoid, you will find yourself trapped in an elevator with them on the second day of your period.

It was inevitable I'd run into Noah. I had even made plans for it.

And this was *not* the plan.

Noah was supposed to bump into me while I was in the middle of laughing at something my drummer had just said on the way to our headlining gig. I was supposed to look stage-worthy, in a costume that would have made Taylor Swift do a double take. I was supposed to look so despairingly hot that when Noah is ninety years old, gumming a spoonful of Jell-O, his only thought is, *River Santos . . . the biggest mistake of my life was letting you go.*

Instead, I'm a sweaty, stinky mess while he stands there with his perfectly fitting jeans, just-the-right-amount-of-tight T-shirt, and bottle-green eyes.

"If you're wondering why I smell like wet fish right now, Tawny accidentally knocked a tray of tuna salad into me." I smooth my hand self-consciously down my shirt. "Try to picture me twenty minutes ago, when my outfit was clean and I still looked like the consummate catering professional." I shove my voice back into something impersonal and casual, like we had homeroom together and it's just *so* nice to see him. Cue the reminiscent laugh, the *remember that one time?*

Noah's expression is unreadable as he surveys the stain. He clears his throat again. "I'm glad I ran into you. I've been wanting to see how you're doing."

*Better before bumping into you,* I think. He sounds so calm. So collected. So thoroughly, wholeheartedly unaffected. It's worse than a slap in the face.

"I'm pretty good, actually." I fight to keep my voice even.

Noah pulls back just a touch to shoot me a concerned look. "You can be honest, River. I . . . I worry about you."

*Pity.* Seeing that in his eyes makes me want to puke. How dare he *feel sorry for me.*

Anger zips through my veins. I hold on to it like a lifeline.

"Honestly?" I say coldly. "I'm doing pretty *damn* good. I've got

Tawny. I've got Tita Anna. And unlike some people, they never leave my side."

For a second, it looks like something akin to pain flickers across his face. But of course, I've imagined it. Because it's gone in the blink of an eye. Because *he's* the one who left. He's just trying to keep from feeling too guilty for breaking up with me right before my entire life went up in flames. And I mean literally right before.

It still stings to think about how completely blindsided I was. I'd thought our relationship was so perfect. For me, being in love with Noah had been the easiest thing in the world. He was attentive but never cloying. He called when he'd said he'd call. He'd remember if I had a biology exam and quiz me beforehand with flash cards. He'd drop by Gertie's and sneak kisses with me out back during my breaks.

God, the kissing. I'd go to bed dreaming of his kisses, lying there feeling the echoes of his arms around my waist.

It seemed so certain.

"We should hyphenate our names when we get married," Noah would say. "Because I honestly feel like a Santos myself." With Noah, it was always *when*. Never *if*.

*When* we have our honeymoon in the Chamonix Valley.

*When* we get a corgi.

*When* we have our third kid.

Noah had an impossible time choosing an outfit in the mornings. He hated making decisions. But he used to say our relationship wasn't a decision for him. It was just a fact. *River Santos, I will marry you.* He would say it like he was reading the time. *It is currently 1:03 p.m., Mountain Standard Time,* and *we're spending the rest of our lives together.*

Which is why I thought he was joking when he said it.

It was supposed to be The Night. He was home from college for winter break. His dad was out of town. It was just the two of us, alone at his place. I'd expected candles and rose petals at least. But instead, I got a quiet Noah. A pale Noah.

"We need to break up," he said.

"Very funny," I said.

He pressed a fist to his forehead, looking tortured.

And then I softened. "I get that you're nervous," I said. "But it's me. I'm right there with you." He didn't respond. I put my hand on his arm. "No matter what, it'll be perfect. Besides. Neither of us would know any better anyway."

He ripped his arm out of my grip. "It's not that. I just don't want to be with you anymore."

When I saw his eyes, saw the cold void of his pupils, all the oxygen left my lungs.

"You're serious," I said, feeling dizzy.

Noah didn't answer any of my questions as he walked me to the door. He was stone-faced, his coldness making his beauty cruel.

I clutched my overnight bag to my chest.

"What did I do?" I whispered, more lost than I'd ever been. "I can fix it." I reached aimlessly for him, and he stepped out of my reach. "I'll fix it."

Noah stared at me, those wide, expressive eyes locked tight. As impenetrable as Fort Knox. Finally, he spoke.

"I'll get you an Uber," he said, pulling out his phone. "You probably shouldn't drive right now."

I knocked it out of his hand. Noah caught it inches before the phone smashed against his concrete front steps. Something wild flashed in his eyes as he looked up at me.

"Don't do me any favors." My voice was unrecognizable from pain. "Don't—don't do anything for me ever again."

I drove home through my tears, and my dad was there, ready with a hug and a batch of my favorite cookies, before putting me to bed, where I cried myself to sleep.

Just three hours later, our house burst into flames.

The sound of raucous laughter from a couple of girls a few feet away brings me back to the present. A gorgeous redheaded girl makes her way toward us down the hall. I motion for Noah to make room so she can pass and use the bathroom. But when he sees her, he stiffens, straightening up and stepping back from me. I'm confused until she stops at his shoulder and frowns at the two of us.

"I thought something happened," she says. She's clearly talking to Noah, but she's studying me.

"Sorry," he says, looking uncomfortable. "I bumped into"—he gestures to me and, for a moment, seems at a loss—"an old friend."

"Oh, hi!" The redhead shoots me a dazzling smile as she links arms with Noah. "I'm Ryan. Nice to meet you!"

Rage and hurt make twin hurricanes in my body. I cross my arms to hide the shaking in my hands. It's so infuriating I have to laugh.

"River," I say with a manic sort of glee. *Wait till Tawny hears about this.* "What a pleasure. I actually gotta go. I've got to get back to my duties. Don't want to keep my coworkers waiting. I'm not as much of an asshole as this guy." I jerk a thumb at Noah.

"Right?" Ryan laughs, nudging Noah with her hip. He looks pale. "We should all get lunch sometime! I'd love to hear all the details of what this guy was like in high school."

What was Noah like in high school? Where do I start?

*He picked me up an hour early every day so we'd have time to make out in his car before class.*

*He made sure to always keep fresh orange juice in his parents' fridge for me because he knew it was my favorite.*

*He told me once that he loved me so much it hurt, like holding red coals in his chest. He told me that loving me was worth fire burning in his lungs for the rest of his life.*

"He was on the debate and chess team," I say. "Unfortunately, he was boring. So there, you're already caught up."

I feel like my toenails are being pried off. I can't take much more of this. I look over at the refill station. Logan is there, and I catch his eye. I look away, but out of my peripheral vision, I see him come over to us, holding his crumpled bow tie in one hand. *Shit. Like this could get any worse.* I do my best to pretend I don't notice him.

But then, as he reaches us, he loops his arm around my waist, pulling me close. All the breath leaves my lungs. *What the hell?*

"Can you fix my tie, Santos? It came undone, and for the life of me, I can't retie as well as you can." His voice is different. He sounds . . . flirtatious.

I gape at him. He raises his eyebrows knowingly. *What is Logan . . . ?* Suddenly, it clicks. The press of his hand is leaving a hot imprint on my lower back, so it takes me a second to find my voice.

"S-sure." It's hard to think with his body heat licking up my side. "Babe." I swallow hard. How does he still smell and look perfect? The only guy who'd find me appealing right now is Tigery. *Why is he helping me?*

"Sorry to steal her away." Logan barely looks at Noah and Ryan. I glance at Noah, whose arms are crossed tightly over his chest.

"Bye, Noah," I say, saluting. "Good running into you."

*Let's never do it again.*

I try (and fail) to get my hands to stop shaking as we head down the hall in the direction of the bathroom. Taking a deep breath, I turn to Logan. "How did you—"

"Your eyes were all but screaming *save me*, and Tawny was busy, so . . ." He ducks his chin, expertly fixing his tie, remote once more.

"Well . . . thank you. I owe you one. Or two, actually," I breathe, thinking of the tuna incident.

"You do owe me," he says, his eyes holding mine. They're ocean-storm tonight, stealing my breath. The question I ache to ask dances on my tongue: *Why? Why help me, Logan?*

"Which is why you'll be covering my shift on Saturday. It's Free Pie Weekend."

*Oh.*

He leans in, smirking. A lock of his hair falls across his forehead. "Pleasure doing business with you, Santos," he murmurs before walking away.

# chapter 6
# logan

Why.

Why?

*Why?*

The car behind me lays on the horn. Green light, shit. Didn't even notice. God, I'm in my head. I don't even care when the sedan passes me, engine snarling, the passenger flipping me the bird out the window. Right now, my brain's only got room for seven words: *Why the hell did I do that?*

I groan. Thump a fist on the steering wheel. Switch on the radio, crank it up, even when it's mostly static. None of it unclenches the fist in my gut, stops the question from kicking my skull, over and over. Fine. I'll face it. So why the hell *did* I decide to go and save Santos?

Because I'm a nice guy.

I'm a team player.

I needed Free Pie Saturday covered.

I . . . just missed my turn.

"Jesus, Logan," I mutter, pulling a U-turn in the next neighborhood. "You're so full of shit."

And, fine, I am. Because none of those things are the real reason. Why did I really decide to save Santos?

Here's the thing: I didn't. Like, it wasn't a conscious choice. There she was, clutching that tuna-smeared tray to her chest, keeping her chin high, ponytail swinging as she nodded along to whatever that dickwad said. There she was, being *so goddamn brave*, especially after all that she's been through and knowing what that silver-spoon asshole did, and then she glanced over at me, and that's when I saw the drowning in her eyes, the agony, the shattering while pretending to be whole.

I dare anyone to look into River Santos's heartbroken eyes and *not* do anything you can to take away the pain.

Not possible.

One glimpse of her sorrow, and my bow tie was already crumpled in my hand. I was striding over, plan hardly formed. See? Not a decision. Not my fault. I'm absolved.

I pull into my apartment complex, put the car in park. I don't get out. I thunk my head against the back of my seat. Wipe a hand down my face, frustrated.

*You're so full of shit, Logan. You broke your own rule. Admit it.*

Here's the thing: It's not like I snapped my rule in one clean break tonight. I'm stronger than that. It's been weeks and weeks of bending, more and more. Santos showing up with puffy red eyes. Days where she's less talkative. Days where she's silent. And then that day when she was crying in the walk-in. Shit, that was tough. I didn't break *then*. I should get a medal. I let her sit on that crate, shivering, trying so hard to stanch her tears as she tried to keep her chin up for me. Sure, I bit my tongue so hard I couldn't eat spicy stuff for a week. Sure, I couldn't stop thinking about it. Sure, I lie awake at night and *regret*.

I didn't break, though. Because if she knew who I really am, what I've done? It would be the end of everything.

So I held strong.

But tonight? I mean, tonight was already a fresh hell for her. I heard what those assholes said about her. I had to hide my smile when she offered them tuna salad, polite as you please. Everything spiraled from there. Her spilling said tuna salad. Me helping her. Being close enough to catch her so-good-it-should-be-fucking-illegal sugar-sweet scent, to see the tiny cluster of freckles on the bridge of her nose.

I almost broke my rule then. Was going to cross the line. Tell her that if she ever needed anything, she could . . .

Well, thank God I didn't say that, at least.

But I'm just a human. I did my best, but I couldn't resist. Even though I really should have. Because now it's going to be a whole lot harder.

I let myself talk to her, so now I know what it's like to put a sparkle in her eyes. I let myself touch her, so now I know how warm her skin is. I let myself hug her, so now I know how it feels to have her body pressed against me.

I'm so screwed. Because if it was hard before, now? Well, now, God help me, I'm not sure if I'm strong enough to stay away.

# chapter 7
# river

I spend the entire Saturday of Free Pie Weekend cursing Logan's name. Maybe he did help me out a couple of times at Tate's, but now I see why. He was just waiting for the chance to screw me over. I can't remember the last time Gertie's was so busy. And poor Tawny has been fighting all day to keep a migraine at bay. It's far easier to worry about her than about the toxic men haunting my life.

"That's it. Please go home, Tawn." I find her sagging against the wall by the back sinks.

"I'm fine." Tawny gives me a weak wave with one hand, clutching her stomach with the other.

"If this is 'fine,' God help us when you're not." I gently rub her back. "It's eight already. The night's basically over. Go home, take some Advil, and get in bed."

Tawny gives me a grateful hug and leaves without much more fuss.

There's a huge concert in town, so the deluge of pie-crazed people slows to a trickle around eight thirty, and the rest of the evening is surprisingly smooth. Anyone who comes in tips generously when they realize I'm the only waitress working these last couple of hours.

Unfortunately, none of them proclaims themselves my secret millionaire donor.

It's so satisfying when I finally get to flip the OPEN sign to CLOSED. I stack chairs and wipe down tables as Gertie and her cooks shut down the grill and kitchen and wave to me on their way out.

It's not until almost ten that I check the time and realize in the rush, I forgot to give Tigery his evening meal. I grab the small bag of Kitty Kibble I keep in my locker and dash outside to find Tigery waiting for me, crooked tail flicking irritably.

"I know, I know . . . sorry, buddy." I grab a fistful of food and drop it in the empty bowl I keep out back, and after an extra little tail flick, he eats his meal, and I head back inside.

I only have a few closing duties left when I hear a huge crash out back. Fear zings up my spine, lighting all my nerves. I creep to Gertie's office and peek out the window, which has a perfect view of the employee parking lot. Except for my falling-apart car, held together with duct tape and a prayer, it's empty.

Maybe it was just a raccoon? A really, really big one. Those exist, right?

Just as I start to relax, there's another crash, closer this time. My mind flashes to Tigery. If it is a raccoon, that's not a fight I want the cat taking on by himself.

Heart racing, I grab one of the big chef's knives in the kitchen. I'm not planning on *using* it. It just makes me feel better to have it on hand. I open the back door slightly, visually sweeping the area. An empty soda can rolls out from behind the dumpster.

I grip my knife tighter, heart thudding.

Then Tigery struts out from behind the dumpster, his eyes forming pleasant half-moons. He bumps his head against my shin.

"Not cool, dude," I mutter. Tigery yawns. I relax, lowering my arms.

A hand falls on my shoulder.

I scream, whirl around, and raise the knife. A strong grip catches my wrist, shackling my arm in place.

"Good God, Santos, what the hell is wrong with you?"

Logan Evans is squeezing me with his fingers, eyes wide like I've got three heads. I snatch my arm out of his grip, rubbing my wrist. But his fingers still burn like a brand, leaving my skin tingly.

"What the hell is wrong with *me*?" I snap, recovering. "You're the one skulking around the parking lot at night like a murderer!"

"Says the girl holding a *butcher knife*."

"Hey, I have the right to bear arms!" I yell, throwing up my hands and cringing inwardly at how stupid I sound. Logan takes a step back. He runs a critical gaze over me.

"What are you even still doing here, anyway?" His voice is accusatory.

I scowl. "I covered for you today. Or did you already forget?"

"Of course I didn't," he scoffs, looking away. "I just can't believe you're not done yet."

I wave a dismissive hand at him. I'm so irritated, I forget it's also the hand holding the knife.

"*Watch it.*" He makes a show of dodging.

"I was nowhere near you, drama queen," I complain.

"Drama queen?" It's nearly comical how offended he looks. "I am *not*— Look, I just came here to do a quick errand. And first thing, I nearly break my neck stumbling over a stupid pile of . . . I mean, why the *hell* is there even a giant bag of empty cans near the dumpster?"

I turn my nose up at him.

"That's Gertie's pile. She collects the cans to make cool art. She doesn't like to keep them in the building, and her apartment's too small for storage." I cross my arms. "You'd know all that if you actually *talked* to any of us more than once every three months."

Logan sighs. "Look. Can you just put that thing away before you hurt someone? Hmm, Killer?" He sounds exhausted. When he lifts his gaze to mine, I'm a little startled at how his eyes are a tinge bloodshot, the thin skin beneath his lower lids dark and shadowed.

"Okay," I say, disarmed by his weariness. I set the knife down on the upside-down bucket Gertie keeps by the door as a seat for her smoke breaks.

He doesn't say thank you, but there's something in the way the tension leaves his body that resembles relief.

I wonder where he's just come from. He looks nice. His jeans are sleek and dark, and he's wearing a simple blue button-up, his shirtsleeves rucked up to his elbows. I try not to stare at the corded muscles of his forearms or the way the fabric stretches over his broad shoulders. I doubt he'll ever tell me why he needed me to cover today, so I ask him a less personal question.

"How did you get here? I don't see your car." I peer around the parking lot.

"I walked. I live in the apartment complex right around the corner." Logan pulls a small Ziploc bag out of his pocket, shaking the contents at Tigery. As soon as he does, Tigery goes on full alert, bleating long and loud, turning in eager circles. "Sorry it's late, buddy. But I got you," Logan murmurs. He dumps out the Ziploc bag on the asphalt, and that's when I register that it's dry cat food.

"Wait." I point at Tigery, who's inhaling the pile of kibble. "You're feeding him?"

Logan shrugs. "If I don't, who will?"

"Me," I deadpan.

"Really?" This time, Logan's surprise is genuine.

"Yeah. I keep Kitty Kibble in my locker."

"Huh." He surveys Tigery with newfound respect. "Well done, you little bastard. You got us both." There's a warmth in his voice that makes my heart jump.

*River Rose Santos, are you actually jealous of a cat?*

"Quick reflexes, by the way," I suddenly blurt to drown that humiliating train of thought. I mimic a stabbing motion, a touch sheepish. A deep laugh bursts out of Logan, and I hate that immediately, I want to make him do it again.

"So is this your thing? Spending time in the shadows, waiting to save people from murderers with your lightning-fast reflexes?"

"You curious about me, Santos?" Logan crosses his arms and raises his eyebrows. There's the tiniest edge to his voice.

"No, of course not," I say, flustered. "Whatever. I don't care."

He sighs. For some reason, his smile is rueful. He takes his time rising to his feet, brushing kibble crumbs from his palms.

"Okay. Agility training in football. A lifetime ago."

Football? Dad's face jumps into my thoughts. Anytime he hugged me after a practice, he smelled like sweat and fresh-cut grass. His hugs were so tight, the whistle hanging around his neck would dig into my sternum. I'd only hug him tighter.

I wonder if I'm showing all this on my face, because when I catch Logan watching me, I swear I see sympathy in his eyes. I clear my throat.

"You and football. I don't know. I can't really see it."

"Yeah, well." He wipes a hand down his face, and all at once, he seems exhausted. "I couldn't either. Didn't last. Wasn't my thing." His voice is quiet.

"So . . . what is your thing?" I chance another probing little question.

Logan smirks. "What is this? Twenty questions?"

"I've asked you *two*," I huff.

"Still." He yawns and stretches, and I lean down to scratch Tigery's head so I'm not tempted to see if Logan's muscles make that V, which Tawny calls *sex lines*. I keep scratching the cat so Logan won't see my obscene blush.

"Well, the boy's been fed. Twice," he muses. "I'm off. My *thing* is getting a full night's sleep." He shoves his hands in his pockets and starts to walk away.

*That's it?*

"You know," I say to his retreating back, "if I didn't know any better, I'd say you were hiding something."

Logan turns his head to call over his shoulder, not bothering to stop. "Here's a tip, Santos. *Everyone's* hiding something. Even the damned two-timing cat."

# chapter 8
# river

Hours later, it's pitch-black out. No streetlamps cast a warm glow. No headlights illuminate with their twin beams. Not even a single firefly lights the air around us. The only light comes from a watery moon above, barely visible through wisps of clouds. Despite the dark, I can see everything around me with startling clarity.

I can see my mother standing next to me, staring at a moldering ruin, her skin pale.

It's unsightly. The haphazard skeleton of a building juts out of piles of rubble. Rebar supports stick out every which way, like metal fangs. Blackened bricks lean against each other, crumbling like a wet sand-castle. It's ugly and chaotic, and I don't know why I'm here.

But then I see the pristine ruby-red mailbox at the end of the driveway.

My mother sighs, shifting on her feet. "The only house for miles that has such a garish mailbox. The color of blood!"

She said that so many times over the years. But still, she'd let my dad paint the mailbox that color and had never insisted he change it back to black.

She tucks a lock of blond hair behind her ear and casts me a sidelong glance. "How did you do it?"

I turn to her, confused. In the moonlight, she looks older than I remember. Tired and pale. Insubstantial, somehow. Like she might fade away into the moonlight itself.

"Do what?" I ask.

Her lips curve in a sad smile. "Survive, of course."

And that's when I realize. I'm not looking at a pile of rubble. I'm looking at a graveyard.

Here lies the Ikea bookcase that took ten hours for Dad and me to put together. The flat-screen TV that Dad saved up for for an entire year. The scrapbooks my mom made, the fourteen thick albums filled with pictures taken before digital, before the cloud. Pictures that no longer exist anywhere in this universe. My dad's record collection, his pride and joy. The stack of twelve ABBA vinyls that sat next to the record player he'd bought as a kid. He kept it all in the kitchen so he could dance while waiting for the snickerdoodle cookies he was making to finish baking.

How did our entire lives, our entire family, become *this*? A pile of black, rotted ash that doesn't even reach my knees?

I stare and stare, tracking wildly over the debris, which once held so much more than even I could possibly imagine. I stare at the wake of the massacre, hungry for any sense of recognition. But as I search, the remains collapse in on themselves, like charred quicksand.

I whirl on my mom, feeling crazed. "Where did it all go?"

"It's gone, River. I love you. But it's all gone." Tears as white and round as pearls cut paths down her cheeks.

I blink in horror. Because as the tears run down her cheeks, my mom is slowly vanishing before me. Growing lighter and lighter until she is no more than a faded outline.

"Mom, no!" I scream, grasping for her hand. But she is already gone, a wisp of smoke curling to the sky.

"No!" I yell again. "Don't leave me!" I scream again and again, until my yells fill the air around me, until the ground starts rumbling beneath my feet, my desperation triggering an earthquake.

In the distance, a siren blares.

And I wake up.

I BLINK INTO darkness, but this darkness is nothing like that of my dream. Light from the parking lot behind our apartment filters through my plastic blinds in thin shafts. My clock glows blue in the corner. And my phone on my nightstand is aglow with a text.

"It was just a dream," I whisper to myself, my heart still racing, my pillow damp with tears.

I clutch my sheets to my chest, listening to Tita Anna's snores from the next room, trying to slow my breathing. "It was just a dream," I whisper again.

But it wasn't just a dream. There are parts of this nightmare that I can never wake from. And there are parts that blur between both dream and memory, so tightly intertwined that I can't separate out fact and trauma.

Parts I haven't told anyone else about, not even Tita Anna.

I close my eyes and call forward the memory that's haunted me for months. Not of the flames or the smoke so thick that I felt like I was drowning.

But of a familiar presence beside me as I collapsed in the hallway outside my bedroom.

I remember calling out for my dad, every breath painful, like there was glass in my lungs. And then I remember the feel of hands on mine, of being dragged from the house into the cool night air. I was so far gone, sliding in and out of consciousness, that I never saw a face. I just saw a shadow and felt the strength of a body as it pulled me through a wall of flames. Whoever it was laid me on the ground before pressing a featherlight kiss to my temple and disappearing once more into the burning night.

Half the time, I'm convinced it happened. The other half, I write it off as a hallucination, as smoke-addled thinking—that I conjured a hero to save me when I couldn't save myself. Still, I can't shake the feeling that there's something real behind it, *someone* real behind it. Someone who loved me enough to walk through fire.

The most impossible person in the whole world and yet the only one who makes any sense.

My mother.

Every rational part of me fights the thought, because if it *was* her, what was she doing there in the first place?

And if she saved me, why wouldn't she have saved my dad?

Why would she have run off and just left me there?

I take my phone from the nightstand, the metal cool in my hand, then guiltily swipe away a text from Tawny, as if she can see what I'm about to do next. I know Tawny and Tita Anna would disapprove, but I can't help it.

I type out a text to my mom.

**River**

Mom. Were you there the night of the fire?
Please answer me. I need to know.

Texting Mom is dangerous in that I never get a response, but I always get my hopes up. It's emotional Russian roulette. Except there are five bullets and only one blank. You'd have to be a masochist to play those odds.

Or just a devastated girl who wants desperately to hear from her mom.

A second later, my phone buzzes in my hand. I jump, hardly daring to believe it. But my heart drops immediately when I read the notification. The text isn't from my mom; it's from Noah.

**Noah**

It was good seeing you yesterday. I hope you know I'll always care about our friendship.

"Oh, *screw* you," I snarl. I delete the message and toss my phone onto my comforter, mad at Noah. Mad at myself for caring. Mad for thinking that my mom would actually write back.

I adjust my pillows and sit up against the headboard. I wish I could talk to Tawny about all this, but my mom is her red line. When it comes to Tawny, you're never going to want anyone else in your corner. She's the fiercest friend I've ever met. It's something I genuinely appreciate, something that makes me feel loved.

But sometimes? Sometimes that loyalty drifts into a more acidic anger. Leaning more toward vitriol than righteousness. It can be a touch scary. Especially when it comes to my mom.

"How do you not hate her?" Tawny has asked me more than once. Usually while pacing like a wildcat in my room as I tuck my knees to my chest, ashamed at how "incorrect" my emotions feel in that moment.

"She's my mom," I would say quietly, scared to meet Tawny's glare. "It's complicated. I can't . . . I can't hate my mom. I'm sure she has her reasons for what she's doing. She'll explain it to me one day. I know it."

"River. There's nothing—*nothing* she could ever say that would justify her abandoning her child." In that moment, Tawny, the human embodiment of a bright day, from her sun-colored hair to her hazel eyes, would be shrouded in darkness. Her voice, her eyes, her face. I'd never know what to say, so she'd clam up, turn away to stare out the window.

I get it. I know where she's coming from. Why she feels the way she does. It's personal for her.

Tawny found out she had been adopted when she was in elementary school. We've talked about it a few times, but it's one of the subjects that's still touchy for her, even to this day. She knows next to nothing about her birth mom, which leaves a giant hole of knowledge for her to fill with her own understandable hurt. Tawny's adoptive mom is wonderful, but her adoptive dad passed away before she could really form memories. In some ways, it just compounds her loss—all these parental figures who are nothing more than ghosts.

Which is why I'm not pushing Tawny to hash this out with me. And that really sucks because Tawny's the one person I trust more than anyone else to help me figure out what went wrong, why Mom left and didn't return.

The cops treated my mom's disappearance with suspicion at first. A missing white woman and a Filipino husband who didn't report it for months? It was basically a *Dateline* headline waiting to be written. They peppered my dad with a million questions about their marriage, but when they heard about my mom's "mental health struggles," they pretty much shrugged their shoulders and wrote it off as a lost cause—albeit with some vague threats about keeping their eyes on my dad.

The cops were useless, but their questions made me think. I grew up believing everything between my mom and dad had been . . . well, good. Not perfect. No one's family is perfect. Mom and Dad had fights. Honestly, it would have been weirder if they hadn't fought at all. But they didn't seem to fight as much as some of my friends' parents did.

Things had gotten a little more stressful in the past couple of years. Money had always been tight, but there had been a few recent budget cuts at Dad's school. He didn't get the raise they'd been counting on. And the interest on Mom's student loans had just increased. A brutal sore spot for her, because she didn't even have the degree to justify the expense. She had to drop out of school when she got pregnant with me, a guilt I walked around with like a rock in my shoe.

When I got a job at Gertie's, I asked to help with bills.

"Never," Mom had said, her eyes flashing. "That is *your* money, baby girl. You save it for college. You save it to build your ladder out of here."

I didn't understand. "Out of where? I don't want to go anywhere." I still didn't understand when she burst into tears and clutched me close, pressing her sobs to the crown of my head.

So, yeah. Now that I think about it, sure. They fought a little more than normal the year before she left. Instead of taking my money, Dad squeezed in tutoring sessions between practices, and Mom picked up extra shifts cleaning houses, though honestly, I think that made it a little worse for her.

Spending her days immersed in the cocoons of the upper class began to affect her more and more. How could it not, when her duties included fluffing pillows on a dog bed with a higher thread count than she had ever seen? Dogs that ate lamb and kangaroo ("Yes, River, *actual fucking kangaroo meat.*") while the three of us eating dinner at Applebee's had become a rare extravagance.

"Mrs. DuPont bought a new rug today," Mom would say as she collapsed on our lumpy couch. "Guess how much?"

"How much?" I would ask, hating how her demeanor would go dull and flat as buttons.

"Two hundred thousand dollars, River. The cost of an entire house." She'd grimaced. "At least it used to be." Then she'd go very far away, losing focus as she'd sink into herself.

I knew where she went every time.

Her daydreams were florid. As vivid as a fresh memory. In them, we were never holding our breath at the end of every month. Mom and Dad never had to decide which would take the hit: the food budget or the student loan payments. We would win the lottery. A sudden windfall of millions, the answer to all our problems.

And she would never spend it on *rugs*.

"What will you do with it?" I would whisper as I watched her lucky penny fly across her weekly lottery ticket. I always made sure to ask it like it was inevitable. Just a matter of time. Mom's fragile hope couldn't take hypotheticals. The amounts she didn't win every week would change, but her answer was always the same.

"I'm going to give it to you, baby girl." She'd lift her head, her sleek blond hair falling across her shoulder. "When I win big, it's all going to you."

This is the other thing I cannot tell Tawny. It's my own little fragile hope, held together by gossamer and spider silk. One Tawny would scoff to pieces in a heartbeat. Something I can barely think, much less speak out loud:

*Has it finally happened?*

*Has Mom finally won big?*

*Has she given it to me? The two million dollars? A ladder out of here that I refuse to climb?*

Even now as I think on this, it feels like a fairy tale. And I'm just an idiot in deep denial, inventing proof that my mother didn't abandon me.

I cling to it anyway. My whisper-thin beliefs.

My mother is protecting me. This is her taking care of me. This is her telling me she loves me, even if she can't be here.

She'll tell me why someday. I know she will.

And when she does, I'll tell her, "It's our ladder, Mom. We can escape together."

*To my baby girl,*

*I know you must be wondering why I left you. And I wish there was a simple answer, some explanation that shows that it had nothing to do with you and everything to do with me and your father. You have no idea how many times I've tried to write it all out, to put it in terms that will make sense to you, to show you why I thought it was the right thing to do.*

*Life deals you a hand, and you play it as best as you can. But sometimes the odds are against you. And they have been against us.*

*Your life started with a tragedy and a secret, and oh, baby girl, I've done some terrible things. Things I will never, ever be able to make up for. I know—I know—it's time to go home. To come clean. To find you.*

*But if I do, I fear I will lose everything.*

*I fear I will lose you.*

*I met a girl on the trail today. She was smart, this girl, in her final year of college. She's exactly how I imagine you'll be in your twenties. Strong. Bright. Charting your own course and keeping your head straight.*

*I couldn't explain to her why I suddenly started crying. Why I'm so very sorry. And I am sorry, sweetheart. I can never say it enough: I'm sorry, I'm sorry, I'm sorry.*

*I'm sorry, and I love you. Even so far away, I love you. Can you feel it?*

*Can you?*

*Love,*
*Mom*

# chapter 9
# river

Tita Anna and I have been talking about the Italy trip ever since our dinner, looking at hotel bookings online and gaming cheap flights. But it turns out that to apply for a passport, you need a birth certificate. Preferably one that hasn't been burnt to a crisp in a house fire. Which is why I've spent my morning at the Arizona Department of Health Services, applying for a copy of a piece of paper that proves that I am indeed River Rose Santos.

It was brutal, writing Dad and Mom's names over and over on the forms. My hand cramped and my heart ached as I wrote their names side by side, like in some alternate reality they're still together, still happily married. It's made stanching the flood of memories impossible.

I can't stop thinking about when I was six and my mom tore apart the living room looking for the TV remote after a particularly hard day. She was sobbing on the couch when I found it under the table, touched it to her hand. Her tears turned to giggles as she hugged me and spun me around the room. The next time she left on a hike, I snuck the TV remote into her food bag, thinking it'd keep her tears away. When she wrote my dad a letter telling him what I'd done, he laughed and wrapped me in a big hug.

The urge to see my dad is so overwhelming that I do a U-turn on my way home and follow the now-familiar path to Ocotillo Ridge Memorial Park.

When I get to his plot, I brush the dirt from the headstone. Sweep the dead leaves away from the base with my hands. I really should have brought flowers. The saguaro I planted is still there, thin but resilient. It barely reaches the midpoint of the headstone, but with time, I know it will tower over it. Fully grown saguaro can reach over forty feet tall. I picture one day pruning a side stem of the cactus and planting it in the backyard of whatever house I find myself living in, a piece of my dad always with me.

Other than the day we lowered him into it, Tawny's never been to Dad's grave. The third time I invited her to join me, she broke down. "I can't," she said, looking ashamed. "It's too painful. I want to be there for you, Riv, I do . . ." I stopped her short because she didn't need to explain anything to me.

My dad was like a surrogate father to Tawny. At dinner once, she let slip that her mother once promised her tickets to see a Taylor Swift concert but with all her traveling, the timing never worked out. Then, on her seventeenth birthday, there was an envelope waiting for Tawny on the kitchen counter. We opened it together as my dad watched, a goofy grin on his face. Inside were three tickets to a Taylor Swift candlelight concert—the kind where an orchestra plays instrumental versions of her songs. I jumped up and down like a little kid, and Tawny almost passed out, she was so excited.

Taylor wasn't actually there, but it didn't matter. We knew every song. My dad even learned the lyrics to sing along with us in the car. We all filled our arms with friendship bracelets and held up heart hands. At least I had him for eighteen years. She only had him for two.

I'm wiping my eyes when I notice a man sitting on a bench a few yards away.

He's bent over a notebook, his foot tapping an agitated rhythm. A riotous bouquet of flowers is propped against the beautiful gravestone by his side. He's drumming a pen against the blank pages, and it's somehow the most relatable thing in the world, even though I've never heard anyone talk about "singer's block." Either way, I find myself wishing the stranger well. *May you find your muse.* I selfishly sneak in, *And may I find my voice.*

I definitely don't want to be caught staring at someone's private moment, so I hold my breath, easing backward, hoping to keep each step silent. Miraculously, I manage just fine.

For about three steps.

On the fourth, my heel snags on a rock, and I tumble noisily to the ground.

"Shit," I grunt, kicking up dust as I sprawl across the ground. The stranger's dark head snaps up, and I know those eyes.

*Shit.*

It's Logan goddamn Evans.

And that's when I see the inscription carved into the ornate face of the marble headstone at his feet. *Helen Evans: May 6, 1977–June 14, 2023. Cherished wife and beloved mother, missed and loved forever.*

Oh God. Helen Evans. Logan's mom. And June 14 was Free Pie Saturday.

That night had been the second anniversary of his mother's death.

There's a quiet snap of Logan's notebook shutting. He rises from the bench and walks over to me. "Santos, when I said everyone has secrets, I wasn't suggesting you stalk me to find out mine."

"Oh God, I wasn't. I mean I'm here to see . . . I'm not. Stalking, I mean." I put up my hands in a placating gesture. "I can go."

"Stay," he says. He offers his hand, and I take it. In one smooth gesture, he pulls me easily to my feet. He finally gets a handle on his face. It's nice and inscrutable again.

I dart a look at the notebook in his hands. "What were you writing?"

I can feel the way he closes up, see the stiffening in his posture. I backtrack. "Look. You don't have to tell me anything you don't want to." I shrug. My eyes flick back to the beautiful bouquet on his mom's grave. Desert bluebells.

My breath hitches and I walk closer, drawn to the bundle of familiar, rich indigo. I brush my thumb against a silky petal. I don't remember the color feeling so mournful. "These were Dad's favorite. Anytime there was a good winter rain, he'd drag Mom and me into the Sonoran the week after. They'd grow thick as blue blankets after a January storm. 'See how they flourish in the middle of the desert, River?' he'd say. 'That's resilience. Even a flower can be strong.'"

For a moment, we just stand in silence. But it feels expansive, like a spool unwinding.

"Sounds like a poetic guy," Logan finally says.

"He liked to think so," I say, smiling. "Dad never loved the whole meathead-football-coach stereotype. 'Why shouldn't a man excel at offensive strategy as well as baking?'" I affect Dad's deep cadence. When the pinch of my heart releases, it feels like some of the pain releases too.

"Your dad . . . baked?" Logan shakes his head. "Can't picture a football guy baking."

I smile. "He did. Cookies were his specialty. He made up his own recipes."

"Anything good?"

"The best." But then my smile dims. "He was old-school, though, and kept his recipes on paper, so . . ." I trail off.

It takes a second, but Logan gets it. He visibly softens. Everyone knows about the fire that took everything.

Even him.

"Oh," he says softly. "I'm sorry. About the recipes. And your dad."

"I'm sorry too," I whisper back, nodding at his mom's grave.

"Thanks," he says. He casts a look toward Dad's grave, his eyes tracing the letters carved into the granite. "I like your dad's headstone."

"Thanks . . ." I chew my lip. "I feel bad about it, a little. It was one of the cheaper ones. Even though I had . . ." I rub my neck, not wanting to bring up the GoFundMe money. "Anyway. I wonder if I should have gotten him something nicer. Gotten over myself and spent more money for a more elegant tribute to him. Like your mother's. Hers is beautiful—"

"I hate it."

I'm taken aback by the edge in his voice. "Why?"

The muscle in Logan's jaw pulses. "Mom was a minimalist. She found simplicity beautiful. That tombstone is expensive only for the sake of *looking* expensive." He deflates, wipes his hand down his face. "Sorry. I'm talking about my dad. Specifically."

"I take it you two don't get along?"

"Understatement." His jaw muscle twitches again. "I moved out last year."

"Wow." I know we're technically adults, but the idea of living by myself feels completely intimidating. "You have your own place. That's impressive."

He waves. "It's tiny. The only thing that sucks is it doesn't allow animals. Otherwise, my little buddy at the diner would be staying with me."

I raise my eyebrows. "Do you mean Tigery?"

He shoots me a withering look. "Don't tell me that's what you named him."

"Hey, he picked it out himself." I raise my hands. "One day I just stood back there saying various cat names out loud. As soon as I said 'Tigery,' he trotted over to me, tail up."

Logan rolls his eyes, but there's something fond in his laugh.

"Tell me about your mom," I say, half expecting Logan to shut down again. But he just looks up at the sky, a thoughtful expression on his face.

"She was amazing. Intelligent and compassionate. A veterinarian. She loved all animals. And I do mean *all*." He tilts his head. "One time, she almost put her hand on a bark scorpion that was hiding in our dishwasher. I would have just stomped on it, but she carefully freed it outside."

"Wow," I say. "I don't think I would have done the same. My dad got stung once when I was little and was sick for two full days. After that, Mom and I were tasked with scorpion chores."

Logan looks at me a long moment before sighing. "All right. I'll bite. What the hell are 'scorpion chores'?"

I raise a brow at him. "It's a privilege not to know what scorpion chores are. Have you ever seen a scorpion under black light?"

Logan shakes his head. "Can't say that I have."

"They *glow*. Light up like a Christmas tree, or some weird alien creature. So during scorpion season, my mom and I would turn off the lights and switch on our black light. We would hunt them with the black light and crush them with wooden dowels." I huff a laugh, shaking my head. "It was terrifying at first. But then my mom told me that we were mighty huntresses defending our fortress. After I killed my first scorpion, she carved a notch into my dowel."

Logan's lips curve into grin. "Wow. What's your body count?"

"Last time I checked, my dowel had sixty-seven notches on it." I have to actively stop myself from picturing that dowel as the pile of ash it undoubtedly is now.

Logan's mouth falls open. "Sixty-seven? I don't know what's more terrifying: the fact that you had *sixty-seven* scorpions in your house or the fact that you tallied your kills on your weapon."

I shrug. "Better sixty-seven kills than sixty-seven stings. Although, honestly, I'm weirdly ashamed that I've never been stung. I'm not sure you're a real Arizonian if you haven't been."

"I've been stung," Logan says.

"And?" I raise my brows.

"I don't exactly count it as a point of pride. It hurt. A lot."

"Oh yeah? How bad?" I ask, surprised that he admitted that. Logan has never exactly been vulnerable before.

A smirk plays on his lips. "You really wanna know?"

I narrow my eyes. "Why, you got a scorpion in your pocket?"

He looks steadily at me. "Give me your hand," he murmurs, holding out his palm.

I swallow hard as he takes my hand and turns it over, touching the tender, pale skin on the inside of my wrist, tracing the blue vein that's there.

"There are fewer nerve endings here," he says, then moves his finger to the center of my palm, "than *here*." He draws a circle at the center of my palm. I can't ignore the way I suck in my breath at his touch, the way my stomach swoops. Logan stops his fingers and taps at the skin just above my heart line, on the space below my fingers.

"This is where I was stung." He cradles my knuckles in one hand and, with the other, gathers a tiny piece of my skin between his thumb and forefinger and pinches lightly.

"That was incredibly anticlimactic," I say.

Logan scoffs. "You think I'd actually hurt you, Santos? Picture that, times a thousand. My fingers swelled to twice their size. I couldn't write for over a week."

"I wouldn't wish that on my worst enemy."

"Is that what I am to you?" He says it so quietly, I almost think I imagined it.

"Honestly, Logan?" He meets my eyes when he hears his name. "That's sort of up to you."

We fall silent then and both turn our heads back to Dad's grave. The sky is unusually cloudy, the monsoons of late summer peeking around the corner. It makes the day a little cooler and darker. It feels intimate, somehow, and I'm aware of just how close we're standing.

As if noticing too, Logan shifts beside me, rustling for something in his bag.

"You don't have to take these. But if you wanted . . ." He pulls out a small bunch of desert bluebells, offering them to me. "Mom never minded sharing. Especially with fellow flower lovers."

"Wow." My voice is thick with emotion as I lift the bouquet from his hands with a gentle reverence. "Thank you, Logan."

He smiles at me, the kindest I've ever seen his face. It makes him even more beautiful, that asshole. It's not fair how the color of his eyes can go from spring's first bluebird to quicksilver in a heartbeat. How a single look from him across the room makes my neurons fire, my nerves light up, the blood race through my veins. It's unfair that there's only an inch between my shoulder and Logan's, but that I still can't breach that distance, even here, even as we both long for people taken from us too soon.

Or can I?

I lean the tiniest bit toward him to barely press against him. I can't tell if I imagine how he stiffens and relaxes, quick as a heartbeat.

But I do notice that he doesn't pull away.

# chapter 10
# river

I'm still thinking about Logan when I walk into the diner for my morning shift. I'd never thought he could be so . . . kind. I keep going over and over our conversation, looking for clues that I read the whole thing wrong. Were we connecting or did he feel bad for me? God, what's worse: his pity or being his enemy? *Is that what I am to you?* he asked. Logan didn't conclude if I was friend or enemy, but he *did* give me flowers. That means *friend*, right? Ugh. Why do I have to care? And *why* do his eyes have to be the same stupid shade as those gorgeous bluebells?

When I push open the door leading to the dining room, the bell jingles above me. As soon as it does, Logan's eyes pop up and meet mine. My body, once more a traitor, reacts immediately to his intense stare. It won't let me look away. His eyes drop first, because *of course they do.*

I clear my throat as I sidle up to where he's counting out the money in the till. I wanted him to say hi first, but I'm *me*, so I say, "Morning, Logan," my voice too high. He doesn't look up from the stack of ones in his hands.

". . . thirty-three, thirty-*four*," he says significantly, focusing on the shuffling bills.

"Ah, shit, sorry," I say.

So it's business as usual. *Ah, but we'll always have the graveyard,* I think morosely, fighting disappointment as I head to my locker to grab my apron.

"You gotta be kidding me." I groan when I tie it around my waist. I'd totally forgotten all about the grease stain I was *supposed* to have washed out after last shift.

"Need an extra?" I look up just as Logan tosses me a brand-new apron. I catch it before it hits my face.

"Thanks." I blink, caught off guard. "So prepared," I tease. "I'm impressed you have extras here."

"I don't." He jerks his head at the closed office door. "Gertie does."

*Right.* I tie the apron a little harder than I need to.

"Well . . . thanks."

"No prob." Logan's eyes sparkle for half a second as he adds, "Scorpion Queen." The smirk he gives me is tiny and brief but is enough to give me an inconvenient, confusing belly swoop. Then he's out the door, arms laden with stacks of pancakes.

The rest of the morning is no less confusing.

Whatever is happening between us—*is anything happening?*—has us both awkward and clumsy. We keep getting in each other's way. At one point, we do that little dance where neither of us knows which way the other is going. Finally, he reaches out his hand on my waist, nudging me to one side so he can get around me. There's a tenderness to his touch that I swear I'm not imagining. I still feel the weight of his hand there when the bell above the front door dings and someone all too familiar strolls into the diner.

It's Dr. Charles Pierce, Noah's dad—and sure enough, Noah is close behind. Dr. Pierce is in a baseball hat pulled low over his salt-and-pepper hair and a deceptively expensive jacket that Noah once told me is not actually "black" but "onyx camouflage." I glance around, hoping Logan can wait on them—I'd rather not have another awkward interaction with Noah—but just as they walk through the dining room, Logan slips into the kitchen, his face tense.

I turn back, pasting on my bright smile. Dad and Dr. Pierce were close friends. We spent this past Christmas (Dad's *last* Christmas) with Noah and Dr. Pierce, and as we were driving away, Dad said, "I wonder if Noah can tell the difference between love and fear."

Because Dr. Pierce can shut down a conversation with a single glance. He rarely smiles.

Except at me, that is. He was always so kind and soft-spoken, clapping Dad on the back as they manned the grill, watching Noah and me play fetch with Pepper, their border collie.

He's smiling right now as he walks up to the counter, sliding off his sunglasses, while Noah trails behind him, hands in his pockets, looking deeply uncomfortable.

"River, it's so wonderful to see you."

I'm surprised how good it is to hear Dr. Pierce's deep, rumbling voice. He's checked in a few times over text since the funeral, but I haven't seen him in months.

"It's wonderful to see you too, Dr. Pierce," I say with a pang to the man I'd been so sure would be my father-in-law one day.

"Hey, River," Noah says. I give him a tight smile.

Dr. Pierce slides onto a stool across from me. Noah takes the seat beside him. "It's *Charlie* to you, River."

"Yes, sir." I slide menus and napkin-wrapped silverware in front of the two. "What can I get you both to drink?"

If he notices that I'm purposely ignoring his son, he has the tact to pay it no mind. "He'll have a Coke, and I'll take black coffee."

When I bring them their drinks, Noah glances up at me. I hold my breath, but he stays silent, taking the Coke without a word. I know he won't drink it. Noah only drinks Sprite.

"So," Dr. Pierce says, scanning over the menu, "I realized this morning I haven't had one of those famous Gertie waffles in a long time." He lifts his gaze. "But more importantly, I hadn't seen *you* in a long time. How are you, kiddo?" His words are enough to make pressure build behind my eyes. I can feel Noah waiting for my answer.

Like I'd admit the truth in front of *him*.

"Oh, you know." I give him a brittle smile. "Hangin' in there." Dr. Pierce gives me a sad smile. I know he understands. He loved Dad too.

"We're family, River." Dr. Pierce puts a hand on my arm. "We'll always be family. You can come to me for anything, you understand?"

If only I could truly take him up on that offer: *I've got something you can do for me, Charlie. Tell me why the hell your son broke my heart.*

"That means a lot to me," I say instead. "And I know that would mean a lot to Dad as well," I add softly.

Dr. Pierce's face flickers again, something like agony contorting his features. I know he misses Dad. And I do know he would do anything for me, no questions asked—and that he has the means to help.

That was the reason Dr. Pierce was the first person I asked about the anonymous GoFundMe donation. The day after the funeral, I waited for him outside the. He finally appeared, hospital looking exhausted and pale, a streak of blood visible on his blue scrubs.

"Was it you, Dr. Pierce?" I asked, holding up my phone to show him the GoFundMe page. "Did you donate the two million?"

His eyebrows shot up, so shocked that he forgot to chide me for using his formal title.

"River," he finally said, painfully sincere. Almost guilty-looking. "I'm so sorry. You know I'll always help you if you need it—financially or otherwise—but it wasn't . . . it wasn't me."

My stomach had plummeted when he said it. It'd made so much sense that it'd be him. Dr. Pierce is rich. He's not flashy about it in the way Tate and Mr. Franklin are, but Noah's house is something out of *Architectural Digest*. He and his dad take amazing vacations all around the globe—skiing in Switzerland, hiking in Patagonia, a guided two-week tour of Japan. They even have a second home on Lake Tahoe. More than that, he's generous—he established a scholarship fund for kids at our high school who need financial support.

And he loved my dad.

It made so much sense—and it would have been so much easier to accept the help, knowing where it had actually come from. Instead, I was left with only my grief and a mystery.

Feeling foolish, I nodded numbly and turned back to my car, walking away from Dr. Pierce before the gathering tears could spill over.

Now I bring them their waffles, a jar of warm syrup, and soft butter. Then, like the mature young woman I am, I avoid them for as long as humanly possible. By the time they've finished, it's almost time for me to clock out.

"This was lovely," Dr. Pierce says, wiping his mouth with a napkin. "Both meal and company."

He pulls a hundred-dollar bill from his wallet. "Here, take this and we're all set. Keep the change, of course."

My jaw falls open. It's like a 200 percent tip. "No way. Sir, I—"

"Don't even try, River." He waves me off, then gets serious. "And, kid? Don't be a stranger."

Dr. Pierce gives me another smile as he leaves the diner. Noah looks like he wants to say something but ends up slinking silently after his father. It's what I wanted: to ignore him and make him feel even a tenth as pathetic as he had made me feel.

But all I want right now is to go home. Maybe cry a little.

Okay, maybe cry a lot.

When I go into the back to punch out, Logan's trying to fit a dented metal tray into the wire rack.

"Here, let me," I say, coming to his side.

"I got it," he snaps. With a final push, the tray slots in. He wipes sweat from his forehead and sighs. When he sees the expression on my face, he softens. "I'm sorry. Just in a foul mood today. Look, maybe—"

"Evans, come back here for a minute, yeah?" Gertie calls from her office. "I need your help with something."

Logan throws an apologetic look my way. "Later, Santos," he says.

I try not to feel hurt. Knowing about Logan's mom makes it easier to cut him slack. I grab my stuff from my locker and head out to the parking lot. I'm fishing out my keys from my bag when I hear someone call my name. I look up. Noah's leaning against my car.

*Great.*

Noah sighs, lifts a hand to ruffle the hair above the nape of his neck. "The waffles are still good. They taste exactly the same."

"Same recipe, same Gertie." I twirl my keys on my fingers. Even though it's nearly a hundred degrees outside, a cold fury rages through my body. Seven months later, and I still feel the punch of his words.

"Right." Noah's shoulders sag. "Look. Can we talk? Dad and I drove separately—he's off to a meeting."

"I don't know, Noah. Can we?" I regret the childish words as soon as they leave my mouth. "Sure. We can talk."

"I, uh. So. Have you decided which . . . are you going to—to college?" His sculpted cheekbones tinge pink, and he rubs harder at the back of his neck.

"College?" I throw up my hands. "I don't know. Someday? I've been a little preoccupied, Noah. You haven't been around, so you wouldn't know, but college isn't exactly priority numero uno at the moment."

Truth is, Tita Anna and I have talked about it. I had a scholarship to University of Arizona for a music degree, and Tawny was going to major in hospitality for her event-planning career. It had been the plan since junior year. We'd room, eat, drink, and be merry together.

But that was before.

UA was understanding and let me postpone my scholarship, but right now I can't even imagine when I'll be ready.

Not that Noah's earned the right to any of that info.

"What do you want from me, Noah?" I snap.

"Ah, right." He runs a hand through his hair, making a floppy blond mess of it. "I am not doing a great job here. I just wanted—needed to make sure you were doing okay."

Frustration spills over my edges.

"Am I *okay*, Noah?" I spit out a cold laugh. "Am I okay now that my dad's dead? And my mom's gone? And I still don't know why my boyfriend broke up with me?" I give my head a vicious shake. "You're a smart guy. What do you think? Or better yet: What does *Ryan* think?"

Out of the corner of my eye, a shadow shifts. Logan's standing there, two trash bags in hand, watching us. He holds my gaze. Grips it, really. And I realize: He's asking if I'm okay. If I need him to step in. I shake my head ever so slightly. Logan hesitates a moment, then, with one last glance, disappears back into the diner. But somehow I know he hasn't gone far.

"I'm sorry."

I turn back to Noah. His eyes are wide and expressive, as green as a field of four-leaf clovers.

"River," he says, "I'm sorry—I mean . . ." Noah presses a palm to his forehead. "Ryan and I," he says, quieter this time. He looks up. "We aren't dating."

"Does she know that?" I challenge. "Because she had future Mrs. Dr. Noah *what was he like in high school?* written all over her."

"I didn't say she didn't *want* to date me," Noah says.

I roll my eyes.

"This is coming out all wrong." He winces. "I just meant—I decided that . . . I don't want to. Date her, I mean." His voice is low and fervent as he takes a step closer. "River, I care about you."

I try to laugh, but it comes out wet and shuddery. "You care about me?" I shake my head. "Because you have a really fucked-up way of showing me just how much you *care*, Noah."

"I fucked up, okay? I made a huge mistake. The way I handled things . . . It was all wrong."

His words echo between us, stretching across the silence above our heads. And I can't help it. My heart lifts despite myself. They're the words I've wanted to hear for so, so long. I've never loved anyone as much as I loved Noah. "Then why did you do it, Noah? Tell me, please."

Noah exhales loudly. "I can't explain it, River, okay? I just—"

"Can't or won't?" I cut in.

Noah just stands there wordlessly.

"God, I'm *such* an idiot," I whisper, half to myself. My lip trembles as I open the door and get in the car.

Noah grabs the car door before I can shut it in his face.

"River, I'm an asshole, okay? Don't let that make you think you're an idiot—"

I yank the door out of his hands, slamming it shut. My driver's-side mirror promptly drops to the asphalt with a clang.

*Ah, shit.*

Noah blinks at me as I sigh and grab a roll of tape from my glove box. "Wait a minute. Is that duct-taped on?" he asks as I open the door and pick up the mirror.

"It's fine. I have a system," I say as I tape the mirror back in place. "It's just been hotter lately. Melts the adhesive."

Noah's face turns red. "River, that can't be—that's not—" He's apoplectic. "Take it to the shop! Get a new car!"

I glare up at him. "Listen, I get that you don't know what it's like to not have a fleet of Cybertrucks at your disposal, but I—"

He throws his hands. "River, you're a *millionaire.* Why aren't you spending it? Why?"

"It's not mine to spend!" I snap.

"What the hell are you talking about?" he asks wildly. "Whose else's is it?"

I can't bring myself to say it aloud, but the moment Noah figures out who I mean, his face fills with pity.

"River," he says, "I know you want your mom to come back. But in the meantime? Spend the goddamn money."

With that, he finally walks back to his own car. The moment he drives out of sight, I lower my head to the hot steering wheel and cry.

# chapter 11
# logan

I'm almost out of Gertie's parking lot when I hear the sound of an engine failing to turn over. A glance over tells me it's Santos's car, because of course it is. I'm torn, for a moment, but when I see that her forehead's against the steering wheel, it's no longer a choice, really.

Of course I'm gonna help her. Especially now that I see that she's crying.

I try not to startle her with a soft knock on her window.

"I don't need your charity, *Noah*," she calls out, refusing to look up. But it comes out thick, her nose blocked: *I don't deed your charity, Do-ah.*

It'd be cute if it were anyone else's name she was saying. She grabs a napkin from the floor and blows her nose discreetly.

I pretend not to hear, then knock again.

"Everything okay?" I ask.

She startles at my voice, peering up at me. Her dark hair turns a gleaming mahogany in the sun. Not that I'm supposed to notice that.

Santos seems to have gathered herself, opening the door and clearing her throat.

"I'm just dandy." She sniffs. Sweat's dripping down her face and neck. I squeeze the jagged edge of my keys to keep from watching a droplet glide to her collarbone.

"Lemme try," I say, waving her out. She brushes against me stepping out, and I try not to flinch away. This girl is driving me nuts.

I reinsert the key into the ignition and turn. The engine groans, trying, and her dashboard lights go haywire, but the car doesn't start. Doesn't seem like it'll be a cheap fix either.

Santos seems to get that. She lets out a loud groan. "Come on, universe, can you please just give me a *break*?"

I close my eyes. I know what I *should* do. Which is to let her call her aunt or Tawny or whoever to help her. It shouldn't be me. But then her voice cracks on that last word, and when I look up, tears are gathering in the thick sweep of her lashes.

Again, it's not a choice, really.

I clear my throat. I can do this. It's fine. Safe. I mean, I'd do the same for Gertie.

Right?

"Look, I don't know about a break, Santos," I say. "But I can give you a ride."

WE STROLL UP to my apartment, just around the corner.

"What is that? A three-minute commute, tops?" she asks.

"A minute and fifty seconds." I slip the fob from my pocket and unlock my car. "If I don't stop to tie my shoe or"—I flick my eyes to her—"rescue any girls in broken-down cars I happen to come across." It catches me off guard when she blushes. I'm busy enough shoving down the heat in my gut that I don't talk again until we're buckled in my car and I'm pulling out of the parking lot.

"Wait. How do you know, down to the second?" she asks. I raise a brow at her and click on my indicator to turn out of the complex.

"You and your twenty questions," I grumble. It's hard keeping the fondness out of my voice. In fact, I'm having to bite back a smile. At the light, I pull out my phone and start scrolling.

*Let's see how she likes this one.*

When I click a button, a familiar raucous guitar riff bursts out of the speakers, upbeat and raw. "This is my commute song," I say over the music. "Or one of them, at least. It's perfect. It always lines up right as I catch that first whiff of bacon grease when I walk into the diner." I catch the frown on her face. "What? Hate it?"

She tries to tap the beat on her knee, but I can tell she can't parse it from the frenetic mix. I hate admitting to anyone when I don't love one of their favorite songs, and I wonder if that's what she's holding in.

"*Hate*'s such a strong word, but . . . I think it's the guitar? It's so . . . *Hey, I'm so cool, I'm the opening credits, look at me.*"

I laugh. She does hate it. "I'll pass that along to Mr. White," I say.

"Okay, it's more than that . . ." River shifts in her seat, turning to face me. "I think, mostly, it's just not my bag. Like . . . it didn't make me want to sing."

Of course. She's a singer.

"Makes sense." I nod. "You wanna sing, not scream." Before I know it, I'm running through the catalog of music I know, trying to find a song she'd like. *Would you be trying to think of songs Gertie would like too, Logan?* says a stupid little voice from the back of my skull. I tell it to shut the hell up. Unless it knows a song Santos might wanna belt.

Why am I having a hard time thinking of a song a singer like her would love? I drum the rhythm against the steering wheel as I make the turn into her neighborhood, racking my brain.

"Hey." River sits up straight. "How'd you know where I live?" She points to the adobe sign we're passing that says COPPER CANYON COVE, the name of the neighborhood where her apartment complex is.

*Shit, shit, shit.* I squeeze the steering wheel so hard, my knuckles pop.

God, I should have listened to that dumb voice of reason. This is why I need to stay the hell away from this girl. She makes me *stupid*.

I better get smart real quick here, or it's all over.

I clear my throat and lift and lower a shoulder, hoping I'm pulling off a casual shrug. "Santos," I say, nice and slow, "I think everyone at the diner knows where you live. You and Tawny don't exactly have quiet conversations."

"Huh." When her expression clears, I let out a long, quiet breath. "So, what you're telling me is you eavesdrop on us?" she says with a wide smile.

I release my held breath and roll my eyes. "Not my fault Tawny McGill doesn't have an inside voice."

"She does so have an inside voice." She sniffs. "She just . . . chooses not to use it."

"What's her catchphrase again?"

Santos looks embarrassed. "Yeah, okay, point taken—"

I put on a slight falsetto. " 'Forget about Copper Canyon Cove. We'll get you out of the "Triple C," that's a Tawny guarantee!' " I shoot her a smirk. "Catchy."

"Wow. Who knew your voice could go that high?"

My smirk gets bigger.

I'm not lying when I say everyone at the diner probably knows that Santos lives in a small, soulless complex. On days she wasn't hankering to clock out to rush back to her neighborhood, Tawny would give her that little speech, always ending with her "Triple-C guarantee."

"I mean it. It really is catchy. Too catchy." I shake my head. "Got stuck in my head all of dinner shift once. Nightmare." I shoot her an amused look, then reach for the glove compartment, pulling out my USB cord. Our fingers brush as I hand it to her, and I ignore the way my skin burns.

"Plug in your phone. Show me a song you would sing to."

She stares down at her phone as I flex her touch out of my hand.

After a moment, she pulls up a song and hits play.

I listen intently to the pulsing, harmonic synth drones. The electronic instruments' bent pitches make me think of malfunctioning equipment, of a low emergency siren, warning you too late. All you can do is hold your family and *wait*. There's no other way to say it: It's a bad vibe.

Santos picks at the cuticle of her thumb, waiting. When the song fades out, I frown.

"That was ambiance. Bleak, bleak ambiance." I study her. There's something sad in her eyes. "And no vocals at all," I add.

She sucks in a breath. "I haven't sung in over seven months." My chest clenches.

"Why not?" I ask.

"Because Dad's gone."

*Shit.* Whatever answer I expected, this wasn't it.

"I didn't notice at first," she continues, "but when my mom left, it got hard to write songs. I didn't open my notebook for months. Didn't have the heart to get onstage. Barely could sing in the shower. I told

Dad I just needed a little time. Just a little more time. But then Dad died. My notebook burned in the fire." She gives me a trembling smile. "No point anymore. You know?"

Memories, dark and disastrous, threaten to suck me into a bad place. I take a breath, blink them away.

"I get it," I say, voice rough.

"Really?" she whispers, peeking up at me. Christ, those warm molasses eyes are killing me.

"Yeah," I say slowly. "You . . . That day in the graveyard? You asked me what I wrote. Still want an answer?"

"Yes," she breathes. "What *do* you write, Logan?" I give her a rueful smile.

"Nothing."

"What?" She blinks.

I massage my chin, fingers brushing my mouth.

"I mean, I've barely written in two years." I turn away as I say it, hiding the way the edges of my face tense.

*That's enough,* I think. *You've already said too much.* But I can't seem to stop talking.

"But before that," I say softly, "I wrote short stories. My mom used to tell me all these amazing stories about her childhood—adventures she and her siblings went on, or the time she got lost in a national park for almost two days as a kid. I didn't have anything like that, so the stories were sort of my way of imagining what it would be like to have grown up like that, where my dad's rules didn't hold me back. Then my mom died, and I just kind of . . . stopped."

Santos's eyelids flutter. "I get it," she says. And she seems like she does. Like she really, really does.

"What kind of music did you sing, back when you used to?" I ask, eager to turn the conversation from me.

Santos bites her lip. I try not to stare at her mouth. She's quiet for so long, I wonder if I've overstepped. Makes sense that she doesn't talk about this. Ever. And I'm probably the last person she *should* be talking to about this.

I open my mouth to backpedal.

"Everything," she finally says, and I shut my mouth. "Anything." She tilts her head. "Okay, that's not exactly true. But it was all over the place. It could be a song I'd heard in the diner on my shift. Or an oldie off of Dad's old records. And sometimes . . ." She tucks her hair behind an ear. "Sometimes, songs that I wrote."

God, I want to know what songs she wrote, what songs she sang. But this subject is tender, and it's *me*, so I keep my curiosity to myself.

"No matter what, though," she continues, "they were the kind of songs that had me freeze while I was wiping off the diner counter. Or sneak down the stairs to hear better while Dad played his records in the kitchen. The kind of songs I couldn't stop thinking about. Songs that would make me say . . ."

" 'I never knew I could feel like that.' " I finish her sentence, getting it completely.

*"Exactly,"* she breathes. I turn, and we lock eyes. My gaze roams her face, because I can't help it anymore. Her beauty is a knife in my gut. My pulse upticks, and when she licks her lips, I linger on the swipe of her tongue.

*Stop, Evans,* I admonish myself.

I shift away from her, toward the driver's-side window, as I turn into her apartment complex and pull into a parking space.

"I'll let you know," I say. "Next time I come across a song like that. Maybe it'll make you feel like singing again."

The smile she gives me is so warm and earnest, I can't help but return it, leaning a little closer to her, chasing that warmth. Santos opens and closes her mouth, words dying on her tongue.

"Go on, Santos," I say, teasing. "Spit it out."

"Why did you help me today?" she whispers, her brows furrowed.

*Shit.*

*What in the fuck am I doing?* I pull away, clenching my fists in my lap.

"Come on, what was I going to do, Santos? Let you die in the heat?" I hate the way she frowns at me.

"So that's it?" she challenges. "You would have done this for anyone?"

*No.*

"Yes," I say, swallowing hard. "I'm a Good Samaritan. What can I say?" I chance a look at her, and it's a mistake. She's leaning in, trying to pin me with her stare. It's working. I can't look away. Believe me, I'm trying.

"You know what, Logan?" Santos tips her chin up, her perfect lips in a defiant pout. My heart rate is throbbing in my ears, my fingers itching to touch her.

"What?" My voice is husky, and I can't stop staring at her lips.

"I don't believe you," she whispers. She closes her eyes and, to my horror, leans in.

For a moment, half a heartbeat, I imagine letting go. But only for a moment.

*"Stop."*

Her lips are so close to mine that, when I speak, her mouth brushes against mine on the *p*. It makes me shiver, nearly reconsider.

Santos opens her eyes, and the hurt and confusion I see is pure agony. But it's still nothing compared to what it could be. I've let this go too far already.

“Santos.” I have to clear my throat twice to get it to work. “We’re coworkers. Friends even. Okay? I’m—I’m sorry. I didn’t mean to give you the—the wrong impression. Or something.”

She crumples back into her seat, her breaths shallow.

“Sorry,” I mumble again. “I should get—”

“Yeah, yeah, me too,” she stammers, stepping out of my car, her cheeks flaming.

My fingers roll a tortured beat on the steering wheel. “You know, I . . .” I clear my throat again and shake my head after a beat. “I really hope the universe cuts you a break soon, Santos.”

“Thanks,” she mutters. She looks nearly as miserable as I feel as she turns and walks toward her apartment.

I put my car in reverse. I need to put miles between me and this girl. But my foot won’t leave the brake pedal until I see her slot her key into the lock and open her front door.

*Okay,* I think. *She’s safe.*

Before she steps inside, Santos casts one last look over her shoulder. She seems surprised to find me still there, watching her.

As soon as her door closes, I get the hell out of there. Because I want her safe. And as long as I’m with her, she won’t be.

# chapter 12
# river

How could I have been so stupid?

Honestly, I don't even know what I was thinking. One moment we were talking about music, and the next, he was *looking* at me in a way that only one other boy has ever looked at me. His eyes were so blue, and suddenly, I was sick of it. Sick of pretending I didn't want him. That I hadn't wanted him for weeks. Months, maybe.

And some part of me knew he wanted me too.

Or so I thought. But I'm such a fool, and I see now, the way I wrote the narrative of what I wanted to be true around reality. He only helped me out at Tate's party because he felt bad for me. He only talked to me at the cemetery because I caught him in a raw moment. He only drove me home because he's "a Good Samaritan." I'm just a friend. Not even. *What word did he use? Oh, right.* "Coworkers." He gave me a ride home, not a promise ring, and I see now where our story goes, how it will only end in unrequited heartbreak.

As if I weren't already heartbroken enough, I woke up this

morning to a calendar reminder on my phone for "Dad's Annual Cookie Experiment."

That means if he were still alive, we would have started the morning off by each of us pulling a piece of paper out of our "Mystery Ingredient" bucket. Then Dad and I would have gone shopping together. Some years, the ingredients were all easy, found in most grocery stores. Other times, we had to check out Asian groceries or markets.

At this exact moment, he would be in the old kitchen, pots and pans clanging metallically as he scurried around the room like a mad scientist, mixing and pouring and stirring, conjuring delicious smells from dubious things. After he had finished several batches of "never-before-seen" cookie flavors (think corn kernel and lime, apple and feta), Mom and I would carefully taste and rate each one, writing our scores on sheets of paper, holding them up like Olympic judges. Some scored surprisingly high, like the olive oil macaroons. Some did not, like the roasted garlic biscuits.

The loss hits me all over again. All these traditions, gone forever. And how alone I feel in it.

Just as I bury my face under my pillow, there's a gentle knock on the door.

"I'm sleeping, Tita," I call from beneath the pillow. I hear the door open. "I love you, but please let me be."

"I love you, but no, I will not. It's almost noon, River."

I lift my head and squint over my shoulder to see Tawny standing there, holding taro bubble tea (my very favorite) and a small white box. She looks wide awake, despite having been the best friend ever and staying up late with me last night, hashing out every single humiliating detail of Logan's rejection. She cracks open the lid and wafts it under my nose. I groan. It smells delicious. Like sugary, buttery coconut.

I eyeball the box. "Is it from Nanay's?"

"Yup. Steamed fresh right before I got there." She plops the box into my lap and settles onto the foot of the bed. The box is still warm. I slide open the cardboard lid and sigh in appreciation at the sight of the pile of ube puto: bright purple rice cakes sweetened with coconut and evaporated milk. I stuff one in my mouth, and it's delicious. Moist, chewy, buttery.

Tawny sits patiently, smoothing out the skirt of her pretty summer dress as she scrolls on her phone. She hands me the bubble tea, which I use to wash down the last mouthfuls of puto.

"Thanks," I say when I've finally swallowed all my food.

"Duh," Tawny says. And her voice gentles even more. "I know what today is."

I nod, giving her a watery smile. If I say anything, I'm going to cry.

"There's another reason too." Tawny flaps her hand, waving away the sad words from the air. "Something more fun. Mom has to do a bunch of back-to-back long legs. She's gonna have to ping-pong from here to Asia like four times." She shakes her head. "Point is, Tate's stupid party got me thinking: Why the hell didn't *we* have a nice, big to-do? We deserve it way more! We can call it Tawny and River's Extra Big Bash Extravaganza!"

Tawny's doing what I call her "Kindergarten Teacher" voice. That bright, happy cadence adults use when they're trying to convince five-year-olds that cleaning up is actually a very fun game, and oh my goodness, broccoli is basically ice cream! I can't help but smile anytime she does it. Not because she's tricked me into thinking broccoli is delicious. But because I love that she's trying so hard to make life a little easier for me.

"A party," I say, nodding. "Okay. Yeah, sure." I'm trying to get used to the idea. At this very moment, with my legs tucked under my sunflower duvet and my body feeling unbearably heavy with memory, with Logan's rejection, the idea of any sort of party sounds *exhausting*.

She must read this in my face because she scoots closer, smoothing my tangled mane of hair back from my cheeks.

"Do you want to talk any more about Logan?" she asks.

I shake my head vigorously. "I don't even want to think about him today."

She nods. "Okay. You'll feel better after a nice, hot shower." She hands me my phone. "I took the liberty of adding a party playlist to your Spotify. Go listen to it while you're showering and tell me what you think."

I look longingly at my pillow. "Why do I need to shower? Where are we going?"

Tawny squeezes my hands, her eyes bright with excitement. "Dress shopping," she says breathlessly. "River, you and I are gonna look hot as hell for our Extra Big—"

"Okay—"

"Bash—"

"You don't have to say the whole—"

"Extravaganza!" She throws her hands up in the air.

"Fine," I sigh. "But I will need more coffee."

WE BROWSE AT the mall and a few other department stores, not really finding anything exciting. I'm on the verge of telling her to forget it, we'll just wear whatever we can find at home, but Tawny is determined that we *must* get new outfits.

And I have to admit, there is one reason I want a new outfit—one hot, sulky, blue-eyed reason. But would Logan want to come to the party after what happened yesterday? Do I even want him there? I'm supposed to throw an extravaganza, not worry about if a gorgeous guy who doesn't want me will show up. Still. It wouldn't hurt to look hot either way, right? Shaking my head, I push the thought away and try to be present with Tawny.

She does some last-ditch googling and stumbles upon a local place, the Desert Rose Boutique. As soon as we walk in, I know we've hit the jackpot.

"Oh my God, everything here is *so cute*!" Tawny gathers the silken train draping from the large bow of a bright pink dress. "How are we gonna choose?"

I shrug, smiling. "Guess we'll have to try them all on."

Tawny dashes from rack to rack, plucking dresses of all fabrics, lengths, and cuts, bright and candy-colored, and stacking them in her arms. Luckily, the girl who works there is friendly and chill. "Knock yourselves out." She briefly glanced up at us from her Kindle to flash us a smile before going back to her reading.

I meander through the aisles, running my eyes over everything. The dresses are cute, yeah. But nothing is sparking anything inside my chest. To be fair, that's a tall order for today.

But then I see it.

Hanging on the wall is a gorgeous ruby-red dress. It has short sleeves that drape elegantly off the shoulder, a corset bodice, and a fit-and-flare silhouette. I lift it off the hanger and hold it up to my body to see where it falls. In the front, the hemline ends at the middle of my thighs, falling longer in the back.

I've always wanted a dress like this. A dress that would go with my black hair and red lipstick. Elegant. Sexy. *Fierce.* The kind of dress I could wear to a rooftop soiree—or onstage as the lead singer of a touring band. The kind of dress that would make men believe I could be an elite assassin. Deadly and beautiful.

“Oh my God . . .” Tawny appears at my right, her mouth hanging open as she looks at the dress. She grabs my arm. “You’re trying it on right now.”

When I step out in front of the three-way mirror, I am shocked to find that it looks even better *on* me. It’s the perfect *just a hint* dress. Bare shoulders. A few inches of thigh. Leave ’em wanting more and all.

Tawny’s sitting on the small fitting room couch behind me. When I walk out, I hear her gasp.

“River,” she sighs. “You look incredible.”

I feel my cheeks heat up, pleased and embarrassed. “Yeah . . . I really like it.” I meet her eyes in the mirror. “It’s not . . . you don’t think it’s too much, right?”

She rolls her eyes. “Definitely not.”

A little thrill goes through me.

“Man, here I am drooling over myself in the mirror.” I turn to her, shaking my head. “Did you find yours yet?”

She grins and dashes into one of the other dressing rooms. “Gimme a sec!” she calls, her voice muffled.

When she comes out, it’s my turn to gasp. Tawny would look hot in a potato sack, but she’s really killing it in a thigh-length silver sheath dress.

“Damn, Tawny.”

“Thanks.” She smirks at me. She examines herself in the mirror, toying with her dyed hair. “I don’t think the green goes with this, though. What do you think? Blue? Teal? Rainbow?”

I feel my smile turn wistful. Mom used to help Tawny when she dyed her hair. We’d do it in Mom and Dad’s bathroom. I’d sit on the edge of the tub while Mom scrubbed the dye out of Tawny’s hair in the sink. The first time we showed Dad Tawny’s new hair, he smiled. “That’s nice,” he said.

"That's it?" Mom yelped. "It's *purple* now, Jay! She looks like a rock star!"

After that, Dad's reactions were always over-the-top. Falling out of chairs. Knocking his sunglasses off. Jogging a lap around the kitchen table. The stoic football coach going full *SNL* actor. It'd leave us in stitches.

Now Tawny turns her head this way and that, her sleek blond hair brushing her shoulders, no doubt imagining herself with vivid rainbow streaks replacing the green. I go to stand next to her, shoulder to shoulder, staring at us in the mirror.

"Mom would love us in these," I say quietly. "Remember how excited she was to take us shopping for prom?" I run my hands down my skirt, my fingers gliding over the silk.

When I'm met with silence, I look up at Tawny. She's giving me a long, searching look. I know we're approaching possible minefields with this subject. But the grief is heavy today, and I feel a little lighter when I let some of it out.

"She would have loved the color," Tawny says, an olive branch. "But she definitely would have said it was too short."

"Definitely."

I meet her eyes and smile. "Tawn," I say, "she is a good mom. She *is*." I shrug. "Everyone goes through crises. I'm sure there's a reason . . ." I swallow. "She's a good mom."

Tawny turns to face me, putting a hand on my cheek. "Good moms don't abandon their daughters, River." She says it kindly. Reluctantly. Like it's a hard truth she'd rather take to her grave than break my heart with.

But a truth nonetheless.

I understand. But it still hurts. Because I thought if anyone knows what I'm going through, it's Tawny. With her mom gone all the time, we basically became her surrogate family. Tawny talked to Mom about her crushes and how she needed a tutor when she was failing Spanish. She rolled her eyes when Mom lectured her or frowned at the length of her skirt.

But it became pretty clear that we were not on the same page about all of this the first few weeks after Mom left. Tawny went the dark, angry, surly route, like the dog at the pound who hoped her owner never came back to get her. Screw them—she was fine sleeping in train yards and digging for scraps.

I, on the other hand, am the kind of dog that returns to the train station every day for ten years, waiting for her to walk off the platform, arms open, calling my name.

Tawny pulls me in for a long, hard hug. And it helps. It does. It's the best she can do, and I appreciate it.

"Well," she says when she pulls away. "What do you think? Have we found the ones?" She looks down at our dresses.

"Absolutely."

We change back into our regular clothes and walk toward the counter, cradling the outfits with loving reverence.

"Should we be worried there's no price tag?" Tawny whispers.

"It's a boutique? So maybe that makes sense?" I say uncertainly.

But Tawny's right. We should have been worried.

"How?" Tawny hisses, bug-eyed. "How is that possible?!" she asks when the salesclerk tells us the price. She looks down at the dresses and actually whimpers. "They were so perfect," she says miserably. "Oh, to have money to spend . . ."

I do some quick math in my head. People have been generous tippers lately—my tips from Free Pie Weekend alone could cover one dress. And I worked a few extra shifts when Tawny's migraine took a few days to fade.

I can afford these dresses right now.

But more importantly, Tawny deserves it. Sure, maybe *we* deserve it, but especially my best friend. She's not only been the life preserver that's kept me from drowning this past year, she's the rescue boat, she's the ship's captain.

Tawny's the only reason I have a shot at building any kind of life worth living. I wish I could buy her a whole damn mall. But a shiny new dress will do.

For now.

Tawny's already put her dress back on the rack, but she can't seem to step away, fingering the sequins on the skirt.

I walk over and lift her dress from the rack.

"Wait. What are you doing?" Her eyes dart between my face and my hand on the hanger, confused.

"They're not too expensive," I say.

She snorts, following me up to the register. "In what world, Riv?"

"The one where we're the hottest girls at the party."

Tawny's mouth falls open as I turn to the girl behind the register.

"Excuse me," I say. "I've changed my mind. I'd like to buy these dresses."

As Tawny envelops me in a hug, I smile, thinking of how amazing we'll look. And wishing, as I always do, that my mom were here to see it.

*To my baby girl,*

*I always wonder if things would have been different if I'd grown up with money. I know: Money doesn't solve every problem. I see it every time I clean a house and accidentally uncover its secrets. Affairs. Drugs. Gambling debts. Life comes for everyone, fast as a hurricane.*

*But money can help you weather the storm.*

*When your father and I met, it felt like I'd won the lottery. Not financially, of course. My parents were long dead, and your father's family wasn't in a position to help. But when we fell in love, we fell hard. And for a while, that was enough. It felt like nothing could touch us.*

*But then I got pregnant. It was the best thing—a baby: you—and the worst, because we were so, so young. We had nothing. No money. No support system. No safety net. A baby needs all those things. You needed all those things.*

*Out here, on the trail, surrounded by the red rocks of the desert, there's nothing to do but think, and I find myself playing out all the different turns my life could have taken, all the different choices, all the different scenarios.*

*In one, I have enough money to give you the life you deserve.*

*In one, I never leave.*

*In one, we are together forever.*

*In one, I don't make a terrible choice that will haunt me for the rest of my days.*

*In one, I'm on my way to you right now.*

*Love,*
*Mom*

## chapter 13
# river

"*Ugh*, River!"

I look up at Tawny seesawing the eyeliner pen between her fingers in an irritated rhythm. "You blinked. Again. How am I supposed to make you a sexy, feline goddess if you're a moving target?"

It's the night of our Tawny-River-Extravaganza-whatever-whatever, and I want to look amazing, for my makeup and outfit to be protective armor. Tawny knows all the tricks to smudgy, smoky eyeliner that will make my eyes look mysterious and sultry, make the muddy brown of my irises pop.

"Sorry," I say, sounding more frustrated than contrite. "I know I promised to stop talking about Logan, but I have to get it out of my system now so I don't make an ass out of myself tonight if he happens to show up."

Tawny purses her lips as she dips a Q-tip into a bottle of micellar water. "Okay, but a reminder that he did say, and I quote, 'I have plans, but maybe I can swing by.' "

"That's not a hard no," I point out.

"It's also not a clear yes," Tawny responds.

"Okay, regardless, he could show up," I say. I haven't had to see Logan since the humiliating ride home, thanks to Tawny pulling a few shift changes with me, but ever since she told me what he said at their shift together, I can't help worrying that he'll show tonight, and I have no idea how to play it.

And truthfully, with each passing day, I feel a little more confused and a little more angry. At first I blamed myself, thinking it was all in my head, but I re-cataloged each event over and over, and unless I'm totally delusional, there was a *vibe*. But why would he pretend I don't exist, then care enough to give me a ride and be flirty, and then *reject me*?

My hands fidget in my lap. Not even the delicate strokes of the eyeliner pen are soothing tonight. But my next question makes it easy to keep still—I don't want to see her reaction. "Is there any scenario where I just ask him about it? In case he's . . . changed his mind?"

I can feel Tawny's sigh against my cheek.

"Look, Riv," she says, her voice close and quiet. "I love you. And therefore, I will be blunt. I think it'd be best if you just . . . forget about Logan."

My fingers spasm into fists on my thighs. "Okay. I hear you. But what if he might—"

I feel a gentle tap on my chin. "Look at me." I peek one eye open. Tawny's serious face fills my vision. "River," she says, "he doesn't. Okay? If he liked you, he'd have done something about it by now. And he definitely would have kissed you in the car."

It's a little humiliating how much that hurts to hear, like all my organs have just crashed to the soles of my feet. Tawny must read it on my face because she leans in to give me a tight hug.

"Oh, River, that doesn't say anything about you. You're *perfect*. Logan is just the biggest douche I've ever met." She pauses for a moment. "Well, tied with Noah, I guess."

"I know," I mutter against her shoulder. "Still." Tawny pulls back and brushes a strand of hair from my face.

"I get it." She shrugs. "Of course it sucks big grizzly bear balls. But forget him. We're going to dance and have a great night."

Tawny's words help, but confusion and hurt still linger. As her fingertips sweep across my eyelids, I imagine it's fairy dust that she's painting on my skin. A magic glitter that makes me beautiful. Makes everything she said come true.

Makes me, as Tawny promised, forget all about Logan.

"Thanks," I whisper, my eyes still closed.

"Duh," Tawny says.

An hour later, Tawny spins me in front of the mirror. "Presenting her royal highness, River Santos." I open my eyes.

My first thought is: *Holy shit. I'm stunning.*

My second thought is: *Mom would love me in this dress so much.*

Tears instantly threaten to spill over.

"River! Don't cry; I didn't use waterproof makeup!"

"Sorry," I say. "Sorry!"

"Don't apologize," Tawny says softly, cupping my chin. "Look. Forget her. Forget about everyone else in this world except *you* and *me*. Tonight, we're all that matters. Tonight, we become goddesses of the desert and dance our asses off. Tonight, with all due respect, everyone else can kindly fuck the fuck off. Deal?"

I wrap my arms around her, tighter than her dress. She squeezes me back, breathless.

"Deal."

Tawny and her mom live in a smallish house on a street of other smallish, unassuming houses in one of the more affordable parts of Scottsdale. It'll be a tight squeeze if half the people Tawny invited show up. Both bedrooms are off-limits, but between the living room and backyard, she insists there will be enough room for everyone to dance their hearts out.

As she flits around the living room making last-minute arrangements of Bluetooth speakers and sodas, I can't take my eyes off her. She looks breathtaking in her diamond-bright dress, the sequins catching and scattering light across the single couch and egg-white walls.

I've got to hand it to her. Tawny's done a decent job turning her mom's house into a makeshift club. The room is lit by several hand-fashioned glow-stick garlands strewn across the ceiling and a few thrift-store-salvaged neon signs, and the entire floor of the room is covered in a wispy vapor thanks to the fog machine I splurged on. Her backyard is decked out with tiki torches. An assortment of lawn and plastic chairs are arranged as seating, some fog from inside the house curling out the patio doors to coat the ground out back.

When everything is arranged as she likes it, Tawny hits play on our party mix. It's when the rhythm rattles my marrow that the promise of the night surges up my sternum. It's a wave I want to chase, grab ahold of, and ride. One that carries me away from the angst of unanswered texts and toxic assholes.

Ignorant, toxic assholes.

When people finally start arriving, it's easy to pretend nothing exists outside this music, this dancing crowd.

As carefully chosen as our playlist was, Tawny's guest list was the opposite. Tawny invited *everyone*. She did a social media blast invite to our entire graduating class. Anyone who came to the diner who seemed cool or cool-adjacent got an invite. Tawny even invited our old friends Audrey and Marissa.

"At least we can still count on them to be fun at parties," she'd said. And I agreed.

By the time Audrey shows up with quite a few cases of Yuengling, there's enough of a crowd to give her a roof-raising cheer. Turns out the guy she's seeing just turned twenty-one and is willing to do anything to impress her.

"Cheers!" Tawny yells over the music, clinking bottles with me. "To us! Forever!"

"Only us!" I scream. Tawny's eyes glow a fervent hazel as she takes a swig of her beer.

I almost never drink, so I'm happily buzzed after the first beer.

Tawny's right. It's easy to push away disappointed thoughts of Logan while I'm dancing. After I've danced enough to get sweat beading my hairline, I tell Tawny I need a break. I grab a second beer, mostly to hold the cold, sweaty bottle against my forehead.

I'd planned on finding a place to sit in the kitchen, but it's packed too densely, no empty seats to be found.

Squeezed to the edge of the living room, I catch a glimpse of the little coat closet alcove. As expected, no one is there. Tawny says her mother hates that little spot, an awkward and inefficient use of space. It's a dead end, nearly too narrow to allow the closet door to swing open.

But tonight, this is what makes it a perfect refuge.

As I push toward that little space, I catch glimpses of old classmates. A few of them do double takes, one or two tell me how much they love my dress, a few more tell me how nice I look. A cute guy who was in my history class gives me a huge smile, his eyes lingering on mine as I squeeze by.

"Hey, beautiful," he says. I feel my cheeks heat with both pleasure and embarrassment. Too flustered to respond, I give him a quick smile and keep going.

Only to stop again when I see Logan.

The look in his eyes steals my voice. Logan is blinking at me like he's never seen me before. He sweeps his gaze over my sleek, glossy hair, the line of my bare collarbones, the corset cinch of my waist.

He clears his throat. "Did I miss something about the dress code? I thought it was just a party, not prom."

I've dreaded this moment all night, but the alcohol buzzing through my veins makes me feel brave. "Some of us just have a little more imagination than others." I look pointedly at his monochrome outfit of dark jeans and a plain black shirt. It's boring.

Or at least, it should be.

It's annoying that I can't help but notice how Logan's shirt skims the plane of his muscled torso, how the black makes the stunning blue of his eyes inescapable.

Thoughts I'll take to my grave, of course.

"Well, Santos," Logan says, regaining his footing, "some of us have more important things to do than spend ten hours getting ready."

"Ha." I poke him lightly in the chest. "Joke's on you. It only took me two."

Logan laughs. A genuine, slightly surprised one that ends in a crooked smile. I return it, and as soon as I do, he breaks eye contact.

"Look, Santos, we shoul—"

But I stop listening, because just then a familiar face appears in the crowd.

*"Noah."* I groan.

"You mean Logan," Logan says, a confused expression on his face. "You sure you're better—"

"Behind you," I cut him off, staring at Noah's towering frame.

Noah and I haven't spoken since Gertie's parking lot. He's scanning the crowd, and I really don't want him to spot me. I've had my fill of painful interactions to last a lifetime. I make a mental note to

Tawny to be a little more discerning in her invite methods next time.

I glance up to find Logan scowling in Noah's direction. If I weren't preoccupied with finding a viable escape route, I'd be laughing at how swiftly Logan's smirk soured at the sight of Noah. But Noah's closing in.

In fact, he's about to spot me.

"Crap," I hiss. Operating on pure instinct, I yank open the coat closet and duck inside. I try pulling it shut, but Logan's hand flies up and blocks the door.

"Wait—"

"In or out?" I snap. Logan frowns.

Noah's head is turning toward us.

"In it is." I yank Logan by his shirt and close the door.

He swears as we crash into the dark, falling against the coats swinging on their hangers. The good news is the closet isn't very big, so there's not enough room for us to fall to the ground.

The bad news is . . .

The closet isn't very big.

"Santos," Logan says hoarsely.

"Yeah?" I whisper.

"You planning on letting go anytime soon?"

He taps the knuckles of my right hand, which, mortifyingly, is still fisted in the front of his shirt.

"Sorry." I yank my arm from his body. I really need to put space between us. But there's nowhere to go.

"Why are we in here?" The soft glow seeping through the door frame illuminates the white of Logan's eyes as he stares at me.

I can feel myself starting to unravel under Logan's smoldering regard. God, I hope he can't read my expression. I pray he can't see how I'm burning from this hot, sticky feeling in my chest, how it's pooling in my stomach.

"You're in here because you couldn't make a decision." I sniff. "I'm in here to avoid . . . people."

"Noah." Logan raises an eyebrow. "You treat him like the killer in a slasher movie. That bad a kisser, huh?"

"You wish," I say, my cheeks heating. I peek up at him. "You sure you're not jealous, Evans?"

"Oh, sure, I'm just *green* with envy over Mr. Trust Fund Fish Lips," he says acidly.

I tilt my head up at Logan, biting back my smile. *He's totally jealous.* Of his money, probably. But still, I'm not turning down a chance to rile Logan up. I've spent all week feeling like crap. It's his turn.

"He has very nice lips, actually," I say. "I miss them." Logan makes a disgusted sound. It eggs me on. "But that's not all I miss."

His eyes narrow.

"I really miss his hands."

"I get it, Santos," Logan growls. "Lay off before I hurl."

"And, honestly, his *thumbs*." I grin up at him.

"That's enough!" Logan's voice sounds like it's been through the grinder. "I don't want to hear anything more about—"

"About what it's like to kiss me?" I cut in. "And why is that, Logan? If we're 'just coworkers,' why do you even care?"

"I don't," he snaps.

"Prove it," I challenge. "If you don't care, why are you even here? At the party? In this closet?"

Logan takes a step forward, backing me against the wall. I stop breathing when he leans forward, his face inches from mine. "*River*, please just—"

I freeze at the sound of my name leaving his tongue for the first time.

"Just what?" I say fiercely, shaking. "I deserve an answer, Logan. For half a year, I'm invisible to you. And then all of a sudden, you're scooping tuna off the floor for me, giving me bluebells, asking what music I listen to, talking to me about your mom." Logan's brows lift, his breath quickening. But I don't care if I'm pissing him off.

"So which is it, then, Logan? Enemy or friend? Because any more whiplash and my neck's gonna snap." I push against his chest. His stormy eyes drop to my hand, rising and falling along with his deep breaths. I take half a step closer. His eyes fall to my lips. The furrow in his brows takes on a different quality. Less frustrated. More desperate.

Logan shakes his head like he's trying to clear away his thoughts. "I didn't even want to— I'm not supposed to—"

For a heartbeat, we just look at each other.

"Supposed to what?" I whisper, my heart hammering. "What aren't you supposed to do, Logan?"

My lips are so close to his that I can feel his breath. For one excruciating second, I think he's going to leave.

Instead, his hands fly to my waist and yank me against him. He kisses me. Hard, hot, open-mouthed.

My body responds immediately, a torrent of lightning and fire flooding my limbs, and I'm kissing him back. Ravenously. My lips move urgently against his, my fingers tangling in his shirt, pulling.

"*This*, River." He groans into my mouth, his voice husky. He sounds so relieved. Like maybe he's wanted this longer than I realize. "I'm not supposed to do . . ." Logan sucks my lip, bites it, like he can't help it, like he's dying and I'm the cure.

My body is on *fire*. Logan's hands are everywhere. He strokes my cheek, cradles my head, slides his fingers down my bare neck, slips them down my body. He pulls me tight against him, and I can't help the desperate moan that slips out.

Logan pulls my hair gently to lift my chin, giving him access to my neck. I shiver against him as he nips from the corner of my mouth down my throat. It's so good. It all feels incredible. It's everything I've wanted Logan to do to me since . . . well, way before I admitted it to myself.

I drop my hands to the hem of his shirt.

"Logan," I finally whisper as I slide my fingers underneath, grazing the skin of his abs.

At the sound of his name, Logan freezes. I lift my head, blinking slowly, unable to think through the lusty haze of Logan's kisses. Logan's looking at me, and even though his eyes are all pupil and half-shuttered, there's a sort of cold awakening happening there too.

"What is it?" I breathe. I swipe my thumb across his skin, and he flinches, stiffening. He disentangles himself completely then, each jerky movement a cold bucket of water over my head.

"Hey," I say, a little clearer and louder. "What's wrong?"

Logan won't meet my eyes. His lips are swollen and red from my teeth, and he won't even look at me.

"Shit. I *really* shouldn't have . . ." His voice is still so gravelly. He steps back as far as he can in the tiny space. "This was a mistake." He puts his hand on the door handle. "I'm so . . . I'm sorry, Santos."

And before I can say anything else, he's gone.

# chapter 14
# river

For a few moments, I just stand there in the strip of light now streaming in through the open closet door, reeling. Heart pounding, I keep staring, unseeing, at the worn jean jacket in front of me, the name EMILY written in faded ink on the tag, no doubt a find from our favorite vintage store downtown. I focus on the threadbare hole near the elbow, the fraying cuff, trying to find something, anything, to ground me. To help me make sense of what just happened.

But *nothing* makes sense. I didn't make up the kiss. The heat of his palms. The way his hands gripped my body. How hungrily he kissed me.

Like he'd been aching to do it as long as I had.

Maybe even longer.

I burst out of the closet, hardly seeing any of the hot, sticky crowd, barely noticing the bodies I squeeze around and through. I head into the kitchen and pour myself a glass of water. I sip it slowly, trying to slow my heart rate, but it's no use.

I touch my swollen lips, and I decide. *No.* I'm not letting him leave me here like he didn't just kiss me within an inch of my life. He owes me an explanation.

"River? You okay?" Tawny spots me from the couch as I march toward the door. "Where are you going?" She sits up.

"To get some answers." And with that, I shut the front door behind me.

I TAKE AN Uber to Logan's apartment, trying to rehearse all my questions in my head. I knock on the scuffed green door with the letter *D* above it. There's no answer. I knock again. This time, louder.

The door opens, and Logan doesn't look surprised to see me. It's like he's been expecting me but is still disappointed I showed up. He leans against the door frame, blocking the entry with his body. His face is stone, his full lips pressed in a straight line.

"Please go," he whispers.

"No," I say, fighting to show none of the hurt I feel.

"River," he pleads. I falter at the way he says my first name.

I want to make him say it again and again. But not like this. Not in this broken, sorrowful way.

"This is such a bad idea, on so many levels. I need you to—can you please just leave?"

"Why? Why is it such a bad idea?" I press. "You kissed *me*, Logan. You can't pretend that you weren't there. That you didn't initiate it. That you didn't enjoy it, because I know you did."

Logan folds his arms and stares at me. "It was *just* a kiss." He leans closer. "It doesn't mean anything, and I never should have done it."

"Bullshit," I say so loudly a neighbor peeks her head out the door.

Logan swears under his breath.

"Come in," he hisses, and ushers me inside. He walks behind the counter that separates the tiny kitchen and living room—that separates him from me, as if he can't even bear to be near me. He crosses his arms over his chest again and leans his hip against the cracked Formica. His hair is still tousled from my fingers, a dark lock falling across his forehead.

"What do you want from me, Santos?"

"The truth," I say, firm. It's all I want. It's all I've ever wanted from him.

"The truth." He licks his lips, his eyes squeezing shut. When he opens them, he starts to pace. In the small space, he seems every bit the panther behind bars. "Santos, you shouldn't be here. You should be back at the party, having fun and forgetting about me. I'll get you an Uber." He plucks his phone from the charger by the fridge.

No. *No.*

I march into the kitchen and yank his phone out of his hand. "You don't get to decide what I want or don't want, Evans," I snarl, poking him in the chest. "Why can't you just admit how you feel? What is so . . . bad about wanting me?" My voice cracks, and Logan's face falters, his cold mask slipping for a second. His eyes flare with something raw—pained, almost.

"River, there's nothing bad about *you*. This isn't about you at all." He rakes a hand through his hair. He takes a few shaky breaths before he laughs darkly, almost despairingly. When he raises his eyes to meet mine, they're a typhoon of wild emotions.

The mask is starting to crack.

"Then what is it about? What are you so scared of?"

Logan tries to step around me, out of the kitchen, but I block him with my body. And just like that, he breaks.

"You deserve so much better," Logan murmurs. "Please. You should go. I am such a mess—you have no idea. You should delete my number from your phone and pretend we never met."

"I don't want to," I whisper back, my lips so close to his that I can feel his breath. "I want *you*."

"You don't—*Christ*." Logan drops his head, the word a ragged breath.

"I do, Logan. I want you. Only you."

I press myself against him. He stiffens and looks away. I put my hand to his cheek and slowly turn his face toward me. Our eyes meet, and everything seems to freeze for a few silent seconds.

Slowly, as if every movement pains him, he takes my hand from his face and pushes it toward me.

"Go home, River." He's hoarse and trembling. He doesn't sound terribly convincing.

I don't let go of his hand. I press my lips to his, featherlight.

"Tell me you don't want me," I say in a hushed tone.

"I . . . I—" He breaks off in a gasp when I swipe my tongue against his. His eyes are wide and pleading.

"Say it," I whisper. "Say you don't want me."

There's a storm in his stare, and when he looks at me, he looks like he's torn in two.

I can feel his pulse beneath his skin, feel his breath on my lips. And then something inside him breaks again.

Before I can register what's happening, he lifts and sets me down on the kitchen counter. His arms bracket my hips. On a broken groan, he surges forward, grabbing my face and crashing his mouth to mine.

*"River,"* he hums desperately against my skin, and I've never heard Logan like this, like he's starving.

"Of course I want you. God, I've wanted you." He pulls me tight against him, pressing our hips flush. I gasp when I feel exactly just how *badly* he wants me. I roll my hips against him, the delicious friction making me keen. With a groan, Logan scoops me off the counter, carrying me to the couch, my legs wrapped around his hips. He lays me down on the cushions and stretches his body over mine, caging me with his arms and knees. It's exactly what I want. Logan's face is raw as he hovers over me. I can see bright hunger as he sweeps his gaze over the dark spill of my hair on the couch armrest, the puff of my kiss-swollen lips. And that face, those eyes . . . I've never seen a more beautiful sight.

"Do you know how beautiful you are?" he whispers huskily. "Do you know how *crazy* you make me?"

The sound of his voice alone has my hips canting upward, his words making my back arch and Logan choke.

"I make you crazy?" I breathe, tugging his hair.

"You've got *no idea*," he says. He pulls me in, then presses his lips to mine.

He's right. I had no idea. No idea at all it could be like this.

Noah was always so quiet, so polite. Noah's kisses were giving. Kind. Controlled. But Logan . . . Logan is ravenous. Like he's so hungry for me, so starving, he can only take. Which works perfectly for me, because when it comes to him, I want to give, give, give.

I want to give him everything.

# chapter 15
# river

When I arrive at Tawny's, the sky is sunrise pink. I can hear the television, the sleek voice of Scottsdale's morning news anchor muffled through the front door. It's Tawny's audio safety blanket. She always keeps the news on in the background when she's by herself. Which means the news is on a lot.

Logan and I fell asleep on his couch after a night of kisses and whispers, only to wake, still in our party attire, once the sun rose and started streaming in through his window. After we kissed goodbye for what felt like forever (and yet not nearly long enough), I got into an Uber back to Tawny's, gazing at his sharp silhouette filling the door frame until his apartment melted into the passing acacias.

Even though I've probably only gotten about four hours of sleep, I feel like I could run a marathon right now. Because:

Logan kissed me.

Logan liked kissing me. In fact, I might go so far as to say that Logan *loved* kissing me.

I can't stop thinking about it. All I want to do is replay every hot moment from last night. I look down at my thighs, and I can feel where Logan's hands pressed, the way he oh-so-tentatively slid his palms up to my—

I press my hands against my hot cheeks, trying to calm my body down.

Gliding down the hall, I find Tawny in the living room, sitting on one of the couch cushions on the floor, a half-full trash bag in one hand and an empty beer bottle in the other. She's sitting with her eyes glued to the TV, and even though I can only see the back of it, her hair is a complete wreck.

As is the entire room. Empty bottles are strewn all over the place. Crushed red SOLO cups are on top of the coffee table, on the couch, scattered across the floor. The speakers are all on their sides, trash crumpled and tossed on the shelves and surfaces. A baseball cap with the Diamondbacks logo is hanging from the ceiling fan. Sunglasses are dangling precariously from a lampshade. A handkerchief with a purple lipstick stain is folded neatly on the counter.

*". . . by a jogger early this morning in a remote area known for its rugged terrain. Authorities swiftly responded to the scene, cordoning off the area as . . ."*

"Who wore purple lipstick last night?" I frown.

*"Holy God in heaven,"* Tawny yelps, leaping to her feet and facing me. She clutches at her chest. "River. I love you. But I swear to God, you actually really almost killed me."

Tawny looks *stupendously* hungover. Her hair is a tangled halo of gold and rainbow. Black makeup is smeared all over her face, her eyes puffy and dark as a bruise.

There's an interview with a firefighter in the background, and his drawl is a comical score for Tawny's slow blinks and dazed movements. She stares down at the empty bottle in her hand. She looks confused as to why she's holding it.

"I think I'm dying," she croaks, snapping off the TV. "It feels like my skull's about to explode."

"You're hungover," I say cheerfully, dancing to her side to tap her nose.

Tawny looks at me like I'm an alien.

"All right. Who the hell are you? Because Morning River is not peppy. And Morning After Late Party River is usually not even up until after lunch," Tawny grumbles.

I thrust a hand out to my best friend. She shrinks back, eyeing it like it's booby-trapped.

"Hi," I say, obnoxiously bright. "I'm Morning After Hooking Up with Logan Evans River. Nice to meet you."

It takes Tawny a second. She looks at my hand. Then looks at my face. Then she stares at my hand.

Tawny shakes her head hard.

"Wait. *Wait.* River." She shakes her head again. "You—you and Logan?"

"Yes." I sigh blissfully. I fall back on the couch with a loud crunch. I frown, digging under me to pull out an opened bag of barbecue chips.

"Lemme get this straight." Tawny blinks slowly, like she's still trying to figure out which way is up or down. "Asshole Logan."

"*Sexy* Asshole Logan," I counter.

Tawny blinks once, twice, and then throws the empty bottle and trash bag into the air with an excited squeal. "Oh my *God*, River!" She dives onto the couch beside me. "You . . . you're glowing! Seriously, you—"

"Can't stop smiling?" I press my hands to my cheeks. "Seriously, I tried."

"Well, obviously, I'll need a disgustingly detailed report. No, no, you think I'm kidding, but I genuinely need to know, like, what his fingernails taste like."

I hit Tawny with a pillow. "Tawny, that's disgusting." I pause. "But I bet they taste like leather. Or . . . or like fresh pine." When she doesn't reply, I look up to find her shaking her head at me.

"What?" I huff.

"Oh, River," she says somberly. "You are *so* screwed."

"Oh God, I know," I say. I fist the crushed bag of chips in my hand. "All right, I know it's an emergency if butt-crushed chips are looking appealing. I'll make you coffee and finish cleaning. Go get ready—I'll tell you the rest over brunch."

"Brunch," Tawny groans with longing. "God, I could destroy some pancakes right now." She stands up. "I'm going to shower the seven layers of party filth off me. Thanks for your help with this wreck. You can choose between IHOP or WaHo, I don't care."

But I have a better idea.

"Hey, Tawn?" I call down the hall, clinking beer bottles into a trash bag. "Put on something nice. It's a celebration. My treat."

Tawny grins as she struts down the hall. "*Ooh la la.* Watch out, Logan. Sure, he got some action, but I'm getting *brunch dates.*"

I pull up Cerulean Mesa Resort's Insta, scrolling through the colorful grid of gorgeous mosaic gardens and sapphire pools canopied by vaulted crystal glass atriums.

It's where Mom was supposed to take us for Tawny's eighteenth birthday. We saved up for months and spent weeks debating hot stone massages versus Swedish ones, trawling through Goodwills for cute spa-worthy clothes. But when Mom disappeared, so did our promised plans.

Tawny did her best to hide her disappointment, but that's the thing with best friends: I saw right through it.

I can't go back in time and plead with my mom to wait just a bit longer to disappear, to remember she'd said we'd all get matching purple pedicures together. But I can take myself, and I can take Tawny, and make up the difference later with a few extra diner shifts. I can bring my friend to the luxurious tablecloths and handsome servers to wait on us hand and foot, stuff her full of lavender and blueberry pancakes, buy her drinks with rosemary syrup and butterfly pea flowers, and spring for a spa treatment after.

I can never undo the worst thing that ever happened to me, and I can never replace what's been taken from me. But I can take what life has handed me and make what's left of my life better, bit by bit.

Because last night, I demanded the truth from Logan Evans, and I got it.

And this morning, I deserve to be nothing more than a teenage girl telling her best friend in the whole world the story of how the hot guy at work kissed her, kissed the hell out of her, as we clasp freshly manicured hands across our side-by-side hot stone massage beds.

This morning, I deserve to be happy.

# chapter 16

# river

Sunday is Logan's and my first shift together since the party. At first, I'm a little nervous. I'm refilling ketchup bottles in the back, on the long, steel counter where the punch-card machine sits, when Logan walks in, smirking as always. He doesn't say anything as he flips through the pile of cards, pulling out the one with his name.

"Hey, Logan," I chirp. God, I sound so eager, so stupid.

Logan looks up at me, and his expression doesn't change. His eyes sweep me up and down, one quick, careless pass before he looks back down at his time card.

"Santos." He pushes the card into the machine, where it punches a hole with a little mechanical whir. He opens the door, pausing with his hand holding it open. He looks over his shoulder at me. "Got enough ketchup there?"

I look down; the current bottle is overflowing, the red sauce spreading over the steel. I swear, pulling back the giant bottle, the sweet, vinegary smell overwhelming. I try to rally. "What can I say? Ketchup is one of my . . ." But when I glance up, he's already gone.

We agreed to keep it secret for now at the diner. It was just easier that way.

But I can't deny it. I'm in a bad way about Logan. I'm not writing *Mrs. River Evans* in any stupid journal or anything, but I have spent an inordinate amount of time imagining his crooked smile, the feeling of his arms around me, his kisses. God, his kisses.

So even if his nonchalance is just an act—*God, let it just be an act*—I'm still shaken. Maybe there's a part of me that's still waiting for Logan to wake up, to remember that I was the girl who irritated him for months on end, and leave.

I'm putting the giant ketchup bottle back in the walk-in when I hear the door open and close. I smell his cologne first, then feel his arms wrapping around me from behind, pulling me into his warm chest.

"How am I supposed to get any work done today?" Logan asks as he kisses the back of my neck. "Admit it, you wore your hair up to torture me, didn't you?"

"Consider it payback for all the times you tortured me at this job." I laugh.

"I see," Logan murmurs, turning me around and pulling me close. "Well, then I'll take my just deserts." He swoops down and slots his open mouth against mine, a hot, quick kiss that leaves my knees shaking. After he gives me a dark look and disappears out of the walk-in, my eyes fall to the crate of oranges on the floor. It wasn't terribly long ago that Logan found me here, crying on that crate, and all but ignored me.

Strange how quickly things can change.

Now it's three days and a couple of hours after our hookup (not that I'm counting), and we both have the day off. I want to hang out with him. I want to do all the things with him. I'm still high off my first hits of Logan, aching for more. But no one likes a junkie, so when I grab my phone off my nightstand, I remind myself to play it cool over text.

**River**

Hey. You're off. I'm off. You up for something?

I wait a few minutes. Should probably clarify.

**River**

Totally cool if you're busy.

Also, probably need to make it clear that I'm not just hanging around waiting for him.

**River**

I have plenty of stuff I can do.

Five minutes pass and I get no response. I grab a pillow and press it to my face, trying to mute my scream of "Why am I like this?"

"River, sweetheart." My door opens, and Tita Anna's sleep-rumpled face appears in the gap. "I love you so much, but can you please have your angsty teenage breakdowns at least *after* my first cup of coffee?"

My phone pings. I dive under the covers, cradling my phone. "Okay, will do, thank you, Tita Anna, love you, thanks, please leave now!"

I hear a snort before my door closes. I don't think I've ever smiled so hard in my life as I open my texts.

**Logan**

Well, good morning—and I do mean morning, beautiful. It's 7 am. I was asleep.

Right. *Right.* I wince. Not exactly playing it cool, binge-texting him at the crack of dawn. My phone pings again.

**Logan**

I will say I can't think of a better alarm though. I'm in. You choose. Anywhere you want to go. You name it, I'm there.

I press my face into my pillow, this time squealing with joy.

"Oh, for the love of—I'm not even done with my first cup yet, River!" Tita Anna yells from the kitchen.

THREE HOURS LATER, I'm knocking on Logan's door, my heart pounding from anticipation alone. And nerves. I pull self-consciously at the yellow sundress that seemed so adorable a couple of hours ago. Are the sleek waves in my hair trying too hard? Am I wearing too much makeup? Not enough?

I'm in the middle of another horrifying *what-if* when the door pops open. Logan leans an arm against the door frame, and the corner of his mouth lifts into a crooked grin as he takes me in. It stops my heart. I'm still not used to feeling his sapphire eyes sweep down and back up my body so slowly, locking back into mine, and I'm helpless. He's dressed simply, in a cobalt-blue linen shirt and jeans. His thick hair is damp, curling slightly at the nape, like he's just gotten out of the shower.

"Hey," I say, my voice already husky. In lieu of a reply, he grabs my hand and pulls me into his apartment. He slams the door shut and presses me up against the back of it. He leans in, and I meet him halfway, our kiss immediately messy and desperate.

Logan's hands go to my bare neck, tracing my collarbones until he reaches the thin straps of my dress at my shoulders.

"Hey yourself," he hums, moving his tongue against mine. "You taste sweet," he says. "Like fresh oranges."

I pull back, suddenly self-conscious. "You can taste the orange juice I had?"

"Mm-hmm." He gives me a lazy, lopsided grin, his lids heavy with desire. He brushes a lock of hair off my cheek and leans in, his lips brushing mine. "But your lips taste like . . . strawberries." Logan brings his tongue to touch the corner of my mouth and slowly, agonizingly, he drags it across the swell of my bottom lip, like he's savoring me. My neck loses bones, and my head falls back against the door in bliss.

"Logan," I breathe.

"That's my favorite." He lifts his head with a wry smirk. "Getting you to say my name just like that."

I lick my lips, loving how his eyes follow the movement. "Like what?"

"Like this," he growls, swooping down to suck my earlobe.

I really didn't want to. I wanted to prove I had some semblance of self-control. But as soon as his tongue licks into my ear, I'm a goner.

"God, *Logan*," I gasp.

"Yes," he whispers. "Exactly like that."

I don't tell Logan that I would be completely fine spending the entire day on the couch with him. Because that would be a little too embarrassing to admit. So when he says, "Where's the place you're taking me?" I suppress the urge to nod behind him and say, *Right over there.*

"It's a surprise." I sigh.

He huffs a laugh. "God help me, being led into the unknown by River Santos." Logan does an *after you* gesture at the door. "All right, let's see what you got, Santos. Keep in mind, I will be filling out a Yelp review at the end. First date, lots of pressure."

My brain explodes at the words *first date.* I try and hide my stupidly huge smile from Logan as we walk to my car.

But I can't help it. I'm a goner.

# chapter 17
# logan

I want to kiss her again. I haven't started driving yet; I could do it, lean over into the passenger seat and just nip at the tender, sugar-flavored skin of her throat. I'm the peasant who broke into the king's coffers. Any minute now, they're gonna find me, drag me away. I want every golden kiss I can pilfer while I still have the chance.

At this rate, we'll never get anywhere.

"You wanna plug something into Google Maps already there, Santos? If you take much longer, I won't be able to resist pulling you into the back seat," I groan, resisting the urge to do it anyway.

"Okay, okay, okay," she repeats breathlessly, keying in the address. I love that she doesn't seem to hate that idea either.

After a thirty-minute drive, we pull into a large parking lot.

"Have you ever been here?" She can't even look at me, weirdly nervous.

"'The Musical Instrument Museum.'" I read the sign aloud. A museum. This, I would not have guessed. It's a surprise, to be sure, but a welcome one. "Nope. I didn't even know this existed. Look at you, expanding my horizons." River seems relieved.

She presses a hand to her chest as we walk across the oven-hot parking lot. She takes a breath. "MIM used to be one of my favorite places in Phoenix. Mom and Dad took me here as often as they could. I was always so happy as I wandered the different floors of musical instruments from every country and era. I've missed this place terribly but couldn't stomach the onslaught of memories. It's different somehow, with you here. The joy of sharing my happy place with you, in this moment, outweighs the grief."

*Wow.* I clasp her hand as we reach the entrance and wrap her in a tight embrace. "I can't wait to see it. With you."

There's an ache in my chest when I think of all that she's baring to me, and all I'm keeping from her. I duck down and steal a quick kiss. It's easy to shove away the bad in my head with her touch.

The lobby sweeps long and tall, all polished marble and sleek white walls. Floor-to-ceiling windows overlook a miraculously evergreen courtyard of manicured grass and flowers. When we walk past the stately grand piano in the lobby center, I pause, drumming my fingers on the polished onyx wood. I bump her shoulder playfully with my own.

"How 'bout it. Gonna woo me with a song, Santos?"

She breathes a laugh, stroking the glossy surface of the white piano keys. "You wouldn't be able to handle it if I did, Evans." She holds a pinkie up to my face.

"Am I supposed to know what you're doing?" I tap her small knuckle.

"I'm showing you the finger you'd be wrapped around. Completely at my mercy."

I laugh, grabbing her hips and squeezing. "*Really.* Just from a song, hmm?"

She shakes her head. "Not just any song. A song from me." A tint of sadness colors the end of her words. She doesn't say anything more.

This won't do. This is supposed to be her happy place. I step into her space, heedless of the other patrons milling about the lobby.

"All right, beautiful." My fingers knead her hips. "I want to hear a song. From you."

She gets on her tiptoes, tilting her head up. I've never been a PDA person, but everyone else disappears when I'm this close to River.

"One day," she says. "One day I'll sing you a song so good, I'll haunt your dreams."

I kiss her instead of telling her the truth: She already does.

We make our way up the stairs, her fingers tangling in mine as we pass through the Indonesia exhibit, where a gorgeous gamelan ensemble is set up, a video of a concert playing, before stopping at the Philippines exhibit.

My eye catches just then on a man in a video playing an ornate guitar that the exhibit calls a laúd.

"He looks so much like Dad," she tells me, pointing to the screen.

"Yeah . . . he does," I muse. When River stiffens beside me, I realize what I've just said.

*Logan, you fucking moron.*

She whirls to face me. "You *knew* my dad?"

I fight to keep all the alarm bells ringing in my body off my face. Christ, *this* girl. That face. Those honey eyes are getting me sloppy. Comfortable.

Stupid.

I lift and drop my shoulder. Hope it's a convincing shrug. "I knew what he looked like," I say. "I actually did go to Mojave Prep. But it was a big school, Santos. Caught glimpses of him in the hall, but honestly, I didn't really know your dad. I mostly heard about him." I study the tips of my shoes, digging for a nugget of truth I can give her. "People . . . people really loved him."

I feel her scrutinizing me as I pretend to watch the man in the video plucking at the stringed instrument. Finally, she sighs.

"Yeah," she says softly. "They did."

"It's not weird, is it? That I didn't say anything?" I wince. "If it is, I just . . . I'm sorry."

River raises her brows. "Logan Evans," she says, "is that the second time you've apologized to me? Careful, your humanity is showing."

When she gives me that smile of hers, I breathe, relieved. *She believes me.*

"Shh," I say, pulling her close. "No one can know."

*There's so much no one can know.*

Our last stop is a big room filled with instruments you're allowed to play. The museum is closing early for an event, and half the lights are off in this room. Technically speaking, we were supposed to leave ten minutes ago.

But how can anyone resist letting it all out on the taiko drums?

"They're gonna come back and kick us out if you don't stop." River giggles. I roll my eyes and finally set the sticks down. She laughs when I make a beeline for a double-strung harp farther into the room. I drag a finger across the strings, inadvertently playing a beautiful glissando, and marvel at the instrument.

"That sounds just like the movies," I say, and she can't help but laugh. I spot an acoustic guitar in the corner.

As I walk over to it, River falls silent.

I pick it up, rotating it in my hands. "Always wanted to learn how to play one of these," I murmur. She hangs back for some reason as I sit on a long bench, a leg on each side, and strum an ugly chord.

"Sounds awful. Now they're definitely going to come kick me out." I strum again, and the guitar is pulled from my arms.

"It's because it's out of tune. Like, *really* out of tune," River grumbles, sitting beside me on the bench. I watch her fingers fly as she twists and turns the little knobs, strumming occasionally to check her work. When she plays a chord and it sounds like a six-part harmony, it feels like something unknots in my chest.

She looks up at me with those big brown eyes, strumming another beautiful set of notes, and it's so gorgeous, *she's* so gorgeous, my lungs ache.

"What?" she says shyly. "You okay?"

"Very," I growl, pulling her snug against me, her back to my chest, my long legs framing hers. I rest my chin lightly on her shoulder, wrapping my arms around her, placing my fingers on the guitar.

"Teach me a chord," I whisper into her hair.

"Why?" She's already breathless for me.

It's hard to think while River's pressed against me like this. With my hands on top of hers as we cradle the guitar together. I nip at her shoulder. "To impress college girls. Obviously."

"Huh. I'll only teach you the boring notes, then." She arranges three of my fingers across the strings in a diagonal line. "Okay, try strumming."

I strum once. It only sounds a little shitty, rattly and metallic.

"Push your fingers in a little harder," River says.

"I can do that." I drag my smile to the shell of her ear.

"Stop it." She breathes a laugh. "Now try strumming."

I strum slowly across the strings, the almost-perfect harmony singing out into the dim room. It's all so perfect, the feel of her against me, the vanilla silk of her skin against my lips. I slide my hands into her hair, gathering it into a bunch and lifting it off her shoulders, and press an open-mouthed kiss to the nape of her neck. River's breath hitches. I can feel her shiver against me.

"What are you doing?" she whispers.

"I used to catch myself staring right here." I suck at the skin just below her hairline. "You'd be at the register, and I'd just want to . . ." I bite her skin, and God help me, she *moans*.

"Christ," I groan, pulling the guitar from her lap and casting it unceremoniously aside. She turns her head, and our mouths meet, seeking and hungry. When my tongue brushes hers, the guitar lesson is already long forgotten.

# chapter 18
# river

**Tawny**
So did you charge for that lesson, or was the strumming pro boner?

**Tawny**
I mean bono 💩

**River**
I hate you.

I'm lying upside down on the couch, television on in the background, laughing at Tawny's text. Tita Anna struts in with the mail. Before I can pull myself up, she frisbees one my way.

"Hide your mozzarellas, hide your gelatos, 'cuz *Eaaat-aly* here we come!" She whoops, an envelope smacking me in the face as I sit up. The return address says ARIZONA DEPARTMENT OF HEALTH SERVICES. I rip it open and immediately frown.

"What the hell?" I say. " 'Request for birth certificate application rejected'?' "

"Gimme that." She snatches the letter from my hand. " 'No matching records found. Please correct and resubmit information within ten business days or you will need to open a new application.' " The paper crunches in Tita Anna's fists. "Oh, my blood pressure. I'll kill them. Every health services in the world. I'll take my frying pan and just . . ." I dodge her mime of swinging a weapon.

"You weren't this mad when I cracked your phone screen." I shrug. "Well, for months people have been treating me like a ghost. I guess it's official now: I don't exist." I'm only half joking.

She sighs. All at once, the fight goes out of her, and she flops on the couch. "Seriously, though, it's unbelievable how heartless bureaucracy is, especially when this is already *so hard*." She massages her temple. "Sorry, Riv. I'll call them. I just want to take you on a nice trip, get out of here for a while."

"Please don't apologize. And trust me, here's not so bad." I scoot closer to her, snuggling in, dropping my head on her shoulder. "Is there really no other place my birth certificate could be? Where do people usually keep them?"

Tita Anna wraps an arm around me, pulling me close.

"Well," she says, "some people have filing systems. Others use safes. I keep mine in my safety-deposit box at the bank. I don't know what your parents did, but . . ." She doesn't need to finish. It's the same refrain from the past seven months.

*There was nothing left.*

"Wait," I say, smacking Tita Anna's arm. "What about Dad's office? At the school? Unless you've already cleaned it out?"

"Ah . . . ha. Jay's office. Right. No. Not yet. And I definitely, *definitely* did not promise the school that I'd have it done months ago." She pats my thigh. "In case you were wondering."

I dig my phone out of my pocket, sitting up. "I'm glad you forgot. Maybe he kept important documents there."

"Maybe?" Tita Anna looks a little skeptical, like she doesn't want to get my hopes up. But she gives me the number, and I shoot Dad's assistant coach, Coach Gillis, a quick text asking if today's a good day to come by.

**Coach G**

On a FB trip, get back 2nite tho. NEtime after that is cool tho!

"Ah, Coach G." Tita Anna reads the text over my shoulder. "So sweet. So dumb."

I sigh. "I know I'm being an impatient baby, but I don't want to wait until he gets back. Now I know why people buy fireproof lockboxes."

"I know, Rivvy, but hopefully you'll find something there tomorrow," Tita Anna says.

Then I sit up straight. "Wait. You keep yours in a safety-deposit box. Do you think my parents could have done that too?"

It's a long shot. I'd spent plenty of time at the bank with them and had never seen anything other than the lobby. But it is possible. Anything's possible.

"It's worth a shot." Tita Anna checks her watch. "I have a Zoom call in fifteen. Do you want to wait until I'm done in case you need help navigating the bank?"

I bark a bitter laugh. "Trust me, Tita. I'll be fine."

I've been to the Scottsdale branch of Mesa Verde so many times, most of the tellers know my favorite Dum-Dum lollipop flavors. When she was feeling up to it, Mom would have me tag along so we could wait in the teller line. I'd squish the maroon velvet rope in my small fists and watch the toes of Mom's dirty white sneakers twist anxiously on the marble floor as she'd beg forgiveness for the overdraft fees, for the monthly penalty levied because we didn't have enough money in our account.

There's no line today, and I recognize Cindy behind the counter. She was one of the tellers who always waived our fees and saved the root beer lollipops for me. Even after forty years in the valley, she's never lost her Southern twang. I'm so thankful she's still here.

It takes a moment for her to notice me standing there, and when she does, her smile is slow, her wrinkles gathering like a theater curtain.

"Goodness me," she drawls. "If it ain't lil' Rivvy." Cindy's always moved a half step behind everyone else, at her own molasses rhythm. "I'm so sorry about your daddy, sweetheart." Cindy's voice is gravelly and Marlboro-low. There's something especially comforting in its rumble as she says, "It's shit, ain't it?"

"Complete shit." I give a hiccuppy laugh. "Kind of why I'm here. I think Dad maybe had a safety-deposit box here, but the key would have been lost in the fire, and I lost my birth certificate and—"

Cindy turns her teller sign from OPEN to CLOSED and fishes a ring of keys from a drawer. "Come on, Bubblegum. I'll take you to your daddy's box right now."

A thrill runs through me. I was right. He has a box.

"But don't you need to—? I don't want you to get in trouble . . ."

"Fuck 'em." Cindy shuffles around the counter, leading me down a hallway. "Your daddy brought me the best goddamn cookies I ever ate, and I've known you since you piddled your drawers in the lobby."

Cindy unlocks a thick plexiglass door to an enclosed room filled with neat little rectangular doors stamped with numbers. She unlocks

Dad's slot and pulls out a long, rectangular box, sliding it onto the cold stainless-steel table.

"Take your time, baby," she says softly as she exits.

My hands shake slightly as I open the box. Sure, it'd be nice if my birth certificate were here. But I want more.

Some new piece of my dad. A family necklace he'd always meant to give me. A letter he'd written, a message from the beyond. One where he'd say, *I faked my death, here are my current coordinates. Come find me.*

Audrey's mom used to keep her grandmother's diamond earrings in a safety-deposit box. I've seen movies where bricks of gold bars lined these boxes, or fat green stacks of hundred-dollar bills.

What's in Dad's box feels infinitely more valuable.

I pull out a stack of small, weathered recipes, the best experimental cookie recipe winners over the years. There's an AA white chip, so old the writing's faded. I imagine Dad keeping it in his pocket, his thumb worrying the surface of the plastic, back and forth, over and over. I press my thumb to the scuffed white, imagine our fingers touching.

The tears start when I find a faded playbill from my first singing concert, the font Comic Sans, probably printed on my chorus teacher's inkjet at home. There's a coaster from Canyon Springs Café, a J + J written in ink in the margins, the back listing Canyon Rock City, AZ. The name of the city shifts in my brain, familiar, but from where, I don't know. A pair of red dice, the white dots cracked and faded. There's a picture of Tawny (wait till I tell her she was one of Dad's treasures), a few rocks from hikes with Mom, and a newspaper clipping of a photo of teenage Mom with a friend at what looks like a fair. Who knew she'd made the paper at my age?

I pull out a tattered copy of a solid, black book. The soft cover is peeling, and I handle it as gently as a newborn, not wanting any part of this to flake away. The Big Book. Dad's AA staple. This must be one of his earlier ones. He always had one on him, tabbed and bookmarked, the inconspicuous cover hiding it in plain sight. When I lift the cover to get a hungry glimpse of Dad's tiny, neat print, a small handwritten note slips out.

*To Jay,*

*Not often I'm on this side of the equation, given my occupation, and I'm having trouble finding the words to properly thank you for saving my life.*

*The day you became my sponsor is the day I was resurrected. It was the day you gave Noah back his father. It was the day you gave me back my life.*

*I will spend the rest of my life endeavoring to thank you for this gift.*

*Thank you, my friend. Thank you.*

*Charlie*

Dr. Pierce. I'd known they met in AA, but I hadn't known Dad was his sponsor. Their devotion to each other makes so much sense now.

I rifle through the whole box, but no birth certificate. I'm disappointed, of course, but at least I'm not leaving empty-handed. I gather Dad's belongings, metal box picked bare, about to leave, when a flash of white catches my eye. I turn the box over and find that shoved in the back is a single white envelope. My birth certificate?

I open it quickly, but I'm disappointed again when there's nothing in there but a few blank scraps of paper. I fiddle with the pieces.

When I turn them over, my blood runs cold.

The ripped pieces of paper are not blank, like I thought. There are handwritten words on them, but it's not my dad's handwriting.

I've never seen these angry block letters before. And the things they say . . .

*I know what you did,* says one.

*You can't hide,* says another.

And then, the worst one of all, a single word:

*Killer.*

THAT NIGHT, I wait until Tita Anna goes to bed to google my dad's name. I love Tita Anna, but I know her. She'll either overreact and insist I call the police, or else she'll deflect with some very well-meaning but very ridiculous attempt to explain away the notes, like it was some elaborate prank. Those notes, like everything else in the safety-deposit box, meant something to my dad, but what?

*Killer.*

There are a million adjectives to describe my father. Resilient. Hardworking. Goofy. Kind. Smart. Creative. But killer? Not even close.

I shake my head hard and type *Jay Santos Arizona* into Google. Unsurprisingly, articles about the fire pop up. An obituary. I scroll a little farther, find plenty of articles about varsity football, coaching awards, school fundraisers he headed. Not much else.

I spend hours googling, combining my dad's name with different key words. Even going so far as to type in *Jay Santos Murder*. I scroll at least ten pages deep into the returned results. But I never see anything I don't already know. I look at locations, organizations, and dates.

That's when I finally notice something interesting. I double-check my work, scrawling notes on a pad next to me. I'm right.

There is nothing about my dad before 2002. Which is weird,

because I'm sure he was coaching since before I was born. I get that people weren't quite as active online back then, but there are multiple sports-related articles with my dad's name every year until it stops cold. Right at 2002.

But what does it mean? And is it related to the fact that Health Services can't find me?

I decide that it's worth playing another round of emotional Russian roulette. And by that, I mean texting my mom. I pull out my phone and type.

**River**

Why is there no record of Dad before 2002?

And now comes the worst part. Where all I can do is sit and wait. Knowing I won't get an answer, but hoping for one nonetheless.

*To my baby girl,*

*I suppose you are wondering about your father.*

*Where to start?*

*At the blissful beginning? Or the bitter end? His amazing qualities? Or his shortcomings?*

*I have always erred on the side of saying less, of protecting everyone from unkind truths. But maybe that's just another form of lying. Maybe it's better for children to know the truth: Parents are human. Who does it help when a child idolizes their parents?*

*Shouldn't we be seen for our true selves, warts and all? God knows I've made mistakes. And God knows I've hidden too many of them. Your father too.*

*Here are some words you should know about your father: Kind. Mischievous. Loving. Daring.*

*Here are some others: Reckless. Angry. Selfish.*

*When we first fell in love, his greatest crimes were youth and ignorance. And yes, maybe idiocy. Never underestimate the imbecilic nature of a boy. But also, never underestimate their earnestness, their ability to love. Love is no less real when it is young. Love is love. Even if you have to end it.*

*Even if the person you fell in love with isn't who you thought they were. Even if you don't get the happy ending you hoped for.*

*My hope for you is a fresh start. My hope for you is to do so much better than I did. My hope for you is to love a person who is good, through and through. My hope for you is a love that doesn't break your heart.*

*Love,*<br>*Mom*

# chapter 19

# river

It's just been Tawny and me working at the diner today. She knew something was up five minutes after I walked in. I could feel her gaze on me when I cut tomatoes. When I gathered the sloppy slices into the metal pan. I shot her a look that said, *Later*, and she got the message, leaving me to brood over the notes I found yesterday.

After my shift ends, I sit out back, hand-feeding tiny pieces of grilled chicken to Tigery, when my phone buzzes. I smile when I see who it is. It feels like the first time I've smiled all day.

**Logan**

So when's my next guitar lesson? Promise I won't interrupt this time. At least not until after I learn a G chord.

**River**

You'll have to be patient, the fingering for G is more complex than A. It may take more than one lesson.

**Logan**

Hm. That does sound complex. For you, I'll be a good student. I'll practice the fingering for as long as I need until I can find that G in a heartbeat.

**River**

Congratulations. You're the nine millionth guy to make a G-chord fingering joke.

**Logan**

Wow, Santos, mind in the gutter much? I'm just an eager pupil, thinking of complex fingering, like how Jimi Hendrix played chords using his thumb over the top of the neck? Think you can teach me that? A way to use my *thumbs* more creatively?

**River**

I knew it. You totally were jealous that night! And sure, Hendrix. I can think of a few ways to use those thumbs.

The back door bursts open, and Tawny's tired face appears. I bite back my goofy smile as Tigery flicks his tail and struts away, unhappy about the sudden slam.

"Oh, good. I wanted to say hi before you left," she says, tying her apron around her waist as she readies herself for the rest of her shift.

"Trouble sleeping again?"

"Yeah." She waves a dismissive hand. "I just feel a little aimless after the party. Maybe I need a new project or something. That's what I was doing, lying in bed and thinking . . . about our next thing."

" 'Our'?" I give her a small smile despite myself.

"Duh, Riv." She snorts. "It's always 'our.' " She eyes me. "Okay, but what's got you all broody today?"

And just like that, my good mood from Logan's texts dissipates. What's got me broody?

*Well, my dad did some shady stuff, apparently. Might be a murderer. Someone knew and threatened him. And the only person I can ask about it hasn't made contact in nearly a year . . .*

The truth is, I don't want to tell her about the notes. Dad was sort of like Tawny's dad too. I want to figure things out more before I tarnish another parental figure in her life.

"I was just thinking," I say. I rub my arm, hesitating. "About . . . my mom."

Tawny's head snaps up, my fiercest protector ready to throw her body between me and anyone who would make me cry. "What about?" There's that hard edge to her voice, the one reserved just for the topic of my mom.

"I don't know. Today is one of those days where I can't decide if I want to send her a million angry texts or just tell her I miss her a million times over." I sigh. "It just . . . hurts."

Tawny gives me a long, concerned look. "River . . ."

"I know, I know." I put my chin on my knee. "I'm pathetic."

Tawny twists her mouth. "Riv," she says, coming to my side to stroke my hair. "You're not pathetic. But you could stand to protect your heart a little more." She lifts a shoulder. "Maybe next time you want to text your mom . . . text me?"

"You're right." I nod, knowing she's only looking out for me. "Thanks. I'll do that."

Tawny brightens significantly. "Good." She stretches and jerks her head at the door. "All right. I should get in there before Gertie has a meltdown."

As soon as Tawny disappears through the door, my mind's right back on my dad.

Where else am I going to get some answers? My options are so limited.

But something occurs to me. I pull out my phone.

**River**

Hey Coach Gillis, sorry its short notice but would this afternoon be a good time to clean out my dad's office?

**Coach Gillis**

Thas cool il be round

**River**

Thank you so much!!!

I put down the phone, my stomach churning. I'm eager to see if there are answers hidden in Dad's office. But I also know that this is going to be hard. Because it's Dad's *office.* His second home. It's like I've been running from a swarm of grief bees, and now I'm willingly walking into the heart of their hive.

"Heya, Santos." Coach Gillis gives me a fist bump in greeting at the double-door entrance to the athletics building. His face and smile are wide and open as he walks me down the hallways. A couple of young boys run past us, throwing hacky sacks at each other, their pubescent voices cracking with laughter.

"Glad you made it out here." His nylon tracksuit, neon green with white stripes, swishes with every step he takes. When we reach the door to my dad's office, he pats the nameplate that reads COACH SANTOS, with a proud grin.

"Here it is," he says. But then his face falls. "Which you probably already knew. On account of all your years of . . . Look, my office is just across the way. I'll be in there running over tapes if you need anything." Coach Gillis offers his fist again, and I bump it, giving him a nod. His retreating swishes grow faint as I turn to the closed door.

I take a deep breath and push it open.

The first thing that strikes me is that Dad's office smells the same. That rubbery smell from a million cleats and ACE bandages and every iteration of sports balls. The cool spearmint of muscle rub. A hint of sweat and the Old Spice spray my dad used to try to mask it.

For a moment, I'm swept away by grief. I forget my mission. I can only think of how my dad held his head at an angle whenever he was working at his desk, going over the statistics from the last game. Growing up, I'd sometimes join him here during the summer, reading on the ratty couch shoved into the corner of his office.

I power through it, force myself to think of the scraps of paper, the dark words, as if the hand penning them was bearing down in rage.

*Killer.*

I sigh. *Here we go.*

The good news is that Dad was organized. No towers of papers that other coaches seem to collect. Dad's desk is neat. Tidy. The only thing on it is a huge desk calendar, still on December. All his holiday plans were laid out—our cookie extravaganza, Christkindlmarkt downtown, and that Christmas Day we spent with the Pierces. He'd highlighted it in pink, which he always did if it was a day he and I'd be spending together.

Tears burn in my eyes, but I force them back. I knew this would be tough. I just need to be tougher.

It takes me hours to pack up his trophy cabinet, his desk, his filing cabinet. Most of it is innocuous, but occasionally I hit a land mine. Like when I open a drawer full of office supplies and see a fine-tip Sharpie with teeth marks on the cap.

Suddenly, I'm back in my living room with Dad sitting in his armchair on a Sunday night, chewing on his pen as he frowns down at his coach's notebook. Mom, Tawny, and I are all watching *Elf*, and the Christmas lights reflect in his reading glasses.

It's a memory so vivid and painful, I have to sit down.

I open another drawer and find scraps of papers and postcards from students whose lives he touched over the years. . . . *I would never have made MVP if it wasn't for you . . . never forget how you stayed after, sharing your story . . . that you're my favorite teacher, ever . . .*

Dad always saw the best in people, even when they couldn't see it in themselves.

When all I've got left is Dad's photo wall to take down, and everything else, the entirety of my father's career, is stuffed in cardboard boxes, I'm exhausted. And completely worse for wear. Emotional land mines aside, nothing here has gotten me any closer to figuring out what the hell those scraps of paper meant, or who my dad was before 2002.

This was a bust. Just a huge emotional-punching-bag session.

My arms aching, I take down several years' worth of team photos, when a familiar face jumps out at me from the frame in my hand. I peer closer at the picture, my pulse ticking up.

And yes. It's definitely him.

Logan.

Logan, early high school Logan, is standing, his hands folded in front of him, looking grim as a prisoner. His hair is short; his face is young. But his pouty lips are the same, those churning blue eyes. No one is smiling in the photo, but Logan looks particularly grim.

*Guess he wasn't lying about hating football,* I think. I consider texting a picture of it to him. But when I look back at the photo, my blood turns to ice.

Standing right behind Logan, with a hand on his shoulder, is Dad.

I think back to what Logan had told me.

*I didn't really know your dad.*

Staring at this picture, that's insanely hard to believe.

I tear down the next year's team photo, searching for Logan. I can't find him. He *did* say he'd only lasted one season. *Wasn't my thing.* But why did he quit? Why did he downplay it?

Why is everyone I care about in my life hiding something from me?

I carry both pictures to Coach Gillis across the hall and hold them up.

"This boy." I point to Logan. "You remember him?"

He scratches his head. "Yeah, that's Evans. He only played for a minute, but it's sort of hard not to remember him." He pauses. "Well, more like, hard not to remember his dad."

I blink. "Logan's dad?"

Coach Gillis sighs, leaning back in his chair. "Yeah. Evans just didn't have his head in the game. If only he'd run as fast on the field as he did to get off the field when practice ended. Your dad cut him. And then?" He whistles, shaking his head.

"And *then*?" He's killing me.

"Evans's dad lost his mind. He was obsessed with football. Played in college, injured himself, was forced to retire early. Apparently, he *insisted* that Evans do what he couldn't." Coach Gillis makes a face. "Except Evans? He just couldn't cut it."

I swallow a few times before I can talk. "What happened? When Logan was cut?"

Coach Gillis lets out a long, slow breath. "It was bad. I wasn't there that day, but Evans's dad showed up. Screaming, cussing. Your dad never told me all the details, just that he almost had to call the cops."

I have so many questions. "How did Logan take it?"

"I don't actually remember. It was his dad's reaction that was memorable. We're lucky no one ended up injured that day."

"Do you remember anything about Logan? Anything at all."

Coach Gillis rocks in his desk chair, his expression far away. "What I do remember is that he was such an angry kid." He sighs. "Can't blame him, with a dad like that."

It takes a minute, but I finally find my voice.

"Coach Gillis," I say slowly, "so, Logan and my dad? They knew each other?"

"Well, *yeah*." He sits up. "He was one of your dad's pet projects. He felt sorry for him, I think. Early in the season, he saw Evans's dad screaming at the kid in the parking lot after a game and had all of us coaches giving Evans extra support and lessons. It didn't really take, though—not everyone is cut out to be a football player." Coach Gillis shakes his head, tilting his chair back again.

I nod, but I don't answer. I'm afraid that if I open my mouth, I'll throw up.

"Why do you ask? You know the kid?" Coach Gillis asks.

Finally, I find my voice. "No. I don't know him at all."

# chapter 20
# river

When I wake up, the cicadas are screaming. An hour later, the sky opens. The monsoons have come late this year. It's exactly the weather I need right now. There's a strange comfort, hearing the thunder wrack the world, seeing the flashes of lightning through the blinds of my bedroom window, the wrecked confusion of my heart reflected by nature.

*Of course* Logan is too good to be true. Someone can't be that incredible without some caveats. And Logan's caveat is that he lies. He lies to me.

Maybe I'm overreacting, though. Maybe it's not that big of a lie. Maybe he just felt awkward talking about my dad because of what happened to him. But it's the fact that it's my *dad*. That subject feels sacred.

I'm supposed to be leaving for my morning shift, but I'm still curled up in bed. It's been too much: the strange notes, cleaning out

Dad's office, and now Logan. The idea of getting up to brush my teeth feels daunting, much less working at the diner *with Logan* today.

I brace myself, dialing the diner's number to tell Gertie I'm sick. She tells me to feel better soon and not to worry before hanging up. It's a kindness that goes a long way.

"River?" There's a gentle knock on my door before Tita Anna pokes her worried face through the gap. "Sweetheart, you okay?"

"Yeah," I say, pulling the blankets up to my chin. "Just sick. I'm taking today off."

She comes in, presses the back of her hand to my forehead. Adjusting her glasses, she asks carefully, "You sure you're okay? Anything you need to talk about?"

But I can't tell Tita Anna that the boy I was absolutely idiotic about just a day ago is already breaking my heart.

"Yeah, Tita," I say. "I think I'm just going to sleep for now."

"All right," she says, mouth twisting. "I have plans with friends tonight, and it might be a late night. But call me if you need *anything* at all. I'll come right home."

I bury myself beneath the covers as soon as she leaves, hating myself for falling too fast, too hard.

But why would Logan even lie? Like, what's the point?

I open my text chain with Logan. He texted me good night last night. Nothing to write home about, just a simple Night, River with a little kissy face.

I haven't responded, and he hasn't texted me since.

As if on cue, my phone buzzes. I'm so startled, I nearly drop it.

**Logan**

You good, Santos? Gertie said you're sick.

I hate how when I see Logan's name on my screen, even now, a shot of dopamine flies through my bloodstream. I hate how I still want to respond.

But I don't.

My phone buzzes again. He sends me a series of texts, one after the other.

**Logan**

Sorry you're sick.

**Logan**

Why didn't you tell me? I could have brought you homemade soup and Gatorade.

**Logan**

The soup being homemade. Not the Gatorade. Let's be clear. Homemade Gatorade sounds disgusting.

I chew my lip, frowning down at my phone. God, there's a huge part of me that wants to text him back. That same part of me feels heartened that he's checking in on me.

The rest of me is screaming, *Are these lovely little lies as well?*

I turn back over into my pillow, feeling miserable.

I still want him. I do. I still can't stop thinking about our first kiss. About his secret smirk when we make eye contact at work. But now there's a film over those memories too. They're tainted. It's hard not to call everything into question. To call his words into question. Did he mean it? Any of it?

Hurricane Logan. The wild tempest. I close my eyes, listening to the actual storm, the one outside, feeling terribly alone. My mom, my dad, and Logan. Even Noah. Is anyone who they say they are? Am I not important enough to have earned my loved ones' truth?

My phone buzzes multiple times: another series of texts.

**Logan**

Alright, Santos, what gives? You didn't reply to my text last night. Didn't reply to the ones today. You call out of work.

**Logan**

Did something happen?

**Logan**

Blink twice if you're being held hostage.

**Logan**

Tell them I know Liam Neeson and *will not* hesitate to call him.

**Logan**

Seriously though. Are you okay?

Finally, I can't help myself. I craft a response, if only to stem the tide of texts.

**River**

I'll be fine. Just sleeping.

I watch as the three dots indicating his typing appear. Then disappear. Then reappear. Even despite the pit in my stomach, there's some distant part of me that enjoys being on the other side of this. Typically, I'm the one anxiously texting, overthinking everything.

Finally, he replies.

**Logan**

Right. Look, I don't know what's going on, but something's up. Let me know when you're ready to come clean.

My blood runs hot. I know I should just ignore it. I try to ignore it for a few minutes. But I just can't. My fingers hover over the keyboard, and before I can stop myself, I fire back a response.

**River**

That's rich coming from you. How about you let me know when *you're* ready to come clean.

As soon as I hit send, I want to take it back. It's that awful, split-down-the-middle feeling. I'm proud of myself for standing my ground. But also, a part of me is screaming, *Tell me I'm wrong. Tell me I've got it wrong.*

My stomach lurches. I walk to the kitchen on shaky legs, shivering, to make myself a cup of tea. I try not to, but every five minutes, I check my phone to see if Logan's replied.

Nothing.

Cradling a steaming cup of chamomile against my chest, I walk to the couch, wrapping a blanket around me, and listen to the thick curtain of rain against our roof, the gentle, giant rumble of occasional thunder joining the storm's symphony, letting it all lull me to sleep.

I WAKE TO a knock on the door. I sit up, the living room dark, the storm still raging outside. I think I've dreamed the sound when there's another knock, followed by the ding of a text message.

**Logan**

I'm outside. Please, I just want to talk.

I peer out the window. Sure enough, Logan's car is outside the apartment. When I open the front door, standing before me is a very wet Logan Evans.

"River." He pushes back his dripping hair, wiping a hand across his face, his eyes like shards of ice. "What is it that I'm supposed to come clean about, exactly?"

I step outside the door, shutting it, not ready to let him in. Logan and I have to stand close so we can both fit under the awning shielding us from the rain.

It's painful, seeing him face-to-face. Heat still radiates from his body, even while he's soaked to the bone, and it's heartbreaking how beautiful he is like this, water falling from dark locks of his hair, his crystalline gaze blazing with fury. I swallow hard, steeling myself.

"You know, Logan, I really don't want to do this. The back-and-forth thing."

His eyes narrow. "What do you mean?"

"Like, I say, 'You lied to me,' and then you say, 'No, I didn't,' and it goes on and on."

Logan stares at me like he's trying to activate X-ray vision to examine my cranial folds. When that doesn't work, he throws his hands into the air helplessly. "Santos. I swear to God, I do not know what you're talking about."

"My dad, Logan." My voice breaks when I say his name. "I'm talking about my dad."

Logan freezes. He opens his mouth, but nothing comes out.

His gaze drops to the ground. "How'd you find out?" He says it so quietly, it's nearly drowned out by the rush of rain. A distant flash of lightning illuminates his face, the darkness in his eyes.

"I cleaned out Dad's office yesterday. I saw your team photo, Logan. The one where my dad's hand was on *your* shoulder." I swallow hard. "And you said you didn't know him." A thunderclap sounds, making me tremble harder. "I just don't get why you'd lie about *that*."

Logan stares at me, holding stock-still. The wind is picking up, the rain blowing sideways, soaking us.

“Santos,” he says. His voice drops. “River. I want to explain.” His eyes flick behind me, to the door of the apartment. “Can we talk someplace less . . . I promise I’ll leave immediately if you change your mind.” He takes a breath, nodding at the ground. “Just hear me out, okay?”

I answer by opening the door behind me and stepping out of the sideways spray. Logan follows me inside and shuts the storm out behind us, his face softening in the quiet. I hate how his look of relief rushes through me, a rosy, golden light. Even after everything, he affects me.

I stand there, shivering in my soaked shorts and tank top, my dripping hair forming puddles on the ground.

“Can I . . . ?” He tilts his head toward the bathroom, and I nod. Logan disappears down the hall, returning with a stack of fluffy cream-colored towels. He tosses me one.

“Thanks,” I whisper, drying myself the best I can. He nods, ruffling his hair with his own towel, leaving it rumpled in my favorite way. I glare at the floor, listening to the rain beating against the windows, the branches of sagebrush slapping at the pane.

“River.” Logan drapes dry towels over the couch, patting the cushion beside him, an offer. Instead, I choose to stay standing, walking to plant my feet opposite him, the coffee table between us.

He leans forward, his elbows on his knees, pinching the bridge of his nose. “You saw a team photo of us together—that doesn’t mean I lied to you.”

Anger rises all the way up my neck and through my cheeks. It feels like he’s elbowed me in the stomach. But I take a deep breath. Yelling will accomplish nothing.

“Omitting information is lying, Logan,” I say.

He nods. “Okay. You’re right. I get that.”

"I know it might seem like a small thing to lie about," I say, my voice trembling with barely tethered emotion. "But, Logan. He's my *dad*. This isn't like lying about your favorite ice cream flavor." I dig my nails into my palm, hoping the stinging grounds me, keeps tears from falling. "He's—he's gone, okay? He's gone, and unless someone else tells me something new, I know everything I will *ever* know about my dad already. And it's not *enough*." I choke on the last word for a moment. "So when Coach Gillis said you were his 'pet project' after you said you didn't know him—"

"Okay, 'pet project'? That's—that's not a thing . . . and have you *met* Coach Gillis? The man's a . . ." Logan cuts himself off, a flash of pain crossing his face. He rises from the couch, his body crackling with that cornered-panther energy I saw the night of Tawny's party as he starts to pace the open space of the living room.

"I told you once, football wasn't my thing. It was my dad's. When he couldn't make his football dreams come true, his thing became making football *my* life. He never stopped pushing and pushing and *pushing* . . ." Logan shakes his head, disgusted. "It was just easier not to fight him *every single day* about it. So I gave up. And yeah. Your dad was head coach." He runs a hand through his hair. "Santos, the school's huge. There were nine coaches for the football team. Nine. You know that. I was bottom of the barrel, third string."

Logan stops pacing and presses his tongue against the inside of his cheek, shaking his head. He won't look at me. "I didn't want to be there, but your dad . . . he said he saw something in me," he says quietly. "Your dad was the one calling the shots. Trying to get the other coaches to give me one-on-one training, help me feel like part of the team. But I hardly spent time with him. Your dad was always busy helping lots of guys out. I'm nothing special."

He still won't look at me as he resumes pacing, faster, more agitated. "I told my dad I was a lost cause when it came to football. Dad didn't listen. Wouldn't hear of me quitting." Logan pauses, swallowing. "So, yeah. Eventually, your dad sat me down and pulled it out of me, why I was always dragging my feet, looking at the time. I told him I wanted out. I could tell he wanted to encourage me, tell me I should 'put my mind to it' and all that crap. But in the end, he did what my dad's never done." Something dark, indiscernible, sweeps across his face as he stares at the ground. "He heard me. He listened. He cared. So . . . he cut me."

It takes a couple of swallows for me to find my voice. "Coach Gillis said that something happened with your dad?"

"Yeah? Did he tell you that my dad forced me to go to practice the day after I told him I was cut? That he grabbed me by the hair in front of everyone and dragged me across the track? Gillis tell you my dad shoved me onto the asphalt, gave me a bloody lip? Your dad showed up, and for a second, I thought my dad was gonna kill him for cutting me. But your dad stood his ground. And when he threatened to call the cops, my dad actually backed down and left."

I wait for him to continue, but he just stands there, his shoulders tight, glaring at the wall.

"I'm really sorry that all happened to you," I say, reaching out to touch his shoulder before thinking better of it and letting my hand fall to my side.

Logan's face finally cracks. "River. I'm sorry. I'm so sorry. For—for lying. And for how I've been handling everything." Logan runs a hand through his hair, leaving it standing on end. "I didn't know how to explain . . . how to even bring up . . . It's like, when you asked me, at the museum, about my relationship with your dad, you just seemed so hopeful . . ."

The windowpanes rattle from the howling wind. The sound of rain stretches between us as Logan shifts uneasily, struggling, like there's something else he needs to say. He drops his voice to a whisper.

"River, I was ashamed. I *am* ashamed. There. That's the truth, and it's stupid. I didn't want to tell you I suck at football. I didn't want to admit that my dad is a piece of shit. I didn't want you to know that the only link I have to your dad is a stupid, ugly snapshot from my life." Logan's jaw clenches as loathing floods his face. "I wasn't even nice to your dad. Back then, I was a miserable asshole to everyone." He wipes a hand across his mouth. "And now I've been a miserable asshole to you."

I reach out, having only enough courage to grab the front of his soaked shirt with two fingers. "You're only an asshole if you're not being honest with me. Don't be scared to be honest with me, Logan."

He drops his gaze to where I'm pinching at his shirt. "Scared?" he says quietly. "You think I'm scared of you, Santos?"

His eyes are starting to get hard to read again. But barely. It's like he's holding the bricks to rebuild his walls, but he can't decide what to do.

I take a gamble.

"Yeah," I say. "I do think you're scared. I just don't know why."

Logan makes a low sound as he walks me back against the wall. "You don't know why? I risk my job and life speeding through a monsoon, just because you're mad at me, and you ask me *why*."

A thunderclap rumbles, and I tremble, my eyes stinging as I stare up into his fervent gaze. In an instant, we're crashing against each other, our mouths tangling messily in a wet, desperate kiss.

I can't believe I get to do this. Taste Logan. Feel his heart slamming against my chest. I run my hands under his shirt.

"*God*, River . . ." He breaks off on a choke as I drag my nails down his abs.

When I slip my fingers beneath his boxers, he makes a frantic, needy sound in the back of his throat, his hand sliding from my hair to my ass, pulling me against him. I gasp when his hips move against my thigh. I press my body harder into his.

"*River*, how can I . . ." Logan presses a feverish kiss to the front of my throat. "How can I keep it together, when . . ." He drags a tongue up my neck, cups my face. "When you *feel* like this, *taste like this* . . ." He pulls back, panting and heavy-lidded. Something despairing flashes over his eyes, like he can't believe what he's seeing. Like he doesn't deserve to. "When you *look* like this?" he whispers, pressing his thumb into my lip. "How do I stay in control?"

"You don't." If my brain wasn't short-circuited, I'd be blushing. But all that's there is *more, more, more*.

And Logan gives me more. As soon as my tongue touches his skin, he groans, and his hands slide to my ass again, lifting me up, my arms thrown around his neck, my legs wrapping around his hips.

Kissing me desperately, he pushes my back against the wall. I squirm against him, his words lighting my body everywhere. All I can manage is one anguished word:

*"Please,"* I whine, not even knowing what I'm begging for. Just "Please."

*"Shit,"* he grunts, sucking on my neck, and he's immediately carrying me down the hall, kicking doors haphazardly until he finds my bedroom. I kiss him hard as we tumble onto the mattress. I wrap my arms around his neck, delighting in the way I'm straddling him, tangling my hands in his hair. Logan pulls back, blinking slowly, his mouth swollen, and his scar (that scar, that *scar*!) flushed pink.

He kisses me deeply. "I need you, River."

"Show me," I breathe, pulling off my shirt. Logan's fingers spasm against my hips. "Show me how much you need me."

As soon as the shirt clears my head, Logan's ravenous mouth is on me. He licks and sucks a trail up the bare stretch of my stomach, dragging a tongue along the edge of my bra. With one hand, he pulls the band out of my ponytail, fisting a greedy hand into my rain-soaked hair. With the other, he squeezes my hip, rocking me against him, an insistent rhythm. I can't catch my breath for how good it feels.

My hands go to his shirt, and he helps me take it off with a low noise in his throat, one that has me pushing him down to the bed. I break our kiss and sit back on his thighs.

"What?" He pants, sitting up on his elbows, confused. "Everything good?" The concerned notch between his brows makes my heart ache.

"Could be better," I whisper. "We could be out of these sopping-wet clothes." Partly because I want to tease him, mostly because I can't help it, I rock my hips against him.

"Oh God—*come here*." Logan flips me over, sounding agonized. Our hands are clumsy as we both try feverishly to peel the wet layers off each other. We're moving fast, but I don't miss the way his eyes get darker, hungrier, when my shorts are off and his gaze is licking down my bare thighs.

Logan surges forward, capturing my mouth as we frantically grasp and yank off soaked clothes, and soon, I'm wearing nothing but my bra and panties, with Logan only in his boxers, each of us breathing like we're running our first marathon.

"Logan Evans in my bed. I've thought about this," I confess in a hot whisper.

*"Really?"* Logan captures my wrists and pins them above my head.

He leans down to drag his teeth against my neck. I never thought I'd want so badly for a man to bite me. "Tell me *everything*."

"W-well . . ." It's getting harder to talk with the way Logan's mouth is trailing down my skin. "I thought about your hands. How you'd be good with your hands."

"Hmm." He releases my wrists and runs his palms down my torso, slipping his fingers beneath the cup of my bra, swiping them eagerly against me.

I arch into his touch, dizzy with pleasure I've never known before.

"Yes, just like that," I breathe. I feel heat spread up my chest and neck, my cheeks burning. Logan tracks the flush of my skin. He leans down, his lips brushing the shell of my ear before capturing my lips.

Kissing Logan is always exquisite. But right now, my skin is on fire, and I need more. I need to feel him everywhere. I break our kiss to sit up a little and reach behind me. In one motion, I unhook my bra and toss it over the side of the bed. Logan's mouth falls open.

"Jesus. You are so beautiful," he whispers, face filled with wonder, before dipping his head to rain kisses all over me, kissing my lips, my neck, and then, finally, my chest.

Every touch, every word Logan is whispering, every press of his rocking hips against me is so good. *So* good. But there is no sating. I'm only growing more ravenous, starving for something I know I want, even never having tasted it yet.

"River," Logan says, as if reading my tumbling thoughts, "tell me what you want. I'll give it to you. I want to give you everything."

I start to tremble. "You," I whisper. "Logan, I want you."

"I want you too, River," he murmurs against me, his hips pressing against me deliciously. His eyes travel up and down my body, as if he's memorizing every detail, every centimeter of bare skin, before tracing his lips over all of me. I clutch him against me. Holding him tight. Because I don't want this to end. I want to capture this, remember this forever. This moment, when the rain is rushing, pouring outside, the lightning and the thunder roaring, and Logan, my tempest, my own hurricane, moving against me, only two thin pieces of cloth between us, his eyes open and naked and raw, and his hand clutching mine.

# chapter 21
# river

Despite the rain, there's a Red Flag Warning announced on the first of July. The desert is greedy this year, the windfall of sudden water still not enough for the sun-choked dust of the Sonoran, the thirsty sage and brush dry as tinderboxes.

Over the past week, temperatures have flared, hitting 110°F nearly every day. Everyone says desert heat is different, more bearable, but this is the type of heat that sucks you dry and punishes you if you stay outside too long. A hiker died of dehydration just yesterday, and even the saguaros are withering, their arms thudding to the ground, their spines sagging as the water within boils them alive in the Arizona sunshine.

"Do you think they'll call off fireworks?" Tawny says, thumbing through her tips at the counter as we prepare to close.

"God, I hope not," I say, and quickly close out of the photo I was looking at of the notes from the safety-deposit box. I've stared at them so many times, I've memorized the slash of each letter. Still, I'm no closer to understanding what they mean.

Logan looks up from wiping the crumbs off his last table. "You like fireworks?"

Before I can answer, Tawny cuts in. "Oh, she more than likes them, don't you, River? She gets downright *hot* for them."

My cheeks burn as I smack Tawny with a menu. "Shut up, Tawn," I mutter.

Logan takes his time brushing at a speck of dirt on his sleeve. "Interesting."

"It certainly was interesting when I stumbled upon her and Noah in the bushes while we were all setting off fireworks in the backyard—"

*"Tawny,"* I hiss. "Enough." At the mention of Noah, I'm reminded of the text he sent me this morning. **Jonah's having a BBQ for the 4th if you want to come**, he'd said. Like I would want to go to that.

"Aw, Riv, I'm just teasing." She kisses my cheek. "As your surrogate sister, it's my job to embarrass you in front of your little boy toy."

When I told Tawny about the other night with Logan, she was shocked but supportive. She kept saying how happy she was for me. But I know her. There was hurt in her voice as well. I tried to ask her about it, but she denied feeling anything other than resplendently happy for her best friend.

But when she says things like this, her teasing has an edge to it. I can't help but wonder if a part of her is wounded that I took such a big step with Logan without consulting her first. Asking for her advice. Even though Logan and I didn't get very far past second base, Tawny is accustomed to me planning every pitch with her, not just giving the postgame highlights.

Logan approaches me as Tawny traipses off to the back to do some dishes.

"'Downright *hot*,' huh?" His voice is dark.

"Don't tell me you're jealous, Evans." I smirk, but my heart's already beating a wild, hungry rhythm as he grabs my hips and pulls me close.

"Of course I'm jealous," he growls against my temple. "I'm jealous of anyone or anything that's ever touched you before me." Logan swipes a thumb across the embroidered diner logo at my chest. "I'm jealous of your clothes, getting to spend all day pressed against your skin."

"Guess you'll just have to touch me enough to erase the memory of everyone else." I'm already lost in the recollection of his hands pulling off my shirt. The things he could do with his thumbs. *God, his thumbs.*

"I don't know." He pulls back. "Not sure there's such a thing as touching you *enough*." I feel his swallow against my cheek. "So you feel better today? Are you . . . good? With everything yesterday?"

I pull back to meet his stare, anxious about the uncertainty I see there. "Are you?"

He gives me a soft smile. "What a question, Santos. You're kidding, right?" He swipes a thumb across my lips. "I'll never look at rain the same again. But it's not me I'm worried about here. I'm checking in on you."

"You know, I'm not too sure." I catch his thumb gently between my teeth. Logan's eyes darken. "I'll need to try again. Just to be sure. Especially since we were interrupted far, *far* too early."

"Too early, huh?" Logan's voice is rough.

"Way too early. Didn't even make it to intermission, much less the grand finale." I flick my tongue against his thumb, nipping it before I release him. His eyelids fall heavy, and he makes a low, rough sound in the back of his throat. It steals my breath, an ache settling deep in my hips, wishing we were somewhere private.

"*Shit*, Santos. You're killing me." His voice is husky. "Come watch fireworks with me. Please."

"Logan Evans, begging for my company?" I try for flirtatious, but my breathlessness kind of ruins the effect. "Who would have thought?"

"Yeah, well." He dips down and bites my neck, making me shiver. "If you wanna compare past records, you're gonna lose." Logan leans in, but when our lips are barely touching, he doesn't move.

He just stays there, refusing to close the agonizing inch between us. I can't stop looking at that scar on his lip. I know what he's doing. Jerk. I won't give him the satisfaction.

But when the tip of his tongue drags over my bottom lip, I break, closing the distance.

"See?" he says against my lips. *"Needy."*

I give him my own wordless counter, and he grabs my hips, pulling me against the hot, hard line of his body. When I pull back and he leans forward, chasing my lips, I giggle. He groans.

"Fine, you make some excellent points. Come with me?"

"I'd love nothing better." I chew my lip. "But we have to invite Tawny."

After earlier, I'm a little worried Tawn's been feeling excluded.

"Of course," he says after a pause. "Invite her. Just prepare her for all the PDA."

"No, you have to be good!" I squeal a laugh as he leans in.

"I'm a man, not a miracle worker," he says against my mouth.

The door bursts open, slamming against the wall. Tawny marches in with a large bag.

"Don't stop on my account, you two." Tawny shoots me a smirk as she heaves the remaining trash into the bag.

"Hey, Tawn," I say, feeling guilty about getting caught kissing. "Wanna do Fourth of July stuff with Logan and me?"

She laughs. "Rivvy, is this a pity invite?"

Does she really think that? "Of course not!"

Tawny takes her time answering, tying the bag tightly before pulling a small bottle of hand sanitizer from her pocket and slathering it on her hands.

"I appreciate the invite, Riv." She smiles. "But I actually already have plans. I had a couple of hot college guys during dinner rush yesterday, and they invited me to their boat party on Canyon Lake. Sounds a little more fun than scrolling my phone while you two dry-hump each other next to me."

*"Tawny,"* I gasp. But she waves her hand dismissively in the air.

"I kid, I kid." She throws her arms around me, squeezing tightly. "Seriously. Thank you for the invite." Tawny pulls back and jams her finger into Logan's sternum. "Just remember who her actual one and only is. Got it, Thumbs?" She struts back into the diner.

Logan raises a brow. "Um, why'd she call me Thumbs?"

I sigh and pat his shoulder. "I'll tell you when you're older."

Logan drives me home after we've locked up. There aren't many fireworks shows scheduled because of the Red Flag Warning, the state not wanting to stretch the fire departments too thin. Luckily, there's a Fourth of July celebration right in Scottsdale.

"They say it's going to be the biggest fireworks display in Scottsdale history! And ooh, look, there's a cheeseburger-eating contest," I tease.

"Ah, explosions and competitive eating. Who says Americans have no culture?" Logan snorts.

"Hey, there's even a lineup of live music! This seems perfect." I scroll through the social media pages and wince when I see the amount of likes and people who have marked *Planning to attend*. "Ugh, it's gonna be so crowded. The idea of being pressed in a crowd of thousands, maybe even tens of thousands, of sweaty people is not . . . my favorite."

Logan hums thoughtfully. "These the fairgrounds just off of Shea?"

I check the map. "Yeah," I say.

He scratches his chin. "I've got a solution, then. If you're willing to trek a little bit. We just need some snacks and camping chairs."

"Okay!" I say. "You have chairs?"

Logan's face tenses. "I don't," he says. "But my father does."

# chapter 22
# logan

On the Fourth of July, I pick River up and drive her to my dad's house. I can barely speak on the way over, barely notice the other cars whizzing past as I make my way to the development where his new house is. My hands grip the steering wheel, and I just focus on keeping the car steady, on breathing.

I can do this. In and out. I don't even have to talk to the asshole.

That doesn't stop my gut from seesawing. Because it's not just about seeing him. It's about River and what *she* sees. And I don't know why it hadn't occurred to me until now what it would look like, not until I pulled into the stone-paved roundabout, lined with topiaries, the marble columns framing the double front door.

"Logan," River gasps, "you're *rich*."

I throw the gear into park a little too hard, jerking the car to a stop. I take a deep breath.

"*I* am not rich." I say it slowly, giving each word its own emphasis. "My dad is."

I glare at the sprawling building, my mouth forming a knot of disgust. "Wait here. I'll be back in ten." I'm out of the car, stalking toward the building before she can reply.

I work as quickly and quietly as possible, punching the door code in, slipping through the atrium and down the basement stairs to the camping storage closet. I grab the chairs and make my way up, thrilled that I may get away unscathed.

I take a moment in the atrium to adjust one of the chairs so it's not digging into my shoulder.

"Those chairs a little too heavy for you, son?" Dad keeps his voice light as he makes his way down the stairs, his walk slow. Powerful. The old knot in my gut comes back, twisting sharp and violent. Maybe it never went away. Maybe it never will.

"No," I say. I straighten my back, let the chair weigh on my collarbone.

"If you say so." Dad's deep bass has always boomed, but here, where it only has porcelain tile and marble to echo against, his voice feels bigger. Colder. Which is saying something.

He runs a critical eye over me, the muscle in his jaw ticking. I don't care anymore. Which is why I don't get why it feels like he's peeling off my skin. He drags a hand through his beard.

"I guess you're working too much to have time to go to a gym." Dad's eyes linger at my arms. I fight the urge to hide them. "If you hadn't thrown away your inheritance, you could lead a more balanced life."

"Guess so," I say.

Something in his expression softens. "It's been a while, son."

"I know," I say.

"I miss you."

I look up, startled. I can't remember the last tender words from him. Can't square the man before me, the one whose once-bright blue eyes are muted, with the man who dragged me from practice, who berated me for not being his vision of a son.

"Your mother wouldn't want this for us."

His words make me stiffen. That's rich, him suddenly caring what Mom would want.

"We both made our choices, and I stand by mine." I don't wait for a reply. I turn on my heel, kick open the door, hope it scuffs.

I march to the car and throw the chairs into the trunk, rubbing the bruise on my collarbone as I get in the driver's seat.

"Mission accomplished. Let's get the hell out of here," I mutter, swearing when my seat belt locks. "Next stop: freedom, fiddles, and fireworks."

"Who is that?" River points out the window to the manor. I'm surprised to find Dad's large frame filling the front doorway, watching us.

"My dad," I say quietly. A million questions silently fly at me, but she keeps her mouth closed. I can see her searching his face, looking for the man she's heard about from my stories. His eyes are dark and cold until they shift over to River. When he sees her, his brows shoot up. I'm surprised when he gives her a tentative wave.

"What?" I say when I see her face.

"You're not embarrassed of me, are you?" she asks, wringing her hands in her lap. "Do you not want your dad to know about me?"

"You're joking. Why would you think that?" I follow her stare out the window to where my dad still has his hand up in greeting. I pause, thinking, before I grab her face, giving her a kiss, quick, deep, and a little dirty.

"There," I say, a little breathless. "Now he knows who you are. But that's all he gets to know."

THE FAIRGROUNDS ARE beautiful in the early evening. Even as the heat clings to us, dry and heavy, the magic of summer is alive. River holds my hand as I buy her cotton candy. When her cheeks get sticky and she asks for a napkin, I lean forward and lick the sugar from her skin. An occasional hot desert breeze plays with the hem of her red dress, and she looks beautiful, like some kind of princess of the desert. I can't believe she's mine.

When we watch the rodeo, I stand behind her, sliding my hands to hold her around the middle. I'm drunk on these little touches, the tiny ones only allowed by a boyfriend, ones now only allowed by *me*.

We walk by a stage dressed in large ribbons of red, white, and blue. The sign says RAMBLIN' RICK'S BIG BLUEGRASS BAND, with a showtime of just after dark, right before the fireworks.

River pauses. The stage is empty except for the instruments arranged around the stage, poised in their stands. She points to the acoustic guitar.

"That's the kind I had," she says, forcing her voice to stay neutral. My eyes flick between River and the stage.

"Yeah? That a good one?"

"The best," she says in a tight voice. "I'd always wanted a Gibson. Best birthday present ever." She chews on the inside of her lip. "Kinda no point in singing anymore without one."

I hum but stay silent. I don't ask where it went. Of course I know. Any memory she's ever shared with me is nothing but ash now.

When the sun starts thinking about setting, I drive us to the parking lot of the McDowell Mountain trail system.

"All right, Evans, spill it," she says as I lug the chairs and her bag up the trail. "Is this a trick? How do you know about this little secret fireworks spot?"

"Mom, actually," I say. "One of our first summers here, we tried doing the fireworks crowd thing. It was awful. I was a little crying kid, Dad complained I was too loud, and it took us hours to get back to the car with all the people. She hiked this mountain a lot that winter, and when the Fourth of July came back around, she took us up here. No crowds, great view. She'd spent all winter scoping out the perfect spot." I turn around and give her a small smile. "It's an Evans Family Secret. Guard it with your life."

She mimes drawing an *X* over her chest. "And I'm *not* going to die, right?" she asks as we veer off the trail, doing exactly what all the signs are telling us *not* to do.

"Trust me," I say, holding out a hand. And she takes it.

The last few rays of the sun are slipping down the horizon as we follow a path that curves around the mountain. To the left is a sheer drop-off, I don't even know how many feet down.

But as soon as we make it around the bend, River's mouth drops open.

We've arrived at a flat stretch of rock that juts out of the mountain, large enough to lay out a tent and sleep under the stars. I start setting up our chairs and a blanket as she walks toward the edge, gazing at the festival grounds below us, marveling at how the wide desert stretches to the horizon.

"For God's sake, Santos," I say in an alarmed voice. "Get away from the ledge."

"I'm not even close!" she protests, pointing at the three feet between her and the drop-off.

"Too close for me," I mutter, grabbing her hand to pull her back. "I'm too young for a heart attack."

She rolls her eyes, letting me pull her to where I've laid out our blanket and chairs, side by side. By the time we've settled into our seats, the first few stars are winking in the purple twilight, and we can hear the sounds of stringed instruments warming up.

"Well, if it ain't ole Ramblin' Rick's Big Bluegrass Band," River says in a surprisingly sexy Western drawl. It takes me a second to find my voice.

"Yeah, okay. Cowgirl Santos. I can get behind that." I raise a brow. "You got a hat? Or better yet, a whip?" Her cheeks heat as she throws a water bottle at me, which I catch smoothly.

The band starts its first song, and I stop mid-laugh to look toward the fairgrounds. I know this song. Suddenly, I ache all over. I guess I'm not doing a great poker face, because River reaches out, touches my arm. It's so soft and gentle—*she's* so soft and gentle—that words start tumbling out of my mouth.

"This song . . . Mom used to sing this song when she'd work in the garden. I wish they weren't playing the instrumental version. If I heard the words, I bet I could remember the name of the song," I murmur. Why can't I remember the words? Why is it suddenly so important to remember?

River's fingers tangle anxiously in her lap. "I know the lyrics," she says quietly.

"Yeah?" I whisper, trying to keep the yearning out of my voice. She nods.

I'm glad the sun's set. That the only light is coming from the stars and the moon. The gentle glow of the lights below. I feel exposed enough as it is—this moment feels like a raw nerve for us both. I'm cracking open my chest for her, and I can't decide if letting her in will heal or hurt.

But if I'm being honest with myself, the truth is, my rib cage is her picket fence. She made a home of my heart a long time ago.

The question is: How could *I* ever be a home for her?

Before I can spiral, River takes a deep breath. She closes her eyes, lifts her head. And then she starts to sing.

From the moment the first word leaves her lips, I'm lost. Her voice is stunning. It's strong and sweet and sad. The kind of voice that stops fights, has both sides laying down their weapons, tearful.

As she sings this old song, River is giving me back pieces of myself. Fragments of memories appear in my mind. I remember the rich soil beneath my mother's nails when she was gardening. I remember the smell of sunbeams and sweat when she'd walk into the kitchen to wash her hands, smiling. I remember it all.

Mom once called this the "first cowboy love song," but as River sings it now, I wonder how could Mom have called it a love song? The words are all about *losing* the one you love. They're filled with longing. The song's message is simple: *Please don't go.*

*"For you take with you all of the sunshine,"* River sings, *"that had brightened our pathway a while."*

I stand to look beyond the edge of the cliff, unable to stay seated. *What happens when the pathway turns dark?* I wonder. *Is brief sunshine worth what it feels like when it's gone?* I turn to gaze at River, and I'm grateful her eyes are closed.

*Can I survive you taking all the sunshine, River?* I think. *When you finally know me?*

*Finally leave me?*

River finishes singing, opening her eyes as the last note hangs in the air. Can she see it in my face? How gutted I am by her beauty? How her voice is so perfect, she's broken my heart? How her voice is so perfect that she's mended it once more?

For a few moments, we're silent, the Sonoran desert stretching out around us, the shape of the mountains rising in the distance. In the quiet, the name of the song suddenly comes back to me: "Red River Valley."

They call this part of Arizona the Valley of the Sun. And now River and I have come here together to mourn all the ones who have left us alone in this valley, taking their love and sunshine with them.

*Please don't leave,* my heart pleads as I stare into River's haunted eyes. *I could never let you go now.*

Overcome, I stride up to her and grab her hands.

"Goddamn you, River. That was . . . your voice . . ." I gaze helplessly at the stars reflected back at me. "I never knew I could feel like that."

Her lip trembles, and she presses her forehead to mine.

I feel words heavy on my tongue. Words that are too much. Too soon. They're there, shooting up from my heart. I swallow them back down.

A sharp whistling sound draws our attention. We turn our heads just in time to watch the first firework burst in the sky, the resonant boom dancing in our bones. A cascade of gold sparkles flutters across the night as another whistling sound gives way to a sharp crack and a shower of red sparks.

"They never get old to me," she whispers. "They're breathtaking."

"Yeah," I whisper back, eyes only for her. "They are."

We reach for each other at the same time, ocean waves crashing together. The air smells like gunpowder and smoke, and she grabs my face and kisses me. I'm surprised at how rough it is, how desperate. I lean into it, wrapping my arms around her, kissing her harder, deeper. She tastes like cotton candy and cinnamon. It's intoxicating. I can never get enough.

"I can't believe I get to have you," I murmur against her lips.

She pulls my shirt over my head, and I take off her dress in one smooth motion, until we are nothing but a tangle of kisses, a haphazard wrestle of undress. When she finally touches me, really touches me, my head drops against her neck.

"Wow," she whispers. Her touch is *magic*.

"You have no idea." I groan, sounding agonized.

We tumble to the blanket, and I roll us over so I'm lying on top of her, kissing her until slowly, too slowly, my fingers slip inside her underwear, finding that button of delicious pressure. The air is hot against my bare skin, and I'm half aware that we're outside, that a crowd of thousands is just below, their chatter echoing in the distance. But here, on our perch, it feels like River and I are the only two people in the world, everything narrowing to her lips on mine, my fingers moving against her. She makes tiny, desperate noises as I feel her climbing, making me pretty desperate myself. My kisses get hungrier. Messier. My fingers speed up.

"This feels so, so . . ." River's eyes fall shut as she gets lost in bliss.

"No, River," I plead. My thumb strokes her cheek. "Stay with me. Look at me. Stay with me."

Her eyes flutter open, and she bears down against my fingers as I circle her.

"More," she pants, and I nearly white out. When she arches up, grinding her hip against me, I choke out her name, my forehead falling against hers. Sweat beads my hairline, and I'm panting against her mouth. Her arms are shaking, wrapped around my neck, her fingers playing with the hair at my nape. She rolls her hips against me again.

"Like that?" she breathes.

"Yeah." I kiss her. "God, yeah." I lick my lips. "Let me try something. Tell me if it's too much." And then I slip a finger inside. First one, and then another. "This okay?" I groan, nearly overcome by the feel of her.

She nods, unable to speak, her jaw falling open.

"You feel so good," I rasp. "God, River, I want this, want you, forever."

"You love it," she whispers. "You're obsessed."

My hips jerk at the needy thread of her voice. "Yeah," I pant against her mouth. "Maybe I am."

Her laugh becomes a moan when I speed up the hand working against her, inside her.

"You feel so good, River." And she does. So, so good. *Too* good. "I love this. A little . . . a little too much." I don't even care that I'm losing it.

She reaches up and kisses me.

"I love that you love it," she gasps again, her voice tight.

"You're my perfect girl, River," I say, and my words undo her.

Above us, the sky explodes. I hold her close as she tumbles over the edge, quivering in my arms. I kiss her through it, stunned by the miracle of her. She says my name, over and over, and I never want to forget this moment, the heavens shattering above us, blazing bursts of dazzling sparks in River's eyes, her hand clutching mine, both of us forever changed.

# chapter 23

# river

**Logan**

Look, I'm just saying, something is seriously wrong with you if you think autotuned electro-pop can qualify as one of the greatest songs of all time.

**River**

Says the guy whose favorite instrument is the accordion.

**Logan**

Um, how dare you?

**Logan**

That was supposed to be just between me, you, and Tigery.

**Logan**

But seriously. Folk, jazz, tango, merengue—you need an accordion for all of that. You can't tell me it's not the perfect instrument. Plus, they're magnificent!

**River**

Dude. Are you gonna leave me for an accordion?

**Logan**

Har har. I guess Mom's the one who got me into them. Weird Al was one of her favorites.

**Logan**

We'd listen to his polka medleys on repeat after she got sick. They made her laugh.

Sick? This is the first time he's mentioned anything about how his mom passed. Even with our growing closer these past weeks, I can tell that the subject of his mom is rife with land mines. As much as I'm dying to ask questions, I tell myself that when he's ready, he'll talk to me. So I offer a little truth of my own.

**River**

I get that. Dad loved collecting old records. His favorite band was ABBA. Dragged us to see tribute cover bands whenever they came through town and yell-sang "The Winner Takes It All" louder than anyone else.

**River**

He's the reason I'm a weirdo who loves oldies more than whatever's on the radio. He was also a tough badass though. He'd be horrified if our ABBA dance routine was public knowledge. He'd play it cool whenever I'd play a cover while trying out guitars at the music store.

**Logan**

Tell you what. How about I take you to Guitar Center and you can finally finish my guitar lesson?

**River**

YES.

**Logan**

Perfect. ABBA covers it is for the inaugural weekly Santos-Evans Jam Night.

**River**

YES AH YOU WILL LOVE IT.

**Logan**

I'm gonna save you some dignity and pretend that your phone got stuck on all caps.

**Logan**

But yeah. It'll be cool. Looking forward to it 😊

" 'Yes, Tita Anna, I'm totally enjoying our day out together, I love you so much!' "

Tita Anna's imitation of a falsetto voice pulls me out of my text chain with Logan back to the present, where Tita Anna and I are in her car driving downtown. It's been a long time since I've been able to spend some one-on-one time with her, so when she suggested we go to the bookstore to pick up some travel books on Italy, I leapt at the chance to hang out.

Before I fell down the Logan rabbit hole.

"Aw, thank you, River. I love you too. What a good and kind thing to say." She clicks on the indicator, checking both ways at a four-way stop before turning left.

"Tita, are you okay?"

She presses a hand to her chest with a mock gasp. "Oh my

goodness, *hello*, Your Majesty! How kind of you to take the time to address your silly little peon of a tita." There's no heat to her voice, and she's smiling wryly. Still, I feel kind of bad.

"Sorry." I laugh. "Logan and I were making plans for this Friday after work."

"Ah." She nods. "Mr. Silent but Deadly."

"Tita!" I slap my thighs. "He's too hot to be nicknamed after a fart!"

"That's what I'm talking about! When a boy is so cute, it's trouble. Their hotness distracts you from their tomfoolery. By the time you've figured it out, it's too late! Silent. Deadly." She makes a face. I roll my eyes.

"So helpful," I say.

"I'm serious! Learn from my mistakes, young grasshopper. Don't just go for hotness. Go for the good guy. Especially if he's anything like Animal from the Muppets."

I scrunch my nose. "Excuse me?"

"Um, Animal is the perfect man, River. Or Muppet. Whatever. I mean, he's passionate, he's an artist, what he lacks in vocabulary he makes up for in *emotion*. I could seriously go on."

"Please don't."

She throws her head back and laughs, a lovely, open-throated laugh, and claps my knee. "I'm sorry, I'm sorry, I'll stop." She shakes her head. "I know I'm teasing you, but honestly?" Tita Anna shoots me a quick smile. "Regardless of what's causing it, it's been nice to see you so happy. Been a while. I'd sort of forgotten what Happy River was like." She reaches over the console and takes my hand. "Not that you should feel pressure to stay happy. I just—well, you know what I mean."

"I do." I squeeze her hand back. "Thanks."

She nods. "It just feels like things are finally turning a corner, you know?"

"I do, actually." I smile. Even though there's still so much unresolved in my life, this is the first time in longer than I can remember that I bound out of bed in the morning.

"Let's take the scenic route today," Tita Anna says, faux-casual, turning in to a neighborhood.

"Uh-huh," I say knowingly.

I knew where we were going a little bit back, when she exited the highway. She's turning in to a neighborhood that's in the heart of the Old Historic District. Canyon Crest Village is her favorite neighborhood to build her fantasy life.

We drive slowly past the spacious rows of adorable terra-cotta houses, the yards lush with prickly pear, ocotillo, and desert lavender bushes. Tita Anna and I take in the view of Camelback Mountain. We roll down the windows. Hot air floods in, but so do the scents of desert willow and citrus blossoms.

Tita Anna hits the brakes, bringing the car to a sudden stop.

"Tita!" I say, thrown by the jolt. I follow her longing gaze to a FOR SALE sign in front of one of the cutest houses we've seen yet.

"Oh, wow." Tita Anna sighs.

I blink at the gorgeous front yard, blooming with cacti and wildflowers, the front porch large enough for two swinging benches. Tita Anna adjusts her glasses eagerly, leaning over me to get a closer look at the yard.

"All right," she says fervently. "So, it's Saturday morning, and I've just finished watching the sunrise from my shaded patio out back. Now I'm finishing my cup of coffee on my front porch." Tita Anna points to one of the white porch swings rocking in the breeze. "I'm pondering what I'll get at the morning market in the town square while Tigery naps beside me."

"Hey," I protest. "Tigery's *my* cat."

"This is *my* fantasy, River." Tita Anna sniffs. "Be respectful." She pauses, falling pensive. "You think the backyard's big enough for a dog? Not a big one, just, like, I don't know. A little medium mutt from the shelter named Balut?" Before I can respond, she shrinks back into her seat and squeezes her eyes shut, shaking her head. "Ah, I need to stop. Getting too carried away." She punches the lever into drive, and we continue down the street.

"Tita . . ." I look over my shoulder. "You know, it's not *that* out of the realm of possibility . . ."

"Hush, River. That's enough. It's a fun little thought experiment, but do you know what a pain in the ass owning property is?" Tita Anna scoffs, and it sounds a bit brittle. "Believe me, when your toilet stops working, you'll wish you were still renting."

It's hard not to get caught up in Tita Anna's fantasy. It'd be nice to live somewhere Tigery could live in the lap of luxury. To live in a space that was soul-giving, not soul-sucking. I think of the GoFundMe money, and for the first time I imagine spending it on something that would make Tita Anna happy.

I'm so caught up in the thought of it, I don't notice where Tita Anna's taking us until it's too late.

"Oh," I say as we pass the rosy brick buildings, the quaint little shops. "For some reason I thought we were going to the Barnes & Noble by Fry's."

"I thought about it," Tita Anna says. "But I was kinda in the mood for some eggs Benedict today and thought we could get brunch after we shop. You ever been to Sunny's?"

"Yeah," I say weakly. "I have." The owners used to know me by name.

"You okay, River?" Tita Anna shoots me a worried look. "What's up?"

“Sorry. Mom took me to Sunny’s a lot when I was little.” I gesture to the bookstore whose parking lot we’re pulling into. “And to the Story Haven. Just makes me miss her.” A lot.

And it makes me think of the days when Mom and I would go out and have a home to return to, one where Dad would be quietly writing in his playbook in the kitchen.

“I’m so sorry, Riv. I should have checked.” Tita Anna puts the car in reverse, but I cover her hand on the gearshift.

“No, no—it’s okay. Honestly? I think it’ll be good for me.” I sigh. “I can’t run from these memories my whole life. I have to face them.”

Tita Anna raises her eyebrows as she straightens the car and puts it in park. “All right, little Zen master. You’re a better woman than I am.” She exhales a long breath. “It’s still hard for me to think about Jay.” I reach out and grab her hand again.

“Me too, Tita.”

*Especially when there’s so much I still don’t know.*

A chilly blast of air-conditioning washes over us as soon as we enter the Story Haven. Mom and I loved this place. Not just for the respite from the Arizona summers. The owners had incredible taste. Or at least, Mom always thought so, due to their penchant for anything romance or romance adjacent. I loved the overstuffed couches, the little tea counter in the back, the cozy nooks meant for hours of relaxing and reading.

But right now, as I walk past a table of adorable bookmarks, I’m not really thinking about if I want to order a matcha latte or see if my favorite love seat is available. I’m not even thinking about Italy, or the books I should buy.

Tita Anna’s mention of my father has dangled a little thread of conversation that I’d love to pull loose. Since I visited the safety-deposit box, I’ve tried bringing up the notes a few times, but it’s never felt like a good time for her . . . or for me. And then, well, I got a little distracted by the best kisser on the planet.

But now I'm thinking of a different approach.

Tita Anna's thumbing through *Eat, Pray, Love* when I sidle up to her.

"You know, Tita, I'm pretty sure she's only in Italy for like a third of the book."

"Oh yeah?" She frowns. "I just want to eat pizza so good I date it. Isn't that what she says? 'I'm dating pizza now'?" She reshelves the book with a sigh. "I only ever saw the movie trailer."

I drag my index finger along the crisp, colorful spines. "Tita, I have a question. But it's . . . sort of random," I start.

"Hello?" Tita Anna gestures to herself so vigorously her glasses slip down her nose. "Have you met me?" She plucks a book off the shelf titled *Pecorino Passage: Sampling Italy's Sheep's Milk Cheeses*. "Oh my God, how do you feel about *cheese tourism*?"

"Uh . . ." I squint at her. "Aren't you lactose intolerant?"

"Shh, Italy doesn't know that, nor does the cheese." She shakes her head. "Sorry, Riv. Ask me your question."

"Yeah." *Why is this so hard?* "I guess I just . . . I think I'm ready to hear more stories about my dad."

Tita Anna's face falls slack with surprise. "Oh."

"And, like, I want all of it, you know? The good, the bad, the ugly . . . I just want more of *him*, even if you think it will upset me. There are a lot of things I wished I had asked him while he was still here." I'm not lying. I would claw through a granite door to get any more pieces of my father if I could.

I just also happen to be searching for answers to these strange puzzle pieces clattering in my brain, particularly the strange notes from the safety-deposit box.

Tita Anna smiles softly. Kindly. "Of course, Riv. Yeah. Um, okay, maybe it's easier if you ask me questions? Otherwise, I'm not really sure where to start."

I nod as we stroll through the travel aisle.

"Okay, well . . . I guess, what was it like growing up with him?"

"I wouldn't know." She scrunches her face. "Sorry. Your lola and lolo moved to Phoenix with Jay when he was like two. My nanay had a good nursing job lined up in New Jersey, so that's where *my* parents immigrated." She sighs. "Between money and jobs and *money*, neither of our families could swing a visit. But we made up for lost time eventually. My parents decided to move back home to Bacolod to take care of my lola sa tuhod, years after your lola had moved back to Baguio, and I decided to go to college at Arizona State." She beams. "When I moved to Phoenix, you were four years old. And already a nightmare. But, girl, they loved you."

My chest tightens a little. "So, when I was little . . . he was a good guy."

"Uh, *yeah*." Tita Anna looks askance at me. "I mean, he wasn't *perfect*—no one is. And I wasn't around before he got sober, so I can't speak to those years." She shrugs. "But I was so happy when Jay and I reconnected. We got to bond over being two full-ass Filipinos who couldn't speak Tagalog. People call me a fake Filipino to this day." She sighs. "Look, I'm not just saying this because he's my cousin."

She stops walking and faces me, her serious eyes magnified by her glasses. "I'm not saying it because he's gone either. Your father was . . . an incredible man. I mean, you know all about how dedicated he was to the people he sponsored. How he was a cornerstone in the AA community here. And he was chosen as Coach of the Year *how* many times?" Her voice softens. "But he was like that at home too." She raises an eyebrow at me. "Did your parents ever tell you that you flushed a hundred-dollar bill down the toilet when you were four?"

*"What?"* I choke. "They said it was a twenty-dollar bill!"

"Nah, sister. It was good ole Ben Franklin." Tita Anna makes a toilet flush gesture, mimicking the sound. "I happened to be over for dinner. Your mother went absolutely apeshit. I thought she was gonna try to flush *you* down the toilet. But your dad didn't yell once. He talked to you calmly. Honestly seemed a little amused. Which—I love you so much, but for once I was more on your mom's side, Riv. It was a slow season for your mom's cleaning business."

"Oh God, this makes me want to puke *now*." I wince. All these years later, it's still agony to hear. I cannot imagine how badly my parents needed that money.

"Sorry, I know it's not a nice story. But it also sort of is? You explained to your dad that if 'toilet paper' goes in the toilet, you thought all paper did. As soon as he taught you the difference, it was good. His motto was, 'It's never the four-year-old's fault.' What's done is done. All we can do is learn. That's just how he was." Tita Anna's face falls serious. "I'll admit it. That first year, I thought it might be some do-gooder-nice-guy act or something. But that time I lived with you guys for a little bit while saving up for my own place . . ." She looks at me. "Your dad was the real deal, River."

It should be a relief. It should be heartwarming. But all I feel is the tangled snarl in my chest growing tighter, tangling even worse.

"Tita," I say. "Is there any chance, any chance at *all*, that there was something that you didn't know, that I didn't know?"

"I really don't think so, River." She sighs. "Honestly, if there was someone I'd be worried about, it'd be your m—" Tita Anna stiffens, cutting herself off. She shakes her head. "Eh, sorry, forget I said anything."

"What about my mom, Tita?" I say calmly, even though my heart's picked up speed.

She shakes her head. "Ugh, me and my stupid mouth. Your mom is nice. She's fine—well, her current behavior excluded. Sorry, Jay never liked me talking negatively about her. It just . . . it never sat well with me that a mother would willingly *choose* to abandon her daughter for *months* just to hide from reality on a hike . . ." Tita Anna stops herself. "Far be it from me to judge someone who struggles with mental health. Point is, it wasn't fair to you then, and it sure as hell isn't fair to you now."

I chew my lip, pondering everything Tita Anna's said. I take a deep breath.

"So, my dad. Just an overall amazing guy?"

"Yes, I'm so sorry to report." She nods formally.

I fidget for a moment, then decide to take the plunge.

"Tita. It wasn't just mementos I found at the bank that day."

"What do you mean, River?" she asks.

I show her the photos I took of the notes from the safety-deposit box. I expect her to be as shocked as I felt, but she just presses her lips into a grim line.

"Your dad did his best to shield you from all this garbage. But after your mom went missing, some people thought . . ." Her shoulders sag. "Well, some people thought he was involved."

My heart clenches. "Do you think . . ." I can't even say the words, can't bring myself to voice aloud the worst possible scenario.

Tita Anna shakes her head firmly. "No, absolutely not. It's just an ugly bunch of nothing. Don't let any of those shitty bullies make you think your dad was anything less than a man who loved his daughter and wife more than anyone else on the planet."

"But why would he keep them?" I ask.

Tita Anna shrugs, letting out a sigh. "I'm sure he kept them as evidence in case he needed to tell the police."

When I still don't look convinced, Tita Anna says, "Look, people aren't just one thing or another. But your dad *cared* about doing the right thing. And his actions were always in line with that."

I nod slowly. "So my dad . . ."

". . . was a better man than Animal from the Muppets." Tita Anna squeezes my arms. "Do you have *any* idea how much that pains me to say? *That's* how good your dad was."

I breathe a laugh. "Fine, I get it. Thanks, Tita." She gives me a relieved smile.

"Now. Do you feel better?"

I nod, finding it tentatively true. It'll take me a minute to process, but so far, it all makes sense. I knew that police had questioned Dad, after all. I just hadn't realized that other people thought he could have hurt my mom. And as for the fact that he doesn't exist on the internet before 2002, maybe there's a similarly simple situation. It was different back then, before social media, before any normal person had a strong digital footprint.

But mixed with my relief is a thread of anger—and for the first time in months, it's at my mom.

*Do you know,* I want to ask her, *the mess you left behind? Do you know what your disappearance did to Dad? To me?*

But there's nowhere for my anger to go except into the gaping void of her absence.

*To my baby girl,*

*Whenever I'm out on a hike, I get philosophical. It's part of my process, how I work through my sadness, through the feelings I don't always understand.*

*One thing I've spent a lot of time thinking about is whether people can change. Or if we are fixed in place, as solid and immovable as the red rocks around me.*

*It's a nice story, thinking that people can change. That we can shed the worst parts of ourselves, the worst things we've ever done. I don't know if that's truly possible, though. You can never escape from yourself, no matter where you go.*

*I know that better than anyone.*

*I've spent half my life wondering about your father, whether it ever would have been possible to dig out the roots that made him hurt. That made him want to drown out the pain with his recklessness. But I think who you are is always there, a darkness waiting to strike, no matter how deep you bury it.*

*I feel that darkness in myself, ever present. And if there's one thing that gives me solace, it is the hope that you are truly better off without me—without either of us—passing that darkness onto you.*

*Love,*

*Mom*

# chapter 24
# river

A few days later, Tita Anna wakes me up from an afternoon nap with a loud knock on my door, a packed suitcase behind her, and a guilty expression on her face.

"I'm so sorry. Emergency business trip. Client's freaking out in New York. I have to go spend the week babysitting them."

"The whole week?" I cry, pushing off my covers and throwing my arms around her.

"I promise nothing's gonna happen in seven days, my friend." She grunts when I give her another tight hug.

"Just bring me back something good," I say to hide how clingy I feel.

"I will," she says. "See if Tawny wants to come over later. Have a movie night."

"She has a date with some college boy—or *boys*, potentially," I say with a smirk. The boat ride went so well that Tawny can't decide which boy she likes. She's going on dates with both this week. "But I'll be fine."

Tita Anna laughs, then gives me another quick hug before she heads out the door.

As soon as I lock the front door behind Tita, the empty house feels cavernous and cold. I sit on the couch, scrolling miserably through my phone. Even though I didn't respond to his last message, Noah texted me again today, about an hour ago.

**Noah**

You working today? I was craving waffles sans awkward dad this time.

Why can't he take a hint? *I* certainly did seven months ago. With help from Tawny, admittedly, who screened all my incoming and outgoing calls and texts for weeks.

I ignore the text and scroll to who I'm looking for.

**River**

Tita Anna had an emergency business trip. Now I'm weirdly sad and lonely and hungry.

**Logan**

I'd come pick you up, but I'm too busy making you a surprise homemade meal.

God, it's intoxicating, the hit of euphoria I get reading that text.

**Logan**

Welp. Surprise! Get dressed. I'm sending a fancy uber to come get you

Who ever thought the too-hot-for-Disney prince of Gertie's would be sending *me* a chariot?

I THANK THE Uber driver as I climb out of the black BMW in front of Logan's apartment. I adjust the hem of my simple black dress. I've left my hair wavy and loose. I can't stop smiling. It's not often I feel lucky or like a "normal" teenage girl.

Tonight, I feel like both.

I knock on Logan's door, wondering if he's closer to Tita Anna or my father when it comes to culinary skills.

"Good timing," Logan says when he opens the door. "I'm still cooking, but . . ."

He stops short as he takes me in, doing a hot sweep over my body.

"Jesus." He grabs my waist and pulls me against him, kissing me deep and hard. "Forget dinner. Can I have you instead?"

*"Ha."* I'm too breathy to pull off sarcasm. "I was promised a gourmet dinner, sir."

"'Sir,' huh? I could get used to that." He clears his throat. "I'm cooking . . . I've got . . ." He gives his head a shake. "Ugh, how do you expect me to get anything done with you looking like that?" For once, I'm the one smirking as he rushes back to the kitchen.

I slip off my flats and set down my bag and purse, sniffing the air. "It smells . . ."

"Fantastic?" Logan says into a steaming pot on the stove. "Mouthwatering?"

Burnt. It smells burnt, actually. He and Tita Anna could make a comedy cooking show.

*"Interesting,"* I say. Logan's head pops up from inspecting bubbling pots, and he puts a hand on his chest.

"Ouch. So lemme get this straight. I send you a car, cook you a gourmet dinner. And you have the audacity to come here looking like *that*"—he waves in my direction—"and criticize my cooking. Brutal *and* gorgeous."

I roll my eyes. "What are you making, Drama King?"

He shrugs, and I swear I see his sculpted cheek flush.

"Ah. It's *supposed* to be chicken adobo. Watched this YouTube video like a million times today. Looked like the easiest Filipino dish to make. I just . . . maybe I got the wrong rice . . . ?"

*Oh my God.* My insides completely melt.

Logan's forehead is beaded with sweat, his thick hair tousled, like he's been running his hands through it over and over. I'm not used to seeing him look so . . . flustered.

I nearly say them right then. The forbidden words. The ones I shouldn't be thinking or saying but ones I'm *definitely* feeling, nearly all the time. Especially right now as he dashes around the kitchen, desperately trying to cook me chicken adobo.

The unflappable Logan Evans completely flapped.

I think I wouldn't feel these feelings any less if he'd perfectly prepared an entire kamayan feast, spread artfully on a table of glossy banana leaves.

Give me Logan Evans burning rice on the stove any day.

I lean in the kitchen archway. "Can I help?"

"Absolutely not." Logan leads me back to the couch. "*I'm* treating *you*. So relax. Put up your feet. Try not to look so hot." He swoops in for a kiss and pulls back, looking pained. "Okay, I know that's impossible, but try. You're distracting me." It never stops lighting me up, the idea that he might want me the way I want him.

Fifteen minutes later, when he hands me the plate of rice and chicken and settles on the couch beside me, I have to bite the inside of my cheek hard to keep from smiling. It's such a beautiful disaster.

I take a spoon and experimentally thwack it against the pile of rice. When it makes a clicking sound, like I'm tapping a shell, I have to disguise my laugh as a cough.

"Oh God. Just give it to me straight, Doc," Logan says.

"I just need water. Stop fretting!" I grab my glass from the coffee table and sip it. Logan's trying to play it cool, but I can feel how earnest he is, in his stiff posture, in the way he's scanning me for any reaction, as I scoop up some rice and chicken and pop it in my mouth.

Logan looks so, so hopeful as I crunch a meal that is supposed to be quite soft. I swallow, feeling the scratch all the way down, and nod.

"Delicious," I say. His eyebrows lift.

"Yeah?" Logan takes a bite. His face shutters as he slowly chews. After he swallows, he turns thoughtfully to me. "Huh. I guess you *do* like me. Like *actually* like me."

"What? Why?" I don't know why I'm defensive.

He leans in. "Because this is not fit for human consumption." Logan kisses me sweetly. "In the future, don't be afraid to hurt my feelings. I'm a big boy. And this big boy is ordering us Tony's."

AFTER WE'VE HAD our fill of gooey slices of cheese pizza, we're snuggled against each other on the couch.

"What do you wanna watch first?" I ask, stretching. When Logan doesn't answer me, I sit up. His right knee is bouncing, and his hands are tapping an anxious rhythm on his thighs. "You good, Logan?"

"I do—I mean, I am. Totally." He wipes a hand across his jaw. "I . . . I've got something for you, actually. Let me just . . . you know what? I'm gonna go ahead and . . ."

I laugh as he leaps to his feet and dashes to the other room.

"All right, close your eyes," he calls.

"This isn't a prank, is it?" I say warily.

"Yeah, it's a huge prank, how'd you know? Was it all the cameramen?" I can hear the mocking in his voice. "Can you just—"

"Fine." I laugh, slipping my eyes shut.

I give a tiny gasp when, a few seconds later, something large and wooden settles in my lap.

"Give me your hands, gorgeous," Logan murmurs, and I shiver at the low rumble of his voice. He takes my hands and places them against what feels like metal strings.

"What is . . . ?" My eyes pop open—and immediately fill with tears.

I'm holding a gorgeous acoustic Gibson guitar. I'm stunned into silence as tears run down my cheeks. Logan glances restlessly between my hands and my face. He's pressing a fist against his tight mouth.

"Hey, totally fine if you don't like it. I got a receipt; you can exchange it for whatever you want." He doesn't seem to know what to do with his hands. "I talked to the lady at the store for like an hour. She said this was the best one. I don't know, was she full of shit? I don't think she was. But was she?"

I still can't find my voice. And if I open my mouth now, I'm definitely going to say it.

There's no way I will be able to not tell Logan Evans that I'm madly, desperately in love with him.

"Hey, look." He squats in front of me. The blue of Logan's eyes makes me think of watching clouds in a meadow, his face like skydiving without a parachute.

How is he terrified when it's me who's falling?

"You don't have to sing, River. Okay? That's not what this is." Logan tilts his head at me, dark hair brushing his brows. "Honestly, you don't have to sing ever again if that's really what you want. I just didn't want you not having a guitar to be the reason why."

I look down at the gleaming wood. I've never seen such a beautiful sight.

Well, except for the one in front of me.

"Logan," I whisper, "it's too much. I can't accept this."

A guitar like this costs thousands of dollars. I can't even imagine how many shifts at the diner it'd take to cover it.

"I know it isn't brand-new, but it's in good condition. She gave me a *really* good deal." Logan flashes me a cocky smirk. "I'll have you know, Santos, that most people find me irresistibly charming."

I laugh, dizzy with the effort of holding back my confession.

"No accounting for taste," I huff. My voice falls serious. "Logan . . . I—"

*"River."* He rises up, presses his forehead against mine. "It's the best money I've ever spent. If it were ten million dollars, I'd say the same thing." He pulls back to look at me. "Well, actually, first, I'd say, 'What the hell, was this Jimi Hendrix's guitar or something?' " He softens. "Then I'd spend all that money and consider it a bargain to see that beautiful smile of yours." Logan takes my hands and gently lays them across the strings. "Just try it. See if you like it."

When I press against the strings, warmth floods my fingers. I strum a chord. It sounds so sweet, feels so good, I strum another. I close my eyes again. It feels a little like coming home.

When I open them, Logan's on his knees before me, his face half bliss, half nerves.

"Well?" He's breathless.

I set the guitar gently aside.

"That bad, huh? Well, I can tell you, from where I'm kneeling it sounded good. Real good—"

But before he can finish, I press a kiss to his lips. "It's perfect," I whisper against his mouth. "*You're* perfect, Logan."

He pulls me tight against him. I can feel his relief in the way he kisses me, slow and syrupy. "I'm glad you like it."

Like it? I *love* it. It feels like he's accepting me for who I am. Bridging that gap between who I once was and who I am now. A Gibson guitar, Old River's favorite possession. But he gives it to me with no expectation for me to use it or sing.

He just gave it to me because he knew it had once brought me joy. It makes me feel hope. Like maybe it can bring me joy again someday.

"I have . . . something else for you. Just a little thing, don't look so excited." Logan laughs, reaching back to grab a small brown package on the floor. I rip it open.

It's a purple notebook, with typeset letters on the cover that read RIVER'S GREATEST HITS. I blink down at it as he explains.

"You said your old songbook got lost in the fire. I can't replace that one, but I thought . . . *maybe*"—he taps a finger on the spine—"maybe it'll feel good to have one in the closet. You know? Just . . . in case."

My throat closes up. I look at Logan, search his gaze.

"Why, Logan?" I whisper, shaking my head. "Why're you being so good to me?"

Logan growls a sound of disbelief.

"*Why*, River?" He inches even closer to me. "You really don't know?"

I can barely breathe. "Please tell me."

His gaze is fierce and hot. "Maybe it's because you're one of the bravest people I've ever met? Or maybe because it breaks my heart to see you cry. That day in the walk-in"—he shakes his head—"I had to grab an orange to keep from grabbing you. It's been torture for way too long, pretending I don't care about you, River, and now it's felt like breathing again. All I want to do is practice cooking chicken adobo every day until I get it right, just to see two seconds of your smile." He cups my cheeks and kisses me hard. "Get the picture, River?"

Before I can utter any words, Logan's on me, kissing me everywhere—my lips, my neck, my chin, my jaw—and pleasure has taken over my body. The notebook falls from my lap as he stands us up and walks us to his bedroom. The only light is the moon peeking through his blinds. He pulls back, just a little. He smiles softly against my lips and says:

"What I'm trying to say, River, is that I love you. I love you a frustrating, lifesaving, life-ruining amount."

I gasp as my heart splits open. Re-forms. Squeezes so hard it makes a new shape.

*"Logan."* The single word manages to be both an answer and a plea. My body is overwhelmed with need. I grab his shirt and pull us onto the bed, his body above mine. I take his hand and slide it under my dress, bringing his fingers to the cotton edge of my panties.

"Please," I breathe, wanting his touch everywhere.

"Yeah?" he whispers as he reverently studies my face.

"Yeah," I say, pulling at the hem of his shirt. His pupil-blown eyes get hungrier.

"I love you like this," he says roughly. "Like you need me as much as I need you."

"More," I say as Logan rips off his shirt and works on his belt. His gaze never leaves mine.

He's only wearing boxers now, and the muscled expanse of his body nearly undoes me. All that sculpted skin. I'm shocked by my urge to run my tongue over all of it. To feel our bare skin pressed together.

My hands go to the bottom of my dress. I start to pull it off when Logan grabs my wrist.

"Wait. I want to." His breaths grow uneven as we scoot higher on the bed and he straddles me, his fingers setting my thighs on fire as he drags them up my body, taking my dress with them.

"I love your knees," he says, cataloging everything he reveals. "I love your hips. *Mm.* And, of course, I love these." I sit up to find Logan smirking as he hovers over my pink panties.

My entire body floods with heat. Especially my face. I cover my face. "I didn't wear my . . . I didn't think . . ." I'm too embarrassed to finish. There is nothing sexy about this underwear.

"Hey." Logan pulls my arm down, lacing our fingers together. "I love these cute, smiling sushi. In fact . . ." He presses a light kiss against the bare skin above the pink cotton trim. I stop breathing, trying not to faint from anticipation. "Yeah. Sushi's my new favorite food." Another kiss. "Pink's my new favorite color." Another kiss.

I feel the wild urge to beg him to kiss me lower.

Logan continues his upward path, baring my belly button and ribs, dragging his lips across my torso, sending static crackles across my skin and growing the hot pulse between my legs.

Logan groans when he unveils my bra. "Okay, blue is tied with pink now. *God*, I can't believe . . ." With a low, rough sound, he presses his mouth against the soft swell above the light blue bra cup, dragging his lips down the dip to kiss the valley in the center.

It feels so good. But it's driving me crazy. The things his mouth is doing, his body above mine, close but not pressing, the hungry sounds he's making, the needy wrench of his beautiful face. It's like the first song at a music festival: It jolts your body, wakes it up, makes you want to move.

But it just makes you want more.

"Trying—" Logan pants against the front clasp of my bra. "I'm trying to take my time. Stay calm and savor. But, *my God*, River." He turns his head, presses a kiss against me, and his tongue darts beneath the cup of my bra. With a moan, I throw my arms around his neck, dig my nails into his back. I arch against his mouth. I wrap a leg around him, pulling his hip flush with mine.

"Oh, Jesus," Logan grunts. In one movement he licks a path to my neck and sucks hard. He rolls against me, and I can feel exactly how *not calm* he is. It's so delicious, I need more.

All of him.

Now.

"Logan." I cup his face with both hands. Lock our eyes. I wonder if I look as lost as he does? He's panting hard now. "Please. I want you. Need you."

Logan's eyes flutter shut. "You're killing me, River."

Seriously? He's killing *me*. I can *feel* him. There's just a couple scraps of cloth between us. My body's never felt like this. This need is nearly despairing. Bordering on panic.

"You're not understanding, then." I raise my hips, and he groans, meeting my friction.

"Logan," I say again. "Do you have a condom?"

That gets his attention.

"Really?" Logan sits up, and so do I.

His eyes flick between both of mine, and now he's starting to shake too.

"Yeah, River?" He swallows. "You're sure? Are you absolutely sure about this?"

*Is he joking?* I've never been more sure. But is he? It never occurred to me that he might not . . .

"Do you not . . ." I lick my lips. "Is it too soon? Do you not want—"

"*God*, I cannot describe how much I want you." He takes a deep breath. Brings our faces close. "But, River. I need to know. Have you done this before?"

"No," I whisper. "But I want to. With you, Logan. Only you."

Logan's eyes go inexplicably darker. Hotter. Hungrier. But there's something else there too. Something intense. Like the earth's molten core beneath a volcano.

"Shit, River," he says in a broken voice. "You don't . . ." He kisses me slow and deep. "I don't deserve you. But I'll spend my life trying. We'll go slow. I'll make sure you . . . We'll go slow."

Logan gets out of bed, rifling through a bedside drawer, pulling out a small, square foil package. When he turns around, facing me, he pauses.

"What?" I murmur.

Logan shakes his head. "Just—I want it to be good," he says urgently against me, stealing my breath. "I want to make it so good you never want anyone else." He gently tugs off my panties. I lie back and lift my hips to help him pull them free and toss them to the side.

When he pulls his boxers off to put on the condom, and I see him, all of him, I make a desperate noise.

"What?" His voice is soft as he joins me on the bed. When he presses the entirety of his hot, hard body against mine, I swear.

"Don't let it go to your head," I say against his lips, "but you are stupidly gorgeous."

"God, I love you." He sighs a laugh. *"Shit."*

He stops talking. Because this time, when I arch my hips, rolling a delicious friction against him, there is nothing between us.

And now he can feel exactly how *not calm* I am.

"I can't wait anymore, Logan. Please? I'm *ready*."

"Yeah," Logan rasps. "If we need to take a break, tell me." He strokes my cheek. His face blazes with love. And need. So much need. Like he's barely holding back.

"I will," I whisper, wrapping my arms around his neck and bringing his mouth to mine.

At first we just kiss, slow and deep. Finally, Logan moves his fingers, dragging them down my thighs, tracing circles on my skin as he works his way to the apex of my thighs, moving his thumb to that spot that has my toes curling already.

When I'm pulling desperately at his hair, whimpering and moving, he shifts. Logan holds himself above me, cupping my cheek as he kisses me.

"Okay?" he asks softly. I can feel him shake.

"Okay," I plead.

And then I feel him between my legs. He presses deliciously against me. And then, gently, slowly, he rocks his hips forward, just the slightest bit.

I suck in breath at the tight, shallow pressure between my legs: It disappears as soon as I feel it.

*"River,"* Logan groans. "So perfect. You feel so—" He breaks off on another groan as he rocks his hips forward once more. I feel that slight pressure again. I wrap a leg around him, pulling, needing more.

In fact, I need all of him. I raise my hips an inch, then bear down against him, pressing him in just a little farther this time. The pain is exquisite, sharp and lemon bright. But Logan moaning above me, his handsome face a portrait of ecstasy, knowing that this is something we are doing together, has me panting and shaking and aching, still, for more.

"You—you okay, River?" he gasps.

I bite my lip and nod, unable to speak from how much I love it. I press harder against him, and Logan chokes out my name, then fills me entirely. "Yeah." I nod, breathing hard. "Going slow is working."

Logan kisses me. "Good. Holy shit . . ." He moves a hand down between my legs and he starts circling his fingers against me, finding that delicious spot. "Feel good?" Logan asks, his gaze darting between my eyes.

For a second, I can't do anything but moan.

Logan breathes a laugh. "That sounds like a yes, but I want to hear you say it."

"Feels good," I manage.

The next time he pulls back and rocks his hips forward, the pleasure helps the pain.

We move like this, slow and incremental and perfect, for I don't know how long. But we finally reach a point where he can move steadily, fully, wholly.

When Logan's above me, pressing against me, I finally find my voice.

"Logan," I say hoarsely. "Logan, I love you too."

His face melts into heartbreaking relief. Into a happiness so acute, it looks painful. With a groan, he pushes into me, and I cry out from the unbelievable pleasure of being physically closer to the one I love than I've ever been to another human being.

"Say it again," he whispers against my neck as he moves, slow and deep. "Say it again, River."

"I love you," I whimper as he tangles his fingers in my hair.

"Again," he chokes out, the liquid snap of his hips picking up.

"I love you, Logan." I nearly sob from the relief it is to say it. "I love you. God, I love you."

Logan makes a strangled, desperate sound every time I tell him I love him. He's moving faster, kissing me everywhere. He grabs my hand, tangles our fingers together, squeezing. Logan's carrying us both up the mountain now. Higher and higher—we're chasing stars. And I'm right there with him. Ready to free-fall as we cling to each other.

"River," he puffs, and he sounds utterly ruined. "You have no idea how long I've—I've loved you." And with those words, I tumble over the edge, dragging him with me.

Logan groans and pulls me close, our arms wrapped tight around each other, gasping in pleasure, before he collapses to my side, our bodies still intertwined.

"River," he croaks. "I think you killed me."

"Too bad," I say. "I was really looking forward to more home-cooked meals."

For an answer, he nips at my shoulder, making me shriek and giggle.

We lie there, limbs tangled, kissing, caressing, pressing as much of our bare skin as possible together. He plays with my hair as we stare into each other's eyes, whispering smiles into each other, as we catch our breath.

"Take a shower with me," he says.

"Next time," I whisper, cupping his face. "I don't think I can move." Logan gives me a quick kiss on my forehead and heads to the bathroom. As soon as I hear the water running, I become aware of my intense thirst.

I wrap a sheet around me and walk, jelly-legged, to the kitchen to fill a glass of water. As I turn to head back to the bedroom, water in hand, I catch sight of the notebook on the ground. I pick it up, setting down the glass so I can run my fingers over the cover and flip it open.

To my delight, Logan's written an inscription on the inside of the cover.

*To River, the girl of my dreams.*

*I was wrapped around your little finger a long time ago. Even without your songs. This notebook is for any new ones you write. Just for when you're ready to have the entire world wrapped around your little finger too.*

*—L*

I press the notebook to my chest and pull it back to read the inscription again.

And again.

And once more.

Because every time I reread it, something's happening in the back of my mind. A little shadow that's growing and growing. A slow realization that's got ice sliding down my spine. My heart starts to slam.

I run my fingers over Logan's handwriting, tracing the shape of his block letter *I*. My eyes snag on the crooked slant of the line of his *L*.

My hand starts to shake. With mounting dread, I pick up my phone from the coffee table, open my photos app. I scroll to the picture I'm looking for and hold it side by side with Logan's inscription.

The handwriting from the notes in my dad's safety-deposit box is a perfect match for the handwriting in the inscription.

*"Please, no, please."*

But no amount of begging will change the truth.

Logan wrote those notes to my dad.

# chapter 25
# river

The world is spinning. I can't breathe. My lungs are shrinking, withering into nothing. I'm afraid I'm going to be sick. The notebook slips from my fingers, and I stagger to the ground, shaking.

What does this even mean? Why would Logan have written those notes to my dad?

*I know what you did.*

*You can't hide.*

*Killer.*

I squeeze my eyes shut, try to get a handle on my breathing. This isn't about some stupid football thing. No way. So what does Logan even think my dad did? Is it what Tita Anna said? Does he think he hurt my mom?

How long ago did he write those notes?

Only one thing is clear: Logan has been lying to me. Over and over and *over*.

I hear the shower stop, and that's when I realize my state of undress. Whatever conversation Logan and I are about to have, I'm not doing it wrapped in nothing but a sheet from his bed.

I scramble around the room and manage to get my underwear and dress back on by the time Logan exits the bathroom, towel wrapped around his waist.

Logan smiles at me, but it falters when he notices the way I'm fully dressed, standing stiffly in the corner of his room, eyeing him warily. He looks around to see if there's something he's missing. "You okay, River?"

I swallow hard and shake my head. Concern floods Logan's face.

"All right," he says gently. "What happened, River?"

I pull my phone out of my pocket and bring up the photos of the notes.

"Did you write these?" I say in a halting voice.

*Please say no. Please, Logan. Please.*

When I turn my phone around, his face bleaches a sickly white. Horror floods his face.

"I can explain," he manages hoarsely.

"Oh *God*," I gasp, clutching my stomach. "You did. You *did*. You wrote them. What the *fuck*, Logan?"

Logan stumbles into a pair of shorts, shaking his head vigorously. "Look, it's not—it's not what it—"

"It's not what it looks like? Really? *Really?* That's what you're going to say to me right now?" I say shrilly.

I had hoped I was wrong. I'm no handwriting expert. But he just admitted it.

"How long ago did you write those notes? *Why* did you write those notes? You lied to me. You lied *again* and *again*, Logan."

I rush out of the room, scooping up my purse, battling a rising wave of nausea.

Logan follows me, his arms out in a pleading gesture.

"River, you need to give me a chance, you need to trust me—" he rasps.

"*Trust* you?" I snarl, whirling on him. "Seriously?"

Logan recoils, looking devastated. Which is rich.

But I'm terrible at compartmentalization. I'm having an excruciating time reconciling that the Logan standing before me, the Logan who was clutching me close, moving above me just minutes ago, is the same Logan who was sending my dad threatening notes.

I can't believe what he's done. What I've done.

With him.

Was he lying about everything?

I bury my face in my hands and sob.

"I don't know who you are." I weep. "I shared everything with you, and I don't even know who you are."

"Please don't cry," Logan begs, his voice close.

My eyes snap up to find him reaching for me.

"Don't *touch me*," I hiss.

"Fuck." Logan clutches his stomach, looking sick. "It's me, River." He takes a step back, gives me space. "It's always been me."

"Is Logan even your real name?"

He pinches the bridge of his nose. "Of course it is."

"Were you blackmailing my dad?"

Logan drops his hand from his face, fear flooding his features. My heart clenches, and a horrible thought occurs to me.

"Logan," I croak. "Did you start working at the diner . . . to get close to me?"

Stumbling, he goes to sit down hard on the couch.

"It sounds so bad when you say it like that," he says.

I start to hyperventilate.

"Oh my God, you actually did," I say tremulously. "This whole time you were—and I just played into it—"

"That's not true, River," Logan says in a heartbroken whisper. "Breathe, or you're going to faint."

"No, you don't get to—to tell me to do *anything*." I point a shaking finger in his direction. His face spasms in agony, and I feel a terrifying urge to make it better.

This is such a mindfuck.

"I'm leaving," I say as I grab my flats by the door. "Don't follow me."

Logan stands abruptly, brows furrowing. "It's late, River. I'll drive you home, okay? It's not safe."

"Leave me alone," I sob. "Don't fucking come near me."

There can't be anything left in my chest. The place where my heart used to sit is now just a charred structure of what was once a home. A pile of twisted rebar and ash.

Logan rounds the coffee table slowly, hands raised.

"You're not thinking straight, Riv," he says. "I can get you an Uber."

"I can get my own Uber," I snap.

I struggle to scroll through my phone, my hands shaking. My stomach plummets. The closest Uber is fifteen minutes away. I can't be in the same room as Logan for another minute, much less fifteen.

I frantically open my text messages. The first name is Tawny, but she's on a date downtown, over half an hour away. I scroll down and jab my thumb on the next name—Noah. Even though I ignored him, I know he won't ignore me if I need him. And I do need him—*now*.

I tap *Share Location* and fire off a text.

**River**

PLEASE COME GET ME

I put my hand on the front door handle.

"Wait. Please? Let me explain," Logan pleads.

I look at him over my shoulder.

"River," he begs, "River, I love you. Okay? That's not a lie. I *love* you."

I lean my head against the door.

"If you think this is love," I say, "then you don't know the meaning of the word." I throw open the door and run outside.

The night is dry. The oven-hot air burns my lungs, like I'm breathing ozone instead of oxygen as my foot catches on a bit of uneven sidewalk. I crash into the ground, skidding across the concrete, my right knee taking the full brunt of the fall. Pain radiates through me, so stunning I don't have it in me to get up and keep running.

Logan rushes to my side, his apartment door slamming behind him. His eyes fall to my knee. He shakes his head. "Shit, are you okay?"

"Leave me *alone*!" I crawl backward away from him.

"River, for God's sake, it's *me*." His face contorts like I've just run him through with a dull blade.

The roar of an engine is overtaken by the screeching of tires as a black Tesla halts right in front of Logan's building. A figure dashes around the front of the car.

"River!" Noah appears above me, and I could cry, I'm so relieved to see him.

As soon as Logan sees that it's Noah, his face curdles with hate. His pale chest shines like a beacon in the night as he stands up. It occurs to me that I don't truly know what Logan might be fully capable of.

Noah crouches to a squat beside me, his hands hovering, as if unsure how to help. "River, oh my God, are you okay? What happened? Jesus, you're bleeding."

Noah sweeps a calculating look over Logan, taking in the state of his undress, then turns to me and clocks my tearstained face. He quickly shifts his body slightly to put himself between me and Logan.

Logan grips his hands in his hair. "River, please. Just let me—"

"River," Noah says, "do you need me to call the cops?"

Logan pales, his face falling slack as he meets my eyes. He's looking at me like I'm pressing the muzzle of a gun to his head. The longer I stare silently at him, the more he looks like he'd rather I just pull the trigger.

"No," I decide. "Just get me out of here. Please."

Logan's shoulders slump. He hangs his head, looking completely broken.

Noah purses his lips, like he'd love nothing more than to sic the cops onto Logan, but he nods.

Logan steps forward one last time. "Please, River. I love you. Please believe me—please talk to me."

A sickening crack splits the air as Noah's fist connects solidly with Logan's face. I scream, my hand flying to my mouth, as Logan staggers to his hands and knees on the sidewalk, blood spurting from his nose. When Logan stands up, Noah lunges at him once more with a roar, taking another swing. Logan ducks it easily this time, countering with his own blow that hits Noah in the jaw.

"Logan!" I sob. "Logan, please don't. *Please!*"

As soon as his name passes my lips, Logan freezes, his arm suspended in midair. His eyes fly to mine, and I gasp at the desperation and pleading I see there.

"Stay away from her," Noah growls, glaring at Logan before scooping his arms beneath me, bringing me easily to my feet. He helps me limp to the passenger side of his car before sliding into the driver's seat.

"You need help buckling?" Noah asks gently.

"No," I whisper. "Just drive."

Logan doesn't move a muscle as Noah puts the car in reverse. As we drive away, I can't stop myself from twisting around to watch Logan's still form shrink in the distance.

Even after everything, it's painful to look away from him.

When we turn a corner and Logan disappears for good, I collapse against the window and begin to sob.

## chapter 26

# river

I tuck my knees under my chin, curling tight against the passenger window, watching the stoplights change in the distance. My tears smear against the glass when Noah breaks the silence.

"Did he hurt you, Riv?" he asks quietly.

"Not in the way you think," I say. "He lied to me."

I can tell Noah wants to ask more. But he bites his lips, keeps silent. After a moment, he swears.

"River, I shouldn't have hit him. I should have just gotten us out of there. I tried not to. But the things he said. You on the ground, crying and bleeding. I just . . ." Noah's fingers spasm on the steering wheel, his face flashing with possessive anger, swiftly replaced with shame. "I'm so sorry."

"Good," I say into my knee. "You should be. The both of you." I turn my cheek to stare out the window. "You were both idiots. What did any of that accomplish? In fact, when has violence *ever* helped more than hurt?"

"I don't know," Noah mutters. "Never, probably."

We fall into a silence, tears still sliding down my cheeks. Tonight should have been special. All I'd wanted was to share my first time with someone I loved, but especially, trusted. I had been so sure that was Logan. How had I gotten it so wrong?

I shiver, picturing his first day at the diner, how infuriatingly attractive he'd been, how withholding. I'd marked him as dangerous, told Tawny I wanted nothing to do with him. If only I had listened to my gut. But I also remember other things:

Logan tucking bluebells into my hand for Dad's grave.

Logan whispering, *I love you*, moving above me, inside me, surrounding me.

Logan admitting his betrayal.

Logan's face, agonized and already bruising.

How are they all the same Logan? Even with the obliterated cavern in my chest, how will I ever make enough space to hold all of these Logans at the same time?

Why do I keep picking boys who break my heart?

I turn and look at Noah's profile. The smile he gives me is so familiar, I could cry.

His car is a time capsule. It smells the same. That woodsy, tanned-hide smell layered with Noah's cologne: a musky lavender-and-vetiver scent. It used to remind me of a fancy barbershop: luxurious shaving cream, the scrape of a straight razor against a CEO's neck.

My heart lurches when I touch the sticky note beside the touch screen, where he's handwritten, "Call Grandma this Sunday."

I started that trend, writing love notes and silly doodles on yellow Post-it notes, pressing them against the brushed aluminum trim of the console. He complained that they'd leave a residue.

I want to ask why he's still doing it, even so many months after we broke up.

Instead, I ask, "How's Grandma Soph?"

"Good. She's good." Noah makes a face. "Still on my case."

"Let me guess. 'When are you getting married?' "

"Well, as impatient as she is, even she knows that's not a one-man job." Noah clears his throat, his voice falling serious as he eyes my bloody knee. "Do you have first-aid stuff at your place?"

"Don't take me back to the apartment." I take a breath. "Sorry, Tita Anna's out of town. The idea of being alone in that place right now is . . ." I shiver.

"Of course," he says slowly. "I can take you back to my house, if that's okay?"

"What about your dad?" I whisper. "I don't really feel like answering a bunch of parent questions right now."

"Dad's in Seattle. Some big surgeons' conference." Noah's mouth twists. "Gone a lot these days, actually. If there's a medical conference, he's there. Started right around when . . ." He cuts himself off, adjusts something on the touch screen. "Well, about seven months ago. Give or take."

We're both quiet for a few seconds. I hear the unspoken thing. That it started after my dad died.

"Well, then," I say, "your house it is."

I'M SITTING ON the kitchen counter as Noah gathers first-aid supplies upstairs. It's a challenge not letting nostalgia twist my muddled thoughts. But it's difficult, returning to a place where you were once given a kind of ownership. Especially when everything in this mansion is the same: the couches, the wallpaper, the magnets on the fridge.

But I'm not the same. And I'm no longer allowed to flop onto that overstuffed love seat in Noah's living room. I can't go to his linen closet and help myself to a spare blanket if I'm cold. It's that strange, cruel loss that's singular to breakups. *We once promised each other forever, but now I need to ask permission to use your bathroom.*

I'd thought I'd gotten past that pain. But here, in Noah's kitchen, where he first said *I love you*, it's harder to brush aside.

A lot's happened since that first *I love you.*

Like another boy telling me those same words. A boy I shared everything with, who gave me nothing but lies in return.

It's easier to fight off these thoughts when Noah gets back, pulling a chair in front of my wounded knee.

"I need to clean it," he says apologetically. "It might hurt."

*Try me,* I want to say. *It'll be nothing compared to what I've felt tonight.*

Noah's hands are gentle and expert as he works on cleaning and bandaging.

"You'll probably bruise a little," he says. "But it shouldn't be serious." Noah's face is inches from my bare thigh. I swing my legs on nervous instinct, and he brings up a hand to steady my good knee.

"Fidgety as ever," he murmurs. He raises a brow. "I'm almost done."

I speak quickly to drown out the awkward, uncomfortable feelings that fill my chest.

"What about you? You okay after taking that hit?"

Noah's mouth tightens. "I'm fine. Nothing bruised but my pride." He sucks his teeth. "Who knew your boyfriend could pack such a punch?"

"Not my boyfriend." The words are out of my mouth before I've decided to say them.

Noah sits back, giving me a long look.

"River," he begins. "You can tell me anything. Even if—even if it's about—"

"I don't want to talk about him. Okay?"

Noah nods and squeezes my calf. "Well," he says, "I think you'll live. You're all done."

An excited bark and the click of nails scampering across the hardwood has me lighting up inside. A beautiful black-and-white border collie rounds the large marble counter and gallops at me.

"Pepper!" I gasp, kneeling on my good leg to wrap my arms around her. I press my face into her coat—just as soft as I remember. Pepper's tongue lolls happily as I scratch under her chin.

"I missed you so much, sweet girl." More than her little doggy mind could comprehend.

Noah watches me. "She missed you too," he says softly. "She missed the *hell* out of you."

I swallow hard, looking away.

"You know what else I've really missed?" I stand up slowly, brushing fur from my shirt.

Noah smiles. "The firepit?"

"Got it in one." I smile back at him.

It's not the firepit itself that I miss, but what we used to carefully hide beneath the largest boulder in the wall that rings the sitting area. Using both of our phones' flashlights, we comb every nook and cranny under the boulder before Noah reaches down and pulls out the bag.

"No way." I laugh when he pulls out a sealed bottle of vodka.

"See if it's still good," he says, offering it to me.

Noah is always careful not to keep alcohol in the house out of respect for his dad, who's been sober almost as long as my dad has. But outside the house is a different story, especially since Noah is the only one who actually uses the firepit.

After opening it, I take a swig. My face pinches.

"Not good?" Noah winces.

"It's just *hot*." I shake my head in disgust. "But it'll still do the trick." I have no designs to get drunk, but I need something to soften the corners of this awful night.

We settle into two Adirondack chairs around the firepit, and I look out at Noah's backyard, what I can see of it in the moonlight. Their property stretches out to meet a beautiful section of the Sonoran Preserve. We used to occasionally ride horses on a trail that leads up a gentle-sloped ridge to where a huge, flat boulder sits, overlooking a valley of saguaro. It was one of Noah's and my favorite places to find alone time. The last time we had sat out here was after a trail ride we'd taken with Tawny—and not long before we'd broken up.

"Do you remember," I say, already feeling warm from the vodka, "that one time Tawny went riding with us?"

Noah laughs. "Tawny," he says, taking the offered bottle from my hands, "is *not* a cowgirl, is she?"

"Nope. Not even a little." I tap my knees. "I thought she'd never talk to me again! You have no idea how hard I worked to convince her to go on one. How was I supposed to know she hated the desert?" I take the bottle back from Noah.

"Or horses." Noah nods.

"God, I shouldn't have made her go." I take a long, burning swig. "I don't think we made it ten minutes before she lost it. But it's not forcing Tawny to go out that I regret the most."

"No?" Noah's watching me, listening in that careful way of his.

"No," I say softly. "I regret that I rushed that trail ride to get her back here faster." I tilt my head back and count stars until the burning in my eyes stops. "I wouldn't have rushed if I'd realized that would be my last one."

There are a few seconds of silence. Noah nudges me with his toe.

"It doesn't need to be the last one," he says simply. "We can go again, anytime."

I lift my head. "You know what I mean, Noah."

"Yeah," he sighs. "Yeah, I do."

I lean back, scanning the night sky, looking for a pattern in the chaotic smattering of stars. "Is it better or worse," I say, "knowing your last time is going to be your last time?"

"Endings are hard no matter what," he says. "Seeing a train coming a mile away doesn't make it hurt any less when it runs you over."

A slightly bitter laugh bursts out of me, and I realize that despite my intentions, I'm a little drunk.

"So, it was hard for even you, then? Our ending?"

Noah blinks, caught off guard, as I thrust the bottle back into his hand. He furrows his brow and stares at it before setting it on the ground next to us.

"Of course it was hard for me, River," he finally says. He says it so quietly, I can barely hear him over the croon of the crickets.

I press the heels of my palms to my brow. I count to three. Ten. But it doesn't help. Rationally, I know that tonight, it's not Noah I'm upset with, that it's not our relationship that needs resolving. But with the two of us sitting out here, alone, under the stars, I need to ask the question.

"Why?" I say. "Can you finally tell me why? Why you broke up with me?"

I half expect him to stonewall me again, or at the very least change the topic. But Noah faces me, his green eyes flickering with something that sort of looks like courage. He squares his shoulders. He opens his mouth. Closes it. Opens it.

Nothing comes out besides a long whoosh of air.

"Because I was dumb, River," Noah says. "Really, really dumb."

I regard him for a long moment, wondering if this is truly all the explanation I'll ever get. It's a cop-out, but I'm too exhausted to force the point, so all I say is "I think you need at least one more *really*. Maybe two."

Noah huffs a sad laugh. "Totally true. Okay, so I was really-to-infinity dumb."

It's vindicating to hear him say that. But to what end? What does satisfaction that he regrets his decision get me now? It's too late. Noah broke up with me, and then my world burned to the ground. There's no coming back from that. And it doesn't change the fact that the Noah I had known and loved for years was not someone I could ever imagine breaking up with me without explanation or warning.

"Why is no one ever who they say they are?" I ask quietly. My eyelids are starting to feel heavy. I curl up in my chair, folding my legs underneath me.

"River . . ." Noah lifts a hand, like he wants to comfort me, but thinks better of it, dropping his arm. "You talking about me? Or . . ." His mouth twists. "Or that guy . . . Logan?"

"All of you. Him. You. My dad."

"Your dad?" Noah breathes.

I shake my head, the world swimming around me. "I used to think—no, I used to *know* that my dad was the most trustworthy person on the planet." I wipe my nose, shaking my head. "I was a daddy's girl. He knew the name of my third-period teacher. He never forgot to sign permission slips. No matter how small the performance, he *never* missed it. There were no secrets between us."

Noah studies my face, his index finger tapping rapidly against the armrest. I'm suddenly overcome by the day and the drink. I close my eyes, exhausted.

"But he never told me about the notes. Or the assholes. Or the racist cops. I was wrong, Noah." I sigh. "Dad hid stuff from me after all. I thought I could trust him, but . . . I was wrong."

I'm on the verge of falling asleep, already brushing the edges of a dream.

I can't tell if I imagine it: Noah's voice, soft and sad, as he says a single word.

"Same."

## chapter 27
# logan

She's gone. She found out and now she's gone.

It's 110 degrees in the Arizona dark, and I can't stop shivering. I count the red droplets as they slide from my nose to the pavement. Blood drop number five splashes on a cigarette butt.

Blood drop number ten has me falling to my knees.

*"Fuck."* Nothing can keep the bullet train of regret and self-loathing from smashing me open.

I press my fists into my eyes, even the bruised one, maybe *especially* the bruised one. I'm glad it hurts, because all I can see right now is River looking at me like I'm a monster, and *I am*, and now she *knows I am, she knows my secret, and now—*

A door slams a few units down. Last thing I need is some random neighbor clocking me, asking questions. I scramble to my feet, skulk back into my apartment, make my way to the bathroom.

Bracing my arms at the sink, I watch the blood drip into the basin, slower now, crimson petals splintering the teeth-white ceramic.

I don't look in the mirror.

*I'm so fucked,* I think, wrenching the hot water on. When steam fogs the glass, I soak the hand towel until it's scalding and shove it against my split lip, my nose, the swelling of my left eye.

I catch my face in the mirror.

The black-purple bruise. The viscera pink of my lip cracked open. The shiny blue of my swollen nose. I look like an oil spill. Not the fucking rainbow bullshit kind. I'm talking the greasy, ocean-ending kind. I'm a disaster that kills innocent, beautiful things.

It feels like breathing in broken glass when I think of River at this second, so I think of *him*.

And as much as I hate him, as much as fury fills me at just the thought of his name, Noah didn't ruin anything. I did.

All at once, I'm flooded with the image of River on the ground, looking up at me like I might—like she genuinely thought I could hurt *her*.

My stomach lurches. I get the toilet seat up in time, retch into the toilet. I realize as I flush, I've never hated anyone more than I hate myself in this moment.

That's saying something.

I stagger out of the bathroom, fall to the bed. And what a fucking mistake *that* is, because of course it still smells like her. I don't deserve to picture it, but I can't help it. River's body, writhing and perfect beneath me. The taste of her *I love you*s on my tongue, over and over. Sharing, with her, a pleasure so good it was *frightening*. That word that rang like a bell to the rhythm of our hips: *Forever, forever, I need this—you—forever, River.*

The best night of my life has become the worst.

And I only have myself to blame.

# chapter 28
# river

Someone is gently brushing my cheek.

"River," says a voice, low and warm. It's a delicious sound. One I find myself chasing, even as I want to sink back into the tar pit of drunken slumber.

"Logan," I whisper.

The touch at my cheek disappears, and I open my eyes. Noah is crouching next to my chair, tapping his fingers against his boot. The moon is low, like she's thinking hard about turning in.

I groan as I sit up, pressing fingers to my temple.

"It'll be dawn soon." Noah straightens, looking everywhere but at me. "We should go inside before the sun comes up."

"Sorry. Passed out." My head and stomach throb like they're radioactive. But nothing feels as bad as the twist in my chest.

"Don't be." He tilts his head back, smiling ruefully at the stars. "A lot happened last night. Makes sense that your brain's a little scrambled." Noah hands me a glass of water. "Drink."

The water is mercifully cold, and after a few gulps, I have the strength to lift myself out of the chair. Noah offers a hand, promising me Advil once we're inside. My stomach roils, but it's not the vodka that's got me queasy. It's the promise of daylight, that harsh light that will make it impossible to ignore everything that's happened with Logan. The step I took with him. That my first time was with someone who has lied to me for months.

Back in the house, I kneel to give the dog a fierce hug, tugging at her soft fur. "I'll miss you, Pepper."

The corners of Noah's mouth curve down. "River," he says, "you're not getting your last rites. Visit anytime."

Pepper licks my cheek. "That would be . . . complicated."

Noah shoves his hands in his pockets. "Doesn't have to be. You miss her? Come see her." He shrugs. "No strings."

It's a quiet ride back to Tita Anna's and my apartment.

"This is where you've been staying since . . . ?" Noah peers out the window at the bleak gray of the peeling paint. The clinical font on all the signs in the complex.

"Well, all the ones with horse stables were taken," I say, though I don't know why I'm defensive. I've always hated it here too.

"That's not what I'm saying." Noah winces. I pause, my hand on the door handle, waiting. But he never clarifies what he *is* saying. Why would he start now?

I step out of the car, adjusting my purse to buy time. There's no way I can find the words for all the things twisting my gut, so I go with the truth.

"I'm grateful you were there last night. You were an idiot. But a helpful idiot." Noah wipes his jaw. I can see the corners of the small, ashamed smile he's trying to hide. I pat the roof of his car. "Thanks for the ride. And for fixing me up. Just . . . for all of it."

I'm halfway to the door when I hear a car door slam and fast footsteps.

"River, wait."

The look on Noah's face as he makes his way toward me on the cracked sidewalk is a familiar one. It's the look he'd get when he was trying to find a new way to call me beautiful.

*I can't use the same words used for anyone else, River,* he once said. *You aren't like anyone else. Ever.*

That was another life, though. Another Noah. Another River. I don't even know who that girl is anymore. So what is he thinking, looking at me like that? And how unfair is it that even without sleep and a shower, Noah still looks as handsome as he does?

Noah fiddles nervously with his collar. "Remember prom?"

"Hollywood theme. You rented a limo with a hot tub. Tawny got in with her gown on."

"No." He shakes his head. "I mean after. When I was driving you home. The sun was coming up. Do you remember what you said to me?"

*Yes.*

"No." I shift on my feet.

"You said, 'What if we keep driving? What if we just hop on the ten, drive until we reach the ocean? Watch the sun set over the Pacific?' " Noah's eyes look very far away. "I think about that a lot, actually."

I pull at some dead skin around my thumbnail, too rough, drawing blood. "There a point to this?"

Noah watches a mourning dove peck at a patch of brown grass a few feet away. Finding nothing, it flies off with a sad, musical sough.

"No," he sighs. "There's not." He stuffs his hands in his pockets, keys jingling. "River, if there's anything you need. Or want. Especially if you need help with . . ." His jaw sets. "With Logan."

"Oh, *sure*. I'll ask for your help if I want to start my own fight club."

He winces. "I'm just trying to say I want you to be okay. I worry if you're not. And no matter what, if you need me?" Noah tilts his head. "I'm there. Believe me."

To my mortification, my eyes start to burn. Haven't I cried enough? But his words hurt, and not in a good way.

"The problem with believing you, Noah," I whisper, "is that I've done it before. And look where that got me."

Noah's face spasms painfully and he nods. "You've got no reason to believe me. But whether you do or not, I'm there for you." He hesitates, like he knows he shouldn't, but reaches for my cheek anyway, brushing away a tear with his thumb.

I quickly take a step back.

He takes a step back too. "I'll check in later. Go get some sleep."

As he heads back to his car, I let myself into the apartment and go straight to the shower. It's a relief to watch the dusty water swirl down the drain. It's a bigger relief to slip into clean pajamas and burrow beneath my cold, clean comforter. I plan on sleeping for at least ten hours straight. Maybe longer. Maybe I'll never get out of bed.

Suddenly, I understand my mom. Like, *really* understand. I can't imagine feeling like this all the time.

I don't even have it in me to text Tawny. I have no energy to relive last night or to talk her down from avenging my honor. I can't think about Noah. And Logan? I *really* can't bear to think about him.

Because when I do, his beautiful face swims into view. And then so does the rest of it: the Gibson guitar, the *I love you . . . you got that, right?*, the dome of rice, hard as plastic, the notebook, his handwriting, *his handwriting*.

It'd be simpler if I hated him. If I never wanted to see him again. As it is, I check my text messages and ache when I see he hasn't texted.

I send Tawny a text instead.

**River**

Did you have fun with College Boy(s)?

The reply comes instantly.

**Tawny**

Meh. Turns out college guys are just as boring as high school ones. Uneventful night.

**River**

I wish I could say the same.

**Tawny**

Oh no, babe. Are you okay? Wanna talk?

**River**

Later. So tired.

I silence my phone and turn the AC down as low as it will go until finally, finally, I sink into sleep.

Two hours later, my phone rings. It's an unknown number. I can't fathom sitting up, much less talking on the phone. But ever since my mom left, I make it a point to answer any call—just in case.

I groan and sit up, reaching blindly for my phone. "Hello?"

"Hello . . . is this River Santos?"

The voice is feminine, but not familiar. I force away a pang and rub my face. "Yup."

"Hi, Ms. Santos, this is Kerry with the Arizona Department of

Health Services. Your legal guardian has been calling us quite often to follow up on our search."

*Oh.* I clear my throat. "Did you guys finally find my birth certificate?"

"We did, actually." I hear typing in the background. "It looks like we mistook some information during the preliminary search. We had your dad down as 'Jay,' not 'Jacob.' "

She says this like I should be laughing. Like, *Oh, you silly billy, of course you got it wrong.*

"But that *is* my dad's name. Jay." There's a long pause on the other line.

"Your full name is River Rose Santos, correct?"

"Yeah." I'm fully awake now.

"You were born on September 18, 2006?"

"Uh-huh . . ."

"Well, according to the only birth certificate we found for a River Rose Santos born on September 18, 2006, her parents are Jennifer and Jacob Santos."

"But my dad's name . . ." I shake my head. "Look, there's not a chance this is a typo on the birth certificate?"

"Unlikely," Kerry says. "Not uncommon for people to go by nicknames, though. Anyway, what address would you like the certificate sent to?"

I tell her the address of the apartment, massaging my forehead. Jay wasn't my dad's nickname. It was his *name.* Mom called him "jaybird" when she was feeling happy. Every formal document I'd ever glimpsed had *Jay* on it. Every single red-stamped late bill.

I'd never heard anyone refer to him as "Jacob" in the entirety of my eighteen years.

*Jacob Santos.*

*Who the hell is Jacob Santos? More importantly . . . is Jay Santos not the same person as my dad?*

When I hang up the phone, I grab my laptop and huddle on my bed. Last time I searched *Jay Santos*. This time, I type in *Jacob Santos*, my fingers leaving sweat on the enter key.

The first thing I feel is incredible relief. Because there, at the top of the page, is a picture of my dad. *My* dad. His soft brown eyes. The mole on his left cheek. It's a picture from when he was younger. Much younger. Like, almost my age young. But he looks sad. Grim.

When I click on the picture for more details, I stop breathing.

Because it's not a picture.

It's a *mug shot*.

My vision blurs as all the words of the headline hit me simultaneously. *Local Man Arrested for Vehicular Manslaughter.*

I stop breathing. I can't stop staring at two words, burnt into my brain forever.

*Vehicular Manslaughter.*

Jacob Santos. My dad.

*I know what you did.*

*You can't hide.*

*Killer.*

This can't be real. I can't feel my face or fingers as I click on it, needing to know everything, but this website is just a collection of headlines from defunct newspapers—no article to be found.

I follow a link to an entry on the Library of Congress website database listing the *Canyon Rock City Times*, published from 1983 to 2002. I click on the *Libraries That Have It* tab to read that the Canyon Rock City Library carries the only copies.

I'm not even thinking as I send the picture of the mug shot to my mom and type:

**River**

What else haven't you told me?

*To my baby girl,*

*I cannot sleep, I cannot sleep, I cannot sleep.*

*Because I'm about to do something terrifying.*

*Something I've waited too long to do.*

*I'm going to tell you the truth about your father.*

*And I'm so sorry, my love.*

*It is a very, very ugly truth.*

*Love,*
*Mom*

## chapter 29

# river

I don't text Tawny again before I show up at her door, banging on the scuffed paint. The door opens a crack, and when she sees it's me, she opens it all the way.

"I love a surprise visit," she says, "but showing up and knocking like a SWAT team after dark—"

Tawny grunts as I dive into her arms, already crying. She smells like bacon grease and sweat. She must have just gotten off from the day shift.

"Oh, Rivvy," she says softly, wrapping her arms around me. "What happened? Your text had me worried all day."

"Sorry," I say into her shoulder. "I wasn't ready to talk about it."

"It's okay, hon. Is this about Logan? He looked awful at work. He didn't say one word. Gertie had to send him home." She pulls back. "That fat lip wasn't you, was it?"

I choke on a miserable, hiccuppy laugh and shake my head.

"People always make tea in movies when someone's upset," Tawny says, leading me in. "Come on. I'll make you tea and bake you something, and you can tell me all about it."

I tell Tawny everything. *Everything.* Her face is grave as she moves mechanically around the little kitchen while I spill my guts. A few times she stiffens, blinking hard, and I clutch the hot mug of chamomile in my hands, ready for her to tell me I'm delusional or stupid. But she just goes back to sifting flour and flattening cold butter with a fork, and I keep spewing my secrets.

I tell her about the notes in Dad's safety-deposit box.

Logan's handwriting.

Noah.

Jay Santos versus Jacob Santos. The mug shot. I tell her about the texts I sent Mom.

I even tell her the one thing I haven't told anyone about the night of the fire.

"I swear I saw her, Tawn," I rasp. "My mom was there. I think she pulled me out, saved me."

Tawny pauses scooping the cookie dough, her eyes locking on mine. "Holy shit. Did you tell the police?"

"No," I say, uncertain. "Should—should I have? I was worried that they'd dismiss it, tell me I'd been hallucinating from the smoke." I start pulling the paper of the tea bag apart. "They weren't very nice to Dad when she first took off."

Tawny nods wordlessly, her frown deepening, the way it does when she's trying to calculate the results of an online quiz in her head. Except this is way harder to figure out than *What do your favorite Taylor Swift lyrics say about your future husband?*

I stay quiet, let her think it all out, stirring my now-cold tea.

Tawny's face doesn't change as she takes scoops of cookie dough and rolls them around in cinnamon, pressing them down on the greased cookie sheet into neat little rows. When the oven door slams shut, she fixes me with a grim stare.

"What do *you* think all this means, River? About your mom? Your dad?"

I groan. "That's why I'm here, Tawn. I don't know. I don't *fucking* know. My dad was the best guy I knew. He was patient, compassionate, and—"

"Technically . . . a murderer?" Her arms are crossed as she leans back against the stove.

"Tawny!" It would have been worse if there had been some disgust in her tone. Vitriol. But no, she says it calmly, quietly, matter-of-factly. Because it's a fact. One, apparently, I still have not accepted. "It was . . ." I lick my lips. "He was . . ."

"We need to start accepting reality here, River. You have such a black-and-white view of your parents, but the truth is, they were hiding things from you. From us." Tawny brushes flour off her sleeve. "We don't know what else they could be hiding. I'd say let's call your mom, but she doesn't care enough to even—"

"Stop! *I know.*" I slam my hands on the counter, upending my cup of chamomile. "Sorry," I whisper, reaching for paper towels.

"River." Tawny plucks the soaked paper towels from my hands, takes over cleaning the spilled tea. "I'm not trying to be cruel. I'm trying to help you understand. And I'm not equating our pain here—in any way—but it's not easy for me either, you know. I cared about your dad too." Her voice breaks, and her face crumples. Tawny throws the soiled paper towels away, and when she faces me, her face is impassive once more. "But the fact of the matter is, he hid things from you. Big things. His name. His record." I flinch at the word.

If Tawny loved me less, her look would be pitying. But as it is, she just looks heartbroken. "Oh, River."

I walk over to the couch and sit down hard, my arms circled protectively around my stomach. "Maybe I should go to the police," I croak. "Tell them I saw my mom. That way they can kick-start the investigation again. Maybe—maybe she'll come back if it's more official, you know?"

Tawny crosses the room and joins me on the couch, taking my hands into hers. She hesitates, running a gentle finger across my knuckles, back and forth.

"River," she says slowly. "Did you ever consider . . . that your mom *doesn't* want to be found? Especially by the law?"

*Don't say it. I can't think that.*

Stubbornly, I raise my chin. "What do you mean?" Tawny winces, but I don't care. I won't be the one to say it.

"River. With all that your dad kept from you . . . well, maybe there's more you didn't know." Her lips are trembling.

"And?"

"*And*, what if his good-guy-Jay thing was an act? What if your mom left . . . to escape *him*?"

My eyes spill over as I glare at Tawny. *"And?"*

"Christ, you're gonna make me say it?" Tawny runs her hands through her hair and clutches the back of her neck. "What if she set that fire to finish him off, once and for all?"

The silence drops between us, violent as an anvil crashing through the ceiling, splintering the floor at our feet.

"No," I say simply. "The fire was an electrical malfunction." I shake my head violently. "Look, I was there that night. She wouldn't have set the house on fire on purpose if she knew I was there."

"River," Tawny says in an agonized voice. "You probably don't remember this, but you weren't even supposed to be there. You were *supposed* to be spending the night with Noah."

"How would she have known?" I throw my hands up. "She wouldn't have. She didn't talk to me *or* my dad."

Tawny raises a brow at me. "Do you know that for a fact?"

When my face crumples, Tawny looks stricken. "Shit, Riv." She throws her arms around my neck. "I'm honestly not trying to pull your nails off with pliers here. God, I'm so sorry. I'm trying to help, if you can believe it." She pulls back and presses her forehead to mine. "Your mom would never have burned the house if she knew you were in it."

Tawny wraps her arms around me as I cry.

But then I remember another fact that has me pulling back with a gasp.

"Canyon Rock City, Tawny. The city from the article. That's my mom's hometown, Tawn."

She doesn't say anything. She just looks at me with a wary sadness.

"Come with me tomorrow. It's only, like, a two-hour drive away. It's where he was arrested. It's where she grew up. All my answers are there."

Tawny sighs, brushing hair from my face. "I work tomorrow, River," she says.

"Well, then maybe the next—"

"And even if I didn't," Tawny says, enunciating her words carefully, "I would still say no. Because I don't think you should go."

"Why not?" I shrink back.

Tawny takes my hands into hers again, staring hard at our fingers. "River, I think you need to think this through. I think . . . I think you might need to let this be."

"Why would I ever—"

"Because if you *don't*"—Tawny's head lifts, and there's a steel to her eyes—"if what you think happened actually happened, you could lose her too. You could be sending your mom to jail. For your father's murder."

# chapter 30
# river

"So, what is it you're looking for in Canyon Rock City?" Noah asks me the next day, his focus on the dusty road stretching to the horizon.

I've considered Tawny's advice. I appreciate where she was coming from. I do. But this isn't really a choice for me—I have to know more. I have to go to Canyon Rock City to look for anything I can find. I just couldn't go alone. Tawny wouldn't go and Tita Anna was still out of town, so my options were limited.

*Logan,* my traitorous brain had whispered.

But in the end, it was Noah who I'd asked and Noah who had said yes.

"I'm looking for *anything*," I answer. "Any microscopic detail that might prove that my dad didn't kill someone and my mom didn't kill my dad." I watch the desert fly by, craggy hills of cacti and boulder. "Proof that my entire life isn't a lie."

"You know," Noah says quietly, "I knew your parents too. Your life isn't a lie."

Those are nice words. Nice, empty words.

"That's sweet, Noah. But call me when you find out your parents might be part-time murderers. In the meantime, pardon me if I have to reconsider the past eighteen years."

Something flickers over Noah's face.

"Fine," he concedes. "I get it. It's complicated. And I . . . well, I can't imagine how awful this whole thing has been for you." He pats my hand, the way I imagine a grandmother might, if I'd ever met either of mine. "Maybe just some music for a little while, hmm?" Noah switches on the radio, and I find myself stiffening against the soft leather seat, the song familiar in the worst way.

There was a time when I sang this song at the Prickly Pear every weekend, and for one second, whether I like it or not, it all comes flooding back—my parents' faces in the crowd, the same thing I've been dreaming of since my first open mic: my name on the sign outside the bar. HEADLINING TONIGHT: RIVER SANTOS.

I turn down the radio, but it doesn't help.

The ghost of my memories is hard to flee and even harder to kill.

My phone buzzes. I know who it is even without looking. Logan. After not texting me for twenty-four hours, he's been blowing up my phone this morning. This is his fourth missive.

**Logan**

Please. Just hear me out.

I can't deal with him right now. Like, at all. So I block him. I'll unblock him when I'm ready to talk. Whenever the hell that may be.

For a while, Noah and I drive in wordless peace, songs I don't recognize filling the silence, the beauty of the Sonoran spread around us.

Canyon Rock City is over an hour north of Phoenix, longer now with the roadwork on I-17. Mom never spoke about it. She's not a dweller in general, and she always brushed off questions about her childhood. I knew her parents died when she was young, but when I'd ask what the house she grew up in looked like, she'd shrug. "Nothing worth remembering, honestly." Or else she'd answer my questions with a proverb. "Honey, I'm an arrow, not a boomerang. I'm only ever looking and moving forward." Or her favorite: "I've already been through yesterday, and once was enough, thank you very much."

Her thoughts, instead, were always focused on the future. A lot of her sentences started with *one day*. "One day, I'm going to learn how to play violin." "One day, we'll go to New York and see every play on Broadway." "One day, River, we'll be rich, and all our problems will be over."

Well, now I have money, and my problems are far from over. With each mile, we're driving farther and farther into the desert and away from civilization, where the saguaros far outnumber any humans. I've never seen such towering cacti, their arms thrown to the sky, some bowing, some bending, all magnificent. The unfurling tapestry of the Sonoran is gorgeous, and I don't understand why Mom never wanted to linger here, how she didn't ache from the beauty of it.

We finally reach Canyon Rock City, and it is the smallest town I've ever seen. Narrow roads wind around cacti-riddled hills, dotted with houses of every variety. Trailers, charming ranches with picket fences, quaint adobe cottages. There are more yellow signs warning of cow crossings than stop signs in this place. Cattle guards bisect the small, single-lane road that cuts through the town.

As if on cue, Noah stops the car suddenly to allow a bull, cow, and two calves to lope across the road.

"That's four cows and zero people so far in Canyon Rock City," Noah says in wonder.

The town center consists of a few restaurants, a Family Dollar, a laundromat, a nail salon, and a food bank. It's hard to picture my mom here, at any age, and finally, I'm starting to understand why she didn't want to look back. She loved the hustle and bustle of Scottsdale, a city girl through and through. No place this small could ever contain her.

"Where to?" Noah says, scanning the vacant parking lot of the local grocery, an ATV rumbling past.

"The library. When I searched, that's where the copies of the *Canyon Rock City Times* are archived. Also, I'd like to figure out if anyone here remembers Mom."

"One parent mystery at a time," Noah says lightly, plugging the library address into his phone.

Unsurprisingly, the Canyon Rock City Public Library is small, but according to the flyers on the bulletin board, it's clearly the hub for social and cultural happenings in the area. The librarian, a middle-aged woman with a pleasant face, takes her glasses off when we inquire about digital archives.

"You're looking for what, exactly, honey?" She polishes the lenses with her shirt. There's a name tag on her cardigan: DEIRDRE MONTGOMERY.

"Old newspapers," I say. "From the early 2000s to start?"

Deirdre rounds the desk, crooking a finger for us to follow. "Either of you kids know how to use microfilm and microfiche?"

"Micro . . . fish?" I ask sheepishly.

She sighs. "Come on, I'll teach you to use the machine."

The archive room is dimly lit, smelling like pots of ink and preservative chemicals, filing cabinets filled with slender reels of microfilms. The microfilm reader itself looks like a large, boxy-monitored computer attached to a microscope. It doesn't take long to learn how to use it, and we spend an uneventful hour flickering forward through headlines like *Volunteers Needed for Annual Cleanup of Agua Fria River* or *Health Fair Offers Free Screenings to Residents.*

I'm about to lose hope when a familiar face catches my attention.

"Stop, go back!" I lean forward, my face inches from the screen.

Noah goes back a few articles, pausing when I breathe, "There."

Below the words *Local County Fair Draws Crowds* is a picture of my mother as a teenager, her arm wrapped around a teenage boy as they stand in front of a bustling fairground.

The same picture clipped from a newspaper inside my dad's safety-deposit box.

But this one has a caption below it that reads, *Jennifer Cole (17) pictured here with her high school sweetheart and fiancé Daniel King (19) about to enjoy the annual cattle show.*

"Did you know your mom was engaged to someone else before your dad?" Noah asks.

"No," I whisper, a knot forming in my stomach. Whatever I was looking for, it wasn't this.

My mom's hair is long and straight, and they've photographed her mid-laugh. The guy she's with is tall, skinny, and good-looking. He wears a rakish smile with deep dimples. The photo is in black and white, but even so, I can tell his eyes are light and bright, his hair a dirty blond, peeking out from under a cowboy hat garishly adorned with the stars and stripes of the American flag.

My mother looks beautiful. She always does. But there's something less burdened about her in this picture that I never saw in real life. As captivating as my mother is, it's the boy that I can't stop staring at.

Her *fiancé*.

He looks familiar somehow, though I'm sure I've never seen him in real life.

"You okay?" Noah asks. "We can take a break if you need to."

"I'm good," I insist, even though my entire body feels cold, a sense of unreality forming with each new secret I uncover.

I snap a picture with my phone before we continue forward through 2001, forcing myself to keep looking for the article I came for. Except for a robbery here, a car accident there, the headlines morph into story after story about the War on Terror once we reach September. I'm turning, turning, my eyes nearly glazing, when suddenly my father's mug shot slides into focus. *Local Man Arrested for Vehicular Manslaughter.*

Noah leans respectfully aside so I can read the disappointingly short paragraph.

*A twenty-two-year-old man was arrested following a fatal crash, Rock City Sheriff's Department reported. The crash happened at about two thirty a.m. Thursday near the intersection of Rock Road and Park Street and resulted in one fatality and one injury. Jacob Santos admitted to having fallen asleep at the wheel while under the influence. Officer Forrest Garrett responded to the scene, with assistance from EMS personnel. Santos was charged with a first offense OWI and vehicular manslaughter.*

"Wait, that's it? Keep going; there's gotta be a follow-up," I demand. "Does it say who died?"

Noah keeps scrolling, but my heart drops when we suddenly reach a December 2001 headline announcing that after nearly two decades, the paper was regretfully going out of print.

Yet another dead end.

Noah sits back in his chair. For a moment, we just stare at each other.

"This can't be it. I can't leave here without finding out who he killed."

"It's a small town," Noah says. "An accident like this is the kind of thing people remember. Maybe the librarian knows what happened?"

I nod, and we speed walk back to Deirdre to tell her what we found.

The librarian looks at us, unsure. "I only moved here about five years ago, but my neighbor Lucy Erikson has lived here her whole life, and her husband was a cop. She's in her eighties now but sharp as a tack. She might know something."

"Great, can we talk to her?" I ask.

Deirdre shrugs. "Swing by her house on Brook Street. Second one on the left. She loves having company."

I head back to the archive room to snap some pictures of the articles on my phone while Noah brings the car around. Then we're off to find Mrs. Erikson.

"Of course I remember that accident," Mrs. Erikson says. We're sitting on her front porch. After we knocked on her door and introduced ourselves, she insisted on bringing out a jug of homemade lemonade and a sleeve of gingersnaps, but I'm too amped up to eat or drink anything.

Her modest home sits on a winding, unpaved street. Away from the endless asphalt and concrete of Phoenix, the temperatures here feel bearable. Noah seemed embarrassed at how fast I'd rushed through introductions, but I *need* to know the truth, and Mrs. Erikson has answers.

"The whole town probably remembers. It was the night of Larry's and my thirtieth wedding anniversary. He was still on the force then, you see. Larry was good police, always put the job first—and he was close with Forrest, the officer who responded to the scene. We heard all about it the next day. The man who died had gone through a guardrail trying to avoid the drunk driver."

"Mrs. Erikson," I say, "do you remember the name of the person who died?"

"The boy driving? He was always stirring up trouble. Still a shame what happened." She hesitates, and I hold my breath as I wait for her answer. "His name was Danny King."

The name drops like an anvil on my chest. *Danny* . . . as in Daniel. With shaking fingers, I pull up the picture of the article I took on my phone and zoom in on my mom and Daniel.

"Ah. Yes, that's him," Mrs. Erikson murmurs, "and there's that poor girl. Yes, I remember her too."

"What do you mean, 'poor girl'?" I say, my heart thundering in my chest. Noah must sense my anxiety spike because he reaches out and puts a hand on my knee. "What happened to her?"

"You know her?" She squints at me.

"That's my mom."

"Oh!" Mrs. Erikson's eyes grow wide and she smiles. "Oh, that's just lovely. You're a daughter of Canyon Rock City. What was your name again . . ."

"River," I say.

"River," she echoes, studying my face. "It is wonderful to meet you."

"Ma'am," I ask, twisting the hem of my shirt, "can you please tell me about her? Even if it's difficult to hear, I'd like to know."

Mrs. Erikson takes her glasses off and rubs the bridge of her nose. "Oh, honey, this was a long time ago. And truth be told, I'm not sure I'm the one who should be telling you this. Haven't you anyone in your family, or relatives you can ask?"

"My father's dead," I say quietly. "My mother is . . . on an extended trip. I can't reach her. And everyone else is gone." I shift forward in my seat, a silent plea. "Anything would be helpful."

Mrs. Erikson gives a sad, contemplative hum as she tucks her glasses back on her nose.

"I'm sorry to hear all that," she says softly. She takes a deep breath and fixes me with a steely sort of melancholy. "Your mother was in the passenger seat of that car."

I feel sick. Impossible and horrible puzzle pieces are slipping into place.

"It was so awful," she whispers. "They were so young, whole lives ahead of 'em. Danny was a fool, in trouble as often as not."

I'm still trying to process all of this when Mrs. Erikson continues, almost musing to herself.

"Everyone in the community was sad about Danny, of course," she says. "And it was so heartbreaking what happened to your mom after . . ." She cuts herself off abruptly, her eyes frightened and owlish behind her glasses.

"What?" I ask.

"It really shouldn't be me that tells you all this—" she begins.

"If you don't, then no one will." My chest feels tight, and I have to swallow before speaking. "Please."

She sighs. "Your mother and Danny were planning on getting married. In fact, they'd already gotten a head start on making a family." Mrs. Erikson takes an infuriating pause. I cringe, hoping I'm wrong about what's coming.

"Your mother was pregnant."

"What . . ." I stop breathing. A feverish wave of nausea rolls through me. "What happened to—to the pregnancy?"

Mrs. Erikson looks out onto the quiet street. "Well, she was pregnant when they took her into the ICU, and then when we saw her around town after that, there was no baby." She looks genuinely sad. "There's only one conclusion any of us *could* come to."

My head is spinning, and I feel like I might pass out. Dad killed my mom's fiancé. He killed her baby. And he almost killed her.

And then, for some reason I can't even begin to imagine, only five years later, she married him and had me.

# chapter 31
# river

I'm in a daze throughout the rest of our visit and while climbing back in the passenger seat of Noah's car.

"You okay?" Noah asks.

I turn my head slowly and stare at him.

"Right. No, of course you're not." Noah winces. He gnaws on his lip. "I'm so sorry, River. I can't imagine how you must be feeling."

"Did she know?" I whisper. "Did Dad tell her who he was? Or, like, this whole time, was Mom just as much in the dark as me? Does she know now, or is she still in the dark? Or did she . . ." I can't finish my thought out loud.

*Or did my mom find out my dad's role in the worst night of her life and take matters into her own hands?*

"She had to have known, River," Noah says gently. "His name and picture were right there in the paper."

But if she knew, how could she forgive him for what he'd done? Who would marry the person who destroyed their life? What am I missing here? I desperately want to text Mom about this. But I'm terrified now to put anything more in writing, just in case.

"I just don't understand. Why wouldn't they tell me any of this?"

He peers at me and grips the wheel tighter. "River. No one wants to admit the worst things they've ever done."

We ride the rest of the way without talking. Noah keeps glancing over at me, his handsome face twisted with worry. He keeps opening his mouth and snapping it shut. I don't fault him for not knowing what to say.

I don't either.

When we pull into my apartment, we sit in silence for a moment.

"I hate this," Noah says finally, his voice full of emotion. "I know this is so selfish, but I hate being here as your friend. I hate seeing you sitting there, so heartbroken, and not knowing how to reach you. I hate that I couldn't hold you when you read about your dad. That I couldn't stroke your hair when Mrs. Erikson told us—told us everything. I hate that I can't—that I'm not allowed to—"

"Noah . . ." I whisper.

The truth is, I've missed having Noah to turn to. I could always text him and know he'd take care of everything. God, I want that. Someone who would want to take the reins for a little while. Someone who could just take care of me and tell me everything will be all right.

I turn toward him, and he leans closer to me. He cups my cheeks and, using his thumb, wipes away a tear forming at the corner of my lashes. Unbidden, my pulse jackrabbits. I close my eyes, savoring his skin against mine. Everything feels so awful now—except for Noah's touch.

"I never should have let you go." Noah's chest rises and falls rapidly. "I'm so, so sorry. I will never stop being sorry for what I did. Never."

Before all this, it would have been so tempting to just climb into his arms and never leave. But as much as I want to give myself over to this comfort, Tawny's words sound in my head. *I just wish you'd be a little more careful with your heart.* With everything going on in my life, with Dad's past and Mom . . . I'm all over the place. It wouldn't be fair to either of us. Any of us.

I lean back, pressing myself into the seat cushion.

Noah holds up his hands as though burnt. "I'm sorry, River. I didn't mean to take advantage . . ."

"No, no, you didn't. It's just . . ." I bite my lip. "Things are complicated. This is complicated. And the timing . . ."

"Right," Noah says slowly. "Of course." He leans back too, tucking his hands in his lap. "Whatever space or time you need . . . it's yours. You know how I feel, River." He turns to face me.

"That makes one of us," I say, half laughing, half sobbing.

His gaze softens. "As long as it takes. I'm not going anywhere."

"Thanks, Noah," I whisper, and he leans forward to wrap me up in a big, tight hug.

"Anytime, Rivs," he says against my neck.

I get out of the car and watch Noah drive away, my stomach churning. There's another universe where he'd drive me back to his mansion. We'd snuggle Pepper on the couch. We'd go to his room, he'd stroke my hair, tell me everything will be okay. Nothing would need to exist outside the Pierce Castle walls.

It's a nice fantasy—but it's just that. A fantasy, one that doesn't quite fit anymore, one that doesn't have a happy ending.

The crickets are singing as I fish around in my purse for my keys.

"River," says a voice in the dark.

I shriek and whirl around. Logan is lounging on the curb of the sidewalk, his legs stretched onto the asphalt of an empty parking spot.

"What the *hell* are you doing here?" I hiss, my eyes darting around nervously.

Logan hangs his head. "I didn't want to scare you," he says softly.

"I just want to say my piece. And then I'll leave you alone. Forever. If that's what you want."

My heart rate slows as I regard him. "How long have you been here?" I ask.

"Not long. Just an hour." Slowly, he rises to his feet. "Or four."

"Jesus." I gape at him as he stretches and cracks his neck.

"I know." His voice sounds so empty. He takes a breath. "Well. We doing this out here? I'll do whatever makes you comfortable."

I jiggle my keys nervously, thinking. "If you do *anything* weird, I kick you out," I say. "And if you refuse to leave, I've got the cops on speed dial."

"Fair enough." He nods.

I flip on all the lights as soon as I step inside, and when I finally see Logan under the fluorescents, I bring a hand to my mouth.

His left eye is nearly swollen shut; the skin around it and on the brow bone is a deep, mottled purple. He's got a split lip, and the bridge of his nose is shiny and red. In his plain white T-shirt and sweatpants, he looks like a young boxer after a lost fight. Maybe one who looks like he wants to quit the sport forever.

"How's your knee?" Logan asks, gesturing to my bandages.

"Fine," I say, still studying his face. "Logan, you look . . ."

"I know." With a long, slow exhale, he lifts his head. "I'm glad your knee's okay."

We both perch on opposite sides of the couch, and he watches me for a long moment, his good eye a bright, soft blue. Then he leans forward.

"I'm just going to get into it," he says. "Two years ago, my mom was diagnosed with lung cancer. She was vegan, and never smoked a day in her life, but somehow ended up on the very wrong side of those odds." He scrubs a hand across his jaw. "They caught it earlyish. The tumor wasn't that big yet. Surgery was supposed to take care of it. Quick and easy, we were told. Quick and easy."

I press my hand to my mouth.

"Mom was still so nervous the morning of. She wanted me to make her laugh, so I kept telling her all these unbelievably stupid jokes to distract her. They were about to wheel her back, and I wanted to squeeze one last one in. 'Why was the skeleton lonely?' She stopped me before I could say the punch line. 'It'll give me a reason to wake up,' she said."

My instinct is to close the distance and comfort him, but I force myself to sit still.

"She never woke up." He closes his eyes. "That," he whispers, "was not a good day."

Logan takes a moment before continuing. "At first we were told that it was just one of those things. There's always a risk under anesthesia. There was like a zero-point-five-percent chance of complications happening. But whaddya know, we won the worst lottery possible."

I'm about to tell him how sorry I am, but he shakes his head before I can.

"Here's the thing, Santos—we *didn't*. My mom didn't die from bad luck." A dark shadow overtakes Logan's face. "She was murdered."

My jaw falls open. "What?" I breathe in horror.

Logan stands up, grimacing when he does it a little too fast for his still-sore body, and he begins pacing.

"I didn't buy it. Mom was healthy. I pushed and pushed. And I finally convinced my dad to push too. It worked. One day, they finally agreed to a meeting. The surgeon showed up with a team of lawyers." Logan stops pacing, his body rigid with fury. "The surgeon's an alcoholic. He'd been sober a long time, but he'd relapsed. The day of the surgery, he'd been drinking. On the job." His fists clench so hard, I hear his knuckles crack. "Get the picture?"

"Oh, Logan." My heart twists.

The fight leaves him all at once, and he collapses back on the couch. "He offered us a fortune for reparations in exchange for our silence. Millions upon millions of dollars." Logan spreads his hands. "All we had to do was sign on the dotted line and let the man who murdered my mom walk away with zero consequences. I told them to go to hell, but my dad couldn't grab a pen quick enough. And that was that. Dad was a multimillionaire overnight. I made plans to move out the next day."

"You couldn't—you couldn't do anything?" I lick my lips, my tongue dry.

Logan leans forward, his elbows on his knees. "No," he says. "I couldn't. I was a minor. My dad signed a lot of paperwork on my behalf. A lot of legal bullshit that will see me in court until the end of days if I open my mouth. So I got to work on finding someone who *could* do something. I did some digging. Found out where the fucker went to AA meetings. I found his sponsor." Logan's eyes flick up to mine, burning. "It was your dad."

Ice floods my body. I lean back involuntarily, my heart rate picking up.

"My dad," I echo.

Logan nods. "Yes. The funny thing was, when I first saw him, I was relieved. I knew him. He'd helped me before. He could help me again. I went to his office at school and told him everything. I told him he *had* to turn the doctor in. At the very least to keep him from doing it again, if not for justice for my mom.

"He was shocked. Couldn't speak for a minute. When he snapped out of it, he told me to let him handle it. He'd take care of it. I trusted him. But months went by, and nothing. Anytime I cornered your dad at school to ask about it, he'd tell me I needed to be patient, that it was 'delicate' and 'anonymous' for a reason. But time kept going on. And that surgeon kept walking free."

Logan hangs his head, his face flooding with shame. "Now comes the part that I'm not . . . proud of. I started to lose it. I slept less and less, got angrier and angrier. And I . . ." He looks anguished. "Oh God, River. I started to follow your dad."

"What do you mean, follow my dad?" I snap.

Logan's expression is haunted. "I just wanted to see if he was actually putting pressure on the doctor. And he was, but still nothing happened. And after that, I don't know, I just kept following him, looking for any kind of way to leverage him to just bite the bullet and turn the fucker in." Logan wipes a hand down the uninjured side of his face. "Nothing was working. It felt like I was living in some evil alternate reality where the bad guys get away with everything. I did deep dives on the internet, searching for anything I could about the doctor, about your dad. I tried aliases. I googled any number of combinations of words. And then I stumbled upon the jackpot."

But I'm already way ahead of him.

"Let me guess. You found the article. Canyon Rock City," I say in a disgusted tone.

When Logan doesn't deny it, the rest of it falls into place. I think about the notes. " 'I know what you did,' " I recite. " 'You can't hide.' " I narrow my eyes. " 'Killer.' "

"I know." Logan's face crumples, but only for a second. He stiffens, and he squares his shoulders. "It sounds so stupid now, but I just wanted to kick him into gear."

"And how did that work out for you?" I bite back.

"Terribly, of course." Logan sets his jaw. "And then I noticed that your dad went to a diner every Friday morning by my apartment. One day after school in early December, I walked in and applied for a job.

I needed one anyway . . . Two birds, one stone. And that first day, I saw one of the most beautiful girls I'd ever seen wiping menus behind the counter." He buries his face in his hands. "I swear to God I didn't know who you were until Gertie told me your and Tawny's names."

Logan looks nauseated. His voice is hoarse. "I felt disgusting immediately, if that helps. I almost quit on my second day. Along with feeling like the world's biggest creep, a mustard bottle exploded on me, and I had two tables stiff me back-to-back. When I fucked something up on the register, that was it. I'd decided I'd walk out and never come back."

I cross my arms tightly over my chest. "So why didn't you?"

Logan gives me a long look. "You got me a spare shirt from the office. Told me to take a break out back while you handled the register. When I went outside, Tigery was sitting there." He sighs. "It sounds dumb, but my mom loved tabbies. Tigery was just her type. It felt like a stupid sign to stick around."

"To spy on me." It's not really a question.

"No, River, I promise. The second I started working with you, it all stopped for me."

My lips part on an exhale. "Why?"

"River, I've been hopelessly in love with you for months." God, he sounds so miserable. "I don't know how anyone could be around you and not be in love with you. No matter how many walls I put up, you were just so *kind*. I snapped back to my senses, and it all just stopped. Watching your dad. The notes. I was preparing to apologize to him, set things right. But then he was gone. And there was no way I was going to go near you after that."

It takes me a few tries to find my voice. "Why not?"

"What happened with your dad . . . it represented the worst moment of my life. My mom was dead, and it turned me into a *monster*. A rage-filled thing I didn't even recognize. And I almost felt responsible for your dad's death, somehow, like my rage had put some kind of cosmic target on his back."

He shakes his head. "And if by some miracle you did let me near you? How would I ever explain my history to you? How I repaid your dad's kindness with blackmail. What if you ever found out?" He quirks a lip. "My, wouldn't *that* be a disaster?"

"Yeah," I manage. "A huge disaster."

"I'm not here expecting forgiveness or even acceptance. I just wanted you to know the truth, ugly as it is. You deserve honesty, and I broke your trust, more than once."

I don't trust my voice, but I force myself to ask the question. "Who was the surgeon, Logan?"

Logan holds my gaze. "I think you know, River."

And I do. I do, I do, goddamn it. But it's so awful I need to hear him say it, just to be sure. Logan can't look at me when he does.

"Dr. Charles Pierce."

# chapter 32
# logan

The cemetery is empty today, which is fitting. It's just me and my ghosts, all alone, which is as much as I deserve.

I lay the bluebells against Mom's headstone and think of the bluebells I laid on River's aunt's doorstep so many months ago. I didn't know back then that they were her dad's favorite. I just knew that I needed to do something.

And I was too chickenshit to sign my name.

I fold my hands in front of me. I've never done the whole talking-at-the-grave thing. Tried once. Felt like knocking on the door of an abandoned house. But I'm so lost now that I'm willing to try that door again.

Did I do the right thing, telling River everything? Did it help? Was it even enough?

She was still deep in thought, shocked into silence by my revelation, when I walked out her door. I must have stood on her doorstep for a full minute, reaching back for the door to knock for one last *I'm sorry, I love you, please forgive me* before wrenching myself away again. Because I don't get to say those things to her. I haven't earned that right, and I have to accept that I might not ever earn it.

"I'm so fucking messed up, Mom," I say, then immediately cringe. She didn't love me using that word. I rake a hand through my hair. "Sorry. I'll . . . get a jar. Throw in a dollar." I wince. "Maybe ten."

A breeze kicks up, and the air's flooded with the scent of rosemary. Mom kept a rosemary plant on her kitchen sill. Put it in almost everything. I can't eat it anymore, but smelling it right now? Well, suddenly, the house I'm knocking at doesn't feel quite so abandoned.

Gravel crunches behind me. I wait to see if the footsteps fade. When they don't, I lift my chin. Stand up straight. When the crunches get loudest, they stop. There's a short pause. After a few seconds, Dad appears at my shoulder.

We stand side by side, staring down at Mom's grave. The silence is stiff. He moves first, stooping and nestling his own bluebell bouquet beside mine.

"Those are nice." His voice booms even as a murmur. But he spoke first, and it feels like an olive branch.

"Yours are too." I pause a beat. "Wasn't sure I'd see you." Dad rumbles a laugh. It's not mean, but there's an edge to it.

"Wasn't me who stopped coming, Logan," he says. Guilt feels like ants crawling through my veins. I resist the urge to fidget in the following silence. I clear my throat.

"Still? Every Sunday?" I can't keep the surprise out of my voice.

"Every Sunday," Dad says quietly. I turn to Dad, and he's already watching me, his mighty features shrouded. Always shrouded. "Are you here just for your mother? Or did you also come to see me?"

"I needed Mom's advice," I say.

"Ah." Something flickers in his face.

"And I came to see you." I keep very still and stare my father dead in the eye. Can't let him see how sweaty my palms are. How the blood's rushing in my ears. "I wanted to let you know I'm going public about Pierce. I'm done hiding. Done being scared." I don't let myself drop Dad's gaze, even though it feels like clutching hot coals. "I wanted to let you know."

We regard each other. This silence is twenty paces long, pistols at dawn. It feels like that second between *aim* and *fire!* He looks at me, *really* looks at me, in a way I can't remember him ever doing. Then he nods.

"His team of litigators is bigger than the Cardinals," he says.

"Makes sense."

"You're eighteen. An adult in the eyes of the law."

"I'm aware."

"Hmm." Dad hums. And then he nods again. "Very well."

I wait for more. For his voice to gather rage and weight. For his shadows to grow long and the ground to shake. The sharp knot in my belly *twists*. But nothing happens.

"That's it?" I breathe. "But . . . you might lose the mansion. Your money." Dad gives me a long look.

"I've lost worse," he says, and peers down at Mom. We're quiet for a while.

"Maybe," I say in a rough voice. "Maybe I need your advice too." I swallow. "How do you deal with . . . if—*when*—you had your perfect girl but then you lost her? How do you deal if it's all your fault? How do you deal with the regret?"

"Ah. Well." Dad's lips quirk, rueful. "Most of us don't get our perfect girl. I just try to be grateful for the time I had." His face crumples, and I imagine this is what it would look like if a full-maned lion flinched. "I've spent a lot of time alone recently, Logan. And I've had a lot of time to think. I have lifetimes of regret but no words of wisdom. I can only tell you that there are many things I wish I had done differently." Dad gives me another lingering, significant look, and the swell of emotions it brings nearly capsizes me.

"Okay, Dad," I say after a minute. "Okay." I check the time on my phone. Start making getting-ready-to-leave noises.

"Was that her, then?" Dad asks. "In the car on the Fourth? Your perfect girl?"

I pause.

"Yeah." I brush the top of Mom's headstone. "Her name's River."

"River," Dad echoes. "I'm sorry you lost her, Logan."

"My fault." I shrug. I startle when Dad puts a hand on my shoulder.

"Let your mistakes make you a better man." He tightens his fingers, then pats the spot twice. "You will endure. Grow. Only the strong can do that." His voice goes quiet. "I see that now."

I don't know if Dad's right. If I'll ever recover from losing River. Doesn't really feel like I will. But as he stands here, gripping my shoulder, giving me something I never thought he'd ever be capable of, I feel a spark of hope. Hope that sometimes the impossible happens. That people *can* change.

That *I* can change. Can stand up for what's right. Accept the consequences of my actions. Do everything I can to repair the damage I've done.

Maybe River will never grant me forgiveness. But I can strive to be a man who might one day be worthy of it.

# chapter 33
# river

For an entire day, I pace my apartment, back and forth, until I know every divot in the tiling, every crack in the walls. I haven't talked to anyone. Sent the bare minimum replies to Tita Anna and Tawny's texts to make sure they don't send over the search parties.

All I can do is think. And process. And wonder how everything got so fucked up.

Logan and my dad and Noah and his dad. It just goes around and around on a loop, until I feel like my mind is exploding, like my life isn't my own. Logan warned me all those weeks ago: Everyone's *hiding something.*

I just didn't realize that everyone was hiding *everything.*

That no one in my life was who they said they were.

There's betrayal in every direction, and finally, on Sunday night, I can't stand it anymore. I get in the car and drive to the Pierces' mansion. On the third ring of the doorbell, Noah opens the door. His mouth falls open in shock.

"River? It's nearly midnight—"

I shoulder past him into the house, not waiting to be invited. I march into the living room and start pacing in front of their ridiculous fireplace, big enough to roast an ox over the flame.

Noah walks over, his brows furrowed with concern. "You okay, Riv?"

I know he's just worried. But it sounds patronizing to my ears. I hold up a hand, and he immediately falls silent.

"I'm going to give you one more chance to answer this question with the whole truth, Noah." I pin him with the steeliest stare I can manage. I give each word its own moment when I ask, "Why did you break up with me? And does it have something to do with our dads?"

I watch Noah cycle through several emotions. Shock. Fear. Realization. Relief. He nods. His face is now calm. Stoic. He takes a seat on the couch and crosses his ankles. He looks like a doctor in his office, trying to be casual, relatable. In the back of my brain, I wonder if he's using this as an opportunity to deliver bad news. I wonder if I'm an exercise on his path to his actual true love: following in the footsteps of his beloved father.

"Let me preface this by reiterating, River: I was a moron," he begins. "I broke up with you because I heard our dads fighting. I didn't mean to listen, but I got nervous. I'd never heard your dad raise his voice the whole time I'd known him. And suddenly, I was hearing him scream: 'I don't want to, but I'll turn you in myself if I have to, Charlie. I'm giving you a chance to do the right thing here!' "

"My dad begged your father to forgive him. He said that if he did whatever your father was asking, he'd lose his license, his career, *everything*. He was practically crying, River. But your dad refused. He wouldn't take no for an answer. My dad lost his cool and threatened him before storming out." Noah shakes his head miserably. "I was terrified that your dad was going to destroy my dad's life. Finally, your dad left, and for the next few days, my dad just . . . imploded. He wouldn't leave his room. He ignored me. He lashed out, told me what a mistake I'd made, tying myself up with a family like yours that cares more about principle than all the lives he saves.

"A few days later was our . . . was the night we were supposed to . . ." This is when I finally see the first sign of Noah's stoic veneer cracking. "You have no idea . . . *no* idea how much I've regretted . . . Oh, River, I broke up with you because I thought your dad was threatening mine, and I didn't know how to handle it. I knew I wouldn't be able to keep it from you. But I also didn't want to drag you into any of our dads' bullshit. I wished I'd never overheard any of it. Especially now. Especially knowing what I know now."

Misery passes over Noah's face.

"I got it all wrong, River. And I was such a fool. I misunderstood everything. I know now that your dad was trying to help mine, that my dad had started drinking again. But by the time I realized all of this, of course . . ." Noah trails off, like saying the next few words is unbearable. But I can finish them for him.

"By the time you realized all of this," I echo, "my dad was dead."

Noah looks at his hands like they're covered in blood. "When I found out what happened . . . that the very night you were supposed to have spent the night with me was the night your house burned down . . ." His face pales. "Oh God, River, for a horrible moment, I thought I'd *killed* you." He closes his eyes. "I thought my dad had your house burned down to stop your dad, and I'd unknowingly sent you into the cross fire.

"When I saw you at the funeral, I just needed to try to make things right with you, make amends any way I could. The longer I was holding Dad's secret, the sicker I got. I eventually just couldn't take it. I confronted my dad. I demanded the truth.

"Dad sat me down, said if I wanted the truth, I'd get it. He told me what he *had* done: Logan's mom, relapsing, the drinking, the settlement, the NDAs. He then told me what he *hadn't* done, which was setting the fire that killed your dad. It wasn't him, Riv. It wasn't him. He's made some very serious mistakes, but he's not a malicious murderer."

Noah wipes a hand down his face and sighs harshly.

"I know my money doesn't make up for anything. But at least now you know where it came from and why—"

I freeze. "What?" I breathe.

Noah pauses, frowning. "The—the two million dollars? Didn't you . . . I thought—"

My vision tunnels. "*You* gave me the two million?" I stagger to the couch as Noah shoots to his feet. "Were you trying to *buy* me back, Noah?"

"*Jesus*, River, I would never!"

Noah reaches for me, and I recoil.

"Don't *touch* me, Noah!" He looks stricken but immediately shrinks back, falling pale. I want to stand up and get out of here, but my legs feel shaky.

"So let me get this straight," I say hoarsely. "You hear our dads fight. Instead of coming to me and telling me the truth, and us talking it out, you, inexplicably, out of nowhere, the day we plan to sleep together for the first time, *break up with me*? And then, when, that night, my entire life burns to the ground, instead of immediately coming to me to comfort me and explain everything in my *extreme fucking time of need*, you click a few buttons at my father's *funeral*, throw a disgusting amount of money at me anonymously, just to stop feeling guilty for being too much of a chickenshit to own up to your mistakes?"

I realize with a jolt that it's *exactly* what his dad did, with Logan's mom.

*Like father, like son.*

"At least admit the truth to yourself. You didn't break up with me to protect me from our fathers' fighting. You broke up with me because you didn't want to disappoint your dad."

I wait for Noah to say something. *Anything.* But he just hangs his head, like I've got his number. It's almost worse than denying it, this rolling over and presenting me his belly.

"You were the love of my life," I rasp. "I trusted you above anyone else. But you lied and tried to fix it with money. Congrats, Noah. You got your dream: You're exactly like your father."

I wait for him to meet my eye. I wait for him to tell me I'm wrong about him. That he's nothing like him. But he keeps his head down, his body folded in on itself. His acquiescence is heartbreaking.

"That's it, then?" I whisper, standing.

"I'm sorry, River." Noah breaks his silence and looks up with wet, red-rimmed eyes. "I'm just . . . really sorry."

What use is a sorry now? Sorry won't mend my heart from all the lying, the months he left me to cry by myself during the greatest losses I've ever experienced. It's somehow more painful than if he'd said nothing.

I walk out of his house, out of his life, again for the last time.

And I don't look back.

# chapter 34
# river

I haven't left the bed for nearly two days. When I got back from Noah's the other night, it all hit me before I could even make it to my room. I fell to the couch crying—that uncontrollable, can't breathe, hyperventilating sobbing that seizes your lungs. I texted Tita Anna, but it was well past midnight by then, so unsurprisingly I received no response. I called Tawny, crying so hard I couldn't speak. But it didn't matter.

"I'll be right there," she said, and showed up twenty minutes later in her pajamas, a big duffel bag of her stuff on her shoulder. She thrust out her hand, obnoxiously bright. "Hi, I'm Your Personal Chef Slash Nurse Slash Therapist Whether You Like It or Not Tawny. Nice to meet you. Also, I'm moving in." Then she wrapped me in her arms.

Tawny worked my shift for me yesterday so I could spend all of it curled up beneath my comforter, tight as a pill bug. She's home from her breakfast shift, banging around in the kitchen, making us food for which I have zero appetite. Not that she still won't try.

"Soup's on!" Tawny calls as she nudges my bedroom door open with her hip, carrying a tray with two steaming bowls and a sleeve of saltines. "Chicken soup. I used my mom's recipe." She sits on the foot of my bed as I drag myself up to sit against the headboard.

"My head's a bowling ball," I groan.

"Don't lie back down." Tawny raises her brows as I pause my slide back under the covers. "Stay sitting up, just for a little bit. Besides, homemade soup!"

"Oh, Tawn," I say softly, noticing the greasy broth and tendrils of floating noodles. "You're so sweet. I really don't deserve you." She rolls her eyes.

"Shut up, that's the dumbest thing I've ever heard."

"As tempting as piping-hot soup is on a hundred-and-twenty-degree bright summer day, I don't know if my stomach will—"

"Just one spoonful, okay?" Tawny dips the spoon in my bowl and blows at the steam. "Just one, and you can lie back down."

Her voice is high and chipper, but I can hear the undercurrent of exhaustion. I feel a pang of guilt. Tawny covered my shift, no questions asked. She's listened to me sob about Noah and Logan for hours, attentive the whole time.

"All right," I say, even though my stomach roils. "Sure. One spoonful." Tawny's face blooms into that gorgeous smile of hers. She holds out the spoon, and I sip the salty broth, smacking my lips. "Not bad," I say, shuffling back under the covers. "What's your mom's recipe?"

"Pretty easy. It's just one can of soup and one canful of water." Tawny grins when I stare at her, deadpan. "Hey," she says, "to be fair, that *is* how my mom always makes it."

I watch Tawny carefully blow on each spoonful, the meticulous way she raises it to her lips, so careful not to spill on the bed, on my favorite comforter.

"Thanks. I mean it. Really."

"River," she says, "*duh.*" Tawny nudges me in that affectionate way, like I've said something very cute and dumb. But then she gets serious. "You don't have to keep thanking me, you know," she says quietly. "I do these things because I love you and look after you, because that's just *how it is*. It wasn't all too long ago that you were the one taking care of *me*."

I can't say anything for a few seconds. When my voice returns, I lift the edge of the comforter.

"You wanna get in here?"

Tawny smiles. "No thanks. You really need a shower."

I laugh hard, loud and surprised. "Rock bottom's not so bad with you around."

A loud knock on the door startles us both. I hold my breath as Tawny goes on full alert, her face tight.

"Was that the neighbor?" I whisper hopefully.

But no, there it is again: three adamant bangs on our front door. Tawny and I exchange uneasy looks. We're both thinking the same thing: that nothing good can come from knocks with such authority.

Tawny helps me out of bed, and I'm immediately dizzy. Whoever this is, I hope they finish up quickly. But that thought goes right out the window when I open the door and see Officer Yeoman's sweaty red face and a man in a worn, dark brown suit and tie with a perpetually furrowed brow staring down at me. I know Officer Yeoman because he was one of the cops who handled our house fire, but this other man has the hair on my neck standing.

"Oh" is all I can manage as Tawny stiffens beside me. She's always been on the don't-talk-to-the-cops-without-a-lawyer side of things.

"Good afternoon, Miss Santos." Officer Yeoman nods at us. "Officer Yeoman again; been a while. This is Detective Rust. Do you mind if we come in for just a minute?"

I wave them in, glad for once to be numb from exhaustion and heartache.

The two men stand awkwardly in the living room. Officer Yeoman takes his hat off and scrubs at his smooth scalp. Tawny slips into the kitchen, preparing glasses of ice water, less a courtesy than a distraction, knowing her.

"Miss Santos, I apologize, but this is a sensitive matter. Do you mind if we speak with you alone?" Detective Rust gestures at the kitchen. Tawny sets down the glasses reluctantly, ready to obey, but there's no way I'm letting her leave my sight.

I need her.

"Anything you need to say to me, you can say in front of Tawny," I snap.

I'm expecting them to tell me something about the fire, so when Officer Yeoman clears his throat and says, "Miss Santos, when was the last time you saw your mother in person?" needles of ice prick up my spine.

My mind immediately goes to the night of the fire, the arms around me, my certainty that it was my mother. *Oh my God. They know.*

"My mom?" I feign taking time to count in my head. "She left my dad and me around . . . well, it's almost a year now, I'd say. Nine months or so, if we want to be more specific."

Detective Rust takes out a notepad and pencil. As soon as I hear the soft scribbling noise, my pulse ratchets up.

"What's going on?" I say quietly, looking between them. I glance over to Tawny, but her gaze is trained on the cops. Officer Yeoman puts his hat back on.

"About a month ago, Miss Santos, we found a body out in the desert. A little ways off one of the sections of the Arizona Trail."

"Okay . . ." Now I'm just confused. What does that have to do with me? Something unseats in my memory. "Wait. Yeah, okay, I think I remember seeing that on the news." I look to Tawny for confirmation, but she's still staring at the officers.

"Yes, well." Officer Yeoman's mouth forms a thin line. "I'm afraid we have some difficult news for you. We've just received confirmation through dental records and DNA that the body belongs to your mother."

There's a crash in the kitchen. I look over and see that Tawny's accidentally knocked over a glass into the sink. I frown and turn back to the officers.

"I'm sorry," I say, "can you repeat that? I don't understand. One of my mom's belongings was found in the desert?"

"Miss Santos," he says, his voice softer, "I'm afraid your mother is dead."

"No, she's not," I snap, because it's true. Officer Yeoman's shoulders sag, and Detective Rust slips his notepad and pen into his pocket.

The two officers exchange glances.

I shake my head vigorously, even though I can feel the blood draining from my body. "No, you're wrong. It's probably another Jennifer Santos. My mom is an avid hiker. She's just out on the mountains somewhere. She's—" My voice catches at the end.

"River," Officer Yeoman says, his voice softer, "I'm sorry, but there's no mistake. I understand this is incredibly difficult to hear. But unfortunately, our forensic team has confirmed it twice over. The body we found in the desert a month ago is your mother's."

My neck suddenly feels very cold. I don't hear any sounds coming from the kitchen.

"Miss Santos, we're opening an investigation," Detective Rust continues. "Your mother was found at the bottom of a ravine without any identification or personal effects. No phone, wallet, or purse. We suspect foul play."

*No, this can't be right. They've got it all wrong.*

"Impossible." I feel like a stranger in my own body. I'm watching a horror movie of myself talking to two policemen, and I can't find the remote to switch the channel. I can barely feel Tawny's arms around me, her cheek pressed to my hair.

"Do you have any proof?" I ask.

"The forensic reports are at the station. You're welcome to come down and—"

"Pictures." I frown at my feet and realize I've crossed the room and am standing near the television. "I need to see pictures. Or the body. Let me identify the body—you've got this all wrong."

Officer Yeoman looks nauseated. "The medical examiner," he says slowly, "would highly advise you against that."

"Why?" I croak, even as my stomach lurches. Officer Yeoman doesn't answer. He just regards me sadly, with pity.

My legs suddenly give out. Officer Yeoman steps toward me, hand outstretched, but Tawny reaches me first.

"You've done enough," she barks at him as she gathers me in her arms. Both cops back up, shockingly obedient.

Detective Rust places a couple of white business cards on the coffee table.

"I'm so sorry, Miss Santos. If you're open to it, I'd like to give you a call tomorrow. If you have any questions before then—"

"How long has that b-body been out there?" I don't realize how hard I'm trembling until I hear the stutter in my voice. Tawny holds me tighter.

"About nine months," he states. "Since October."

I hear a strangled gasp. Tawny. Tawny is sobbing. "Oh, River," she says through her tears.

It's that, more than anything, that makes me believe. I was ready for Tawny to laugh in their faces, kick them out. But Tawny is crying just as hard as I am.

This is what ends me.

Losing my dad was impossible. But I still had my mother. She was out there, and there was always hope.

Except she never was, was she?

She never even left Arizona. She's been dead this entire time.

# chapter 35
# river

Three a.m. is the worst hour for grief.

I give myself an hour before I leave Tawny's bed, not wanting to wake her with my rolling, and move to the couch.

I couldn't stay in Tita Anna's apartment. I had to put as much distance as possible between myself and the place where I found out that my mother was dead.

Now I'm on the lumpy cushions, trying to tuck into myself, fantasizing that I can become a perfect spiral, like a snail shell, so tight, no one could ever unfurl me. So tight, I could disappear, just like my parents and my memories of them.

No matter how hard I try, I can't remember the last words my mother ever said to me. Was it *Bye, guys,* or *Don't forget to take out the trash, River*? Or was it just *Bye*?

It's been almost a year since I last heard my mother's voice. I'm terrified I've forgotten what she sounds like completely.

What's the last conversation we had? I'm sure it was nothing profound. I'd probably asked if she could pick up spaghetti for dinner. A selfish, pointless demand. Or I'd said something bratty or snarky. Something worthy of a lifetime of regret.

What I should have said was *Tell me again why purple is your favorite color?* Or, *You know what, I'll go to that candle-making workshop with you.* Or, most importantly of all?

*Stay, Mom. Stay and tell me everything.*

I get why she didn't tell me about the car accident. But I wish she had. I wish they both had. There's so much more I want to know. *Need* to know. And not just the big stuff.

I wish I'd asked Mom the name of her best friend in kindergarten, or how she liked to wear her hair when she was sixteen. I wish I'd asked what she and her mom fought about, and what the scariest moment of her life was.

That one feels like a kick to the stomach, because it's not hard to believe that the scariest moment of her life happened just before it ended, somewhere out in that desert.

Anytime I think about the texts I sent Mom over the past months, my stomach roils. There was no phone found on her body. Is it still out there in the desert? Or does somebody have it?

Have I been pouring out my heart to her killer?

I start shivering, and I can't stop. If the cops are right, then the killer is still out there. They're out there, and they know who I am, where I live, what I think.

Who could it be? Someone Mom knew? Someone *I* know?

And what about the night of the fire? Now I know for sure my mom didn't start the fire. She never even got to see New Year's Eve.

Was it an accident or not? And who pulled me out of there? Or did I imagine it all and pull myself to safety? I've been holding tight to so many fantasies, I don't even know what's true anymore.

I lie awake until the glow of morning's first light starts to sliver through Tawny's kitchen blinds. She's going to get up soon. I'll hear the doors open, the faucet in the bathroom, the spray of the shower. Tawny will be worried that I didn't sleep, but what no one understands is that it's easier not to.

If I could go the rest of my life without sleep, I'd do it. There would be no dreams where Mom walks in, goes, *Why are you crying? It was all a big mistake!* Or where I bump into Dad at a Costco and he seems embarrassed. *Sorry,* he says, *I've been waiting for you to find me. I forgot how to get home.*

And there would be no devastating moment when I wake up and they're not here, and I remember everything all over again.

A door opens down the hall, and I'm so relieved that Tawny is finally awake. I follow the audio trail of her morning routine. The electric toothbrush. The squeak of her nearly empty shampoo bottle. The tiny roar of her blow-dryer. The ringing of her phone. She's working from lunch to close at Gertie's today. My stomach drops at the thought of being alone.

After a moment, a door opens, and Tawny's voice filters down the hall.

"Yes, of course. No, I know, I know." Tawny enters the room, her brows jumping when she sees I'm awake. "Actually," she says into the phone, "she's up, wanna talk to her?" She crosses the room and holds the phone to me. "It's Anna," she says quietly.

"Hey," I say, pressing the phone to my ear.

*"River."* Tita Anna's delivery is breathy, and I know she's fighting her tears tooth and nail. "Oh, my sweet, sweet girl. I'm so sorry, my love."

"Thanks."

"Sweetheart, I'm coming home early. I'm so sorry, but there are no flights until late tonight. Can you hang in there until then?"

I nod before I realize she can't see me. "Yeah."

"That's my strong girl. Rivvy, I know it feels like it will never be okay again. But you've got me. You've got Tawny. We're not going anywhere. Ever. I love you. I'll see you soon."

After we hang up, I stagger to the kitchen, where Tawny's pouring herself a fresh cup of coffee.

"Here," she says, handing me the mug. Coffee sloshes over from her trembling hands. Her eyes are red. "I'm so sorry. I'm so sorry for everything I said about her. I was so mad at her for leaving, but underneath it all, I wanted your mom back just as badly as you did."

"Tawny." I set the cup down sloppily, spilling all over the counter, pulling Tawny in. She presses her face into my shoulder and cries. Tawny rarely cries. It's starting to make sense why Tawny was so angry with Mom.

She was hurt too.

I squeeze her hard. If grief is a prison, at least Tawny's my cellmate.

"I don't want to be alone after the sun sets," I whisper.

"You won't be," she says softly. "You need rest. Catch up on sleep. I'll be back before you know it."

I've never felt this clingy in my life. Tita Anna's coming home tonight. I need to remind myself that I can wait it out. Her plane lands in sixteen hours. I won't be alone for long.

What can happen in sixteen hours?

THE DAY GOES by in a melancholy blur. I spend most of it watching a nature show about the Arctic, trying to focus on David Attenborough's voice. I try to name the colors of the birds I see. I try not to think of the killer who murdered my mother, try not to picture them carrying around my mom's phone, that strange, invisible wavelength connecting them to the little rectangle in my pocket.

I do a half-decent job. I'm only thinking of the killer once every five seconds until my phone buzzes, and I jump. But it's just Tawny.

"You on your way home?" I say breathlessly as soon as I pick up.

"Oh, River," Tawny sighs, and my heart sinks. "I'm so sorry. Got some bad news. It's gonna take me some time to close tonight. The new line cook took off without cleaning the grill and Gertie says I have to do it."

She lets out a rough sigh. I know her knuckles are currently white from how hard she's squeezing the phone. "I won't be done until after dark, Riv. I'm sorry."

"Oh."

"*But* I was thinking, why don't you come here? You can just hang out while I finish, so you don't have to be alone. Just come in your coziest pajamas, bring a pillow and blanket, and snuggle up in one of the booths. Bring my Bluetooth speaker and we can listen to all our favorites. What do you think?"

"That sounds . . . pretty good, actually."

"Awesome! Ooh shit, Gertie's calling. She's gonna tell me how to do the grill over the phone."

As I make my way to Tawny's room, I pass the familiar little coat closet alcove. When my eyes land on the door, I freeze. It's such a bizarre feeling, trying to reconcile the River from that night, getting the hell kissed out of her by Logan, in that exact little closet, and the River I am now in this moment, afraid of the dark.

*Honey, I'm an arrow, not a boomerang.* My mom's words come back to me like a gut punch.

Unconsciously, I take out my phone. And without fully being able to take in why, I call my mom's number. I can taste the relief I would feel if she answered, and it makes my heart ache. *Hey, baby,* she'd say, or *It's my sweet girl.* Alone in the hallway, I swear I can hear it—her voice. But then I snap back to reality. And all I hear is ringing, and ringing . . . but then . . .

*Buzz. Buzz. Buzz.*

I hang up, and the buzzing stops.

I stop too. What phone could be ringing? Tawny has hers at the grill.

I call my mom's number again.

*Buzz. Buzz. Buzz.*

I follow the sound down the hall. It's coming from the other side of a shut door. *Tawny's mom's room?* It's always closed—Tawny says her mom is very particular about her space. "She'll freak if anyone even thinks about sitting on her bed in anything but clean pajamas," she said once.

Still, I reach for the metal handle to open the door, but when I push down, there's no give—it's locked.

I run back into the kitchen. The phone still pressed to my ear, I rifle through the junk drawer and pluck out a single bobby pin.

*Buzz. Buzz. Buzz.*

I can still hear it beyond the bedroom door. I shove the bobby pin into the lock, jimmy it once, then twice. With a soft click, it unlatches. I push the door open. The room is wide with plain white walls and a large, curtainless window on the far end. It's hard to tell where the sound is coming from. I grow more frantic. I move to the bureau and start opening drawers.

"What the fuck . . ."

They're empty. They're *all* empty. I stagger back toward the closet and wrench it open.

The closet's empty too. This entire room looks untouched.

"What the fuck, what the fuck," I whimper in a high-pitched whisper, clutching my head. My vision is tunneling, and I'm getting dizzy. In the background, the buzzing continues.

I take a few steps forward out of the closet, and the buzzing grows louder. I call my mom one more time and walk forward until the buzzing becomes the loudest.

I'm standing beside the bed. I inspect the side of the mattress, pressing my ear against it. The buzzing tickles the shell of my ear. I run a hand along the side, slipping it under the sheet. After a second of dragging it along the side, my fingers find a neat slash in the fabric, and when I reach in, my fingers close on a hard, flat rectangle.

I pull out my hand, and when I turn it over, I'm clutching my mom's phone.

A cascade of thoughts flashes through me. I've never seen Tawny's mother in person.

Tawny's mother doesn't exist.

Tawny has my mom's phone.

I unlock the screen and scroll through the texts I sent to Mom. The ones I'd been desperately hoping she'd answer.

I'm going to puke.

I'm going to faint.

I'm going to scream.

I suck in deep breaths, but nothing helps. I'm not getting enough oxygen. The walls are going to crush me.

Tawny has my mom's phone.

Tawny has my *dead* mom's phone.

In a daze, I unlock the phone and scroll through all the pictures. A swift kaleidoscope of beautiful agony. Dad pointing to a carpet of desert bluebells. Mom with her arms around Tawny and me, her fingers threaded through mine.

And Tawny's.

There's a calendar notification showing two hundred and ninety-one days snoozed: *Hike w/E.*

My phone rings, splitting the air. With the picture of Tawny, Mom, and me still in my palm, I pull out my phone, hands shaking badly, and answer.

"Hello."

"I almost forgot—bring socks, please. I spilled dishwater on my shoe, and now it's squishing with each step."

Tawny.

*Say something, River.*

"River? You okay?"

"Socks," I rasp. "I'll bring socks."

"Aw, Riv, you sound awful. Just come to the diner. It's gonna be okay, honey. See you soon."

How did she do it?

I need to know. I need to know who the *fuck* I've spent the last two years with.

I've got nothing left to lose. I stumble out of the house and get in my car.

No more secrets.

I'm going to look Tawny in the eye. Ask for the truth.

# chapter 36

# river

When I get to Gertie's, I burst through the back door of the kitchen to find Tawny on the dirty tile floor. Her clothes are covered in grease and dishwater as she cradles her phone. It takes me a second to notice the cracked screen.

"Oh, hey," she says, falsely bright. "Don't mind me. I was an idiot and dropped my phone."

She looks so small and sad, gingerly testing her phone screen. If this had happened an hour ago, I would be giving her a hug.

"Oh well." Tawny slaps her thighs and gets to her feet. She turns on the grill. "It needs to heat up for a while. Gertie says it's the only way to get the gunk out." Her rueful smile slips as she takes me in. "Hey, I'm sorry. Come here." Tawny closes the distance between us and wraps her arms around me.

I freeze, unsure of what to do for half a heartbeat. When Tawny tightens her hold, I crumple, pressing my face into her shoulder.

*Please, God, don't let it be true. Please let me have gotten it all wrong.*

When we pull apart, I go straight to the dining room to collect myself. I reach into my pocket and pull out Mom's phone. I stare at it madly. How in the hell am I supposed to do this?

Tawny pops her head through the order window. "Real quick, what kind of toppings do you want for your pizza? I'm gonna order now."

I can't stop looking at the phone in my hand. I start to shake.

"River?"

I hear the kitchen door open and suddenly there's a hand on my shoulder. I'm so keyed up, I whirl away, stumbling against a chair.

"Hey, are you okay?" Tawny's face pinches with a flash of hurt. "Riv, what's the matter? Why are you looking at me like that?"

"Like what?" I say shakily.

Tawny frowns. "Like I'm a stranger."

I have no words. But I don't need them to ask her my question.

I hold out my fist toward Tawny, pressing the button on the side of the phone. Tawny frowns, her eyes on the illuminated lock screen photo.

"Oh no! You broke your phone too?" Then Tawny's mouth snaps shut, and she blanches. It takes her a few seconds to respond. "Oh my God. Is that your mom's phone? Holy shit . . ." She looks at me, her brows creasing. "But how do you have it?"

"Don't . . ." I lick my lips. "Don't fuck with me, Tawny."

"What are you talking about?" she asks, taking a step toward me. When I flinch, she freezes, pain flashing across her features. She holds up a conciliatory hand. "Okay, okay. Where did you get it, River?" She says it slowly, like she's talking a man off a ledge.

"In your house," I say in a broken voice.

Tawny puts her hand over her mouth. "Oh my God," she whispers. "How the hell would it get in there . . ."

This is killing me. I want her to stop.

When I remain silent, some slow horror dawns in her expression. "Wait a minute," she murmurs. "River. *River.* There's no way you actually think that *I*—that *I would*."

I squeeze my eyes shut against the agony twisting her face.

"Come on, River," she pleads. "No one knows me better than you. *You know me.*"

"I don't, actually." My voice breaks. "I found it in your mom's mattress—and by that, I mean *your* mattress. Because your mother's not in Norway, is she? She's not anywhere. Did you kill her too?"

"River," Tawny chokes, "what the fuck?" Tears start to fall down her face. "Please stop. I don't know what you're talking about." She approaches me, holding out her hands, beseeching.

I shrink back from her, working through all the grotesque pieces that are slotting together in my head.

"You've been living alone this whole time," I say faintly. "Everything I've ever known about you is a lie, isn't it? Who is that woman in your pictures?"

Tawny's outstretched fingers flicker. "It's my mom. The woman who adopted me," she says urgently.

But I'm barely listening.

"It was you that night," I whisper. "You set the fire. You killed my father. You—*you almost killed me*—"

"I *saved* you!" Tawny screeches, throwing out her hands, knocking into my mine in the process, sending Mom's phone to the floor. Her eyes are wild, and I finally get a glimpse of a different Tawny, at the raw fury spring-loaded in her body.

She suddenly slumps, deflating all at once. Wiping a hand down her face, she sighs.

"Sorry," she says raggedly.

Slowly, like she's in a daze, Tawny walks behind the counter, ducking out of sight to rummage through the cleaning supply cabinets.

"Not sure if you knew this," she says, "but Gertie's glass cleaner? She makes it herself using her own recipe."

Her voice sounds strange. Disconnected.

"For God's sake, Tawny." I take a step forward, pleading. "Just tell me the truth." I swallow hard against my rising nausea and ask the impossible. "Did you kill my mom and my dad?"

"River," Tawny says, ignoring my words, that odd lilt to her voice rising, "let me finish. Gertie's glass cleaner is made out of water, vinegar, soap, and . . ." She pops up into view, holding a glass bottle of Everclear. "Booze! What *can't* it do, am I right?"

She reaches by the coffee maker, grabs a mug, and fills it with two healthy splashes of the alcohol.

Tawny points a finger at me, her smile brittle enough to snap at any second.

"Did you know that if a dog drinks antifreeze, you can give it Everclear as an antidote?" She laughs. "Amazing! So versatile." She looks admiringly at the mug and takes a drink, flinching. "God, it does taste awful. But worth it, for all the things it *can* do. It keeps windows shiny; it saves canine lives." Her eyes flick up to mine. "It helped your dad take *human* ones."

"You don't get to say shit like that," I snarl. "Dad's got nothing to do with this."

"On the contrary," Tawny says, taking another swig. "Your dad has . . . *everything* to do with it."

"What are you even talking about right now?"

Tawny's eyebrows pop up, her mouth dropping open. "So you haven't figured it out yet. Hmm. Guess that makes sense. How could you have? Mom was so careful. So, so careful and secretive."

"Your mom?" I whisper, confusion and sorrow stealing my breath.

"No," she says patiently. "Our mother."

I blink once. Twice. "You're delusional," I say in a low, strained voice. "I really don't know who you are."

"Yes, you do," she says. "I'm your family. The only family you have left, in fact."

Fury rises in my chest.

"Tita Anna is my family. You," I say, dripping poison, "are *nothing* to me anymore. Especially not my *family*."

Something swift and violent flares in Tawny's glare. The hand clenching the Everclear bottle shakes. There's a tight silence, like the one that follows the cocking of a gun.

"Do you know what I've done for you? What I've gone through? Just for you?" She lifts her head, her lips trembling. "How can you not know that the important stuff is all true? You're the best friend I've ever had." She closes her eyes. "I would do anything for you. Just like any loving sister would."

I feel bile rise in my throat.

"In fact, it's time we truly, officially met." Tawny holds out her hand. "Hi, River. My name is Emily King. Your sister."

I look at her hand like it's got teeth, feeling dizzy. "Twenty years ago," I say slowly, putting the pieces together. "My mom. Her pregnancy."

"It was twenty-three years, actually," Tawny says, frowning down into the mug. "From the pictures I've seen, it's clear I look more like my dad than our mom. Especially in that newspaper photo you showed me."

So that's why he had seemed so familiar. The same blue eyes. Same high cheekbones.

"Mom gave me away." Her voice falls hollow. "And it was a closed adoption. When I finally got the chance and asked her why, she told me that she'd been eighteen and had just lost the love of her life. She had no parents. No siblings. No one to help her with a little baby. She knew she wouldn't be able to take care of me." Tawny rounds the counter, pulling up the chair of a nearby table and sinking down into it.

"I was *born* unwanted. You know what that does to a person?" She leans forward. "Every night I'd lie in bed, wondering about my birth mother. I *knew* that if I could just find her, show her how much I loved her, what a good daughter I could be, my life would finally be okay.

"But I couldn't really do anything until I turned eighteen. As soon as I could, I started my search." She wags a finger. "It was tough, let me tell you. Our mom did *not* want to be found. But I finally got her name and address. Oh, little eighteen-year-old me poured her heart out to her in a letter. Handwrote it, even, to make it more sincere." She leans forward in the chair. "Can you guess what she said?"

My heartbeat roars in my ears. I barely manage a single, trembling shake of my head.

"Nothing." Tawny flicks her hand. "*Nada.* I sent her three more letters. Ignored. I thought, well, maybe I got it wrong, the address. So I came here to see for myself. Went to the address I had and—boom. There was Mom, exactly like I'd pictured. I saw the whole family. Your dad and . . . you." She gestures to me grandly. "When I saw you, I was so . . . happy."

Her eyes turn glassy with tears, but something in her face twitches. I get the feeling happiness wasn't the only emotion that came to her.

"I had a sister," she says reverently. "I had always wanted a real sister. One of my blood. One who couldn't deny me or leave me—because no matter what, we would share this." She taps a vein on her wrist. "The address on the letters was right. Mom was getting them. She was just . . . ignoring them. It hurt. I didn't understand. Why wasn't she thrilled I'd reached out? So I thought . . . well? Maybe I can meet my sister first. Your mom knew my real name from my letters, so I went by my childhood nickname—one of my childhood friends couldn't pronounce 'Emily' and called me 'Tawny' instead."

I shake my head back and forth, the horrible truth sinking in.

"Come on, River. You were there. You felt it, that first time we talked. What happened wasn't forced. It wasn't a lie. You know that." She looks at me, and for a moment, I see the Tawny I've known for years, that earnest love. "You can't fake what we have."

"Maybe no one knows me as well as you do. But that's not a two-way street. I've never known the real you."

"Yes, you have." Her voice is eerily calm. She stands abruptly. "You have," Tawny insists again. "When I enrolled at your school, yeah, I had planned to just fake a friendship to get close to Mom. But nothing was smoother than us becoming friends. It was meant to be, truly. I genuinely became a part of the family. I got to love my mom, finally. Even your dad, before it got complicated for me.

"I was too scared to say anything for the longest time. I didn't want to ruin our little family. But the longer it went on, I started feeling like I *had* to say something—it looked worse and worse the longer I kept the secret. Last year, I finally got up the guts to do it. I told Mom who I was." Even now, hurt shines in her eyes.

"She . . . wasn't as receptive as I would have liked. She didn't insist I leave all of you alone or anything like that. But she was so secretive about it. We would get lunch or coffee and talk—she didn't want to tell either you or your dad. I didn't—didn't *get* why she was so resistant!"

Her face falls, and she gets up, shuffling napkins, turning her back to me. Her voice drops. "About nine months ago . . . she finally told me why."

The hairs on my neck prickle. I can barely breathe.

"At the beginning of October, she asked to go on a sunrise hike.

Mom had something big she wanted to talk about. I got so excited. *This is it,* I thought. *She's going to tell me she's ready for me to officially come out as her daughter.* The drive there, I fantasized about moving in. Sharing a bathroom with you. Fighting over who gets to shower first in the morning.

"We hiked for a while, just shooting the shit. I couldn't stop shaking with excitement, waiting for her to bring it up. Didn't want to be pushy, though, you know? We finally get to a part of the trail with a nice little view. Perfect for a daughter proposal. Mom stops us, gets serious. *Here it comes,* I'm thinking. *Will you officially be a part of the family?*"

Tawny turns around, and tears are streaming down her cheeks. "Instead, she confessed why she'd been cagey. Told me the man responsible for my father's car crash started writing to her when he was working the Twelve Steps. It started off as letters of apology, but soon they were exchanging letters of *love.*" She curls her arms around her middle, rigid and protective.

"Can you blame me for getting upset? My rage and heartbreak and agony just . . . took over my body. I couldn't keep still, I just kept thinking, 'How could she have done this to me? She chooses the murderer over me?' Mom asked me to calm down, be careful, I was going to trip on something, fall over the edge of the cliff. I could barely hear her over all the buzzing in my head. And then—and then she grabbed my arm."

Tawny cries. Thick, soft hiccups in her throat. "River, you have to understand. You have to believe me," she squeezes out. "It was an accident. It was a complete fucking accident. When she grabbed my arm, I—I lost it. I ripped my arm out of her hands and shoved her away from me. I hadn't noticed how close to the edge we'd gotten."

*"God."* My knees buckle, and I sink to the floor. She takes a halting step forward but thinks better of it.

"It wasn't even that far of a fall, Riv. When I climbed down to the ledge to check on her, I thought she was just knocked out. But then I noticed . . . then I saw . . ." Tawny squeezes her eyes shut. "She looked like she was sleeping. It was quick. At least it was quick."

*"Mom,"* I wrench out, squeezing my legs to my chest, rocking and rocking. I've never felt more like a child. I've never felt more alone.

I've never *been* more alone.

"It was quick. At least it was—" Tawny breaks off on a sob. "I—I panicked. I did consider turning myself in. But I thought about what that'd do to you. Losing your best friend and your mom in one fell swoop? I . . . I didn't want to do that to you." Tawny gives me a look full of regret and love.

I want to claw it off her face. I want to collect her skin under my nails for what she's stolen from me.

"Maybe I deserve that," she says softly, taking in the hatred in my face. "But I don't regret choosing you."

"Don't you dare," I rasp. "Don't use me as your fucked-up excuse."

"No," she says, "not an excuse. You want to know why I had to do what I did. I never wanted your dad dead. I—I may have hated him after I found out what he did. But I never wanted to—to *kill* him. But I had to. He was onto me. I . . . I went through his phone, his notebooks. He'd started to figure it out. He had that picture of our mom and my dad. He was making a list. He didn't have much yet, but he was figuring out who I really was, what I had done. I don't know how, maybe shit Mom had left behind? I was cornered. Had to make a choice."

"Let me guess," I say acidly. "Me again."

"You were supposed to be at Noah's," she says. "I never would have if I'd known . . . When I read your text that you were *back at home*, I nearly died. Thank God I got to you in time."

I stagger to my feet, swaying. I feel like I've been carved out, my insides scraped away with a spoon. I don't know how I'm able to breathe and stand when I'm nothing but a husk of skin.

I lift my head to Tawny. My best friend. My sister.

*Emily.*

I lick my lips, tongue rough as Sonoran sand.

"How could I ever feel anything but—but revulsion and horror about you?" I say. Tawny flinches. I take a deep breath. "Rationalize all you want. But the facts remain. You killed my mother. You killed my father. You burned down my childhood home." I lean close. "You have given me the worst moments of my life."

Tawny snaps. With a shriek, she shoves me back. I catch myself on a nearby table before I fall to the floor.

"And you?" Now it's her expression that's filled with rage. "You stole the best ones from mine."

"I can't steal something that was never yours."

Tawny explodes.

*"It was mine,"* Tawny roars, bloodcurdlingly high. "If your dad hadn't gotten behind the wheel that night, you wouldn't even exist! That life was my birthright!"

"You don't even exist, Tawny! Everything in your life is a lie. *Everything.*"

Tawny grabs a mug, cocks an arm, and for one terrible moment, I'm sure she'll hurl it at my face.

But then the fight leaves her. It slips from her fingers and splinters on the floor. She buries her face in her hands.

"We had everything," she whispers into her palms. "We were a family. I had my mom, my sister." She lifts her head. "I would have done anything to hold on to it. To hold on to *you*, River. *Anything.*"

In that moment, when I look into Tawny's eyes, I see my mother coming home after a long day, talking about what she'd give for the two million dollars that could help pull us to a life without strife. That desperate gleam.

Tawny didn't want to win the lottery. She only wanted what every child deserves: a family who loves them.

"Shit," I say, my hands going to my head. I look madly at Tawny. I can never forgive her. I hate her. And?

I still love her. She's the best friend I've ever had.

A best friend who can read my mind.

"Good," Tawny sighs, taking a few ragged breaths. "That's all I can ask. Is that you understand." She wipes her eyes and straightens, oddly calm. "I need you to leave, River. Go home. Okay? Please go." There's a moment of hesitation at the kitchen door, but she slips into the back without another word.

I stare down at my hands. They've stopped shaking. What am I supposed to do? How am I supposed to make space for these coexisting impossibilities? How am I—

*What the fuck.*

I know that smell. I still smell it in my nightmares.

Smoke.

# chapter 37
# river

Black smoke has started to billow through the order window. I burst into the kitchen to find Tawny standing in front of the grill, feeding rags into an already large fire on the grill.

"Tawny, what the *fuck*?" I look around for a fire extinguisher. Tawny whirls around.

"River?" She sounds panicked. "I said *go*! Fucking *get out of here*!" Behind her, the fire is spreading on the kitchen wall, licking at the papers there, the wooden hodgepodge decorations caught on fire.

She drops the remaining rags and sprints to where I'm stooped under the sink, searching blindly for the extinguisher. Tawny yanks me to my feet.

"River, one more minute and it's too late for you. *Please, please go.*" She grabs my shirt and drags me toward the back door, but the flames are already too close to the door handle.

"Not without *you*." I cough, grabbing her arm and pulling her out of the kitchen. We're hit with a wall of smoke and heat. I'd scream, but my lungs are cooking, shriveling in the heat. The fire is spreading, engulfing the dining room.

Suddenly, it's seven months ago.

*My bedroom is filling with smoke.*

*Fireworks explode like bombs.*

"River!" Tawny's voice pulls me back. I'm on the ground, shoulder aching from where I must have collapsed.

"Come on, River, I got you." Tawny's arms go around me, and when she pulls me up, I know, I *know* that this is the second time she's done this, lifted me, pulled me up to save me from the flames.

She really did save me that night. I grab her hand.

"Let's go," I yell over the creaks and groans of wooden beams splintering. Thank God she doesn't argue.

It's hard to see where the front door is anymore. I can barely keep my eyes open, the smoke stinging. In halting steps, we make our way to the front, kick over plastic chairs, distorted and melting from the flames.

I stumble forward, Tawny slipping from my fingers, and nearly sob with relief when I catch a glimpse of the door.

Behind me, Tawny screams, followed by a deafening crash. I whirl around. I can't see her through the clouds of smoke and dust filling my throat.

"Tawny!" I scream.

No answer.

Freedom is one step ahead of me. I have a split second of hesitation before I turn back toward the hellfire and brimstone, looking desperately for Tawny.

In two seconds, my foot hits something soft. It's a limp hand belonging to Tawny, who's pinned beneath a pile of debris.

She's not moving.

There's another crash behind Tawny, louder this time. I've got no choice.

I grab her arm and pull.

Her eyes shoot open. *Thank God,* I think.

"What the fuck are you doing?" I can only see half her face, the other side coated in blood. *"Leave me,"* she moans, her face twisting in pain as I ignore her. She screams in agony as I yank her up and throw her arm around my shoulder. One of her legs is dangling at an impossible angle. I look away, my stomach lurching.

The front door's no longer visible in the black wall of smoke, but I know where it is. Just a few more hobbling steps, and we'll be free.

I can't breathe through the smoke, and fire, and pain. Flames dance all around us, swallowing the pictures of Gertie from thirty years ago, the torn red seats, the worn carpet runner that took me months to stop tripping over.

"We're gonna die here," Tawny chokes out.

It's happening again. Things I love turning to ash.

*But not me.* I refuse.

"We're gonna make it," I grunt. "Hold your breath." Digging deep, I lunge into the wall of smoke. But then a support pillar to my right cracks in half. In the blink of an eye, it swings wildly, smashing into my knee. Something snaps inside my leg, and ungodly pain explodes from a point under my kneecap, sending Tawny and me crashing through the front door and onto the ground.

We take a collective gasping breath, sucking in the clean, sweet, oven-hot Arizona night. I try to pull Tawny along, clawing across the asphalt, away from the giant fire that was once Gertie's Diner.

Tawny looks half-dead as she hacks so hard she vomits, a yarn of red spit dangling from her charred lips. The pale bone of her skull glows in the throbbing light. I catch a glimpse of her ruined, wrong-way leg, and my hacking turns to retching as well.

Police sirens howl in the distance, getting louder and louder.

Tawny's pinkie brushes my hand. My fingers twitch, but I don't pull away.

Tawny's lips move, forming silent words: *I'm sorry.*

# chapter 38
# logan

I toss my garbage into my complex's dumpster. The breeze shifts, and that's when I smell it. The sour stink of garbage morphs into smoke. I shut the door to the waste enclosure, perturbed. Smoke's not great at the best of times, but this smell during a Red Flag Warning feels like a harbinger of calamity.

When I round a building toward the parking lot, the smell grows stronger. A police siren cuts through the silence of the night, then another, too loud, too close.

I'm already sprinting toward the road. Those sirens are coming from the direction of the diner. I turn the corner and see the column of smoke, the sky glowing. I sprint harder.

The fire comes into view first, an infernal monster that's eaten the sky. Then the smoke. Then the diner, or what's left of it, being consumed, burned alive. My lungs will explode, but I dig deep, run faster, while my brain is going haywire with fear.

*River.*

I have no idea if she was working tonight, no idea what I'll find at the scene.

Just as I arrive, two figures burst through the front doors in a shower of glass shards and blackened splinters and collapse onto the pavement.

*"River!"* I scream, mindless with terror. She doesn't hear me, but she's alive, dragging Tawny behind her.

Thank God, thank God, thank God.

By the time I'm on my knees beside her and Tawny, she's limp, unconscious. They both are. There's a wooden crack and the threatening groan of collapse behind us.

The sirens are closer but not close enough. I don't know how much time I've got, so as swiftly and gently as possible, I lift the girls, one with each arm, and pull them a safe distance away.

As soon as I've laid them down carefully, I fall to my knees at River's side, touching her ash-streaked face. Tawny's leg is facing the wrong way. I can see her skull. River's knee is twice the size it should be. Bloody.

There's blood everywhere.

I'm suddenly desperate. Half out of my mind. I touch her neck, but my fingers are shaking too hard. Can't find a pulse. I bring my ear to her mouth. Her nose. Listen like my life depends on it.

It does.

The crackles and roar of the fire and the siren are too loud. I can't hear her breathe.

"River," I croak. I bring my forehead to hers in a featherlight touch. *"River,"* I beg. I wipe red spittle from the corner of her mouth, feel no movement. Her beautiful face is still. I press my nose to her hair. She smells like fireworks. I nearly lose it right then and there.

"Don't do this to me, Riv," I whisper urgently. "Please. *Please don't do this to me.*"

"We need you to step back, son." An EMT is hovering above, motioning for me to give them space. I sit up but keep a hand on River's arm. That's when I notice the crowd around us—neighbors, rubberneckers, first responders. Everyone is watching, but I can only watch the EMT opposite me, kneeling on the other side of River, hooking up instruments to check her vitals.

"Is she alive?" I whisper.

"Kid." Another EMT kneels beside me. "I need you to get back, okay?"

*"Is she alive?"* I say, voice breaking.

"I've got a pulse!" shouts the EMT across from me, pressing an oxygen mask to River's face, and I'm so overwhelmed, so relieved, I nearly collapse.

Tawny's already on a stretcher getting loaded into an ambulance, and I catch sight of her right before they close the doors. A loud hiss bursts behind me, and I whirl around, disoriented from the feeling of being suddenly surrounded by firefighters as they wield the spewing arc of water from the fire hose. Not even two fire trucks can pull my attention away from River.

When they load River on a stretcher, I stay close, just outside the orbit of paramedics and EMTs surrounding her. They load her into the back of the ambulance, and even though they're doing a great job, I have to suppress the irrational urge to scream. *Be more gentle, goddamn it.*

"Can I come with her?" I ask one of the EMTs as he leaps into the back beside River.

"Sure," he says, adjusting the oxygen tank. "Go sit shotgun with Mikey up front."

I don't move. He looks up, sees me. Frowns.

"Please," I say quietly. "I won't be in the way. I won't say a thing. I just need to be with her."

*"What's the holdup?"* crackles a voice from his radio, and he sighs.

"Get in, kid. But not one goddamn word, got it?"

I lift myself carefully into the back. The doors close as soon as I've cleared them. I spot a seat in the corner where I'll be out of the way.

I feel a touch at my wrist, faint as a whisper. I look down and take a hitching, wet breath.

*"Logan,"* River breathes, her swollen eyes finding mine.

"I'm here." I touch her face, her fingers at my wrist. "I'm here, River." But her eyes close again, her fingers slack and sliding to the gurney.

"All right, kid. We're moving. Go sit." His voice is kind.

I have no problem obeying. Hearing River's voice will get me through the ambulance ride. Because it means she's going to be okay. River's going to be okay.

She *has* to be. There's no universe I can live in where she isn't okay.

Because there's no universe that exists where I don't love her more than anything.

*To my baby girl,*

*Here it is. The truth I've been promising. I met your father when I was only fifteen. By the time I was seventeen, I was pregnant. Danny, your dad, was full of life. He laughed with his whole body. His smile lit up his whole face. But he was a complicated man. His childhood had been hard, so much harder than any childhood should be. And I think some part of him felt he didn't deserve to be here. He tempted death at every turn. He jumped off cliffs into lakes without knowing how deep the waters were. He drove fast, too fast.*

*I'd always worried your father would accidentally kill himself, but in the end, it was a drunk driver who ended his life, and suddenly I found myself alone, barely eighteen, broke, and desperate. I was not fit to be a parent. I agonized every second of every day, but I knew, deep down, I wasn't ready to be your mother. I knew someone else, someone older, more stable, less sad, would love you better.*

*I made the hardest, best, and worst choice of my life: I gave you up.*

*Then the man who killed your father wrote me a note from jail, apologizing profusely, devastated at what he'd done. His name is Jacob Santos. At first I was furious. Who was he to write me? He had destroyed my life. But when I wrote to tell him that, he wrote back again, and again, and again. And I found myself writing back again, and again, and again.*

*And I found myself forgiving him. And then I found myself falling in love with him, this man who had worked so hard to make up for this awful thing he'd done. And soon I found myself pregnant with a new baby girl.*

*I have had so much trouble living with my decision to give you up. And whenever I feel that sadness coming on, I leave for the hills, to hike, to protect my other daughter from this pain that eats me alive.*

*I've been wanting to find you for years. But how could I ever explain that I fell in love with the man who killed your father? That just a few years later I had a baby that I did keep? How could you ever forgive me?*

*All I know is this: I love you. I will always love you. And one day, I hope we will find our way to each other. I will give you these letters. And then, maybe, if I'm lucky, we can begin anew.*

*Love,*
*Mom*

## chapter 39

# river

A knock sounds on my door, and Tita Anna and I look up to see Officer Yeoman hovering in the doorway, a bundle of papers in his hands.

"This an okay time?" he asks.

"I have nowhere else to be," I say, gesturing to the various tubes coming out of my arm and the hospital bed beneath me.

Being back in the hospital is the worst sort of déjà vu. Once again, I have survived a fire. Once again, my life has shifted beneath my feet.

I have lost my mother.

I have lost my father.

I have lost part of myself.

And now I have lost my best friend. My *sister*.

Yes, Tawny—*Emily*, I correct myself—survived the fire. She's in the hospital too, somewhere, on a locked ward. They'll take her to prison once she's well enough. Officer Yeoman told me that the last time he was here.

"Since you've been doing better," he says, "I thought you might like to take a look at these."

He puts the bundles of papers on my lap. I pluck a frail, yellowed page from the pile, blinking.

"We found them in the pocket of your mother's hiking jacket," he says softly. "They're letters. Lots of them. We didn't understand them at the time, but now . . ." He trails off. "Your mom, she was writing them to her 'baby girl.' To Tawny. There are also letters between your parents, and letters to you . . . Well, you'll understand when you read."

I nod, my eyes starting to water when I unfold the first piece of paper and see my mother's handwriting there.

"She didn't want to leave you, River," Officer Yeoman says gruffly. "The letters . . . well, she says it all in the letters."

He bows his head and heads back into the hallway.

Tita Anna looks at me with concern. "Are you sure you're ready for that?"

I nod. "I've been waiting for answers for nearly ten months. It's time."

And with that I fully unfold the letters and begin to read.

*Dear Miss Cole,*

*My name is Jacob Santos, and I am the man who fell asleep, drunk, at the wheel, blocking Mud Springs Road last October. I am the reason your fiancé had to swerve on that winding road, and I am extremely sorry.*

*If you are still reading at this point, I am deeply grateful. You see, I'm working through the 12 steps of AA and am making amends to those I have hurt while I was in active addiction.*

*I have not hurt anyone as much as I have hurt you.*

*I am truly sorry for my behavior. I regret the trouble I caused you. It was never my intention to hurt you and your family. These are the best words my sponsor could help me come up with when I told him it was you I was writing.*

*I told him these words were a pebble when I needed a boulder. I cannot find words to encompass how sorry I am: I tried. I spent two days Asking Jeeves and combing through Webster's.*

*I take full responsibility for my actions and everything that happened that night. My alcohol addiction was a significant factor in this tragedy. I am committed to my recovery and changing my life so this never happens again, as long as I live.*

*I would like to make things right, if possible. In any way.*

*And I'm here to listen to anything you need to say. I know my apology will never be enough to heal the hurt I caused. But I will do anything to try.*

*Very sincerely and forever sorry,*
*Jacob Santos*

My eyes blurring with tears, I'm about to reread this letter when a small, yellow, aged paper slips out from the haphazard pile in my hands. A letter in Mom's handwriting. It's undated, and I don't know if it was her first letter, her third, or her last. But it's the one that says everything.

*Jacob,*

*Thanks for being so patient while I took my time responding to your letter. I think I finally have figured out my answer to your question.*

*The truth is, forgiving you for that night feels impossible.*

*But one day, I think: I will be ready to try.*

*Jen*

The tears spill over, and I put the stack of letters down. I will read them all, every last heartbreaking word, because it's the story of my family. The real one. The one I thought had died with my parents.

I've lost so much, but this shows that I haven't lost everything. Because this pile of letters contains more than I even knew to hope for:

The truth.

# chapter 40
# river

The next time I wake up, Logan is here.

He's pacing at the foot of my bed, chewing his thumb. I've never seen him do that, Mr. Unflappable. It makes everything inside me, from collarbone to belly, do a somersault. Even after everything, Logan's got a direct line to my heart.

"Hey," I whisper, because he's still pacing. He startles and stands frozen at the foot of my bed. For a moment, he gazes at me like I'm a miracle. But then he clears his throat shakily and makes his way to my bedside, grim once more.

Logan sinks down into his chair, his perfect face tense. He swallows hard, pressing a hand over his forehead for a moment, wiping it all the way down his face. He takes one of my hands, tracing a finger along the back of my knuckle.

I have the thought once more that it's terribly unfair how Logan's so beautiful. Like right now? Shadows weigh down his bloodshot, red-rimmed eyes. His injuries aren't healed, his skin still a canvas of violet and liver yellow. Anyone else would look haggard, decades older.

Logan looks battle worn. If a casting agent caught a passing glimpse of him right now, in two months he'd be playing a warrior prince, dashing in dirty armor after a brutal victory.

"I thought I lost you," he croaks. "For a moment there, I really thought . . ."

"Wait. Logan. Were you . . ." I have to talk slow. My throat's killing me.

Logan's face flinches. He nods once, his fingers spasming around mine.

"You scared the shit out of me, Riv. If you'd . . ." Logan inches forward in his chair. "I never would have recovered. Losing you. Never." I squeeze his hand hard, and he squeezes back harder.

*Holy God*, my blood sings, *do I love him.*

"I'll never let anything happen to you again," Logan whispers.

I start trembling, and Logan turns my hand over, maps the tender place on my palm where he once pinched. Taking my wrist, he drags his thumb lightly across the sensitive underside, tracing my veins. It's so, so good.

The heart rate monitor's beeping increases.

Logan's gaze flies to the readings, face flooding with panic. He drops my hand.

"Should I go get a—?" He lunges for the nurse call button, but I stop him with my hand on his arm. He frowns, confused. But then his gaze falls on my embarrassed face, my spreading blush, the rise and fall of my chest, and his expression clears. Then turns heated.

Logan's smirk is so hot and completely insufferable.

The beeping ratchets up again.

He leans close, his breath rustling the hair at my temple.

"You all right, there, Santos?" he murmurs. "Can't help but notice you're looking a little . . . *flushed*."

I can barely lift a finger, but Logan's voice has my entire body clenching from a fierce surge of arousal. My lips part, my eyes fluttering. I'm aching to kiss him, to feel his hands on my body. There's been so much pain, a whole lot of back-to-back *awful* in my life. Is it so bad to want to feel good for once?

Logan's mouth barely brushes mine, and the machine sounds like it's about to explode.

"Wait," I gasp, shocking us both.

Logan freezes and pulls back. The confusion on his face swiftly melts into shame.

"You're right. Shit, I'm an asshole." He puts distance between us, taking steadying breaths. "You almost died, and here I am trying to steal a kiss. God, I'm so sorry." He rakes a hand through his hair, back and forth, back and forth. "Okay. I won't touch you until you feel better." Logan lifts a hand, as if taking an oath.

"No, Logan." I take some deep breaths, and the beeping finally slows, fading into the background.

Logan blinks rapidly. He ducks his head, but I still catch the flash of hurt. This is excruciating. Because I *do* want all of those things with him. He broke my heart, and still I want him. I know how sorry he is, how much he regrets everything. How he would do it all over if he could. My parents have shown me that we are more than our worst moments, and that with work and trust, forgiveness and healing are possible.

But if I want to grow, if I want to learn to trust myself, my decisions, my gut . . . if I want to learn how to be brave, I'm going to need to learn how to take care of myself. And to do that, especially after everything I've been through this past year, I need time and space.

"I'm sorry," I whisper. "I can't."

Logan flinches like I've knifed his guts. Agony floods the blue of his eyes, confusion wrenching his face. He takes a step back, pulling his arms tight against his body.

I have to look away; otherwise I'll change my mind.

"Not saying never. Just not now. Not yet." There's a long silence. When I peer back, Logan's face is unreadable. "I need time, Logan. Space. After . . ."

I wave a hand to indicate, well, *everything.*

Logan nods, giving me a long look, his tongue pressing against the inside of his cheek. Something rises in his eyes, something that looks like heartbreak.

In a halting movement, he steps forward, reaching for me, mouth open. He looks desperate, and for a moment, I think he might beg. I'm not proud that a part of me sort of wants him to.

He deflates all at once, nodding to himself. Chuckling softly, he drops his chin.

"Of course you do, Santos." Logan gives me a brave smirk. "Take all the time you need." He pats my hand. "You'll need it. Recover that voice. Write some songs. Sell out some stadiums." Logan clears his throat, grimacing. "And we should all probably get therapy. Lots and lots of therapy." He rubs the back of his head.

"Especially you," I tease.

Logan raises a brow but concedes a soft laugh.

"Especially me," he says before falling serious.

"I'll call. When I'm ready." I sink back into my pillows, exhausted. I could sleep for decades.

Logan gives me a long, searching look.

"River, I . . ." He cuts himself off, turning his face over his shoulder.

After a moment, he huffs a warm laugh. On his way out, Logan pauses at the open door. "Take care of yourself, Santos. I'll be here. When . . ." He takes a breath. "*If* . . . you're ever ready." He gives me a lopsided grin, and I can't help but smile back. I hope he can see it there. Everything I feel for him.

*You'll be okay, Logan,* I think.

*And one day, maybe, so will I.*

# six months later

## chapter 41

# river

It's January in Scottsdale. It feels like everywhere else in the world is covered in snow, but here the days are clear and steady, perfect seventies stretching out in front of us, just like the desert racing past our car on the freeway.

In the passenger seat, Tita Anna is zooming in on a picture on her phone.

"River, I'm *serious*, it's him."

"No way. I do not believe that Ryan Gosling just happens to be in the background of one of your Italy pictures." I laugh.

After a few seconds of staring, she tosses the phone aside.

"Okay," she says sullenly, "maybe it wasn't Ryan Gosling." I snort and see Tita Anna shoot me a glare in my periphery. "Don't laugh—they could be twins, I swear! You didn't get to see him. You were off getting your fourth gelato of the day. He was like an *Italian* Ryan Gosling."

"If you say so."

"All right, all right. It's your turn. Favorite moment: go."

I drum my fingers on the steering wheel thoughtfully.

"Let's see . . . I loved when that pigeon pooped right into your coffee cup." I make a splashing sound, pantomiming the splatter with my fingers.

"You are very lucky that happened, young lady." She sniffs. "We were about to get fined, but the polizia were far too charmed by me and my pigeon poop to follow through."

"I liked when it snowed on Christmas Eve and we drank mulled wine and bought five bags of candied chestnuts at the Christmas market." I shoot her a soft smile.

"Ah," she says, "good choice. That was the best." Tita Anna hums "Good King Wenceslas" under her breath, caught in a happy memory. "Your dad," she says, "would have eaten his weight in those chestnuts."

"Oh God," I say, "he would have made us hide bags of them from Mom inside our luggage."

"Ooh, she would have caught us too."

"Naturally. And Dad would have gotten a talking-to about the risks of diabetes, the dangers of sugar . . ." I let out a bittersweet sigh. Tita Anna looks out the window, her smile soft and tender.

"Yeah, but then he would have used them to make the best damn cookies in the world, and all would have been forgiven."

I nod. "That's exactly how it would have played out."

We sit in meditative silence for a minute or two, content to watch the desert fly by us, dazzling in the winter sun.

It's nice being back in Arizona. There's room to breathe here. The Sonoran feels infinite. *Take all the space you need,* the saguaros seem to say, bowing like butlers. It's exactly what I've needed. Space. Space to process my feelings. Space to feel my feelings. Space to have absolute, magnificent breakdowns.

But also space to rediscover joy and hope.

The sign for our impending exit flashes by. Before I change lanes, I do a quick check of my blind spot. The way I brace my leg sends a quick, sharp pang through my knee. I wince, rubbing at the area.

"I was gonna ask how your leg was doing," Tita Anna says.

"All that walking in Italy probably didn't help. Worth it, of course." The pain still comes and goes. But the good days are finally starting to outnumber the bad. I'm starting to see the possibility of this thing healing one day.

I take the next exit ramp and we pass by Gertie's—the new Gertie's. The rebuilding was completed while we were away. Tita Anna and I smile at each other. It's new, but it looks familiar in the best way. I still recognize the diner where I ate my first Belgian waffle at the age of seven. The same one I'd worked at since I was fifteen.

It's the last standing remnant of my childhood. And I didn't lose it after all. In fact, for my contribution, Gertie made me the only other owner. It'll give me some passive income to fund my music, my eventual schooling, and lend a helping hand to those who find themselves drowning in the cost of life.

And it's healing. I'd thought it gone, the years in those booths with Mom and Dad, the carrot cakes, their laughter over black cups of coffee, all made ash. But we'd brought it back.

At the next red light I hit, I reach into the middle console and pull out a long, slim strip of cloth.

"Put this on, Tita Anna." I offer her the cloth, and she looks at me like I've asked her to eat a live frog.

"Put it on what?" She raises a brow. "Is this a thong?"

I snort. "It's a blindfold."

"Oh, good," she says, wary. "Way better."

I stamp my good leg impatiently. "Titaaa," I whine. "This is a nice surprise thingy, okay? Can you just do it? We're almost there, and you *have* to be blindfolded."

"Sheesh, fine, fine. Anything for a nice surprise—thingy." She points a finger at me. "But if this is some sort of prank where you drop me in the middle of the desert—"

I roll my eyes. "I'd never do that. You wouldn't survive three minutes out there."

Tita Anna scoffs but ties the blindfold on just the same. I wave my hand in front of her face, and when she doesn't ask me to quit it, I know it's secure.

My heartbeat kicks up a notch in anticipation.

The Old Historic District still has its Christmas decorations up. It's a good sign. They're kindred spirits who hate letting go of the holidays just as much as I do.

I turn into Canyon Crest Village, and after a few more turns, I roll to a stop.

"We're here," I singsong.

"And where, O niece of mine, is 'here' exactly?"

I leap out of the car and run to open her door.

"Home," I say as I help guide her out of the car.

When she's standing right where I want her, I say, "Okay, blindfold off!" She rips it off eagerly, and her face falls slack with shock.

I've placed her squarely in the center of the brick path that leads to the steps of the front porch—the front porch that's large enough for two swinging benches. They're currently swaying in the gentle breeze. Tita Anna's face stays frozen as she sweeps her gaze over the front yard, lush with clusters of prickly pear, bushes of desert lavender, and multicolored native wildflowers.

Tita Anna looks at the house, looks at me, then looks back at the house.

"River?" She frowns. "I don't understand. What is this?"

“This,” I say, taking her hand, “is our new house.” I press a key into her palm. “The good news is, the morning market isn’t until tomorrow, so you have time to make a grocery list.”

Tita Anna stares at the key, blinking rapidly.

“This house,” she says slowly, “is my dream house. In my dream neighborhood. Did you buy it? For us?”

“Merry belated Christmas, Tita,” I say warmly, throwing my arms around her neck.

“Holy shit, River,” she says tearfully against my hair. “I can’t even. I don’t know what to . . . this is way beyond . . . *I got you an Etsy gift card for Christmas, River.*” She pulls back, her fingernails digging into my shoulders, her eyes bulging. “You never have to get me a present again. Jesus, Mary, and *Joseph*.”

I laugh. “I wanted to live here too,” I say. “Technically, it’s also a gift to myself.”

Noah told me everything that happened. In a shocking team-up, Logan and he joined forces. Together, they’re going to tell the state medical board about his dad. Then he told me in no uncertain terms that he would not be taking back his donation. So I did what he told me months ago. I spent the goddamn money.

I lead Tita Anna to the front door. “Would you like to do the honors?” I gesture to the lock.

She vibrates with excitement as she slots the key in the hole and unlocks it with a satisfying click. As soon as we step through the front door, Tita Anna gasps.

I don’t know if I’ve gone overboard, but after living for so long in a soulless, gray-spirited rental, I figured we desperately needed bursts of color. And eclectic decor is Tita Anna’s exact taste, so I went all out.

The foyer walls are covered in a luxe wallpaper featuring a dramatic tropical vista, a vibrant emerald splashed with colorful rainforest foliage. A bright yellow table sits beside the door to hold keys and wallets.

"Come on, the living room is so fun." I pull at her arm.

"I'm not done staring at this wallpaper," she says.

"You live here now. Make staring at the wallpaper part of your morning routine."

The living room is a favorite of mine. It has high ceilings and huge windows next to French doors that open to the patio and backyard. Our view is an infinite stretch of red desert and far-flung mountains—and a saguaro pup, culled from the one beside my father's grave.

The floor is beautiful wide-plank white oak. Accent rugs are scattered throughout the room, all shaped like slices of fruit. Two oversized teal velvet couches are bracketed by bookshelves on either side, stacked with all of Tita Anna's books and then some.

Tita Anna's head is on a swivel. She can't seem to decide whether she wants to look out the wall of windows at the mountains or at the giant plush tomato slice on the floor.

"How the hell, River? *When* the hell?"

"I arranged for it all to happen while we were in Europe." I smile.

Tita Anna wraps me in a hug. "It's perfect."

We stand there together for a beat, taking it all in. Above the couch is the gallery wall I designed: pictures of me, Mom, Dad, and Anna are arranged in a collage of smiling faces. In my room, I know the guitar Logan gave me is leaning on its stand, waiting to be played. Somewhere in the house Tigery is curled up, napping.

Tita Anna is right. It is perfect.

## chapter 42

# river

It's almost seven months to the day since I saw her loaded into the back of an ambulance, her face bleeding and her leg mangled.

The moment the correctional officer leads her into the visitation room, her eyes find mine. I wonder if, even after all this time, something within me calls to her. I have the sudden urge to pull my hoodie's zipper up to my throat. So I do.

Her hair is shorter now, the tips brushing her shoulders. Her eyes still blazing hazel. She's not allowed to dye her hair here, so she's back to her original, lemon-bright blond, identical to our mother's. Her skin is pale, wan.

And then there's the scar. It runs like a pink, puckered river along the left side of her face from her crown to her chin.

She is so beautiful.

Her gaze never leaves mine as the CO brings her to me. I can't tell if her limp is from the injury or the tight shackles on her ankles, bunching up the fabric of her orange jumpsuit. As soon as she's touching my table, she loses her nerve and looks down. We stay silent as she slides into the chair across from me.

It takes me a few moments before I decide what to say.

"You got a haircut."

She lifts her gaze from her lap.

"You got a piercing," she says. I touch the tiny green stud in the left side of my nose. "I like it," she adds.

"Really?" I twist the jewel uncertainly. "Thanks."

We fall back into a brittle quiet.

On the drive here, I had wondered which of us would be the braver of the two. Which one of us would have it in them to say the first real thing to the other.

I had assumed her. Easily. So I surprise myself.

I jut my chin at the CO. "He seems fun," I say. "He look that constipated all the time or just on days that end in *y*?"

For a moment, she doesn't react. I worry it wasn't the time to joke, but then suddenly, she lets out a laugh. It's loud, surprising, and achingly familiar. The CO startles and shoots a frown our way. She shakes her head.

Her eyes dance across my face, and for a moment, *there she is*. Then bit by bit, her smile fades. She clears her throat and rolls her shoulders. She falls into what must be Default Prison Emily.

"So what's . . ." I clear my throat. "How are you?"

"Well," she says solemnly, "I'm right where I deserve to be." Her cuffs rattle as Emily rubs at a smudge on the table. "I've been learning braille, actually. We turn textbooks into braille for blind kids who can't afford them. Did you know that just five chapters of a braille science book is like fifteen grand? Like, how the hell do these assholes expect anyone to afford that?"

"No idea," I say. I can't look at her when she sounds like that—like Tawny.

"Yeah." Her eyes flick nervously to me. "I'm doing some therapy too. Anger management. DBT. And I go to group when I can." Her bottom lip trembles, her voice dropping to a whisper. "I know it's not much. Not yet. But I hope . . ." Her voice breaks.

I don't know what she wants me to say. I shift in my seat, uneasy. I accidentally knock my bad knee into the table.

*"Shit,"* I hiss, sucking in a rough breath. Pain shoots through my shin and up my hip.

"Still?" Emily stares down at the table, as if she can see straight through to where I'm rubbing my kneecap below.

"Yeah. But it's getting better." I recall how her leg dangled that night, bent into unnatural angles. "Yours still hurt?"

She stretches her mouth into a thin-lipped smile. "Every fucking day," she says.

Another silence.

Emily leans back in her chair. "Why did you come to see me?"

I pull out the stack of letters—the ones my mom wrote to Emily—and place them between us.

"These were found with Mom," I say. "They're letters to you."

"What?" Emily asks.

"She wrote them on her hikes. She was always thinking about you, Emily. She never stopped loving you."

Emily blinks rapidly. Part of me wants to stay, to be with her when she reads them. But I can't. I just can't. Because it should've been Mom giving these to her—it would've been if—

I scoot my chair back, clapping my thighs. "Well," I say, "good luck with—"

"Wait." Emily leans in. "I know I shouldn't ask." There's the faintest sound of chains tinkling, and I realize her hands are shaking. "Is there ever a chance, even the tiniest one, that you could . . . ?" She slumps in her chair. "Fuck, I can't even say it."

I smooth my hands on the table, wondering how many hundreds, if not thousands, of people have sat in this very seat and squirmed through this exact conversation.

"You want to know if I could ever forgive you."

Emily's face floods with shame. "Yes," she whispers. "Not anytime in this decade or anything. I just want to know if it's possible."

I study her face.

"Forgiving you feels impossible," I finally say.

Emily bows her head. "Of course."

*"But,"* I say. She tilts her head up slightly. "But one day, I think: I will be ready to try." I chew my lip, seeing how true the words feel suspended between us.

Emily's shackles clink as she wipes her cheeks.

"Thank you," she says quietly. And maybe it's my answer that's given her enough courage, enough hope, to ask her next question.

"River," she breathes. "Why did you save me that night?"

I shake my head. Because I don't really know the answer to this question either. It wasn't a decision I made consciously. We were surrounded by an inferno, and I had seconds left to escape.

I think back to that moment seven months ago, when the world was crumbling into fire and brimstone around us. I picture myself turning back to save Tawny—*Emily*—buried in the rubble behind me. And I know even after everything, I would do it again.

I would still save her.

"I don't understand myself," I confess. "I can only tell you that when it came down to it?" I catch Emily's eyes. "I couldn't let my sister die."

There's a moment of silence before Emily crumples and begins to weep. The CO barks at Emily to be quiet, and she sucks in her sobs.

"I should go," I say, and she nods, staring at her hands. The drag of the chair is a terrible, screeching sound.

"Hey, River?" Emily calls. "Are you . . . okay?" The smile she gives me is so gentle and earnest, I feel my heart sink. Because there she is again—the old Tawny. Those big hazel eyes that never looked more worried than when I was hurt or crying or sad. That same face framed by our mother's golden hair.

The longer I look at her, the more I realize: There's no "Old Tawny" and "New Emily." They aren't two different people. The person I knew and loved is the same person sitting here now, shackled and draped in orange.

My sister.

And just like that day I was crying in the walk-in, huddled on a carton of oranges, she wants to make sure I'm okay.

"Yeah, Emily," I say, "I will be."

When the CO opens the door for me, I pause, unable to resist one last look over my shoulder. Emily's looking at me like I knew she would be.

The smile she gives me is as reverent and hopeful as an Arizona sunrise.

## chapter 43

# river

This is the last song.

All the lights dim in the Prickly Pear. This stage once held too many ghosts for me to return, but now the lone spotlight cleanses me, the mic, and my guitar in a beam bright as a solar flare. The stage lights are hot, and my pulse is thrumming, delicious and electric.

I begin the song by picking a naked, earnest melody on my steel strings. With the lights in my eyes, I can't see the crowd. But like any higher power, I don't need to. They hear me and see me and are waiting for my worship to begin. So I lift my head and begin to pray.

Thinking of my music as a religion feels apt. Because every time I start singing onstage, I'm sure this is what heaven would feel like.

My voice starts out soft and slow. I hear a few voices singing along with me, the words I've written on their tongue.

Then I shift the energy, my voice rising, louder and louder. The crowd claps and cheers as I lift the neck of my guitar, then swing it down. Just as I do, the entire stage lights up and the crowd erupts.

This is what it's like to fly. I know it.

I throw back my head, full-throated and feverish, and I sing. I sing for my dad and my mom.

But especially, I sing for me. This is what will heal me and how I hope to heal others.

With a final chord ringing out, the song ends, and the crowd goes wild.

"Excuse me?"

I look down to see two girls, one redheaded, the other brunette, both with bold eyeliner and shy smiles, leaning over the edge of the stage. They can't be older than fifteen.

"We just wanna say we loved the show," the girl with red hair says. She's dancing from one foot to the other, nervous.

"I've seen you here three times already," the brunette says, blushing.

I kneel on the stage so we're at eye level. "You don't know what that means to me," I say. "Thank you so much for coming."

"Will you sign this?" The redhead holds up a shirt. I grab the proffered Sharpie, choked up from the ask.

"We love this shirt design—we couldn't stop talking about it, and we were wondering . . . where'd you get the inspiration for your name?"

I smile, smoothing a hand down the front of the shirt.

The designers, Claire and Lindsey, really did do a good job. The shirt is a light amethyst, and the words UNBURNED ISLAND are in a deep, royal purple. Underneath the name is a logo: the silhouette of a cluster of trees in the center of a large fire.

"Well," I begin, "in biology my junior year, I learned that it can take a forest up to three hundred years to recover after a wildfire. That broke my heart. But my teacher offered up a kernel of hope. She said after a wildfire sweeps through forests, occasionally a section of land will remain untouched. A tiny forest of untouched trees, surrounded by acres of ruin, stands resilient to the flames." I look up at the two girls, who are listening with rapt attention.

"Those are the unburned islands," I say, "and they work together to help speed up the recovery of the forest. The remnants help rebuild everything that's lost. Hence, the logo." I trace the outline with my finger.

"Amazing," the brunette says.

After I sign their shirts, I watch the girls go. My pocket buzzes. I pull out my phone and see I've gotten a text from Tita Anna.

**Tita Anna**

Was the show amazing? Of course it was! Can't wait to see you in action. Speaking of, question: am I too old to crowd surf?

I laugh and text her back with a definitive No!

I'm carefully wrapping my microphone cord when the overhead lights begin shutting off. The owner, Mitch, must be getting impatient.

"Look, I'm so sorry to bother you, miss," says a warm, deep voice behind me.

My pulse soars. I straighten my spine and flip my hair when I spin around.

Logan's leaning against a wooden column at the side of the stage, his hands tucked into his jeans. He's wearing a dark button-up, his sleeves rucked to his elbows. I love when he does that. His forearms are mouthwatering, much like the rest of him.

"I was just wondering if you could help me. I'm conducting an experiment." His mouth twitches.

"What kind of experiment?" I close the distance between us, his eyes darkening the closer I get.

"Well." Logan's eyelids narrow. "I have a theory that the better the singer, the better the kisser." He jerks his head toward the open room. "I caught your show tonight, and now I'm thinking you might just be the best kisser on the whole damn planet."

I slide my hands up his chest, following the dips and contours of his muscles. Logan's jaw clenches. Seeing how a simple touch of my hand still affects him nearly has me breaking. But Playful Logan is so fun. I want to keep it going as long as I can stand resisting him.

Which is probably for about thirty more seconds.

"You know," I say, my voice already husky. "I already have a boyfriend." Logan takes on a possessive gleam. He hooks a finger in one of the belt loops of my shorts, pulling my hips close.

"Of course you do." He drops his head, brushing his lips against my earlobe. "What if I told you I don't care?"

*God.* The spicy smell of his skin has my knees near buckling. But then there's everything *else*. His voice, his hands, his lips, his eyes, his face—ugh, his *everything*.

I keep waiting for my appetite for Logan Evans to cool even slightly. You'd think several months of indulging our mutual insatiability would take the edge off, even just a little.

As I run my hands underneath the back of his shirt, I decide that I'm happy to keep trying to get my fill of Logan, even if it takes me the rest of my life.

"You're bad news, aren't you?" I brush my top lip against the tender underside of his jaw. His breath hitches.

"The worst," he murmurs, capturing my mouth with his. I press the entire length of my body into his, fitting against him like we were made for each other.

Logan slides his fingers up the back of my neck, burying his hand in my hair and pulling. I make a keening sound in my throat, swiping my tongue against his lips.

"Let's get out of here," Logan murmurs. He drops his hands to the waistband of my jeans and pulls me tight against him.

"But my equipment—"

"Can wait." He dips his head and bites my neck. "*I* can't."

A floodlight flicks on, and Logan and I jump, holding up a hand to shield the blinding light.

"I swear to God, I'm gonna get a hose installed just for you two idiots." Mitch scowls at us as he emerges from the shadows, grabbing at cords and wrapping them up violently. "It's late. Go home. Fantastic job. See you in a few days."

"Thanks, Mitch—" I begin.

"Goodbye. Go home." He waves me away, stalking back into the shadows.

Logan helps me gather my equipment, and we're out the door in less than ten minutes. He shifts everything to one arm, freeing up a hand so he can lace our fingers together. My pulse flutters like a hummingbird.

"I saw people crying in the audience tonight, during that last one." Logan squeezes my hand. "You're the real deal, River. They loved it."

We load all the equipment into the trunk, slamming it shut.

"What about you?" I say, giving him a wry smile. "Did you like it?" Logan gives me the eye roll of the century before sweeping me up and gently setting me on the back of the car.

"I still can't find the top of my head." He kisses me. "I loved it, and

I love you." He kisses the tip of my nose. "So much." He snags my bottom lip between his teeth.

"Ha," I say, the effect ruined by how breathless I am. "You're obsessed with me."

"And what of it?" I feel Logan's chuckle against my neck.

"Hey." I cup his cheek and pull back to look at him. "I was thinking about running some numbers for a tour." My palms start sweating. "Local at first, of course. Then maybe the Southwest. After that, who knows? But what do you think about that?"

"Hell yeah," Logan says without hesitating. "Give the people what they want." He squeezes my hips. "Honestly? It's a no-brainer. You've been killing it in such a short time."

"Thanks," I say, anxious. "I was thinking I'd be traveling to all these small venues in all these cool cities, there'd be plenty for you to write about. So if I did, would . . . would you join?" Logan's eyebrows raise.

"Become an official groupie? An Unburned Island roadie? What do you think, gorgeous?" He smirks. "You think I'd pass up the chance to shack up with a rock star?"

"So, yes?" I'm already beaming. Logan shakes his head, laughing softly.

"You still don't get it." He leans down and kisses me, slow and tender. Breaking off to press his forehead to mine, he sighs. "Wherever you go, I go."

My heart is overflowing. I bite my lip, smiling.

"See?" I tease. "Obsessed."

Logan leans in and brushes his lips against mine. "For the love of my life? Always." I can't tell him what he means to me, so I press my lips to his, hoping he can feel it.

He is my own unburned island. Every kiss brings me back to life.

The moonlight bathes us in bright gold, the color of my mother's and sister's hair. The night sky stretches infinite above us, the same dark magic as my father's eyes. I now know I can survive their loss. It won't take me three hundred years to recover.

I know that soon, my trees will be tall once more.

# acknowledgments

Y'all, there were points during the writing of this book that I didn't think I could do it. But if you're reading this, that means *it happened*, and I have so, so many phenomenal people to thank for that.

First, thank *you*. Yes, you, reading this right now. It still blows me away that someone out there is reading my words, so thank *you* for reading. I also want to thank all the people who've sent me such kind messages! I can't imagine I'll ever get used to how wonderful it is to hear from people all around the world. It's an honor, and if I could, I'd bake each and every one of you your favorite cake. But I, unfortunately, do not have the time nor the kitchen to pull this off, and I do not know how to bake. But please know the sentiment is there, because none of this would exist without *you*.

I want to take a moment to thank everyone who supported me during my debut novel launch. To the *incomparable* Kathleen Glasgow, who so generously helped me on my first B&N Live: Thank you for being so kind and encouraging to this new (and nervous) author. Thank you to the incredible people at Tombolo Books and the amazing staff at B&N Town Center Prado. Thank you to every single person who came to see me: Each one of you helped make those days some of the best of my life.

A very special shout-out to my lola and all my Filipino and West

Coast family for sending love and support from afar. I love you all so much. Brynn, I hope you were able to read this while not grounded.

To Lanie Davis, my editor, creative collaborator, and guiding light: *Thank you.* Thank you for buoying me through my trenches of despair and for teaching me how to trust the process. I am so lucky to get to work with you. Thank you also to Jess Harriton! Your brilliant insights honed this story into what it is today. A warm thanks to Romy Golan for doing *all* the things (and for sharing my love for black nail polish)! Again, thank you to everyone at Rights People for continuing to be my champions worldwide.

Thank you to all the miracle workers at Penguin Random House. I have not yet stopped pinching myself over getting to work with the creative powerhouses of Jen Klonsky, Simone Roberts-Payne, and their teams. Special thanks to Natalie Vielkind for ushering this book through production and to Janet Rosenberg for her masterful copy-editing. Thank you to Cindy De la Cruz for the beautiful interior design and to Kelley Brady for yet another jaw-dropping cover! A huge thank-you to Jordana Kulak, who helped me navigate uncharted territory. A big, big thank-you to Felicity Vallence and her incredibly talented team for guiding me through the petrifying lands of social media.

Thank you to all my friends for your support and love. Claire and Lindsey, thank you for letting me cry on your porch and eat all your Cheez-Its. Love you two so much. Thank you to Matt and Julie for being so encouraging and creatively revitalizing. Love and thanks to Mia and Angela for supporting my work, even when it was just a twinkle in my eye. Thank you to John and Jay, two sunbeams in human form. You tease magic out of everyone who surrounds you. Thank you to Si and Raven for supporting me, even when we don't get to see each other nearly enough. To my beloved Annie D., thank you for lighting up my life whenever we're together. Thank you, Bex Carlo, for supporting me even as I struggle; you're a beautiful human.

So much love to all my Bandits. Thank you, Cat, for always making me laugh and making sure I'm in the know about the current whippersnapper trends. Kevin, I love you, man. Thanks for everything, you ole ledge-talker-off-er, you . . . though I'm sure you'll agree nobody compares to John Lasavath. John, thank you so much for always reading everything I've ever written. Truly, you are the wind beneath my wings.

To my GFF soulmates, Allison, Amaris, and Joanna. Thank you for your radical love. You are my loves. My lifes. My roommates forever. My future co-signers on the mortgage for that compound I sent you on Zillow that we're all going to move into in six months. I've already booked the moving trucks, so . . .

Michael and Will, you've got a house in that compound too, obvi. Thank you, Michael, for always managing to make me laugh so hard I snort and fart, even when I'm in the trough of sorrow. You are, and always have been, a constant source of joy in my life. Thank you for helping me get up the mountain even when it felt impossible to keep climbing. Love you forever. Will, thank you for being an endless fountain of kindness and laughter in my life. The world needs more people like you, people who can discover light in a starless cave, people who understand that sometimes that light can be a fancam of Kovu from *The Lion King II: Simba's Pride*.

Speaking of, thank you forever-and-ever-amen to Jess, who never judged me for writing "I <3 Kovu" on my reading binder when we were eleven. There are so many things I could never have gotten through without you, and the crushing self-doubt I felt while writing this book is one of them. Thank you for our Jedi dates. I love you. And chips. Oh, and also thanks to Jess's husband.

Thank you to my genius father; I won the lottery having you as a dad. Thank you for the two million ways you've supported me my entire life. But especially, thank you for teaching me self-care is most important, and that if you are at Six Flags and you are tired, it is valid to stretch out on a bench and take a nap.

To my beautiful mother, you've always given me what I need to succeed, and this book is no exception. Thank you to infinity's moon and back. Thank you for befriending the real-life Tigery, pampering him, and giving him a home so he could live on in this book. You've taken me to the most beautiful places in the world, but my favorite spot will always be wherever you are. Even when it's a ninety-degree hotel room with no air-conditioning.

To my dearest Peetz, thank you for always being there for me, specifically to carry my dead body out of the basement in *Lethal Company*. Thanks for still playing with me, even when I die five minutes in (or when I don't have enough stickers!).

Thank you, Vic, for being an all-around Best and for your solidarity in *Lethal Company* when you also die five minutes in. I'm still just a puddle of cheese because I love you so, so much. Oh, and please tell Tim thank you for politely participating in the debate whenever I pose a deeply philosophical question like, *"Who's hotter, Kovu or Balto?"* at Thanksgiving dinner.

And finally, thank you to Pabu, my co-author, for keeping me company throughout the months I found myself writing consistently at four a.m. You always make the loneliest hours feel cozy as a hearth, which is why I forgive you for insisting that the best time to nap on my keyboard is the hour right before my deadline.

Oh, and Babs?

Thanks.

**Turn the page for a sneak peek into Sloan Harlow's thrilling and sexy *NYT* bestselling debut.**

At 3:15 p.m., the bell rings.

*Finally.*

I'm sprinting toward the front doors when a voice stops me.

"Ms. Graham! I've been looking for you." Ms. Langley, the pottery teacher, is beckoning to me from the doorway of the art room. I glance longingly at the double doors at the end of the hall, at the flickering EXIT sign, then walk over to her.

"Hi, Ms. Langley," I say, readjusting the bag of books at my shoulder, every one of my polite Southern instincts at war with my desperation to leave.

"I just wanted to give you something real quick." She holds up a finger, and then reappears a moment later with a small cardboard box in her hands. On the side, handwritten in Sharpie, are the words ELLA AND HAYLEY. Inside are two handmade ceramic mugs.

And just like that, the tiny rowboat that I'd managed to keep upright all day starts to go under.

"I thought you might want these," Ms. Langley whispers, sounding nearly as sad as I feel. "They didn't get fired in the kiln until after . . . Well, I've been holding on to them for you."

"Um," I say, blinking down into the box.

It had been Hayley's idea to make mugs for each other. Coffee cups for when we roomed together at the University of Georgia. Hayley had been so proud when she'd shown me her design, a mug with an ornate *D* stamped into the side. *D* as in . . . *denture*. When I'd protested that I was *not* going to be drinking out of a *denture mug*, she'd held up a hand.

"Wait, listen. This is a mug you'll use for life. I'm just preparing for the best phase of our friendship: when we're old and senile. Think of how fun that'll be." Hayley's eyes had flashed their green mischief. "Every time we see each other, we'll be new best friends all over again." She'd shrugged. "And you'll have a place to keep your dentures."

Both mugs had turned out beautifully.

I barely register saying goodbye to Ms. Langley. I exit the school in a daze, unable to stop looking down at the mugs, clinking against each other in the cardboard box. I'd like to look away. I want to, I do. I want to chuck them into a ravine, but I know it would be like pulling out an organ and stomping on it. I somehow need these mugs to keep going.

I run my hand over the one Hayley made. There's an indent on the bottom, one she forgot to smooth. I peer closer and see little swirling lines, a pattern.

Hayley's fingerprint.

Distantly, I register that there is a world around me. Maybe some grass, a sky. Raised voices from far away.

But right now, all I can focus on is pressing my finger into that little indent.

It all happens so fast.

One moment, there are headlights in front of me, a bus barreling at my face. There are screams, the bellowing of a horn like a great dragon. My heart is in my throat, my last thought, *Protect the mugs,* and then I'm flying backward.

I don't die.

I slam back into something solid. My brain thinks, ridiculously, of a brick wall, but this wall is warm and has a heartbeat. Someone pulled me out of the way. Someone saved me.

I tilt my chin up to find myself looking into the wide, panicked eyes of Sawyer Hawkins.

"Sawyer!" I gasp, stumbling out of his arms to face him. My book bag has spilled onto the school lawn, but I'm still clutching the cardboard box, mugs miraculously unbroken.

"Ella." Sawyer's panting, his face slack with shock, one hand on his chest, the other pulling at the roots of his thick hair. He takes a few steadying breaths, closes his eyes. When he opens them once more, they're blazing with anger.

"Ella," he growls, "what the *hell* were you thinking? You could have *died*. Like, literally *died*. If I hadn't been here, if I hadn't been watching? *Christ.*"

"Why were you?" It takes me a minute to realize I've said this out loud.

"What?" He stops short, confused.

"Watching me? In fact"—I swallow—"why even save me?" Horribly, my eyes spill over. I can't pretend I'm fine anymore.

Color drains from Sawyer's face. The anger in his features evaporates, and if it's at all possible, he seems more stricken by my words than by my near miss. He licks his lips, mouth dropping open, but nothing comes out.

I want to hear his answer. A microscopic diamond of hope embedded in my stomach is begging me to stay, to listen to what he has to say.

But I don't. I can't.

I know the answer. And anything kind out of his mouth would be pity, or a mercy I don't deserve. I whirl around and walk away.

He doesn't call after me. That tiny prick of hope wants me to look over my shoulder, just once. But I don't.

And I vow to never speak to Sawyer again.